FALLEN STARS

STONE BAY SERIES

BOOK THREE

USA TODAY BESTSELLING AUTHOR

PERSEPHONE AUTUMN

BETWEEN WORDS PUBLISHING LLC

FALLEN STARS

STONE BAY SERIES

BOOK THREE

USA TODAY BESTSELLING AUTHOR

PERSEPHONE AUTUMN

BETWEEN WORDS PUBLISHING LLC

CONTENT WARNING

Fallen Stars is a contemporary romantic suspense story. Graphic content, human trafficking, physical assault, sexual assault, and post traumatic stress disorder in certain scenes may trigger emotional distress in some readers. If you are sensitive to the listed triggers, this story may not be for you.

Please use your own personal judgement before proceeding.

If you or someone you know is a victim of human trafficking, please reach out to the National Human Trafficking Hotline for support. All contact is confidential.

In the US:

- Website humantraffickinghotline.org
- Call 1-888-373-7888
- Text INFO to 233733

A Love So Bright

<u>Artist Duet</u>

Blank Canvas

Abstract Passion

<u>Novellas</u>

Reese

Penny

Stone Bay Series

Broken Sky—Prequel

Shattered Sun

Fractured Night

Fallen Stars

Stolen Dreams

Raptured Souls

Standalone Romance Novels

Sweet Tooth

Transcendental

In Knots For You

Poetry Collections

Ink Veins

Broken Metronome

Slipping From Existence

Poisonous Heart

Beneath Wildflowers

PUBLISHED UNDER P. AUTUMN

Standalone Non-Romance Novels

By Dawn

CONTENTS

PROLOGUE

OLIVER

Past—Age 16

Every damn day, I fight like hell to not stare at him. Levi West. My best friend. The one person I feel most at ease with. And one of the few people in town who's transparent and genuine and accepts me exactly as I am.

What I should do is look away.

What I shouldn't do is ruin our friendship.

But fuck is it hard to focus when he's in the room.

Hitting pause on the game controller, I toss it on the table and lean back in my gaming chair. An arm's length away in the second gaming chair, Levi types furiously on his laptop, his eyes hyperfocused on the screen.

When he's like this—rapt and in the zone—it makes not staring at him more of a challenge.

"Mind if I work on a song?"

His fingers pause and hover over the keyboard as my question registers, then his fingers fly over the keys again. "Not at all."

I pop open my guitar case and take out the acoustic guitar that's seen more of the world than I have.

A gift from Grandpa Giuseppe, I tend to play this guitar more in private or around people I trust. In mint condition, I have this irrational, niggling fear of damaging the antique instrument. Not that anyone has messed with my shit before but this guitar is irreplaceable.

Bowing over the guitar, I close my eyes and strum the strings as the fingers of my other hand slide along the neck. A soft, slow, intimate melody floats through the air, but I don't dare sing the few lyrics I've paired with it aloud. Words packed with longing and lust and a hint of desperation.

I keep those words bottled up. Sealed tight and shoved in the furthest recesses of my mind.

Because giving those words a voice would change everything.

I'd rather have Levi as a friend, my best friend, than not have him at all.

Opening my mouth and spilling secrets to him would flip our worlds upside down. Forever alter our friendship, and unlikely for the better.

"Fuck, yes."

I stop playing, lift my chin, and lock onto Levi's profile. A devious smile tugs up the corner of his mouth as he stares at the computer screen.

Levi doesn't smile often. Most mirror the one on his lips now—minimal, dubious, vain. Not because he's an asshole or thinks he is better than anyone. No, this smile is for those moments when he *sticks it to the man.*

As for his other smile, I've only seen it twice.

The first time was when he hacked into the health teacher's laptop remotely and fucked with the PowerPoint presentations during sex education week. He'd ducked his chin and pressed a hand to his mouth, but not before I saw that brilliant smile.

And the second time, it was in my garage last month.

A friend from music class suggested we start a band with his girlfriend. All three of us play guitar, but I also have a love for drums. Before our first jam session, we discussed the style of music we wanted to play. It didn't take long for us to agree on our passion for rock music. Shortly thereafter, I sat behind my drum kit while Trip and Hailey shouldered their guitars.

And then the garage rattled with the thumping bass and wail of our instruments as we played a song from an early Nirvana album. It had been pure bliss.

Or so I thought.

Until I peered up and was captivated by the massive, blinding smile on Levi's lips. Aimed in my direction.

Fuck... I see that smile every time I close my eyes now. I jerk off to that smile no less than three times a week. I lose myself in fantasies of the future because of that damn smile.

My lungs expand as I silently, slowly suck in a deep breath. Swallowing on the exhale, I set my guitar down. "Wreaking havoc on the town?"

Smile still firmly in place, Levi twists in my direction and cocks a brow. "Nothing that'll burn it down." With a shrug, he averts his gaze back to the screen. "Just deactivating security cameras and alarms in town hall."

Eyes wide and jaw slack, I stare at his profile in pure awe.

A true mastermind, Levi's ingenuity is unmatched. Not many are aware of his level of talent. Not many comprehend the machine that is his mind. He has the ability to dismantle the most secure computer systems created with a few lines of code.

Hell, I don't completely understand it. Not that I need to.

I see the real Levi. The complex guy with an endless

labyrinth for a mind. The guy always in his head, deciphering what he sees into bits and pieces rather than taking it in as one whole object.

"On a mission to piss off your dad?" I chuckle.

It's no secret that the West family—one of the Stone Bay founding families referred to as the Seven—has taken on a mayoral role more years than not in Stone Bay. Oftentimes, they rotate through which West will hold the seat. Not that the residents don't get a say or vote. They do. But it's rare to have anyone run against the West family for the position.

As of now, Jefferson Thornhill-West is in the running for town mayor. Not that he has much competition.

No surprise to anyone, Mr. West is on a mission to shape Levi into someone he's not. All in the hopes that Levi will one day step into the role as mayor, keeping the West name high in the town ranks.

Politics and superiority aren't priorities for Levi, though.

If anything, Levi wants to tear the world apart and put it back together better than it was.

"Pshh." Levi shakes his head. "Is there anything I do that *doesn't* piss him off?"

I've known Levi long enough to know his question is rhetorical. So I wait for him to continue.

Levi scoffs. "Did I tell you what he said the other night?"

I jog through my memories over the past week and come up blank. "No. What'd he say?"

Closing the lid on his laptop, he sets it aside and reaches for a game controller. "*'You're a dead weight bringing this family down. That changes after graduation,'*" he says in a mocking tone. He holds his hand high and flips his middle finger up at the bedroom door. "Fucking asshole. As if he's God or some shit."

Living under the roof and thumb of generations of town founders is something I will never fully grasp. His frustrations,

I get. His anger at his family for trying to mold him into someone he's not, I comprehend. But bearing the burden of an invisible crown, carrying the weight of generations' egos on your shoulders, is far beyond my reach.

All I can do is be here for my friend. In whatever way he needs.

Even if it isn't in the way I want or need.

Levi resumes playing the game and I pick up my guitar and play the song from the beginning. Humming to myself, I recite the lyrics in my head.

You're a brand on my heart, a tattoo on my soul.

You hoard all the game pieces, tight fists of control.

The darkest of shadows, please let me be your light.

I'll take the long road, forever on your right.

"That new?"

I startle in my seat as my eyes shoot to Levi. "What?"

Eyes focused on the screen as he plays the game, he tips his head in my direction. "The song. Is it new?"

Shit. Did I sing it out loud?

"Kind of…" I say with zero confidence.

I study his face for any indication I did more than hum the lyrics. Had Levi heard the lines of the song, I'd be answering a different set of questions. An endless inquisition over who the song is about.

But his expression is passive, his frame relaxed as he taps various buttons on the controller.

"Just something I've been toying with in my spare time," I clarify.

He widens his legs and leans back into the chair farther. With that simple move, my gaze drops to his legs, slowly traveling up his thighs until I reach his crotch. Saliva pools in my mouth and I swallow as my dick twitches against my leg.

Don't fuck up your friendship to appease your dick.

"It's slower than what you usually play." His frame stiffens as he jerks the controller right and smashes a combination of buttons. A beat passes before his whole body relaxes again. "Like a ballad."

At this, I tense.

Essentially, a ballad is a love song, no matter the genre of music. And that's exactly what that song is… a love song. Written for him. That I'll never sing in the company of others.

Needing to shift the direction of the conversation, I do what I do best. Mask my feelings with humor. Or at least what I consider humor.

I set the guitar back in the case, twist in my seat, and arch a brow. "Are you saying I'm the next rock ballad legend? That I'll be on the wall next to Queen, Poison, and Led Zeppelin?" I let out an exaggerated sigh. "Now that I'm rock 'n' roll royalty, you should cater to my every whim."

Levi snorts. "Didn't take long for that to go to your head."

"You said it, not—"

A voice in the hall cuts me off. Thick with false authority, Levi's dad argues with whoever else is in the hall. The other person talks softly enough to not be heard, and I assume it's Levi's mom.

"He will not sit in this house all day and play video games. It's time he grows up, Felicity. Not fuck around with his queer friend."

"Jefferson," his mom scolds loud enough for us to hear. "Oliver is not the problem. And Levi deserves time for himself before he leaves for college."

The muscles in Levi's jaw flex as he tosses the controller down and curls his fingers into fists in his lap.

Unfortunately, this is nothing new with his parents. His dad spends every minute they're together shoving his ideologies down Levi's throat. Then his mom swoops in, telling Levi he can be whoever he wants and not to worry, that she'll deal with his dad.

It's this vicious cycle filled with stress and agony, followed by alleviation and temporary bandages.

"College." His dad scoffs. "Are you aware of how many times I've called the dean of admissions?" A pause of silence. "Five, Felicity. Five goddamn times."

"Lower your voice and don't speak to me like that."

A mumble filters through the door and I assume his dad is apologizing. "Political science should be his major. He should be focusing on what's best for this family." His voice rises again. "Instead, he's switched his major to computer information technology. Every time I have it changed, he has it switched back." He huffs loud enough to be heard through the wall. "I'm done with his juvenile behavior, Felicity."

Every cell in my body rushes to my arms and hands and begs me to reach out and comfort Levi. To tell him he can do whatever the hell he wants with his life. That he has the right to choose his own future.

But I clasp my hands in my lap. Focus on the stretch and sting of my knuckles as I resist.

"Your word is not law, Jefferson," his mom declares. "The hyphenated addition to your surname does not make you above the law." Seconds tick by in silence, and I hold my breath. "You bear *my* name, Jefferson. Do not abuse it with your ego."

Oh shit.

A mumble floats through the air a moment before Levi's door swings open and his dad enters the room. Cheeks flushed with anger, Jefferson straightens his spine and looks down at Levi, whose eyes are on the television.

"Say goodbye to Oliver," he states with practiced control. "The Calhouns and Kemps will be joining us for dinner soon."

His eyes flick to the screen. "The time for games is over." He swings his gaze back to Levi. "You're an adult now. Start behaving as such. Clean yourself up and be downstairs in thirty minutes."

I drop my gaze to Levi's hands in his lap and watch as his nails dig into his palms. Obvious to anyone paying attention, rage oozes from his pours.

Under normal circumstances, Levi is chill. He's the quiet observer in the room. The one person you think is bored or uninterested. In reality, he picks up on every minor detail and only gives his attention to what he feels matters.

More often than not, people take advantage of him. They take all he has to offer for granted.

As much as I want to defend him in this moment, as much as I want to rise up and tell his dad to go to hell, I sit in silence and wait for Mr. West to leave the room. Because if I get up now, it will only provoke a yelling match between them.

"Not in the mood to schmooze the townsfolk," Levi mutters.

His dad steps farther into the room, closes the distance between him and Levi, and bends down to hover just above Levi's head.

"I really don't give a damn what you're in the mood for. You're a West and you'll behave as you're told." He straightens his spine and aims his attention my way. "Goodbye, Oliver."

"No, Ollie. Stay. The dick-swinging contest is always a good laugh." Levi tips his head back and sneers at his dad. "Plus, we aren't done hanging out."

Perspiration dampens my skin as my heart pounds in my chest.

It's not the first time I've been figuratively trapped between Levi and his dad. I doubt it will be the last. Regardless, it makes me want to shrivel in the corner.

Levi's dad stares down at him with nothing but fury. "Thirty minutes," he grits out. "Be downstairs. Preferably with a better attitude." The hint of a devious smile tips up the corners of his mouth. "Jasmine, Sara, and Abigail will be joining us as well." His gaze flits to me for the briefest of seconds before returning to Levi. "Fine young ladies." He spins on his heel and starts for the door. "Who knows. One of them may be your future wife."

A spasm ripples through my body at his words.

The hasty glance my way, his comment in the hall minutes ago, the bite in his voice as he said *future wife…* it was all intentional. Mr. West brandished a sword in the form of words and ran it straight through me. He did it to hurt me and piss off Levi.

"I should go," I mumble after Mr. West walks out the door.

A groan echoes through the room. "Ignore him, Ollie."

I pull my phone from my pocket and type a text to my mom, asking her to pick me up. Seconds later, she responds that she's on her way.

Sifting through my backpack, I double-check I have everything I brought over. Then I secure it on my shoulder, bend down to grab my guitar case, and pause a few feet from Levi.

"Sorry you're dad's an asshole."

I lift my gaze from the floor to meet his and my mouth goes dry. Luminous blue eyes with that small hint of green around the pupil lock onto my darker greens and hold me captive.

My limbs are lead weights; my feet rooted to the rug. With one look, with *that* look, every rational thought vanishes from my mind. My tongue is heavy in my mouth.

I should leave before I say or do something stupid and irreversible. I should walk away before I ruin our friendship.

But the way he's looking at me… it's like he's reached

inside my chest and wrapped his fist around my heart with the promise to never let go.

I need to go. Now.

A half-hearted smile tugs up one corner of my lips. "Text me later?"

He inches forward and rises from the chair. I suck in a sharp breath and step back to add more space between his hand and mine.

"Yeah." He audibly exhales. "When the circus ends."

I start for the door but don't make it far. His hand lands on my shoulder and I stop breathing.

"Seriously, Ollie. Ignore him."

My back to him, I nod.

"He's a prick. Don't let him get under your skin. That's what he wants."

I peer over my shoulder. "I know." I want to add that I hate how his dad treats him. That he shouldn't put up with his bull-shit either.

But I remain tight-lipped.

"Want me to walk you out?" His hand falls away from my shoulder.

Much as I do, I shake my head. "Nah, I'm good. Mom should be here any minute."

I start for the door again. This time, Levi doesn't stop me.

Just as I pass the threshold, a whispered "Later" hits my ears.

June 28th

Today was shit. Well, it wasn't total shit. It started off great. Like many days, it was just me & L hanging out. Games and hacking and music. What we do most of the time. Also, I saw him smile again. Damn I love his smiles. Sounds immature or silly of me, but his smiles make my heart skip and skin sweaty. Ridiculous, I know. But it's true.

Then his asshole of a dad trashed it. He stole his smiles. He stole his peace. And it just pisses me right the hell off. L is one the best people I know and his dad treats him like property. Like he doesn't matter.

He does fucking matter!

And what was that look he gave me before I left? That wasn't friendship. That wasn't sympathy. It was something else. Something more. Or maybe it was my imagination. Maybe it was me seeing something on his face I've wanted to see for months but haven't.

Other friends have said I'm too young to know what love is. That my feelings for him are just a phase. But they're wrong. In my own way, I love him. Even if all he sees me as is a friend. His best friend.

L may never be mine, but my heart doesn't care. I love him. And I will love him in secret and as a best friend if that's all he'll ever be.

ONE

LEVI

Present

All it takes is a stalker and some serial killers to make every resident of Stone Bay want a security system installed or a private investigator to spy on questionable loved ones.

Shit news for the town.

Great news for Tymber Woulf Security and Investigative Services.

Even better news for my bank account. Not that I *need* the money. But it is nice to know I have backup funds for the random occasions my father decides to throw a holier-than-thou tantrum and threaten my financial future. A future he technically has no control over.

Five years ago, when I was neck-deep in studying for sophomore finals at college, I met Tymber. In a coffee shop not far from campus, I sipped on caffeine, blocked the world out with noise-canceling headphones, and fixated on my notes. Tymber sat down at the table next to me, opened his laptop, and started futzing with a program he was writing.

When I came up for air and sat back in my seat, I glimpsed

his frustration and the lines of code on his screen. Sliding off my headphones, I introduced myself, told him I was studying computer sciences, and asked if he needed help.

Though I'd learned more about computers prior to college, there were some ethical components to the technology that were new.

That day in the coffee shop changed my life. Other than Oliver, I'd never formed such a fast friendship.

Now Tymber is more my brother than my friend.

As for Oliver... our connection has always been stronger than friendship. Indescribable and far from familial. Constant. Intimate.

Shortly after Tymber's cyber security program took off, he asked if I wanted to join the business. If I wanted to be a part of the next big thing. Fresh out of college and eager to get my hands dirty, I said yes without hesitation.

When he wanted to expand from cyber security to residential, I expressed my lack of enthusiasm. I didn't want to live in the city—not that being near my father was a better choice. I also didn't want to do what's already been done. There was nothing new in home security.

Wanting me on his team and refusing to take no for an answer, Tymber pestered me every waking hour until I agreed. But I had stipulations. The biggest one... I would not deal with customers directly. I was in it for the tech, not the people.

Late last fall, Tymber Woulf Security boomed again.

Wanting a physical location for the ever-expanding business, Tymber mentioned buying land and erecting a brick-and-mortar space in Stone Bay. Though he loved the city, it'd become too noisy, too in your face. And after a long day, all he wanted was quiet.

To sweeten the deal, I told him I'd chip in if he added investigative services. He jumped at the chance.

Just after shit hit the fan in Stone Bay last year, we opened the doors to the new business. With me as a partner with Tymber, I assumed one of the founders would come to us to help investigate the murders.

Not a single one did.

Had they, they would've had answers much sooner. There would've been less death on their hands.

Live and learn, I suppose.

A knock on my closed office door steals my attention and I growl. Tymber never knocks. He always shoots a text or an IM if he needs something.

"What?" I bark out.

The door slowly opens and a newer employee pokes their head inside. "Sorry to bother you, Mr. West. It's just…"

When they don't continue, I peer up from my screens and take in their worried expression. "What?"

They cringe. "I think the server is broken."

Not fucking possible.

My molars gnash together and I audibly exhale. "For fuck's sake," I mutter.

They are obviously unaware the servers we use are in the cloud. Yes, in some undisclosed remote location, there are physical machines running, processing, and storing all our data. In a server farm. In a controlled environment capable of handling our programs and networks.

And last I checked, we have more than enough storage and security to meet our needs.

I shove my chair back, rise from my seat, swipe up my phone, and head for the door. "Show me."

They lead me to their desk and show me how the account they're working on continues to crash.

Eyes scanning the screen, I find the problem before I reach the bottom. The crashes have nothing to do with servers. They have nothing to do with machines at all. No, the issue is one-hundred-percent user error.

Which irritates me more.

I point out the issue, tell them a resolution, and then remind them of the reference manuals we have readily available for all employees.

Sheepish expression in place, they thank me.

I don't let it pass so easily. I don't have the time, patience, or money to deal with incompetent people. Were this a basic job that didn't require intelligence, I wouldn't give a shit.

But it's not.

We deal with private information and people's safety. Blood, sweat, frustration, and several years of planning built this company. Pleading with and schmoozing high-end clients for years to gain trust was far from easy. But eventually, we won them over and rightfully earned their confidence.

After all the work Tymber and I have put into the business, the last thing this company needs is for shit to go haywire, information to leak, and to be hit with millions of dollars in lawsuits.

I'm not an asshole. But I refuse to put up with incompetence.

"I'm s-sorry, Mr. West. I'll d-do better."

Yeah, you will. Or I'll fire your ass. That's what I want to say.

Instead, I give a gentle dip of my chin. "See that you do."

As I turn back for my office, I spot Tymber on the opposite side of the open floor plan. He lifts his chin in way of greeting, then tips his head toward the conference room.

I love what I do, I love running this business with my friend, but damn do I loathe the meetings and office politics. Just let me sit in front of my computer and do what I do best—research and code.

"Wanted to talk with you first." Tymber closes the door as I pass.

"What's up?"

Tymber pulls out a chair and sits. Folding my arms over my chest, I stand near the head of the table.

"I need to shift their tasks." He tips his head toward the large glass wall separating us from the cluster of cubicles in the main room.

"Okay…" He doesn't need my approval to change employee tasks or workload.

He reaches up, presses his thumb and finger to his brows, then strokes the length of them until he reaches his temples. On an audible breath, his hand falls away. The lines of tension near the corners of his eyes and between his brows steal my attention.

I want to ask what happened. What has him frustrated. But I bite the inside of my cheek and wait. In time and when he is ready, Tymber will share what's eating at him.

"Got off the phone with a buddy of mine from the city." He leans back and stares toward the ceiling, eyes unfocused.

Minute-long seconds pass as I wait for him to add more. To clue me in on what has him so distressed.

Did someone pass away? Is he taking leave and putting me in charge of everything until he returns?

Before I agreed to partner with him, we talked about this shit. I don't want to be the person people come to about petty bullshit.

Technical problems? All good.

Issues requiring sympathy? Not really my area of expertise.

Heartless, I am not. A hermit that speaks when he has something worth saying or is comfortable with the present company is a better description. I'm not *not* a people person. I'm just selective about who I choose as *my* people.

"He hired us for investigation work."

If Tymber is this frazzled after the conversation, it isn't because his buddy wants to spy on a romantic partner. Whatever this case is, it's legit. Important. A big deal.

A shot of adrenaline hits my bloodstream and sends my pulse into overdrive. The voice in my head screams in victory as I give a mental high five to the powers that be. It's about time a substantial job landed in our laps.

The corners of my mouth twitch as I fight the start of a smile. "That's incredible, T."

"It is." He nods. "And it isn't."

My enthusiasm dies. "I don't understand."

Rolling back his chair, he rises and runs a hand through his hair. "I'm lightening your workload so you can focus on this."

I nod. "Yeah. Sure, man."

He levels me with a steady, unreadable gaze. "I'll explain more after I reassign your work. But Levi…" Swiping a hand over his jaw, he adds, "No one can know what you're working on."

Most days, the only person familiar with the tasks on my docket is Tymber. My current workload isn't classified or hidden from employees. I just don't make it my business to share every facet of my life—professionally or personally.

"Not a problem."

On an exhale, he jerks his head toward the door. "Let me deal with them." Eyes unfocused, he nods. "Meet you in your office after." And then he disappears from the room.

"There's been an uptick in missing persons in the Northwest." Tymber sits in a chair opposite me at the small table in my office. "My buddy in the Washington missing persons division says numbers have doubled in Washington and Oregon since last year." He tips his head back and stares at the ceiling. "Government funding means limited resources and access."

A soft growl fills the room.

"And since someone higher up deprioritized the recent missing persons for other tasks, the cases have been left to collect dust."

My brows pinch in confusion. "So missing persons stopped searching for missing people?"

Exasperation and disbelief mar his forehead as he levels me with his gaze. "Seems to be the case."

What the actual fuck?

I get that the unit may be overwhelmed. I get that they may have lost funding or staff. But what a piss-poor excuse to stop looking for missing citizens. Seek outside resources. Fundraise to help pay workers. Invite others to aid in research.

But never stop looking.

"What part do we play in this? If they've lost funding, are we doing this pro bono?"

"Our focus is one individual in particular. But finding them may lead to others." Tymber sits taller in his chair and pulls his phone from his pocket. After a few taps on the screen, he sets the phone on the table and spins it to show me the screen. "Sydney Messer. Fourteen years old. Last seen two weeks ago outside a burger joint with friends in the city."

I pick up his phone and study the photo as Tymber shares more details.

"Her friends got on a different bus, but no one thought anything of it. They'd done it countless times. And her bus was scheduled to arrive at the stop five minutes after the other."

"She never made it on the bus, did she?"

Tymber shakes his head as his face turns a sickly gray. "No.

Her father, James, checked her bus pass when they couldn't get ahold of her. The last time it was used was on her way to meet her friends."

I sit back in my seat and lace my fingers on top of my head. "The family is paying us?"

He nods. "I told him it wasn't necessary. He's a friend. I'd help without compensation."

"Wouldn't take no for an answer?"

He scoffs. "Rich bastard," he teases then sobers. "I think he thinks if he doesn't pay us, we'll stop looking too."

"Like hell."

Tymber doesn't say a word but nods in agreement.

Does the business need money to thrive? Of course. The same as every other business.

But when it comes to the people we call our own, it isn't about the money. It's about doing the right thing. And finding this man's daughter is at the top of the list.

"Do we have more than the picture?" I point at his phone.

Tymber scoots his chair away from the table, rests his elbows on his knees, and drops his forehead to his hands. "On the way. James is emailing over everything they have as soon as he gets more from missing persons."

"Forward me what you already have and I'll get started."

College taught me several legitimate ways to work with computers and software. I busted my ass for four years and made several professors proud to call me their student. I have a wall's worth of accolades praising me for my accomplishments that sit in a box in my closet. Hell, I still get the occasional call from one professor in particular, asking if I'll mentor a student for the semester.

College was the first place I truly felt accepted for who I was and what I had to offer. It was the first place I felt respected. Most people would show that off by hanging their degrees and certificates on the wall. I keep them stowed away and safe. Locked up tight. They're worth more than a cheap frame that someone could damage.

In the past twelve years, much of what I've learned is from a shit ton of trial and error. Seeing what would happen if I tweaked programs. Digging deep into the development of websites and messing with code, fucking it up for a laugh.

My professors wouldn't be proud of that.

But with how fast technology evolves, sometimes shortcuts and illegal methods are necessary to get the job done. And in this case, find a lost loved one.

My phone buzzes in my pocket.

"Sent." Tymber rises from his seat and shifts his gaze to mine, eyes solemn and lips in a flat line. "This case stays between you and me, L. I'll exhaust my resources and let you know what I find. As far as updating the family, I am the only point of contact for James and Estrella Messer."

I push up from my seat and head for my desk, ready to start my search.

"Understood."

"Ultimate confidentiality."

"T…" I scoff. "Don't you know? I'm the master of keeping secrets."

TWO
OLIVER

A MOAN MORE APPROPRIATE FOR THE BEDROOM SPILLS FROM MY lips as I shove another bite of bacon and gouda macaroni and cheese in my mouth. "So good," I garble around the bite.

Out of the corner of my eye, Skylar shakes her head, then follows it up with a muted snort. "You're ridiculous, Ollie."

I swallow the bite, twist in her direction, drop my chin to my shoulder, and smile. "You love my brand of ridiculous."

Skylar positions a monstrous burger, sweet potato fries, and a milkshake on the table. After she finagles a few things, she holds her phone up high over the meal and snaps a few photos. Sifting through the images and seemingly satisfied, she shifts the food aside.

While she sets up her next shot, I take a long pull of the milkshake. Again, I moan and garner more stares from customers trying to enjoy their lunch.

"Sorry." I wave to an older couple and the woman rolls her eyes.

Grumps.

After Skylar takes the final photo, she sits in the booth across from me and starts nibbling.

For the longest time, I've asked her to take me with her on work photo days. She promised she'd make it happen, but over the last year, something always got in the way. Conflicting work schedules, band practice, plans one of us made with someone else, our friends' lives being in danger.

But I held on to hope.

Sure, I've lived in Stone Bay my whole life. Without a doubt, I've probably tried almost every menu item from every restaurant in town. But not once have I gotten to eat a mountain of delicious calories for free. Today, I got to sample two new dishes coming soon to RJ's Diner and Dive. It's a win in my book.

"Sky," I draw out her name after I swallow a bite of burger. "Feels like I never see you anymore. Has Law been cuffing you to the bed?"

A faint dusting of pink colors Skylar's cheeks and before she says a single word, I already know the answer. Because Lawrence is a kinky bastard.

"Lower your voice, Ollie." Her eyes dart around the diner to see if anyone is paying us attention. "And maybe." She tucks her lips between her teeth to fight a smile.

I load up another forkful of macaroni and cheese and bring it to my lips. "That's what I need." I narrow my eyes, nod, and shove the bite in my mouth.

Her brows bend inward. "What?"

I wash down the bite with a sip of Cherry Coke. "A kinky father figure."

Skylar chokes on the food in her mouth and several sets of eyes turn our way. I rise from my seat, move to her side of the table, and smack her back a few times. She shoos me away as her coughing fit dies down.

"Seriously, Ollie?" She takes a long drink of water. "At least wait until I've swallowed."

"That's what he said."

Elbows on the table, she drops her head in her hands. "Why do I love you again?"

I hold up a hand and tick off the answers on my fingers. "Because I'm funny, sweet, talented, devilishly handsome, and the best gay friend ever."

Lifting her head, she drops her hands in her lap. With a subtle tilt of her head, she arches a brow. "I guess so." She plucks a fry from the plate and slathers it in sauce. "How're things with Levi?"

It's no secret my friends are aware of how I feel about my best friend, Levi. On the nights I hang out with Skylar, Kirsten, and Delilah and drink too much or get sucked into their love stories, I spill too much of my heart. Thank goodness what I share is vanilla and common knowledge among our circle.

But the more time that passes with Levi and I as nothing more than friends, the more I dread the possibility of divulging all the things left unsaid.

My friends would never hold my feelings against me or use them as a coercive tool. They would, on the other hand, use what they know to give me a nudge. Push me to talk to Levi and tell him how I feel.

Badly as I'd love him to be more than my best friend, I also don't want to lose him forever. Opening my mouth and confessing how I feel about him may do exactly that.

So for the past six years—almost seven—I've bottled up my deep affection for Levi West.

"Fine." I slide the milkshake in front of me and take a long pull from the straw. "He's been working a lot."

"The new investigation company, right?"

I nod. "Yeah. Runs it with a friend he met during college."

Skylar's lips turn down at the corners a moment. "Wish they would've been here a year earlier." Her eyes lose focus as she stares over my shoulder. After a deep inhale, she blinks and meets my gaze once more. "Things might've been different for many of us."

Too true.

Had Tymber been in town even a few months earlier, had the town and police known Levi worked with an investigative team, maybe our town wouldn't have lost some of its citizens to tragedy. Maybe the culprits behind several heinous acts would've been located sooner.

But if I've learned anything over the years, it's best not to question what might have been after the fact. All it does is drive you mad.

"Agreed." My stomach cramps, so I shove the milkshake away. Leaning back in the booth, I give Skylar a sympathetic smile. "But things might not have turned out the same if all that shit hadn't gone down."

Skylar mirrors my position across the booth as her brows scrunch together. "How so?"

How do I say this without sounding like an asshole? I don't think it's possible.

Fingers drumming against my thigh, I swallow and do my best to soften my voice. "If you were never abducted and the" —I lean forward and barely whisper the next word—"embezzlers were never caught, do you think you and Law would be where you are now? Blissful, living together, and not constantly looking over your shoulder."

Confusion wrinkles her forehead. "Of course—"

"Would Kirsten have decided between Travis and Ben so easily without her stalker thrown in the mix?" My lips twist up as I shrug. "Probably not. Without the additional stress, she would've had more time to get to know Ben better. The pissing match for her affection might still be happening had her stalker not made them go into protector mode."

Skylar scoffs. "So the intensity of someone's protection level determines who you love?" She crosses her arms over her chest. "I don't believe that for a second." Skylar shakes her head for emphasis. "Chemistry speaks volumes."

At this, I laugh. Not because Skylar is wrong. Chemistry is vital between romantic partners.

The reason I laugh at her comment has everything to do with Delilah and Phoebe.

For years, their chemistry was one-sided. Delilah never came across as miserable regarding her unrequited love for Phoebe Graves. Occasionally bummed? Yes. Consistently hopeful? Absolutely. But never depressed. Somehow, Delilah knew *something* would happen between them.

"It does," I agree. "But chemistry also changes in certain situations. When life gets shitty, you look at the world through a different lens. You also see people in a different light." I reach for the straw wrapper on the table and roll it between my fingers. "If Dee Dee hadn't been taken, would she and Phoebe still be in relationship limbo?"

"No, they'd be—"

"You don't know that for sure." I shake my head. "Yeah, Dee Dee and Phoebe were headed in that direction. But the possibility of finding her dead in the forest like the others… it flipped a switch in Phoebe's brain." I curl my fingers into loose fists, hold my hands up on either side of my face, and pop them open as I make a detonating sound. "Tell me I'm wrong," I dare her.

"If you'd let me speak." Her brows shoot up as her lips flatten into a line.

I clamp my lips between my teeth to hide my smile.

"Thank you," she says after a moment. "And yes, those situations sped up the process of our friends falling in love." Her attention falls to the table for a beat as she mulls over her next words. When she meets my gaze again, I see the resolution in her thoughts. "I still believe we'd be where we are had those events not happened." She rocks a little in her seat. "Would it be exactly the same? Of course not. But I firmly believe we'd have the same outcome."

"Really?"

Skylar narrows her eyes as she studies my face. "Nice try, Ollie."

I tilt my head. "What?"

With a shake of her head, she mumbles, "Always steering the conversation away."

From Levi, she means but doesn't say.

And maybe I am. I don't see the point in carrying on a conversation that will lead to the same point it always does—my friends giving me that gentle, nonchalant push to tell Levi how I feel.

Bless my friends for wanting me to have the same happiness as them. But it will never happen.

Levi has never seen me as anything more than what we are. Though he hasn't been in a relationship with anyone, I'm not oblivious to the women he gawks more than in passing. I've never seen him check out a guy. Not even a little. If he had, I may not be as hesitant to open up that part of myself to him.

As it stands, things between us are good. Best to keep it that way.

I ignore her comment but do as she says. I steer our chat in another direction.

"Coming to the show tonight?"

Sympathy curves her lips up momentarily. But as quickly as it makes an appearance, it shifts into a bright and excited smile. "Of course. Law and I will be front and center with everyone else."

"Cool, cool."

"How many shows are scheduled?"

As I sound them off in my head, I tick them off on my fingers against my thigh. "A dozen or so."

"All at Dalton's?"

If we played a dozen shows in our local pub in such a short period of time, the residents would get sick of us. Not that we aren't constantly adding songs and covers to our roster. But people like variety, and listening to the same band in your favorite hangout would get old fast.

"Most of them. But also a few town festivals. And a couple in Lake Lavender and Smoky Creek."

"Let me know the dates. I'll convince Kirsten and Dee Dee we need to be your groupies and follow you town to town."

I roll my eyes. Opening my mouth, I'm about to tell her how comical that is. But the words die on my tongue as RJ— Ray Jr.—sidles up to the table.

"Skylar." A wide smile brightens his expression. "How was everything?"

Skylar scoots out of the booth, steps to RJ and wraps him in a hug. "Perfect and incredible, as always."

His arms tighten around her shoulders briefly before falling away. "Glad to hear." RJ's attention drifts in my direction. "And I see you brought an assistant today."

Rugged laughter shakes his frame, and we join him for a beat.

"Food waste is a disgrace." I bow my head and then meet his gaze. "Just doing my part, sir."

Skylar scans the diner. A small crease forms between her brows before she looks to RJ. "Where's Tré? I didn't see him when I came in. Usually, he says hi."

It takes me a moment to remember Ray's son, Ray III, is often referred to as Tré. Rolls off the tongue easier.

"Surprised Pops didn't tell you already." When Skylar

doesn't say anything, RJ continues. "My son, the online food celebrity."

Chuckles echo around us as the three of us snicker.

Not long ago, Ray III reached stardom online. Through his love for food and natural charisma, he gained millions of social media followers. According to a post, it started as something fun. A spoof created as a dare. But after the video went viral with millions of views, likes, and shares, Ray III gave the people what they wanted. More. He posts titillating cooking videos packed with endless visual innuendos.

"The sous-chef position opened up at Calhoun's Bistro and Chef Beaulieu requested my boy." RJ glows with pride as he speaks about his only son. "I miss him like hell in my kitchen, but I'm so damn proud of his accomplishments."

Skylar gathers her phone and purse. Stepping into RJ's side, she wraps an arm around his shoulders and hugs him again. "As you should be. How's Tucker?"

I shove a few more fries in my mouth and finish the last of the milkshake as they wrap up their chat. Scooting to the end of the booth, I wait until Skylar signals it's time to go.

Pulling my phone from my pocket, I open my text history with Levi and type out a quick message.

coming to the show tonight?

My focus bounces between my phone and Skylar's conversation with RJ. When he asks if we want anything boxed up, I lift my gaze and nod. Then I drop my attention back to the screen.

Minutes tick by before his response pops up.

Wouldn't miss it

The hint of a smile tugs at the corners of my mouth as I stare at the screen. In my periphery, food is shoved into boxes and then a bag.

"Ready?"

I lock my phone, shove it in my pocket, and meet Skylar's waiting stare. Rising from the seat, I nod. "Yep. Where to next?"

"Your place."

My lips push out in a pout.

"Unless you want to sit in Poke the Yolk on your day off."

"Oh." I shake my head. For whatever reason, I assumed she wouldn't visit where I work while I tag along. "Yeah, no. I'm good with skipping." I hook an arm around her shoulders as we cross the parking lot for her car. "Going anywhere after PTY?"

"Back to the office."

"Damn."

She unlocks the car and we slip inside.

"When are you going to the bistro or confection place?"

Calhoun's Bistro and Calhoun's Confections are the two high-end food establishments in Stone Bay. Works of art, the meals and desserts will make a dent in your bank account, at least for us common folk.

"Wednesday."

Of course, it's on a day I work. I grumble under my breath. "Figures."

Starting the car, she buckles her seat belt and rolls down the windows. "Promise I'll bring you goodies."

"Yeah?"

Skylar puts the car in reverse, but doesn't ease out of the space yet. Instead, she glances my way. "That's what friends are for." She backs out, puts the car in drive, and aims for the lot exit. "Besides, wasting that food is definitely a crime."

Maybe it's the warmer weather, maybe it's the influx of tourists—I have no clue—but for whatever reason, Dalton's is at capacity tonight. Although not everyone is here to listen to us play, the adrenaline spike at seeing the crowd has me bouncing on my seat behind my drums.

My eyes drift to the table near the front of the stage. Smiles light up my friends' faces as they chat and wait for us to start. One by one, I scan each person at the table. When I reach the end, my heart plummets.

No sign of Levi.

He promised he'd be here.

Why isn't he here?

God, how I hate my heart sometimes. *Stupid, useless organ.* Always sets me up for disappointment.

I don't *need* Levi here, but I want him here.

When Levi and I are in the same room, this intense and extraordinary thrill pumps through my veins. Nothing compares to the high I experience when Levi is nearby. But in complete opposition, he also grounds me in a way no one else does. For some inexplicable reason, when he watches me play, it gives me focus. It centers me. His presence pushes me to play better.

The jukebox music abruptly cuts off and everyone in Dalton's cheers.

The buzz of the crowd fuels me, but I need that extra boost of epinephrine. The surge only Levi delivers.

Guitar hanging across her chest, Hailey steps up to the mic. "Holy shit, Stone Bay." She shields her eyes and surveys the massive crowd. "I have to admit, this is a bit overwhelming."

Cheers and whistles echo throughout the pub.

"But I've never been shy."

"I love you, Hailey," someone yells over the crowd.

Hailey rests a hand over her heart. "That's so sweet. I love you too." She glances at Trip—who lightly strums the strings of his bass guitar—and jerks a thumb in his direction. "But this guy has my heart."

A unanimous *aww* from the crowd fills the place.

She waves them off. "Enough of the sappy stuff." She plucks a few chords on her guitar. "Who wants some rocking fucking roll?"

The crowd roars at a deafening level and it's like nothing I've experienced. It's intense, phenomenal and life-altering.

I press the bass drum foot pedal as we prepare to kick off the first song. When Hailey plays a specific set of chords together, it starts a silent countdown between us. Seconds before I lift my sticks to start the song, my breath catches in my lungs.

Weaving through the throng of people, Levi makes his way to our table. The buzz in my chest moments ago amplifies tenfold. And when he glances up at the stage and our eyes lock for one, two, three seconds, time stands still. For a blip in time, the pub, the crowd, my bandmates and friends... it all disappears. For a split second, it's me and him.

He gives me exactly what I need.

That extra boost.

Him.

On the next breath, I bang my sticks down and start the song. And for the next hour and a half, I casually glance in his direction. Every single time, Levi's eyes are on me.

Such a simple act, but it's what keeps me hooked. It's what gives me hope.

May 3rd

Something about tonight reminded me of years ago. Of the days when L & I hung out in his room for hours. Every once in a while, I'd look up from whatever the hell I was doing and notice his eyes on me. There was no longing or frustration or sympathy on his face. Maybe curiosity. Maybe admiration.

But I lived for those moments. Those tiny moments made me believe in the impossible.

We still hang at his place, only now it's in the pool house. We still do a bunch of the same shit. But it's been years since he's looked at me like that. Often and relentless. Like there's something he's trying to figure out in his brilliant mind, but he just can't.

For a while, not having those moments ate at my memories. It sucked away my hope. Until tonight.

I don't know what the hell made tonight different. I don't know why he suddenly couldn't take his eyes off of me. It was addicting as hell. It fed my starved soul. It rejuvenated my hope for more.

L & I are like the tide. Up then down. Certain then questionable. Connected then disengaged. There isn't any one thing we've done—together or individually —to make our friendship... fluctuate like this. It just does. And I've gotten used to it. I accept it.

But is it so wrong for me to also want more stability? Is it wrong for me to also want more than what we share? I don't think it is. Selfish? Yes. But not wrong.

L & I may never be more than this, more than two friends that enjoy each other's company. This should be enough. This should be fulfilling.

But the way he looked at me tonight... I'd be a fucking idiot to let go of the possibility we could be more. But how long is too long to hold on to hope?

THREE

LEVI

Electronic music blares through the living room as I smash the buttons on my controller and turn it slightly to the right. Beside me, Oliver mimics the action as we both fight to make it to the finish line first. We're neck and neck as I fist the controller tighter.

His knee starts to bounce as we round the last corner on the map.

For a moment, I let him think he has a chance of winning.

He scoots to the edge of his seat, a hint of a smile grazing the corner of his mouth.

I let that faint smile distract me for a split second. Then I punch the button for my final booster and fly past his car on the screen.

"Seriously?" he bellows over the music as he tosses his controller in the direction of the table. It lands with a *thwack*.

Setting my controller aside, I swipe up my phone and turn down the music. "Not like you didn't know I had it." I shrug then point at the television.

He leans in my direction and shoves at my shoulder.

"Dick." The word comes out in a playful tone, but hearing it roll off his tongue sends a surge of heat through my veins.

I swallow down a retort and rise from my seat. The last thing I need to do is feed the beast that lives between us. The one that knows what we both want, but neither will move on. I know why I hold back. Why Oliver does is a mystery.

Since the day we met, there's been this underlying current in the air whenever we exist in the same space. I was unsure how I felt about it in the beginning. But as time ticked by, as the buzz grew undeniable, I accepted it for what it was.

Oliver is my person. My best friend. The one person I trust above all others. The only person I can spill every secret to without fear—not that I've shared *everything*. For now, some secrets are still under lock and key. But even those secrets are inching closer to the surface.

Ambling toward the kitchen, I toss over my shoulder, "Hungry?"

His feet pad over the tile in my wake. "I could eat."

I open the fridge and stare at the sparse contents—water, soda, milk, eggs, bread. But also leftover pizza. I pull out the two boxes from when we grabbed pizza after Oliver's show two nights ago.

I'd had an appetizer at the pub to hold me over until the set ended. Most nights, I watched Oliver play—whether in his garage or on stage—we typically grabbed a bite after. When the server boxed up our leftovers the other night, Oliver told me to bring them to my place.

We don't spend every nonworking hour together. But we spend enough time together that he knows his food will still be edible when he wants it.

"As is or heated up?" I turn the oven on and set it to the suggested temperature on the box.

"Heated enough to take the chill off."

I cover a pan with foil, add the slices, shove them in the oven, and rip the lids off the boxes, tossing them in the recycling bin. Oliver sits on a stool at the kitchen island bar as I return to the fridge and grab us some drinks. I slide him a can of Cherry Coke before I crack open a Pepsi.

"Thanks." A faint smile curves the corners of his mouth. His eyes lift and meet mine as he pops the top. "Saw Tymber at Poke the Yolk yesterday." Oliver takes a swig of soda. "He seems... unsettled." His brows twitch. "Everything okay at work?"

Considering we talk about almost everything, work isn't off-limits when it comes up. I never mention the fine details or share names—confidentiality and all—but I never shy away from job details.

With the most recent job we took on, the company is being held to a higher level of discretion. Which means I need to be vague with Oliver. My skin crawls at the idea, but it's not like I have a choice.

I lean forward and rest my forearms on the island across from Oliver. Eyes focused on my drink, I slowly spin the can on the counter.

"Yeah. Tymber's just stressed." I take a long pull of my drink. "More clients. Some slightly incompetent employees."

With a subtle nod, Oliver hums. I expect him to say something—a joke, perhaps—but the room quiets. He simply stares at the can in his hands.

Silence with Oliver is never uncomfortable. But a muted Oliver is rare, as notable and rare as he is.

As the silence stretches on, I steal the occasional glance across the island. Trace the sharp angle of his jaw with my eyes. Visually dance over his olive skin until I reach his lips.

Fuck... I love his lips.

I continue my visual perusal of his features—the bow

between his top lip and nose, the soft flare of his nostrils and dramatic slope of his nose. My gaze shifts to the side and I stop breathing when my eyes collide with his.

How long has he been watching me ogle him?

My cheeks heat under the delicious scrutiny of his bold, vivid green irises, but I don't dare look away. If he wants to call me out, let him. I'd love to hear the words leave his lips. I'd love to hear him ask me if I was checking him out.

Will I confess if he asks? Doubtful. Not because I'm scared of Oliver knowing how I feel about him. More like it'd do neither of us any good for me to share my truth.

My father would rather me fall off the face of the earth than be seen with a "commoner"—his word choice. Add in the fact that the person I am attracted to is a guy and my father is a semi-closeted homophobe... we can all picture how that conversation would go down.

The timer on the oven buzzes and garners my attention. I blink out of my thoughts and grab the pan from the oven. Transferring the pizza to the bottom half of the boxes, I slide Oliver's food across the counter and then move to take the stool next to him.

We eat in relative silence for the first two slices. Every now and then, I *feel* his gaze on my profile. His addictive basil-green eyes studying the lines of my face.

I fight off a smile as a subtle buzz floats through the air. There is no way he doesn't feel the hum. That potent and vital electricity I only feel with him. He must feel it too.

Finishing the last of my pizza, I shove the box away. I sit taller on my stool and twist a little toward Oliver. As he drops a piece of crust in the box, I open my mouth to apologize.

"Ollie, I—"

A knock on the pool house door cuts me off. "Levi?"

Another knock, this one softer. "It's Mom," she says, as if I don't recognize her voice.

I swallow down my apology and save it for another day. Chin over my shoulder, I holler, "It's open, Mom."

On my next inhale, the gentle clap of her heels echoes throughout the open pool house. She crosses the room, the epitome of elegance and grace. A kind, warm smile highlights her face as she reaches my side.

Wrapping me in a side hug, she kisses my temple. "Hi, darling." After a squeeze of my shoulder, she releases me. "Hello, Oliver. How are you?"

Oliver reaches for the towel on the other side of the counter and wipes his hands off. "Hey, Mrs. West. Good, thanks. And you?"

Her smile doesn't falter once. Unlike my father, Mom has a heart and unabashedly wears it on her sleeve. She is the only reason I haven't packed my shit and moved out.

"Wonderful. Thank you for asking." She averts her attention back to me, her fingers brushing my hair off of my forehead. "You need a haircut," she says with no strength behind the words, knowing full well I won't cut it unless *I* want to. "Just came by to remind you of dinner tonight."

Fuck.

I keep my gaze on Mom but see Oliver staring at me in my periphery.

In the last decade, my parents have tried to mold me into something I'm not. Mostly, it's my father. First, it was politics. When he realized that was a battle he would never win, he focused his energy on something else. Meddling in my love life—not that I really have one.

The minute I turned eighteen, my father started inviting the Calhouns or Kemps over for dinner more often. Growing up, we'd shared meals with the Calhouns and Kemps as regularly as we did some of the founding families. I assumed the uptick was more business than personal. Then, I started putting the pieces together.

Initially, I played along, somewhat oblivious to the arranged relationship my father was trying to orchestrate. It only took dining with them once a week for less than a month for it all to click into place. The questions my father asked the daughters of two other financially secure families in Stone Bay made my stomach sour. It's one thing to ask your own child how they picture their future—career, marriage, children. But the tone my father used as he asked Abigail Calhoun, Sara Kemp, and Jasmine Kemp was borderline creepy.

Though I missed Oliver like a limb, the four years I was gone for college were a reprieve from my father's constant need to find me a bride I didn't want.

Sick of the spectacle, I sigh. "Is it necessary I attend?"

"Of course not, darling."

My entire body relaxes. And I don't miss how Oliver's does as well.

"But your father and I would like you there. Abigail is joining us with her parents. It's been a while since we've all shared a meal together."

"Not long enough," I mutter.

Mom lightly swats my arm. "Be nice. She's a wonderful young lady and a good match."

Oliver stiffens and balls his fingers into fists in his lap. A painful knot forms beneath my diaphragm and renders me speechless.

I hate this. God, I fucking hate this so much.

At twenty-five, my parents still try to rule so much of my life. Mom doesn't dangle the West name and our millions over my head. But put her in a room with my father for five seconds and she goes along with whatever he suggests. And for some absurd reason, he has played matchmaker with me for the past seven years.

Inhaling deeply, I remain even-keeled as I speak. "Yes, she is a wonderful *friend*." I wrap an arm around her shoulders. "And one day, she'll find the right person for her."

Mom steps out of my hold and nods. "That's what your father and I are hoping." Without another word, she spins on her heel and heads for the door. Hand on the doorknob, she peeks over her shoulder and meets my gaze. "Dinner is at six." Her eyes flit to Oliver and I suck in a sharp breath, but then relax when she smiles. "Was nice to see you, Oliver."

Anguish-filled silence smothers me the moment my mother exits the pool house. Inches from where I sit, Oliver won't lift his gaze from the counter. His hands fidget in his lap as both of us figure out what to say or do.

His despair is a hot blade in my chest.

I detest my father for his insistence. Every cell in my body screams to get off the stool, step outside, and yell to the heavens. To storm through the gardens, rush into the main house, and tell my parents I can't fucking do this anymore.

But I don't move. I don't mutter a single word. Now isn't the time, but oh, how I wish it was.

Another apology sits on the tip of my tongue, this one different than the one left unsaid earlier.

"Ollie, I—"

Wood grates tile as he abruptly shoves back on the stool. "Just remembered I have band practice," he says, eyes downcast as he shuffles toward the living room.

Lies.

Unless Hailey or Trip scheduled an impromptu practice, they never meet on Sundays. The weekday practice days may vary, but Sunday is always certain. It's the one day they all get a break. On Sundays, Oliver spends most of the day with his parents.

But I won't call him out. He's upset. I would be too, were I in his shoes.

"Sorry I distracted you from the time." Still on my stool, I swivel in his direction.

On his gaming chair, he laces up his Converse. Lost in the way his nimble fingers tie the laces, I fail to notice his gaze shift. I don't register the fact that he's watching me stare at him. Again.

Still for too long, I glance up and read everything his eyes and expression are saying that his words will not.

Pain. Oliver is in pain. Inexplicable, excruciating pain. All because I fear the repercussions of speaking my truth.

One foot in front of the other, he slowly crosses the room and stands a foot away.

Every breath, every heartbeat, every nerve ending in my body reacts to his proximity. My mind screams for me to be brave. It points a proverbial finger at the man in front of me and implores me to reach out and haul him closer. Breathe in his leather and musk scent mixed with something distinctly him. Nuzzle the crook of his neck and confess my truth in soft whispers on his skin.

Then my father's dreadful voice enters my mind and steals every ounce of joy. Not an occasion passes that I don't hear my father mutter something homophobic when he's aware Oliver is here. The way he says it so casually—guests present or not—tells everyone in the room the type of person he is.

My father doesn't have the standing to outright threaten my future as a West. Though he takes his role in the family quite seriously, only a biological West is capable of making certain changes in our family. According to the prenuptial agreement he signed before he and Mom exchanged vows, he has no control over West family financials.

Since I won't conform to his rules or way of life, his speaking cruelly about someone I care for is his form of punishment. Forcing me to have dinner dates with the daughters of wealthy families in Stone Bay is another form of punishment.

But it hurts more than me, and I despise my father more for his insensitivity.

"Don't worry about it." Oliver shrugs. His eyes drop to my lips for one heartbeat. "No one will be mad if I'm late."

Because there is no band practice.

I slip off my stool and he inches back, but not by much. The heat of him blankets my chest and steals my breath. My pulse whooshes in my ears as I swallow, his gaze dropping to my throat.

"Sorry," I whisper.

Sorry for my asshole father.

Sorry my family continues to parade me around available women in the hopes I'll choose one to marry.

Sorry I am too much of a coward to tell you how much you mean to me.

Sorry I continue to torture us both, but mostly you.

Sorry, sorry, sorry.

With a nod, he licks his lips and takes a step back. "Nothing to apologize for." He pivots on his heel and moves toward the door. "Text me later?"

My chest spasms as the distance grows between us.

"Yeah," I choke out.

No sooner than the word leaves my lips, Oliver steps out the door. And like every other time we go separate ways, the fissure in my heart deepens.

Dinner dishes are cleared from the table as coffee and dessert are set in front of us, neither of which I plan to consume.

For the past hour, my father has glanced in my direction from his end of the table with an insistent look in his eye. As I've done every time he insists on hosting these asinine dinners, I remain stoic. It pisses him off and, in turn, makes me happy.

Muted conversations happen over the final course. On my left, Abigail is silent. If I had to guess, she is as equally displeased about this bullshit as I am.

Immobile in my seat, I stare at the crème brûlée with pity. *What a waste.*

"Levi."

I inhale slowly and shift my gaze to the end of the table. There is no point in responding. Whatever I say will be ignored.

"Since you and Abigail are done eating, why don't the two of you walk through the gardens and catch up."

My molars grind as I narrow my eyes at my father. The hint of a smirk curves one corner of his mouth. It pisses me off. I shove back from the table and huff as the wood legs of the chair glide easily across the marble floor.

"Sure." Then I give everyone my back and walk away.

Goose bumps dance over my skin as I step outside. I pass a tall hedge, tip my head back, close my eyes, and mentally scream at the heavens.

The soft click of the door closing meets my ears and I straighten. Quiet on her feet, Abigail comes to stand beside me. For a moment, we both stand there, unspeaking, staring out at the ornately groomed shrubs and flower bushes.

In my periphery, she crosses her arms over her chest and

shivers. Were I trying to court her, I'd offer to get her something to keep her warm. I'd pull her into my side or rub the length of her bare arms.

I offer her nothing. Not even my voice.

"This sucks," she mutters.

Uncertain what it is she's referring to, I don't respond.

"I don't want this. Do you?"

Now, this catches my attention.

I pivot slightly and glance down at her. Fists clenched under her arms and jaw muscles tight, Abigail Calhoun appears just as irritated by this whole charade as I am.

"Not at all." I shrug. "No offense."

She waves off my comment. "None taken." Peeking over her shoulder toward the house, she gives a curt nod. "My parents don't know, but I've been seeing someone."

My brows shoot up in surprise.

"Please don't say anything."

I relax my expression and give what I hope is a sympathetic smile. "I won't."

"Thank you." Her whole frame sighs. "I'm in love with him."

"Why don't they know you're with him?"

Abigail rolls her eyes. "Anyone in this town with our kind of wealth is trying to find suitable matches for their children." She looks me dead on. "We may not be a founding family, but we're as close as they come. Daddy may be laid back at times, but he and Mom still want us to marry *good* people."

"Fucking bullshit," I mutter. "I'm twenty-five, and you're, what?"

"Thirty."

"We're grown-ass people. Why do they keep shoving us together like cattle?"

"Sometimes I wonder if they actually care about *me*." Her emphasis on the last word comes out so softly.

I wish I could assure her things will be fine. But I have a feeling this horse and pony show will go on until our families get what they want.

I hate this for me, for her, for the people we care about and who care about us. Sure, I could walk away and move into my own place. Hell, Oliver or Tymber would happily offer me a place to stay. But running away won't solve the problem; only exacerbate it.

I stay because it is the only way to consistently express myself, not that my father hears a word I say. I stay because no one should be bullied into something they don't want or need in their life. I stay because, dammit, I have a say in how my life goes.

And Jefferson Thornhill-West does not own me.

He wants to shove Abigail Calhoun down my throat? Fine. I'll give him what he wants but on my terms.

My eyes meet hers.

On our terms.

"Want to get our parents off our backs?"

Her whole face brightens. "Yes."

I glance over to the door to make sure we are alone. "What if we make our parents believe we're dating, but we're not?"

"You want to... fake date?" Her forehead wrinkles with confusion.

"I don't *want* to, but it'll shut them up." How blissful the silence will be. "We carry on as we have been. Live our own lives. Go out for the occasional dinner to keep up appearances. But other than that, we do whatever the hell we want. You go out with whoever you're dating. I'll do my thing. We can coordinate in texts when our parents think we're together, but we're not."

Abigail bounces in place. "This is brilliant."

I shrug. "Beats being forced to have awkward dinners with our families."

"We're fake dating?"

"Yep."

She squeals. "I can't wait to tell Desmond."

"As long as he won't tell anyone else…"

"He won't."

I take my phone out of my pocket, unlock it, open a new contact, and hand her my phone. "Add your info and I'll shoot you a text."

After she keys in her name and number, she returns my phone. We move farther into the garden and talk logistics for a bit. Once we are both on the same page with the major details, we head back to the house.

We tell our parents we decided to give this a shot, and both families are overjoyed.

A half hour later, I drop to my knees in front of the toilet and lose my dinner.

FOUR

OLIVER

Do you ever feel like the rest of the world is moving forward while you're stuck in a perpetual cycle of the unknown?

Oblivious to my surroundings, I stare down at the server kiosk with an unfocused gaze. My breaths come in quick, shallow bursts as a light sheen of perspiration blankets my skin. Everything is foggy—the restaurant, the people, my thoughts.

I've cashed out customer's orders countless times over the years. I could probably do it with my eyes closed. Yet my hand is immobile above the screen. My fingers twitch every other breath but otherwise remain motionless. As though I'm broken.

In a way, I am broken.

If anyone is to blame for my malfunctioning brain, it is one-hundred-percent me. Because no matter how much time passes or how many times I attempt to drill reality into my head, I never see the truth for what it is.

Levi West is not mine.

Not in the way I want him to be.

My heart tells me to quit being pessimistic. My soul weeps then smiles and says to hold on to hope a little longer. But my mind… he's a fickle bastard as he says it's time to let go of fantastical dreams.

A hand on my shoulder startles me and I jump.

"Sorry." Kirsten pulls her hand away. "You zoned out for a bit. Wanted to make sure you were okay."

Shit. How long have I been standing here? Thank goodness I don't need to return a card or change to the customers.

I close out the order, stow the cash in the till and tip in my apron, then shut the drawer. I take a deep breath and blink away my incessant thoughts about Levi and the fact I haven't heard from him in almost a week.

Everything's fine. He's bogged down at work. He told you as much on Sunday.

"You are okay. Right?" Kirsten shifts until she fills my vision, a heavy dose of concern written in the lines of her face.

I hate lying to people, especially family and friends. But the occasional sprinkle of fiction to appease their hearts and avoid conversations I don't want to have is best for us all.

The lump I've felt for days in my throat swells as saliva pools in my mouth. My brows tug together as the backs of my eyes sting. It all happens so fast. And on the next breath, I shove it all away. I meet Kirsten's waiting gaze and force myself to smile as I nod.

"Yeah. Of course." I move past her to grab a cleaning rag from the bleach water bin. "Why wouldn't I be?"

Before she's able to answer, I exit the server alley and dart to the vacant table in my section.

But Kirsten is not easily deterred. On my heels, she weaves between tables and across the dining room. Every other table, she pauses to ask patrons how their breakfast tastes or if they need anything. The regulars love her. Most of them come in for the company over the food, though both are excellent.

Sidling up to me, I feel her curious stare on my profile as I stack dishes and wipe down the table. While I work, I keep my gaze fixed on what I'm doing. The last thing I want is to see her pity.

"Talk to me," she whispers softly to avoid catching the attention of the gossipmongers. "You haven't been yourself for days." She grabs one of the two stacks of dishes. "It's okay to be sad or upset or angry." The light weight of her hand rests on my shoulder. "It's also okay to let others in. Give us some of that weight to carry."

Kirsten makes it sound as though I'm imprisoned in a dark cave with no escape. I love her for wanting to help. I love her for not giving up. And I love that she doesn't mention Levi once.

With this, though, there isn't much to unload. There isn't much to share unless you count my irrational, relentless thoughts and feelings.

So what if I am upset about Levi's parents constantly thrusting him toward wealthy young women in town. Me telling Kirsten, Skylar, or Delilah won't make it any better. Telling them won't make it stop. What is the point of complaining? It will only make it hurt more.

Tossing the rag on top of the other stack of dishes, I scoop it up from the table and head for the kitchen. "Everything's fine, K. I swear." I push through the door, hold it open for her to pass, and then follow her to the dirty dishes rack by the dishwasher. "Things have just felt... off." I shrug.

"Is it Levi?"

My eyes dart to Maxine—Max to those close to her—the lead cook at Poke the Yolk. In the zone at the stove, she pays neither of us any attention.

I gnash my molars for one, two breaths before I relax my jaw. "Is *what* Levi?"

Kirsten's eyes widen as she lifts her hands in surrender and takes a step back. "Just trying to help."

A sigh leaves my lips as frustration bubbles in my chest. "Sorry." I hang my head. "Sleep has been shit."

An arm slips around my shoulders and Kirsten hugs me to her side. "Chin up, Ollie." She shakes my frame. "Nothing a little caffeine and chocolate chip pancakes can't cure."

At the mention of pancakes, Max peers over her shoulder. "CCPs for Ollie. Check."

I laugh.

A minute ago—hell, ten seconds ago—Max paid us zero attention. One mention of food... bam! She hears every word.

"Thanks, Max."

She tosses me a wink. "Sure thing."

Kirsten and I exit the kitchen and get back to our tables. Max calls out my order and I collect it from the kitchen pass-through window. I fill a mug with coffee, dump several packets of sugar and a heavy hand of creamer in, and sit on a stool at the end of the diner counter.

As I unravel my silverware, the bell over the door jingles. I look up to greet whoever walked in and spy Skylar with a bright and cheery smile on her face. It doubles when she sees me sitting down to eat. She winds her way through the restaurant and parks on the stool to my left.

"Morning." I shove a forkful of pancakes in my mouth. "Here for work?" The question comes out garbled and I apologize.

Skylar chuckles as she leans into my side and gives me a hug. "Morning, Ollie." She shakes her head. "Nope. I missed breakfast this morning, so I'm strictly here to eat."

I point my fork at my plate. "I suggest the chocolate chip pancakes with a healthy dollop of whipped cream."

Skylar eyes the disappearing pancakes on my plate and hums. "They do look good, but the banana and Nutella crepes have been calling my name for an hour."

"Another favorite of mine." I nod.

Kirsten finishes up with a customer then comes over to greet Skylar. They chat for a few minutes—mostly about their boyfriends (insert eye roll)—before Kirsten walks off and inputs her order.

Skylar swivels in her seat to face me. "I know you're short on time, but we should all get together soon. It's been far too long."

The jealous part of me wants to say, *Yeah, because you're all too busy with your significant others.* But I bite my tongue.

Truly, I am happy for Skylar, Kirsten, and Delilah. They found love. They've started the next phase of their lives with someone they care about. Life has never been better for them, and that's a good thing.

But damn, do I miss them. I miss seeing them more often than not.

Yes, I've spent a significant amount of time with Levi over the years. But I've spent just as much time with Skylar, Kirsten, and Delilah.

And now… time is all I have. Except it's mostly alone.

"I'd like that." I sip my coffee. "Text the group with dates and we'll sort it out."

Skylar riffles through her purse and pulls out her phone. Her fingers fly across the screen. A moment later, my phone vibrates in my pocket. Then it vibrates again.

Wiping my hands off, I fish my phone from my pocket to see two text notifications. One from Skylar and the second from Levi. My pulse soars in my chest as I stare down at the screen, unsure which to read first.

I tap on Skylar's message.

SKY

Movie night, next week, my place. What days are good for everyone?

I type out a quick response.

Monday, Tuesday, Thursday, Sunday

After I hit send, I close the group chat and tap on my text history with Levi.

LEVI

Sorry I'm a dick. Work has been insane. Feels like I never leave my desk. Hang tonight?

For days, my brain has spiraled. I've replayed last Sunday again and again, overanalyzing every minute. His eyes on me as the food reheated. How it looked like he wanted to say something but wouldn't or couldn't. The mention of Abigail Calhoun by his mom and how she'd be a *good match* for Levi. The way his mom's words shredded me as Levi agreed to dinner. But most of all, that undeniable electricity in the room as I prepared to leave.

I swear it's all in my head, but maybe it's not. Maybe Levi feels *something* for me too.

Days of silence from him has been torture. I thought he ghosted me or finally caved to his parents' persistence, or maybe he and Abigail clicked and decided to give a relationship a try.

I went on some mind-bender while he has been swamped at work.

Idiot.

Sucks about work. Band practice tonight.

Mind if I watch?

Fire licks my skin from head to toe. I fucking love when Levi watches me play, whether it's with the band or solo in my house or his. If only I were brave enough to tell him half the songs I write are centered around him or us.

Not at all. Same time as usual.

He reacts with a thumbs-up but doesn't say anything else.

"Who ya chatting with, Ollie?" Skylar singsongs. "You look a little flush."

I lock my phone, shove it in my pocket, and chug the last of my coffee. "No one." I set the cup on my plate with my napkin and utensils and push it away. "Just wondering how long movie night will last before one of y'all starts making out."

Skylar sets her fork down, her expression deadpan. "Really, Ollie. You were thinking of your friends making out? And blushing because of it?" She shakes her head. "Doubtful. But I'll let it slide." A wicked look takes over her face. "For now."

"Whatever." I rise from my stool and walk around the counter until I'm opposite her. Pointing at Skylar, I add, "No romance movies. Seriously. I'm not in the mood to watch you guys get handsy."

I take my dishes to the dirty bin then return to wipe down the counter and put out a new place setting.

"Ollie?"

Tossing the rag in the water, I meet Skylar's waiting stare. "Yeah?"

Her features soften. "Do we make you uncomfortable?" She waves a hand animatedly. "When all of us get together, I mean."

Yes. No. Sort of.

I shake my head. "Of course not. I'm just giving you shit."

The look on her face says she isn't buying a single word. The corner of her mouth twitches, but she doesn't smile. "Please tell us if we do."

I swallow and shove down the emotion building in my chest. "Promise I will."

"Love you, Ollie."

Warmth wraps around me at her words and that she didn't push the subject. "Love you too, Sky."

Hair damp and clinging to my forehead, I slam my sticks down on the drums again and again. Trip plucks the strings of his base, occasionally leaning forward to belt out the chorus. A powerhouse as always, Hailey assaults the strings of her guitar as she bounces inches from her mic and belts out lyrics. Individually, our music sounds questionable. But once everything comes together, it is rock and roll perfection.

Our followers say it's the quintessential blend of alternative and contemporary rock with a dash of classic.

As our last song for today's practice starts, the side door of the garage opens. I falter a moment as Levi walks in with three large pizza boxes but quickly get back in my groove. And for the rest of the song, I keep my head down and focus on playing.

It isn't long before the song ends and the hum of the amps fills the garage. As per usual, at the end of practice, Hailey, Trip, and I discuss what we loved and what needs work. We aren't perfectionists by any means, but we also want to play music we are proud of.

Grabbing waters from the fridge, I join everyone on the couches facing our makeshift stage.

Initially, my parents weren't keen on turning part of the garage into my band's studio. But the more I played and loved music, the more willing my parents were to gift us the space. Especially after we struggled to find places to practice. Being an only child, more often than not, I tend to get what I want. In the end, they agreed to let the band use the last bay of our three-car garage as long as we kept it clean and didn't let our stuff drift into the other bays.

I hand Trip and Hailey water bottles before I take a seat next to Levi. Opening my water, I guzzle half the bottle then sigh in relief as my body cools. I twist the cap back in place and set the bottle on the floor between my feet.

Sweeping my sweaty hair off my forehead, I turn toward Levi. "Hey."

Half a slice of pizza in one hand, he covers his mouth with the other. "Hey." He finishes the bite in his mouth. "Good set?"

I shift my focus to the three boxes on the coffee table in front of us. After a quick mental game of eenie, meenie, miney mo, I grab a slice of veggie lovers and sit back. "Yeah. Still some shit we need to tweak, but we're pretty solid otherwise."

I shove the pizza in my mouth and moan when the salty cheese hits my tongue.

Beside me, Levi tenses. The sudden jerk silences me and stirs up a dozen questions.

My eyes flash to Hailey and Trip, but they are lost in their own conversation as they eat.

Did that really happen? Or is my mind playing tricks?

Hour-long minutes tick by as neither of us says a word. Per

usual, it isn't uncomfortable. Time with Levi is always worth every second. It's the leaving that sucks.

"Sorry about this week." He covers his face with his hands, rubs his eyes, then drags them down his cheeks. "This new client..." He drops his elbows to his knees, clasps his hands, and turns his head to meet my gaze. "I think it's bigger than they or Tymber knew."

I don't ask for details because Levi can't share them. But he and Tymber both need someone to confide in when work gets heavy. They shouldn't have to keep it bottled up.

"Wish I could help."

The corner of his mouth twitches as he nods. "You do." He sits up and inhales deeply. "This"—he waves a hand toward the stage—"being here with you, it helps."

Warmth blooms in my chest as I absorb his admission. Uncertain *how* exactly I help, I allow myself to fantasize it is more than just giving him a place to hang out after work. I indulge in the possibility that I am more than his friend.

"Ollie, man." Trip rises from the couch and holds a hand out for Hailey. "We're gonna head out." He looks to Levi. "Thanks for the grub. Appreciate it."

"Anytime."

As we exchange goodbyes, I confirm our next practice. After a hug from Hailey, they disappear out the side door.

Silence echoes through the garage as I reach for another slice of pizza. Usually, when it's quiet like this with Levi, it's nice. Peaceful. Easy.

But today, the energy in the room feels *off*.

"I need to tell you something."

Ding, ding, ding.

"But I don't want to upset you."

Fuck. This is going to hurt.

I chew the food in my mouth and reluctantly swallow as I

set the rest of the slice down. "Okay..." The word is a mile long as it leaves my lips. My stomach churns, and I inhale a slow, deep breath.

His fingers dive into his hair before they fall to his lap. "Not saying you won't, but I need you to hear everything." A pained look consumes his expression. "Please," he whispers.

Leaning back, I nod. "Yeah. Of course."

Knee bouncing, he looks anywhere but at me. His hands fist in his lap, then relax. "Dinner last Sunday was an overzealous show like usual. Fancy meal, wine, dessert." Sinking into the couch, he tips his head back and stares at the ceiling. "Every time is worse. And not just for me." He shakes his head. "For whoever my parents force to sit next to me too."

I study his profile as he gets lost in his head a moment. Without looking too hard, it's easy to see how this whole situation with his parents is slowly eating away at his soul.

If I were able to make this better for him, I would without hesitation.

"Mid-dessert, I left the table." He pauses and swallows. Then, this indescribable emotion twists his expression. "Abigail followed me outside."

My stomach knots, and I fist my shirt.

Levi rotates his head against the back of the couch. His luminous blue eyes lock onto my greens and hold me captive.

I forget how to breathe.

"She's in love with someone else."

Cool air fills my lungs as I mentally sigh with relief.

"Like me," he continues, "she doesn't want this. Her family doesn't know about the guy she's dating because they wouldn't approve of him."

At this, my heart breaks for Abigail Calhoun. No one should have to hide who they love.

But who am I to think as much? I've hidden my love for Levi for years.

"I came up with this crazy idea. Then we walked the gardens for a bit and shared our sides of this whole ordeal."

The reprieve I felt a moment ago vanishes.

I shift my gaze from his as my eyes lose focus. The world wobbles beneath me and I close my eyes. Suddenly, I'm teetering on a rocky cliff near the bay. Curiosity has me eager for more details, while anxiety begs me to plug my ears and ignore what he says next.

"To get our parents off our backs, Abigail and I made a pact. We agreed to pretend we're dating."

Bile crawls up my throat as sweat coats my skin.

"It's not real." His voice blends with the white noise in my ears.

I'm going to be sick.

It shouldn't bother me this much. Since I've known Levi, his parents have been trying to marry him off. He has been on several dates with women over the years. He never bragged about them or shared much of what happened. Thank goodness.

Each and every one of those dates and dinners with his family made me ill—physically, mentally, emotionally. But a piece of me always knew the dates and dinners were solely at his parents' insistence.

This… feels different. Irreversible.

"Ollie." My name is a whisper on his lips. Soft. Distant.

My fingers twitch in my lap as I process his news over and over.

I want to twist in my seat, grab him by the shoulders, and shake this ridiculous idea out of his head. I want to cup his cheeks, haul him forward, and press my lips to his. Tell him how much I care about him. What he means to me. That I love him.

But I can't.

Doing those things—saying those words—will ruin us.

Warmth grazes my forearm from my elbow to my wrist and I suck in a sharp breath.

He's touching me. Really touching me.

"Ollie, please look at me."

Fire ignites under my skin as his finger slowly trails up and down my forearm.

"Please," he says, a breath above a whisper.

Nervous energy swirls beneath my diaphragm as I face him without hurry. Our eyes connect and I see so many conflicting messages.

I don't know what to believe.

"It's. Not. Real." His knuckles brush my skin. "I swear."

Damn, I want it to be true. I want this farce he and Abigail set in motion to be a hoax.

His hand falls away. "All I ask is for you to remember that, no matter what happens."

My brows pinch together. "What does that mean?" The words come out scratchy and accusatory.

"If our families think we're dating, we have to act like we're dating."

I bolt up from the couch with the need to move and plunge my fingers into my hair. My Vans clap the concrete of the garage floor as I pace the length of the stage. Over and over and over, I shake my head.

"Dinners and movies are what I mean."

I fist my hair and tug.

Don't ask. Don't ask. Don't ask.

"Time with her and…" I bite my tongue and force myself to

not add *kissing and sex*. "And less with me. I get it." I stop and stare at Mama's car. "Need to keep up appearances."

The couch creaks behind me, and then I *feel* him at my back. His heat, his energy, *him*. His clean, cedar scent fills my nose, and internally I weep.

Why is life so fucking unfair? Why did I pick someone impossible to love?

"This changes nothing," he whispers inches from my ear.

God, he is so close.

"I promise."

"How?" I barely recognize my own voice.

"We talked logistics. We set rules in place for each other. Limits."

I scoff. "And when your parents expect more?" I drop my chin to my chest and inhale deeply. "You know what? Forget I asked." Spinning around, I hold his heady blue eyes with mine. "It doesn't matter." I swallow. "We're just friends." The last three words rub my throat raw.

Nimble fingers wrap around my forearm. "Ollie, don't be mad. I can't..."

Against every instinct in my soul, I take a step back. Then another. "I think you should go."

His eyes glaze over as hurt swallows his expression. "It's not real." He shakes his head. "Please understand."

Neither of us has once confessed we are anything other than friends. More recently, there have been questionable moments between us—like the one in his kitchen less than a week ago. Nothing more, though.

In this moment, while Levi begs me to see his side of the situation, my hopeful heart wonders if he does feel more for me than friendship. I don't want to let go of the possibility. But it would literally break me if I made a move and he rejected me.

With an imperceptible nod, I cross my arms over my chest and close myself off. "I'll try," I promise. "Just… give me time."

He takes a step back, and my heart splinters. "Whatever you need." *Step.* "You know where to find me." *Step.* "Anytime, no matter what."

And then he turns away from me, crosses to the door, and leaves.

Fingers curled into painful fists, I storm forward and kick one of the open pizza boxes across the garage.

May 10th

Today was shit. I hate every damn thing about today. Well, not everything. Okay, maybe 99.9% of everything.

For a split second, he felt like more today. And I don't mean my one-sided feelings. I'm talking about him.

It hurt him to tell me about the charade he and her are putting on for their parents. He says it's not real. I want to believe him. But I just can't. Something about it doesn't sit right. Maybe because I don't know what it's like to have parents that constantly force you on dates you don't want. Especially since they're both grown-ass adults. It seems bizarre.

What does her boyfriend think? If he's not mad, he must not love her. Not like I love him.

I hate that I told him I need time. The last

thing I want is time away from him. This whole thing is fucked up.

He touched me tonight. <u>Not like a friend</u>. I don't know what the fuck it means. And I can't ask him. Because I told him I need space and time.

This is fucked!!!

FIVE

LEVI

In times like this, I wish I wasn't so good at my job.

Since Tymber handed over the Messer file weeks ago, I've been neck-deep in research. I sifted through the national missing persons database for any information they had on Sydney Messer. Then I filtered the database for other recent missing persons in the Northwest under age eighteen. As of Monday, the four cities I'm focusing on—Seattle, Tacoma, Olympia, and Portland—have reported more than a hundred missing persons in the past sixty days.

To some, an average of twenty-five missing minors in each city isn't high. They might argue that thousands of children go missing every year.

But this is different.

The hundred-plus faces I've burned into my brain aren't toddlers lost in a store. They aren't delinquent children mad at their parents who pack a bag and run away. Each of the missing persons is between twelve and seventeen years old. Majority of them were out with others their age, then abducted once alone.

Last week, in coordination with James Messer, Tymber and

I set up a website for people to submit information, anony-mous or not. Though Sydney Messer is who we are being paid to locate, the website has images, names, and minimal details of the other children reported missing.

Every morning, when I check the submission log, there are no less than twenty new entries. Some submissions contain repetitive information. But at least once a day, we get new intelligence. Minor yet major clues such as height or hair color or someone struggling near a specific location. Each new piece is added to the ever-expanding file and compared to other tips submitted.

But as the hours have dragged on with no significant leads, as desperation to find these children has eaten away at my soul, I've started digging in the darkest pits of hell.

Accessing the dark web is no easy feat. It takes specific programs. You need to be friendly with people that lurk in those grotesque, shadowed places. Worst of all, you have to pretend to be one of them. Dive into this deplorable mindset. Speak their language without hesitation.

Needless to say, I haven't eaten much in the past couple of weeks. And most of what I've eaten hasn't stayed down. I wish I could say it's strictly the morbid images and vile conversations I've seen online that have me vomiting once or more a day. But it's not the only reason.

As promised, I've given Oliver space. Let him do his thing while I do mine.

But it's been twelve fucking miserable days since the day in his garage. Since I told him about my *brilliant* idea to fake date Abigail. Since I wanted to take his face in my hands, press my lips to his, and show him where my heart really lies. Where it has been for several years.

Other than work, my focus has been shit. If anything, since Oliver and I entered limbo, all I do is work. Sleep is a joke.

Keeping up pretenses with Tymber, my parents, and Abigail is a challenge.

I fucking hate it.

A ping echoes through the room and I shift my attention to the top right screen. Rows of code fill the screen and I scan each line. Hunt for the smallest of clues.

"What is that?"

I inch closer to the screen and narrow my eyes. Scan a section of code again and again. Lose focus as I read the jumbled, nonsensical words for the fifth time.

"A code within the code," I mutter then laugh. "Smart, sick motherfuckers."

Anyone with expansive coding knowledge should pick up on it. See the intricate details sprinkled throughout several lines. On an actual site, they'd be Easter eggs hidden in images or random text. Something these sadistic bastards would know how to find.

But not everyone in government offices has programming expertise or the right brainpower to decipher these hidden messages. The front end of missing persons is your average investigator. A person with a badge and ambition.

I screenshot the lines and add them to the file. Then, I spend the next hour decoding it. And when I finally have what I believe is the clue, I question if I got it right: *golden wings overhead.*

"What the hell does that mean?"

I stare at the words until my eyes cross and my mind warps. A riddle within deciphered code. A phrase that sends a message to all who land on this page. But what the hell is the message?

Sifting through my memory bank, I search for yellow or golden-colored birds and their names. When I hit a dead end, I scan the web. Nothing makes sense.

"Maybe it's not a bird…"

My phone vibrates on the desk and I glance at the screen to see a text alert. Hope soars in my chest that Oliver is breaking the silence.

Ignoring work, I swipe up my phone and see the message is from Abigail. Instantly, I deflate.

Should I be the one to reach out first? Or would I upset him for overstepping?

Fuck. I wish I knew.

Tapping on the notification, I read Abigail's message.

ABI

Sorry to bug you at work. We should grab a bite tonight. Mom asked me how things were going. She didn't like my lack of details.

A little more than two weeks have passed since we agreed to fake date. Since that night in the gardens, Abigail and I have spent maybe two hours together for dinner. And, of course, our parents were present. After the night ended, she texted to suggest we get to know each other better. That way, we can answer mundane questions our parents ask when we're not in the same room.

So we've been texting almost daily. Nothing life-changing. More like the small details—favorite foods, music, sports, things we've done recently. Considering she works with her mom, she has a higher chance of being asked questions.

Over the past couple of weeks, a friendship has formed as we've chatted. It's nice to add another person to my small list of friends.

No worries. I needed a break. I'm good with dinner. Where?

Anywhere our parents won't be lol

At this, I laugh.

We both come from wealthy families with high expectations, though her family is a bit more laid back than mine. A lot of people think money equals happiness. For us, it's a prison sentence with unattainable expectations.

I can't wholeheartedly speak for Abigail, but all I want is to be myself. Just Levi. Not some stuffy politician with an overinflated ego. Not someone deemed town royalty because his great-times-however-many-grandfather was dubbed a town founder over a hundred years ago.

All I want is a simple, normal life. One that includes Oliver.

Sloppy's BBQ

My family wouldn't set foot inside the local laid-back barbecue joint. Abigail's dad or brother, maybe, but unlikely.

Good choice. 7?

7 works

Meet you there. Have a good day ☺

I react with a thumbs-up, lock my phone, and toss it aside.

Elbows on the desk, I drop my head in my hands and fist my hair. Pinch my eyes closed and groan at the reality of my life.

Secrets. So many damn secrets. My own concealed truths. The ones I unearth at work. And now this… pretending to be with someone I have zero interest in romantically just to appease my parents and hers.

It's too much. A weight that grows heavier by the day. A weight I won't be able to support forever.

———

"Last weekend, we went to Lake Lavender for some R&R." Abigail sighs from her side of the booth. "It was so nice to walk around and hold hands and not worry about people seeing us together."

I pick at the baked beans on my plate and hum.

"Have you been there?"

Swapping my fork for my drink, I take a long sip and shake my head.

"Such a cute town. Small like ours, but less pretentious." She laughs.

I remain mute on my side of the booth.

Has Abigail always talked this much?

I think back to every occasion we've been in the same room together. Not once do I recall her prattling on like this. If I'm honest, it grates my nerves.

She blathers on about her romantic weekend in Lake Lavender with her boyfriend, Desmond. I nod and hum at all the right times but otherwise disengage from the conversation.

Am I the asshole for basically giving her the cold shoulder? Yes. Without question.

Do I give a fuck that I've detached myself from the situation? No, not a single fuck is given.

I made my stance in this situationship abundantly clear. It's all for show. A way to shut our parents up and get them off our backs. Period.

Sure, I should be friendlier toward Abigail. At least act as though I'm interested in her life. Be a *friend*.

But why add another lie to the stack? It's not as if I'm

outgoing and chipper with Tymber or Oliver. Why be someone I'm not for her? If anything, that'd make it worse.

When she realizes I have yet to engage in conversation, she asks about work. How it's going. What project has me so busy and exhausted. I give her brief, vague answers and tell her I'm not at liberty to share details.

And then, somehow, the conversation feels lighter.

She tells me about her boyfriend and what he does for a living—retirement home nurse. That they're saving up and hope to move out of Stone Bay in the next year or two. She talks about her nephew, Tucker, and the hardships he's endured since his mom abandoned him with her brother.

Surprising myself, I tell her I'd like to meet her boyfriend. That we should all hang out together sometime. Make this already awkward situation a little less uncomfortable.

When the suggestion leaves my lips, I immediately think of Oliver. How I wish it was him across the table instead of Abigail. How I wish I could bring him along when Abigail brings her boyfriend.

The rest of dinner is a blur of more one-sided conversation. Unfortunately for her, I don't feel bad for my silence.

This is all a farce and I don't need to know her. Nothing more than basics. We can be surface-level friends without spilling all our truths or secrets.

We skip dessert and I pay the bill. Roughly an hour after slipping into the booth, we head for the exit. I hold the door open and let her walk out first.

The wind whips her hair and she laughs, tucking it behind her ears. A few steps into the lot, I turn in the direction of my car, ready to leave.

"Thanks, Levi."

Not wanting to be a total dick, I turn around. "No problem."

She takes a step in my direction, but there's still a solid two or three feet between us. "You've made this whole thing a little less weird." She laughs.

I don't know what to say or how to react to that, so I remain silent and still.

When she takes another step and reaches for my arm, I inch back. And as I do, movement in my periphery draws my attention. Shifting my gaze across the side street, I freeze.

Just outside the pizza restaurant, Oliver stands impossibly still, his eyes glued to my face. He may be several feet away, but the hurt in his eyes is undeniable.

With a subtle shake of his head, he wilts.

The sight is a jagged knife to the heart.

Abigail forgotten, I walk toward Oliver. When he starts to move, I lengthen my stride.

"Ollie!"

He picks up speed, and so do I. And then I'm running across the street, ignoring traffic and pedestrians and everything else trying to stop me from getting to him.

I just need to reach him.

Please let me make it to him before he drives off.

"Ollie!"

SIX

OLIVER

My calves burn as I weave through the parking lot for my car. The occasional person blocks my path and slows me down, but I don't stop. I can't.

Rage fuels each step forward. Funny enough, I can't pinpoint what pisses me off most. Seeing Levi with Abigail. The fact that I've ignored him for so long. That he hasn't reached out the entire time. Or that I had to park so damn far and he'll probably catch up.

For twelve damn days, my life has been utter shit. I've replayed the night in my garage too many times to count. His telling me the whole scenario with Abigail is fake has been on a stomach-churning loop. By now, I hoped it would've sunk in —the situation and his truth.

For whatever reason, it won't.

And now… seeing them in public together… it fucking hurts.

Neither of us has been celibate over the years. I've had my share of fun. Fucked random guys, pretended it was Levi, then never saw them again. He went out with women in college and has gone along with the arranged dates his parents set up.

We've never outright discussed our sex lives, but there's not a chance in hell Levi is still a virgin. Maybe when it comes to men, he is, but not sex in general.

"Ollie!" he shouts again as I near my car. "Fucking wait!"

I reach my car and curse as I fumble with the pizza to dig out my keys. Before I hit the unlock button on my fob, Levi is at my side. He shoves my shoulder and knocks the box out of my hand.

"What the hell, Ollie!" He bends at the waist, clutches his knees, and tries to catch his breath.

My gaze drops to his heaving frame and every ounce of fight or flight leaves my body.

I want us to go back to the way we were. Ollie and Levi. Levi and Ollie. Two halves of a whole, neither of us complete without the other.

His breathing settles as he rises to his full height. When his blue eyes slam into mine, so does his anger, his pain, his disbelief. He inches closer and I step back, smacking into my car.

"Why the hell did you run?"

I want to laugh, scream, ask him why wouldn't I run? But nothing comes out. My eyes refuse to look anywhere but at his eyes. I refuse to miss a single damn moment of him this close. Shadows may mask us from others, but I see every line of his profile. I see the faint glint in his eyes. Every twitch of his muscles.

He's so damn close.

Levi gives the subtlest shake of his head as he inches impossibly closer. His clean cedar scent invades my nose.

I fight the urge to lean forward, drag my nose up his throat, and inhale deeply.

"I told you," he whispers. "It's not real. Don't be mad."

It's on the tip of my tongue to tell him I am allowed to be

angry. At him. At the situation. At what it has done to us, whatever we are.

He swallows and my eyes drop to his throat. Countless fantasies of my lips on his skin spark to life. Dreams of licking a path up the column of his throat and sucking the pulse point beneath his ear.

My dick swells behind my zipper. I lift my gaze back to his and watch as his eyes widen. Without a doubt, he reads my mixed thoughts.

"It's not real," he repeats. Softer. Pleading.

His eyes dart around us, scanning the street and parking lot. When his eyes meet mine again, they're loaded with conflict and uncertainty. Muted, I give him a moment to articulate his indecision.

When what feels like minutes pass, I clench my fists at my side. I should leave. I should pick my pizza up off the ground, drive home, and lock myself in my apartment.

This... us... we are going nowhere except in circles.

I extend my arm for the door handle but only make it inches before Levi presses into me. I suck in a sharp breath as his weight crushes me against the car.

"What are you—"

"Fuck it."

His lips crash down on mine as his hands fist my hoodie. It takes a moment before my mind and body get on the same wavelength. But the moment they do, the world disappears around us.

I reach for his hips and haul him forward. Return his kiss with equal fervor. Moan as his tongue darts out and licks the seam of my lips. Melt when my tongue grazes his and I taste him for the first time.

Holy. Fucking. Shit.

Levi is kissing me. Not some simple peck on the cheek. Not

some virginal kiss on the lips. No, his damn tongue is down my throat. His hard dick is grinding against the length of mine. And his moans… it's as though he's starved. Ravenous. Greedy for more.

I bring a hand to his cheek and cup his jaw. Tilt his head and deepen the kiss.

And as quickly and unexpectedly as the kiss comes on, he breaks it and takes a step back. His brows bend in confusion. Wide eyes locked on mine, he covers his mouth and shakes his head.

The bravery he had moments ago disappears. In its place, his mask slips back on.

He is losing control and that scares the shit out of him.

As well as I know Levi, there is no perfect way to handle this situation. This is something he has to sort out on his own. All I can do is support him and his decision.

"Levi, it's—"

"No." He shakes his head and retreats farther. His hands ball into fists as his whole expression tightens. "I'll…" He rolls his lips between his teeth and takes another step back. "I'll text you later."

Before I get a word out, he whips around and runs across the street. Frozen next to my car, I stare after him as he unlocks his Ferrari, slips behind the wheel, and speeds away seconds later.

Several minutes pass before I unstick my feet, grab my pizza, and head home.

May 22nd

L fucking kissed me! And not some lame, half-ass

kiss. Like a full-on, I-won't-be-able-to-live-another-day-without-kissing-you kiss. God, it was so much better than I imagined. The way he held on to me. The way he pinned me to the car and gave me all his weight.

Fuck... it was heaven and hell and the best form of torture.

And then he freaked out and bolted. Not that I expected anything else. For a long time, I hoped L would show some level of attraction for me. Before this whole fake dating bullshit happened, I got a glimpse of it. Or so I thought. I'm not sure if my mind was playing tricks. If I'm confusing what I thought were signals.

But after tonight, I'm less confused. L, on the other hand, is probably more confused than ever.

Please don't let it be another two weeks before we talk again. I can't handle it. As much as I needed that time and distance to think, not talking with him every day was hell. Not hanging out was pure torture. Even if we never kiss again, I want L in my life.

If he only wants to be friends, I'll be his friend and nothing more. I'll go back to the way things were before. Loving him in secret.

SEVEN

LEVI

I STUMBLE THROUGH THE POOL HOUSE DOOR, MY EYES HEAVY BUT mind buzzing. The further I dig into the dark recesses of the web for this case, the more I question my sanity and if I will be able to finish this assignment.

I've never been one to throw in the towel. Admitting defeat is a last resort. The evidence trail has to have been desolate for weeks or reached a point where my mind can no longer handle the monstrous content I unearth. Only then will I concede.

Tossing my phone and keys on the kitchen island, I amble to the fridge, open it, and stare at the bare contents.

When I moved into the pool house after college, I lost the perks of living in the main house on the estate. Housekeepers don't tend to my needs. No dusting, vacuuming or laundry services. No trips to the grocery store to stock my fridge or pantry. All of which are fine. It's a rare occasion to see any part of the pool house messy.

What I do miss, though, is access to the personal chef. Someone to make meals for me and store them in the fridge. Simple dinners to reheat. Grab-n-go lunches I can take to work. Light and quick breakfasts to eat in the car or after I get to the office. A few days during the week when I don't have the wherewithal to cook anything myself.

I snatch a can of Mountain Dew and a box of questionable leftovers from three or four days ago. Cracking the lid, I do a sniff check. Satisfied with the smell, I open the box and scan the remnants of the lasagna Bolognese.

"Looks safe." I shrug.

Fetching a plate from the cabinet, I transfer it from the box and reheat it in the microwave.

While it warms, I cross to my bedroom, swap my work clothes for sweats and a T-shirt, and grab my laptop. I situate myself with dinner at the island, crack open my computer, and dive back into case work while I eat.

Should I take a breather from all this shit, even if only for a night? Absolutely. My mind needs the break as much as my soul.

Will I listen to my body and take the night off? Good question. I'd like to say I will. I know that I need to. But more often than not, curiosity or determination or being close to a resolution steer my answer.

Remotely connecting to my work computer, I pick up where I left off at the office. While I eat dinner, I sift through topics on a forum I discovered earlier today. Most of it is sick assholes looking for disturbing pictures or like-minded people to speak with. As of now, I have simply scanned the topic titles. Unless one piques my interest in reference to the assignment, I don't open the thread.

I finish the last of the food, shove the plate aside, and shift my laptop front and center. Hunched over the keyboard, I study the screen closely as I scroll, scroll, scroll. Get lost in the dark subjects some of these fuckers talk about with too much ease and delight.

My phone buzzes on the counter and I startle in my seat.

Straightening my spine, I close my eyes and take a deep breath. When I open them, I disconnect from my work computer, shut the lid on my laptop, and sit in silence for a beat.

"Take a break," I chastise myself. "Even if it's just an hour."

I reach for my phone and wake the screen to see a text notification. Tapping it, I wither when I see who it's from.

> ABI
>
> Parents are asking if we're going to the Memorial Day Fest together

My phone digs into my palm as I stare down at the screen, my knuckles burning and tight.

This whole setup was concocted so our parents would *stop* interfering in our lives. So they'd stop forcing us to attend dinners and events on their schedule. So we could live our own lives and let them believe we were fulfilling their twisted, unpleasant, undesirable fantasy.

Now they want us to put on a show for the entire town. Flaunt the eldest West son with the youngest Calhoun heir. Give the gossip mill new Seven falsehoods to whisper about.

Fuck.

Why the hell did I propose fake dating? Seemed like a brilliant idea at the time. A way to get my father off my back. For a couple weeks, it worked. The relentless thrust toward a wealthy, well-known and well-loved member of the Stone Bay community ceased. For a couple weeks, life felt normal.

But I suppose that was the calm before the storm. It was foolish of me to expect it to last, but I did. And now we've hit the other side of the storm.

After kissing Oliver two nights ago, I no longer want to play this game. Though I made this bed, I no longer want to lie in it. I want to rip the sheets off and burn them.

Not my scene, but I suppose we have to.

Fire singes my veins as I stare at the screen. Not a single cell in my body wants to do this—fake date, attend town festivals, smile for people I don't give a shit about.

It'll be fun! Food, drinks, music. Let's make the best of it

She sounds more excited than she should be, especially since she has to attend with me and not Desmond.

I read her message again and pause on the word *music.*

Immediately, my mind drifts to Oliver. To his band and the night they played later in the garage than usual because they'd just heard back from the town. Along with other musical talent, Hailey's Fire had been asked to play during a few town festivals this year.

I sift through my memories for which festivals they're scheduled to play. Is Memorial Day one of them? Will I be able to talk with him before then? I need to, especially if I'm required to make an appearance with my fake girlfriend.

I don't bother replying to Abigail. The whole situation has me ready to puke up my dinner, no sense in adding fuel to the fire.

Instead, I open Instagram to check Hailey's Fire's page for their schedule. As the app loads, the story icon indicates the band is currently live streaming. I tap the circle and squint a moment as my eyes adjust to bright lights filling part of the screen.

As rock notes and Hailey's raspy voice float through the speaker, I stare at the small stage on the screen. I glimpse past Hailey and Trip and zero in on the man behind the drum kit.

Oliver. Per usual, I lose myself in fantasies as he hammers his sticks on the drums.

Years of watching and listening to Hailey's Fire, I sing each of their songs to myself or in my head as they play. All artists have their own twist. Hailey's Fire writes their songs with this interesting blend of rock and soul. You get the grit of rock 'n' roll with this deep, emotional undertone. When they play a new song, I focus with more attentive ears. It usually takes hearing it a few times before I pick up on the hidden meanings in the lyrics. But they are there. Loud and clear.

I have yet to ask Oliver who writes the songs or the significance behind certain ones.

For years, part of me has feared the answer. That the songs were one of his other bandmates' creations. That he only chipped in with the musical concept for the songs and nothing more.

But every now and then, the smallest sliver of hope in my veins whispers to ask anyway. Because that small sliver swears those songs are written by Oliver about me or us.

I exit the live video and go to their main feed. Tap on the pinned post with a list of upcoming dates and read the May schedule. There, in black and white, I have my answer.

May 27th – Stone Bay Memorial Day Festival

Seeing him play, having the chance to hang out with him in public for a bit, is a perk. Being at the festival with my fake girlfriend, on the other hand, puts a damper on spending any true time with him. I easily picture my father scowling as I ignore Abigail to speak with Oliver.

"Fucking bullshit," I mutter as I swipe up and close the app.

I tap on the photos folder, then click on videos. And because I obviously have masochistic tendencies, I choose a video I filmed a while back in Oliver's garage as the band practiced. Over and over, for far too long, I stare at the screen, at Oliver, and watch him play. Without shame, I play it muted on repeat for close to an hour.

When I close the video, I open my text history with Oliver. My fingers fly over the keyboard. And before I second-guess myself, I hit send.

> Saw part of the live in LL. Sounded great. Not sure if you're back tonight or tomorrow. Would like to hang before MD fest.

A light sheen of perspiration dampens my skin as I read my text to him again and again. My message feels generic and lifeless. Like I don't know what to say. Like I don't know how to speak with my best friend.

But I guess that is what happens when you kiss said best friend. The world around you—every word, every glance, every touch—is different. The lightness you once had morphs into something more complex.

And since we have yet to discuss what this all means or where we go from here, the earth is less stable. The future is more uncertain. The friendship Oliver and I have shared for almost seven years is in limbo.

I toss my phone down, drop my elbows to the counter, and let my head fall into my hands.

Please tell me I didn't fuck this up.

Oliver kissed me back. He pulled me closer and wordlessly begged for more. I may have been reserved about my feelings for Oliver for years, but I picked up on every single one of his signals. He wanted me. He *wants* me.

Not opening up to him about how I feel has been tough as hell. Countless sleepless nights have passed when I wanted to call or text him at three in the morning and reveal all my secrets. Spill my heart.

Seeing Oliver with other guys… it chipped away at my soul. Made me question if I'd misread him all these years. If I'd misinterpreted the smiles he gave me and no one else. If I'd misunderstood the way he flirted differently with me than other men.

Fingers crossed, Oliver's silence is just his way of processing this major revelation. Uncertain what our kiss means, he needs time to sort through his thoughts and feelings. To adjust to this new side of us.

If there is an us.

Quit overthinking.

I get up, rinse my dishes, and put them in the dishwasher. Grabbing my laptop from the island, I go to the gaming chair in the living room and crack open my computer again.

Much as I need a break from all the work chaos, I need a distraction from my wayward thoughts about Oliver more.

After I reconnect to my work computer, I pick up where I left off in the forum. Line by line, I scan through the feed and read the topic captions. My eyes grow heavy and my limbs weak as I sift through endless dark chats. Topics written in creeper code that I spend minutes deciphering before reading the next.

As I'm about to close my laptop and call it a night, a title catches my attention.

Fresh catch from port at market price.

To the layperson, it sounds like fishermen offering fresh fish to markets and restaurants. To sick motherfuckers, this is something way darker, more sinister, and the ultimate prize.

I take a few deep breaths to center myself. Calm as possible, I click on the topic and read through the thread. Nausea roils in my belly as I wade through the posts. As I read comments from others with off-putting user handles asking how *fresh* the catch is, if it's *ripe*, I question if I am able to do this. If I can pretend to be one of these disgusting pieces of shit to find missing children.

I shove down the bile climbing up my throat.

This is for Sydney. Set aside your feelings and find her.

My fingers hover over the keyboard as I think of what to type. Can't seem too eager. Can't be too clean.

Keep it simple. Talk their lingo. Earn their trust.

> *fall_or_rise39*
> *sampled recent catch from a buddy*

Not too eager. Vague yet straightforward. In their words and hinting that I know someone in their circle.

I can do this.

I *have* to do this.

A new line fills the screen and I hold my breath as I read it.

hook_n_release_cap
@fall_or_rise39 welcome. which buddy? don't want
them to miss out on their referral bonus

Are they serious? Is this their way of verifying if I'm a cop or creepster? Either way, the lasagna is about to make a comeback.

Swallowing, I type out my reply with the user Tymber got from his buddy at missing persons and hit send.

> *fall_or_rise39*
> *@hook_n_release_cap @night_angler54*
> *would have my head if I didn't mention*

The feed quiets for several minutes. No one chimes in with a single word or reaction. My heart thrashes in my rib cage as I wait for *something*. Breath caught in my throat, my lungs burn as I wait for *anything*. My knee bounces as I bite the corner of my thumbnail.

Still, I wait. For a response, for the site to kick me out.

Hour-long minutes tick by as I stare at the blinking cursor on the screen. On the cusp of saying *fuck it* and shutting down my computer for the night, a new message pops up on the screen.

hook_n_release_cap
@fall_or_rise39 verified referral. check out the
market place. new members are encouraged to
wade through the surf and explore before sampling catch.

I just got accepted into an underground human trafficking ring forum. Via a fake referral. For my job. To find missing children. And the person on the other end is telling me to *explore before sampling*.

I react to the message with a simple *will do*.

Then I set down my laptop, bolt for the bathroom, drop to my knees, and lose my dinner.

EIGHT

NUMBER 263

Day One

Blinding, debilitating pain pulses in my skull. A persistent, breath-stealing torture bouncing in the confines of my mind.

I inhale, the action stilted as my ribs scream and scrape my lungs. A pungent smell wafts up my nose—a nausea-inducing mix of bleach, filthy bathrooms, mildew, and metal. Reaching up to cover my nose and mouth, weight tugs at my wrists. Metal clinks and grates the ground and I wince.

Confusion swirls with the pulsing pain in my head as I try to recall anything before I woke up. As I try to figure out what happened and where I am. But the harder I think, the more it hurts. All I feel, all I think, all I am is pain. Burning and screaming and paralyzing pain.

Easing my eyes open, darkness greets me as I survey what little I can see.

Lying on my side on the ground, I notice divots in the concrete floor. Damp spots not far from where I lie. Gradually, my gaze drifts to my wrists and the metal binds mottled with dark splatters.

My stomach churns and cramps.

Without hurry, I press my palms to the ground and push myself up to a seated position. I dizzy with the simple action and close my eyes, taking a deep breath, followed by another. When I open my eyes again, the room spins and wobbles less.

My gaze falls to my wrists once more and this time I notice the chains linked to the cuffs. Following the chains with my eyes, bile claws at my throat when I spot the large metal ring anchored in the floor. Fear crawls across my skin when I see a second ring with chains that lead in my direction. Before bearing witness, I already know where they go. I already feel the immeasurable weight around my ankles.

And when my eyes land on my bare, dirty feet, the reality of my situation sinks in further. I may have no idea what happened or where I am, but I'd be a fool not to accept what I see with my own eyes.

Someone has me locked in a basement or old, abandoned building.

Goose bumps pebble my skin as my limbs start to shake. The chill in the air blends with the bitter truth of reality and settles deep in my bones. Carving itself in my marrow and spreading like an uncurable virus to my soul.

I scoot away from the floor anchors, fantasizing the distance will turn the situation into one huge nightmare. Radiating pain wraps around my spine when my back smacks the wall. It's a brief reprieve from the pulse in my head but doesn't last the same.

A groan rattles in my chest and scrapes the inside of my throat.

Turning to face the wall, I run my hands over the surface. A softer stone. The tips of my fingers graze over small indentations, long and slightly spread out. When I run over them again with a finger over each, it dawns on me what they are.

Claw marks.

Someone in my same position dug at this wall often and hard enough to leave a lasting trace. An echo of who they were and the life they'd been robbed of. One final plea for the world not to forget who they are, who they were.

Is that what will happen to me? Will I go mad? Will I claw at the walls in the hopes of escape?

The notion has me moving faster around the room, my hands on the wall and mind racing as I search for a way out of wherever I am.

Muted voices hit my ears and I stop. Closing my eyes, I focus solely on my sense of hearing. I do my best to ignore the pain in my head and turn every ounce of attention to my ears.

The subtle sound of metal on concrete. A loud clap followed by a howl. Distorted laughter. Then it's quiet a moment.

I feel my way around the room until I discover what feels like a doorframe.

Thrill spikes my bloodstream as my hands fly over the surface in search of a handle. But after feeling every inch within reach, I come up empty.

Then I hear it again. Someone speaking. It's faint, but a voice filters through the air.

"Hello?"

Jerking the chains, I clutch my throat. Bewildered by the scratchy, unfamiliar sound of my voice, I swallow past the dryness and try again.

"Hello?" Stronger, but still so foreign. "I need help."

The voices fade then disappear. With them, all other noise vanishes too.

I bang a fist against the door, feel it boom under my hand, but barely hear the sound.

What the hell?

Stumbling back, I stare into the darkness as my mind races. I reach for my ears, jab a finger in both, and wiggle. Still no change. So I slap my palms over my ears and hum. This I hear. This small realization brings me an inkling of comfort.

The second I pull my hands away from my ears, a discombobulated feeling washes over me. Swallows me. Drowns me. As though I am underwater.

On my next shuffle backward, I bump one of the anchors on the floor and fall down. A howl claws up my raw throat and spills from my lips as my tailbone hits the concrete. I roll onto my side and reach for the newly inflicted pain.

As the fire in my backside calms, it's then that I register my missing clothes. All except my underwear.

Before I have the chance to question my lack of attire, the door swings open. I jerk back and squint as bright light filters into the space.

Lifting a hand to shield my eyes, I am met with the silhouette of a person. Tall. Muscular. As large as the doorway.

Boots thump the floor as he steps into the room. My eyes adjust slightly as I scoot away from him and crash into the wall. I ignore the stabbing fire in my back. Ignore the fact I still can't hear properly. Ignore the way the room sways a little.

My gaze drifts up as I bring my knees to my chest. Dark fabric hugs his face and masks him from the neck up.

"Welcome to your new home, Two Sixty-Three," the man says, his voice warped, distorted, robotic. And then he hooks a hand under my arm and hauls me up off the floor. "We're going to have so much fun with you."

I flail my arms and kick my feet but barely make contact. The weight of the chains keeps me from truly gaining any sort of momentum. Yet, still, I fight. I kick. I scream. I try to knee him between the legs.

The entire time, he laughs.

Then he fists my hair, yanks my head back, and looks me over. His extensive perusal of my face twists my stomach in unnatural ways.

"It's not often we get pretty ones like you," he says in the robotic voice.

He leans in close and the scent of cinnamon pierces my nose. It throws me off. Muddles my thinking. And then he drags his tongue up my cheek from my jaw to my eye.

Vomit hits the back of my throat a second before I drop onto the floor and my hip screams from the landing. I puke on the floor, on myself, in my hair.

Laughing, the man steps out of the room then tosses a bottle of water. It hits my head with a *thwack,* followed by a handful of loose crackers.

"Keep your strength up, Two Sixty-Three. Gonna need it."

The door slams shut, and once again, I'm blanketed in darkness.

NINE

OLIVER

For the first time, I don't know how to respond to Levi. As if him kissing me short-circuited or rewired my brain.

Perhaps it did.

Years and years of fantasies, of daydreams, of imagining me and Levi as something other than friends. So much more than friends. Those small figments of my imagination, those made-up scenarios of him and me and the life I pictured us living if we took that next step. For years, those minor glimpses and what-ifs gave me hope. A glimmer of sunshine in the lonely moments.

But part of me never expected them to be anything other than what they were. Fantasies.

Then, he kissed me and *poof*. Peace out, coherent thought processes. Au revoir, rational mind. Sayonara, mental comprehension, knowing how to act or what to say.

It's been three and a half days since he muttered *fuck it* and took me by surprise. Approximately eighty-five hours since he pinned me against my car and claimed my mouth. And close to thirty-six hours since he sent a text and said he wants to hang before the Memorial Day festival.

And because I am now incapable of thinking clearly when it comes to Levi, his text remains unanswered.

Ignoring him after the kiss twists my insides. Makes me jittery. Ignoring him feels wrong on so many fucking levels. The polar opposite of what I'd do in normal circumstances. With each passing day, my silence undoubtedly comes across as rejection. A slap to the face. As if I didn't want him to kiss me. As if I never want to see him again.

But that is the farthest thing from the truth.

I want to kiss him. *A lot.* I want him to kiss me. God, do I fucking want that. His lips and tongue and hands on my skin. His warmth, his taste, his scent overwhelming my senses.

But my brain hasn't figured out how to connect the damn dots. Not in the correct order. It refuses to blend years of fantasies with reality. Refuses to believe it happened. Instead, my mind works overtime. Steals my sleep as I lie awake at night and overanalyze every minute Levi and I have spent together the past few years.

Hopes and suspicions were all I had throughout the years. Now… I don't know what it is that I have. An insignificant taste of what *could* be.

I rip the comforter away from my body, throw my legs off the bed, sit up, and fist my hair.

"Text him later. After practice," I mutter to myself.

After a quick shower, I dress and exit my apartment over the garage. I punch in the code on the door beneath the stairs and enter the mudroom between the dining room and garage. Kick off my shoes and stow them beneath the bench.

A notable grumble sounds from my stomach as the scent of fresh bread, seasoned meat, corn, and cheese hit my nose. When I reach the kitchen and see my parents working in harmony on a late breakfast, my stomach gnaws at my insides.

"Smells good." I sidle up to Mama and kiss her cheek. "Anything I can help with?"

"Good morning, dušo." Her gaze sweeps over my face a beat before the corners of her mouth turn down. "You need better sleep." She wipes her hands on a towel and cups my cheeks. The soft pads of her thumbs stroke slowly as her green eyes hold mine. "Too many late nights and early mornings are catching up."

I lean into her touch, her warmth, and rest my hands over hers. "Just a lot on my mind right now." I drop my hands and step into her, wrapping her in a hug. "After the festival, I'll catch up on sleep."

When I release her from the hug, she holds me at arm's length and studies my eyes. Not that I've ever lied to my parents, but when Mama sees me out of sorts and I tell her I'm okay, she looks at me like this. A little longer. An inquisitive look in her eye. It isn't out of mistrust. More from a place of concern. She wants her only child happy and loved. So I don't shrink away or wave off her examination. It's just another way she says I love you.

She rests a hand over my heart. "After the festival."

"Promise, Mama."

Washing my hands, I join my parents at the counter and help with breakfast.

On Sundays, we cook traditional foods throughout the day. Breakfast or brunch features Mama's favorite recipes from her childhood with the occasional twist of her own. Bosnian recipes handed down from her mother and grandmother and so on. Though she doesn't need them, she has each recipe written down in her neat handwriting and stowed in a hand-carved box her grandfather made when she was a girl, *Emina* etched in the grain.

She saves those recipe cards for me. So she can pass them

on one day. Not that I need them either. Decades in the kitchen with my parents without a single written recipe has taught me all I need to know.

Late in the afternoon, Papa will come in the kitchen and blanket several surfaces in flour as he makes fresh pasta. Soon thereafter, the house will smell of capers, basil, garlic and oregano, followed by the salty aroma of cheese. Fresh red sauce gets made once a month and canned. On those Sundays, the house smells incredible all day. Papa tends to rotate through a menu in his head, but we usually have fish, chicken, or vegetables during Sunday dinner.

Unless I'm with Levi, I help Papa with dinner too.

Being in the kitchen with my parents is a balm for my soul. Not only are they sharing family history and traditions, they're also teaching me a way of life. Reminding me that we exist beyond computers and phones and trends. That we aren't robots in a maze. And food is as much a love language as what you say or do.

This time with them reminds me I am human and loved and capable. It hits the refresh button on what's important in life—spending uninterrupted time with people you care about. I wouldn't exchange it for anything.

We carry platters of food to the dining room table, sit in the same seats we have since I was a kid, and dive into the fruits of our labor.

Mama mentions an uptick in business at Zen Den—the town's most popular massage studio—and how she's needing to do extra self-care before and after each client she works on. Papa shares recent chats with the townsfolk in the post office. Since the Stone Bay post office is the main hub for packages, snail mail, and additional professional services, Papa sees most of the town's residents weekly.

They ask how Trip and Hailey are, and about the band's

show lineup. Although it isn't part of our usual routine to practice on Sundays, my parents are excited for us to play at tomorrow's festival.

With natural ease, the conversation shifts and Mama asks about Levi.

"It's been ages since he's joined us for dinner. Would be nice to share a meal with him again." Mama lifts her mug to her lips and sips her coffee. "Ask him for me the next time you talk?"

I swirl the tines of my fork through the last bit of čimbur on my plate, my eyes following the action. With a stilted nod, I mutter, "Yeah. Of course, Mama."

Near my twelfth birthday, I told my parents I had a crush on a boy in my class. At the time, I didn't think much of it. I'd never thought my attraction to boys was different or weird. I hadn't seen many gay or lesbian couples in Stone Bay, but it never occurred to me that love had limits or boundaries regarding *who* you loved. My parents didn't raise me with closed-off ideals.

My parents have always been accepting of who I am without hesitation. They have always gifted me the space to grow and flourish so long as I was safe. Over the years, I've dated several guys. Some incredible, and others I'd rather forget. Neither of my parents laid judgment on me for my choices. All they asked was that I be careful and only give my heart to someone deserving.

I didn't miss the way Mama watched me and Levi during family dinner. Nor did I miss the small smiles she sent in our direction when we spoke on passionate topics.

Mama is not oblivious to my feelings for my best friend, but she keeps them under lock and key.

After I help wash dishes, I head out to the garage and get in the mindset for practice. Trip and Hailey come in through the side door moments later. We go through our individual warmup routines and then go over our setlist for tomorrow.

The *thump, thump, thump* of my drums bounce off the garage walls, the wail of Hailey's guitar vibrates the air, and the low and sultry tone of Trip's bass pulses beneath our feet. Song by song, we go through each without hurry. Not wanting to exhaust ourselves before tomorrow, we take several breaks and hype each other up for our first major show.

Near the end of our second to last song, the side door of the garage swings open. Still playing, the three of us glance toward the door as Levi walks in with a large brown bag. We continue to play as though nothing happened. No greetings or gestures are exchanged. It's like any other band practice when Levi shows up.

As we go through the final song, I keep my head down and try to focus. But I can't help but peek at Levi every chance I get.

When the final song ends, Hailey bounds over to the couches, her eyes on the spread of take-out boxes. Trip sidles up to her a beat before they open boxes and get lost in the Thai buffet. As for me, I remain glued to my stool behind my drums.

The minutes pass with stuttered breaths and congested thoughts. It irks me that I feel so out of my element now. That I don't know how to act around Levi.

But I can't just fucking sit here.

Inhaling deeply, I rise from my stool and cross the room to join everyone on the couches. As I have hundreds of times in the past, I sit next to Levi and lift my chin in greeting.

"Hey." A corner of my mouth twitches. "How'd you know Hails and T were here?"

Levi is quiet as I scan the boxes filled with noodle or rice dishes, fried spring rolls, and satay skewers. When he doesn't answer after a moment, I shift my attention to him. What I'm met with steals the breath from my lungs.

Brow cocked and lips slightly puckered, his blue eyes bore into my soul. My eyes dart between his before dropping to his lips for one, two, three erratic heartbeats. I swallow as my gaze returns to his. A desperate, feral need to taste his lips and tongue again simmers in my veins and makes my groin swell.

"Big day tomorrow," he says as his tongue darts out and licks his lips. "Makes sense to practice."

His words hit my ears, but they're indiscernible white noise. Because all I can think about is his mouth on mine again.

Fucking hell. Get your shit together.

Needing a distraction, I grab a satay skewer from the box and give my mouth something else to focus on. Conversation about the festival sparks, and Hailey becomes highly animated as she speaks. And for a half hour, the four of us munch on takeout and chat like we do any other day.

"We're going to head out," Trip says as he balls up a napkin and tosses it in the bag. "Thanks for the late lunch, man."

"It's no problem. Can't wait to see you all on stage tomorrow." Levi closes up the boxes with food in them. "Want the leftovers?" He pushes a few boxes toward Trip and Hailey.

Trip looks to me and I shrug. He gives his own shrug in return. Then he grabs the boxes from the table. "Thanks, Levi." He lifts a hand and flashes two fingers. "Deuces. We'll be here bright and early to pack up."

"Later." I give them a half-hearted wave.

A foreign silence echoes around us once Hailey and Trip exit the garage. Once Levi and I are truly alone for the first time in several days. I'm still not feeling like myself, but also not uncomfortable. Nervous, perhaps?

Considering I never anticipated Levi reciprocating my feelings, I'm just... out of sorts.

He walked in here almost an hour ago as though nothing happened. As if we are still the same Oliver and Levi we were a week ago, a month ago, a year ago. But it's impossible to be the same. After that kiss, we will never be the same. How can we be?

Does he regret the kiss? Is him coming here today, sticking with his same routine during band practice, because he wants things to go back to the way they were?

God, I hope not.

Now that I've tasted him, now that I know what his weight feels like against me, I want nothing less. I refuse to settle for anything less.

"Hey." He bumps my knee with his.

I take a slow, deep breath before I lift my gaze to meet his. "Hey."

He gives a quick tip of his head toward the main garage door. "Let's go for a drive."

What little I ate churns in my stomach.

This is it. This is the end of our friendship.

I swallow and shove the dreadful thought to the back of my mind.

Uncertainty pulses through my veins as I nod. "Sure."

I collect the trash and deposit it in the garbage as we leave. Levi unlocks his fast as fuck Ferrari Spider and slips into the driver's seat with ease. Seat belts buckled, he reverses out of the driveway and weaves through the neighborhood at a painfully slow pace.

As we pass the Northcott farm stand, I expect him to turn left and drive into town. But he continues north, driving through more neighborhoods at a moderate speed. At the end of the street, he makes a left and then veers us onto Aarluk Bypass.

The houses disappear and tall evergreens take their place. Sun filters through the trees as he picks up speed on the windy road. Soon, we merge onto Bloodstone Blvd, then turn right onto Granite. Mashing a button on the steering wheel, he cranks his electronic music playlist all the way up as the car goes from thirty-five to eighty in a matter of seconds.

We fly down the highway, the adult store on the northern outskirts of town a blur as we pass. His tires eat up the miles as we drive away from Stone Bay and through national forest lands. Indistinct stripes of green and brown whiz by, and I try not to focus on any one thing as Levi drives faster.

Over the years, I've learned to not study anything outside the car when Levi pushes the car past eighty. I end up dizzy and borderline nauseous. When we take these rides, I sit back and let go. Allow myself to get lost in the blur. On these drives, I used to dream about all the what-ifs—the scenarios that'd follow if we took the next step.

Now that he's kissed me, and we haven't talked about where we go from here, my what-ifs have taken on a life of their own.

What if I royally fucked up our friendship? What if we're unable to go back to the way we were? What if I lose him?

Then it dawns on me that I've been the quiet one for days. I've been the one avoiding the subject. I am the one that has put us in limbo.

The car slows and I peek at Levi from the corner of my eye. He downshifts and slows further. Before I get the chance to ask why, he turns left onto a road somewhat obscured by overgrowth. I stare up at the tree canopy and take in the narrow lanes as we continue forward. After less than a quarter mile, the road opens to a small gravel lot with a park bathroom, an elevated view of the Pacific, and not a soul for miles.

He parks the car, cuts the engine, and drops his hands in his lap. Silence swallows us as we sit unspeaking. But it isn't the same kind of silence we shared weeks ago. It isn't *our* silence.

"Ollie, I..." He takes a deep breath as he searches for what to say.

I turn my head his way, but don't look at him head on. I'm not prepared for the possible rejection on his face.

"About the other night."

Here it comes. My heart bangs viciously in my rib cage.

"About the... kiss."

Fuck. Why is this so damn hard for us? If you're done with me, just rip the bandage off already.

"I don't regret it."

My brows tug together as I narrow my eyes and twist to face him better. "What?"

His luminous blue eyes riveted to my greens, he worries his bottom lip. With a simple shake of his head, he repeats himself. "I don't regret it." His gaze roams my face and studies the skeptical lines in my expression. "Do you?" Those two simple words are shadowed by tangible fear.

"No," I say immediately. "Never."

"Are you sure?"

Does Levi not know me at all? If he's picked up on how I feel for him—even if only a fraction—he already knows the answer. Although I've done my best to keep my attraction and emotions toward him in check, it'd be impossible for him to not sense any of it.

Pulse whooshing in my ears, I hold his radiant blue gaze. "No regrets."

It's funny how saying two straightforward words changes your entire life.

"No matter what happens, no matter what you see or hear, I promise you the whole thing with Abi is fake."

Relief and alarm punch me in the solar plexus simultaneously. The way he says the shortened version of her name… as though they've been chummy all their lives. I hate it.

"What I see or hear?"

His gaze shifts to look out the windshield. He rolls his lips between his teeth then swallows.

I stare at his profile, the sharp line of his jaw, the slope of his nose, the pout of his lips. I visually trail down his neck, roam over his Adam's apple, past the collar of his shirt.

He's so damn still, I swear he isn't breathing.

"Her parents asked if we were going to the festival together."

Of course, they did.

Head against the seat, he rotates until our eyes meet again. "I hate organized events as it is. Attending with someone I have no interest in is ten times worse."

"So don't go," I blurt.

"Wish it was that easy." His brows bend inward. "I started this whole fiasco. I need to figure out how to end it too."

Gaze unfocused, I nod. "Yeah. Okay."

Warmth grazes my cheek and snaps everything back into focus. My eyes widen and jaw slackens as I stare at Levi. I stare awestruck as his eyes follow his caress of my cheek. Slow and soft and curious. His fascination and tenderness are a shot of adrenaline in my bloodstream.

His fingers drift to the angle of my jaw and down the length of my neck. "Are you nervous?" The words are barely a whisper.

Saliva pools in my mouth as his fingers stroke the collar of my graphic tee. Swallowing, I nod. "Yes."

His eyes flit to mine. "Why?"

What a loaded fucking question? Truly, there is no simple answer. Not when it comes to me and Levi.

Inhaling a methodical, ragged breath, I spill one of my biggest fears. "I don't want to fuck this up."

His fingers drift along my collarbone and down my arm. Drawing a few swirls near my elbow, he continues his exploration as he traces over the half-sleeve tattoo on this arm. Like the kiss, his fingers on my skin is the headiest mix of heaven and hell.

"Me either." His hand returns to my cheek, the tips of his fingers curling firmly around the nape of my neck. "We'll figure it out as we go." Gaze on my lips, he eases forward and eats up the space between us.

"Why now?"

Lips inches from mine, his brow furrows. A beat passes before his expression smooths and turns to awareness. "This whole situation woke me up, I guess." He inches back, but remains close. In light, measured strokes, his thumb caresses the angle of my jaw as he holds my stare. "Ollie, I've wanted this"—he pauses and swallows—"I've wanted more than friendship with you for a while."

"You have?"

The corner of his mouth kicks up in a subtle half smile. "Yeah, I have. For years."

"Oh."

How the hell did I miss this? Maybe I was too busy in my own fantasyland to see the forest for the trees.

"With my father the way he is, I've been biding my time. Waiting for my trust to kick in so I can move out and on with my life however I want."

I hate that his life is so wrapped up in the politics of Stone Bay. That he can't live his life how he chooses without his dad interfering or trash-talking his choices.

His grip on my neck tightens. "Can we talk about it later?"

I nod.

He licks his lips. "Thank fuck."

And then his lips are on mine, hungry and wet and warm as he kisses me senseless. A click echoes through the car, followed by another. My seat belt eases from my shoulder and I shrug it the rest of the way off.

My hands go to his cheeks, his stubble scratching my palms as my fingers slip into his brown locks. His tongue swirls mine once, twice, before he deepens the kiss and sucks the length of my tongue. It's a shot straight to the dick and I moan in appreciation.

All the sound does is spur him on further.

One hand in my hair guiding the kiss, his other travels down my neck, my pecs, my abdomen. He pauses inches from the aching erection beneath my zipper.

As much as I want him to wrap his fingers around my cock, I won't pressure Levi into doing something he may not be ready for. It's one thing to admit your feelings for someone. It's something wholly different to confess your feelings, reveal that you're gay or bisexual, and then consensually grope someone in a public parking lot during the day.

I want his hands and lips and mouth on every inch of me. But I also don't want to rush this.

Whatever this is between us, it's been a long time in the making. Going from zero to a hundred this fast… I don't want hurried, spontaneous decisions to ruin us before there truly is an us.

Against every molecule in my makeup, I break the kiss. He instantly hauls me back to him and crushes my lips once more.

A smile ghosts my lips as soft laughter spills from my mouth. At this, he pulls back and stares at me with confusion in his gaze.

"Did I do something wrong?"

My cheeks sting as I widen my smile. "Not at all." I tug at the length of his hair. "More than perfect."

"Then why stop?"

"Truth?"

He nods. "Always."

My gaze drops to his swollen, red lips and I lick my own before leveling him with my gaze. "I don't want the first time we do something other than kiss to be in a crampy car in a parking lot. And…"

When I don't continue after a moment, he nudges me. "And?"

"And if we take the next step and you start to feel uncomfortable, I don't want you to feel trapped." I shrug. "If you need space to digest it all, I don't want you to feel stuck."

The corner of his mouth twitches a beat before he leans in and presses a chaste kiss to my lips. But he doesn't pull away after the kiss. Instead, his lips hover over mine. I curse every fucking deity in the heavens as he lingers in my orbit, deliciously torturing me and making me second-guess my decision.

"Touching dicks other than my own may be new for me, but nothing about touching yours will scare me off."

Frozen in my seat, my heart beating a turbulent rhythm in my chest, I forget how to speak. Levi mentions touching my dick and that's it… I'm done for.

Light laughter floats through the car as he inches away. He trails the tip of his finger over my lips, his eyes following the action. When his hand falls away, I immediately miss his touch.

"Guess we should head back." He buckles his seat belt and starts the car.

I adjust myself, not missing his subtle groan, and buckle myself in. Needing to take my mind off my erection, I try to think of anything other than the kiss and Levi wanting to touch my dick. I glance at the time on the dash—early evening—and it jogs an earlier conversation with my parents about inviting Levi over. It's an instant cold shower to my system as we exit the lot and drive south.

"Got dinner plans?"

He shifts gears and the car picks up speed. "No." He glances my way for a split second. "Want to grab something?"

"Mama misses you. She said it's been too long since you had dinner with us." I stare at his profile as the trees pass in a darker blur than earlier.

He rests his hand on the gearshift as we coast down the highway. Silence stretches out between us and has me wondering if I should rescind the invitation.

"I miss Sunday dinners too," he finally says. And as we exit the national forest near Stone Bay, he eases off the accelerator. "Maybe I should join more often."

Thrill buzzes in my chest.

Yeah. You should.

May 26th

I've dreamed about this for so fucking long. And now it's happening. I think. He kissed me days ago. Today, he kissed me again. He wants me. I really fucking wants me. And it's so surreal that I had to be the one to slow us down earlier. If I hadn't stopped us in the car earlier, my dick would've been in his hand. Just the thought of it has me hard. And it wouldn't have stopped there.

Fucking hell! My spank bank got a million times better today.

All those old fantasies... psh. After the way he sucked my tongue earlier, now all I can think about is fucking his throat. Or him fucking mine.

Sweet fucking hell, I am screwed.

TEN

LEVI

Driving through the Stone Bay amphitheater lot, I steer the car toward the section designated for Seven members. Barely after ten in the morning, the place is packed.

Shuttles transport residents and tourists in from the overflow parking at town hall and the performing arts center. Clusters of people swarm the gates. Children dance and talk animatedly as they tug their parents toward the carnival games and rides. Hints of fried food and sugar and salt float through the air. Upbeat music bounces off the amphitheater and echoes for miles.

I loiter next to my car near the entrance and compose myself. Mentally prepare to walk around with Abigail all day and appear genuinely happy to be her *boyfriend*.

Thinking of anyone other than Oliver as mine makes me queasy. Although the shift in our relationship is new and we haven't put a label on what we are, the idea of being with anyone else is unfathomable.

But this thing with Abigail gets our families off our backs—mostly—and allows us the freedom to spend time with who we want to without being lectured.

After dinner with Oliver, Emina, and Nero, Oliver and I hung out in his apartment for hours. Sat pressed against each other on the couch and watched a movie. And then another. When he took my hand and threaded our fingers, I held on to his tighter than comfortable.

Opening myself up to him is the best decision I've made. Scary as hell, too, but worth every terrifying second.

Late in the night, I held his face in my hands and devoured his lips once more. Every cell in my body screamed to stay at his place. Pleaded with me to strip him bare and get to know him in a new way. Whispered in my ear to lie with him and fall asleep with our limbs tangled until the sun came up.

But Oliver needed to be up early for the festival, and I didn't want to fuck up this incredible opportunity for him or the band. So, I went home. Alone.

Before my head hit the pillow, I sifted through and cleared out notifications on my phone. It's then that I noticed a missed text from Abigail, the timestamp during dinner at the Moss house.

ABI

We should ride together tomorrow. For appearances.

Well after one in the morning, my reply was simple.

no

When I woke a couple hours ago and checked my phone, she hadn't responded. Not that I care either way. It's best to keep the lines drawn and visible. If that upsets her, it's not my problem.

Inhaling a deep breath, I head for the gates, enter the

pandemonium, drop a couple hundred dollars in the charity donation box, and linger in the periphery of the crowd. This isn't the first town event I've attended—as a member of a founding family, we are more or less obligated to appear—but I am one of the few Seven that shies away from the crowd.

"There you are." Voice saccharine sweet, Abigail approaches with her parents, brother, and a young boy. She invades my personal space and hooks her arm around mine. Glowing smile on her face, she leans into my side. "Have you met my nephew, Tucker?"

I force down the urge to yank my arm free and shove her away. This whole situation is my fault, but I never gave her consent to touch me without advanced warning. Something we will discuss today.

Lips pursed, I shake my head. "No, I haven't."

Ray Calhoun III—also known by many as Tré—extends a hand my way. "Been a while."

I ease out of Abigail's hold and take his hand. His grip is firm, a hint calloused, but otherwise benevolent. "Nice to see you again."

Hand on the boy's back, Ray nudges him forward. "This is my son, Tucker. Tucker, this is Levi West, Aunt Abi's boyfriend."

I mentally cringe and pray it doesn't show on my face.

"He does all kinds of cool stuff with computers."

A spitting image of his father, Tucker doesn't give me an ounce of attention. "Can we play games now?" Annoyance laces his tone and I bite my cheek to keep from laughing.

I'm over it too, kid.

Ray III shrugs and chuckles. "Priorities." And then he steers Tucker away from the group and heads for the row of games.

Abigail shifts closer. I counter her move, add a few more inches of space between us, and cross my arms firmly over my chest. Her smile falters for a beat, but returns fast enough for others not to notice.

"Levi," Angel Calhoun says, my name sunny and refined on her tongue. "Abigail says you've been working a tremendous number of hours recently." She sips the mimosa in her hand. "Is it on a project with your father?"

I resist the urge to roll my eyes. Undoubtedly, my father continues to give the impression I will follow in his footsteps and assume a role in town politics. As though what I do professionally is unsavory.

"No, ma'am. Politics aren't my thing." Nor is my father. "I'm a partner at Tymber Woulf Security and Investigative Services. We recently took on a large case and it's kept us quite busy."

"Busy enough to lessen your time with Abigail." It's more a statement than a question and she says it with practiced finesse. Though her tone doesn't come across as irritated, I read between the lines effortlessly. Angel Calhoun wants the best for her daughter.

If only she knew I am not what's best for her. Unless she wants a friend.

"I barely have time for myself."

As the words leave my mouth, my parents, brother, and his girlfriend enter my periphery. My mood instantly plummets.

Less than an hour into the day and I want to rip my hair out. The facade, the elitist mentality, the mountain of bullshit… I am more than over it.

Artificial smile on his face, my father pats my back. "Stubborn, this one. But we'll get him in town hall sooner or later."

"Or never," I mutter, stepping away from him.

The group sparks up generic conversation about things that

don't hold my interest. As my father gloats about himself and what he's done to improve Stone Bay, an uneasy sensation sparks to life in my chest. Seeing as my attention isn't focused on the group chatter, it isn't anything they've said that has me ill at ease. No, this feeling is… different. As though I'm being watched.

I scan the group and find no one looking my way. So I widen my search. Visually roam the bustling crowd. Flit from one person to the next and search for anyone with eyes on us. One face after another, I come up empty.

A hand on my forearm startles me and I catch the last of Angel's words. "…leave these two be and let them have the day together."

"Thanks, Mom." Abigail kisses Angel on the cheek, then her dad, Ray Jr. "Love you."

"Love you, too."

The families disperse and we are left alone. Abigail inches closer to me, but I skirt away from her and maintain a comfortable distance.

"Sorry," she mutters. "Just trying to keep up appearances."

"Whatever." The word comes out a little cold. I take a deep breath and try to dial down my inner asshole. "This was my idea, I know. But I'm not comfortable with touching. At all."

She pulls her phone out of her pocket and drops her attention to the screen. "They think we're a couple, Levi. Couples touch each other."

Although she has a point, my counterpoint is better. "True. People that *want* to be in a relationship do touch each other."

A soft hum dances over my skin and I scan the crowd once more, looking for Oliver.

"But we were forced into this," I continue. "Fake dating was a solution to shut our families up. This, our fake relationship, is all for show. Remember?" I glance at her out of the corner of my eye. "You have a boyfriend. And I have… my own life."

"Yes." A smile brightens her expression. "I know this is fake. I know I have a boyfriend." She scans the crowd. "But shouldn't we be a little more convincing around our families?"

"No." I widen and cut that invisible line separating us deeper. "Not all couples do PDA. Considering neither of us wanted this for years, it wouldn't be weird for us not to touch."

"Fine," she huffs out as a man in khaki shorts and a navy button-down approaches. In a blink, her entire mood shifts. At the sight of him, Abigail comes to life.

"Hey, baby." He steps into her, wraps his arms around her waist, and hoists her off the ground. "Fuck, I've missed you."

Abigail giggles as he peppers her neck with kisses. "Put me down." She playfully slaps his shoulder but has a look that begs him to never let go.

When her feet finally hit the ground, he hooks an arm around her shoulders and tugs her into his side. "Hey, man." He extends his free hand. "You must be Levi. I'm Desmond."

Strange as this is, I take his hand. "Nice to put a face to the name."

"Same." He presses his lips to her hair, kissing her often. As if he will never have his fill. "Thanks for doing this for her." He waves a hand around. "The fake boyfriend thing."

"It's not weird to you?"

He glances down at Abigail at the same time she looks up at him. "At first, yeah." His gaze returns to mine. "But after hours of explaining it, I get it. Quid pro quo." He shrugs. "Abi's still mine and her parents aren't on her ass every day to marry some rich guy she barely knows."

Guess that's a good way to look at it.

Desmond changes the direction of the conversation and

asks questions to get to know me. I do the same in return. And the more we chat, the more I like him. A nurse at the retirement home, he's quite passionate about caring for others, especially the elderly. Overall, he's a pretty chill guy. Likable. Kind.

The hum from earlier is back and stronger than before. I scan the crowd and, after a moment, spot Oliver. Our eyes meet and the low hum morphs into this endless rush. I can't help but smile as I wave him over.

Oliver sidles up to me, a bright, toothy smile on his handsome face. "Been looking for you. You just get here?"

"Half hour or so ago." My hand twitches at my side, desperate to touch him. So I shove it in my pocket. "Ollie, this is Abi and her boyfriend, Desmond."

They exchange hugs and handshakes. Desmond studies Oliver a moment, his brows pinching together. My stomach knots the longer he looks, as if he's trying to puzzle him out. Maybe who Oliver is to me.

"You the drummer in Hailey's Fire?"

Relief washes over me at his question.

"I am." A blinding smile lifts the corners of Oliver's lips. "You've seen us play?"

"A couple times. Love the sound. Like old school and alternative with a twist."

Oliver reaches up and grabs the back of his neck. It's not a nervous habit of his I've seen. But maybe it's equivalent to my hand in my pocket.

He wants to touch me and can't. Not here.

"That's the vibe we're going for." He nods, then turns his attention toward me. "I need to get back." He gestures over his shoulder with a pointed thumb. "We go on soon. But I wanted to find you and say hi. Maybe we can hang after?"

I *feel* Abigail's eyes on us. *Hear* her unspoken questions lingering in the air. I do my best to ignore it and focus on Oliver.

"Sounds good."

Unexpectedly, Oliver closes the distance between us, wraps his arms around me, and slaps my back once. A hug most would see as friendly. But I don't miss the extra squeeze at the end before he releases me.

"Cool." Turning to Abigail and Desmond, he gives a brief wave. "Was nice meeting you. Enjoy the show." And then he jogs off.

Desmond releases Abigail, cups her cheeks, and kisses her as if no one is watching. It's uncomfortable to witness and ends quickly. Thank goodness. He rests his forehead on hers. "I should go too. Shift starts in an hour."

Giving them privacy, I walk to the pretzel cart nearby and order two pretzels and lemonades. As I'm handed the order, Abigail approaches the cart. I hand her a drink and pretzel then grab us napkins.

"Thanks," she whispers, her sunny disposition gone.

We wander over to a cluster of shaded picnic tables and sit across from each other. Several minutes pass in silence as we pick at our pretzels and get lost in our own thoughts. As I pop a piece of pretzel in my mouth, she speaks up.

"So, Ollie…" She stares down at the table. "He's your boyfriend?"

I clutch my throat as the bite of pretzel gets lodged and cuts off my airway. Repeatedly, I smack my chest. Fire flames my face as sweat coats my skin.

Abigail bolts from her seat. "Oh god." A second later, she hits my back. Hard. "Shit." *Thwack.*

Someone at a nearby table comes over, my face hot with embarrassment and lack of oxygen. Arms band around my chest, fists situate beneath my ribs, then there's a forceful thrust up. In one go, the bite dislodges and I gasp for air.

"Slow and steady," the man coaches.

Once I catch my breath, I guzzle half my drink and thank the man. Soon, the chaos and excitement at the tables dies down. I do my best to ignore what prompted my near-death experience in the first place. Abigail's question.

But of course, she isn't having it.

"I'm right, aren't I?"

I don't answer.

"No one knows, I assume."

Still, I remain tight-lipped.

She reaches forward and sets a hand near me on the table. "I won't say anything." A softness fills her expression, something akin to sympathy. "Promise."

My molars gnash together. "Can we talk about something else? Anything else?"

"Sure. Sorry." She winces, then lifts her hand from the table and holds it between us. "Let's agree now. Friends, and nothing more."

Personally, I want to throw this whole situation in the trash. Forget I ever brought it up. But Abigail is a nice person. Her boyfriend is a great guy. They deserve happiness. As do I. We need to make this work for a little longer. Until I wrap up this case at work and have time to sort out my personal life.

I can do this. Be friends with Abigail.

For her. For me. So she can be with Desmond. So I can be with Oliver.

Reaching across the table, I take her hand. "Friends. Nothing more."

Will this day fucking end already?

What I thought would be two or three hours of schmoozing and appeasing my and Abigail's parents has turned into an all-day event.

When Hailey's Fire started their set, Abigail and I moved closer to the stage. Teens and adults cheered and whistled and sang along with their songs. Hailey riled up the crowd as Trip plucked the strings of his bass, his gaze on Hailey more often than not. And Oliver... fuck, he looked fantastic behind the drums. Sweat beading his skin and dampening his hair. The way his muscular arms contracted and flexed as he got lost in the music.

Every show I've been to, every practice I watch, my eyes are locked on Oliver most of the set. I admit my attraction to him plays a major role in my ogling. But it isn't just that. When Oliver sits behind his drums, something magical and inexplicable happens. He isn't just playing music. He *is* the music.

But it's been hours since Hailey's Fire played their last song. Hours since I've seen Oliver. And too many hours of close proximity with my family and the Calhouns.

My father has informed no less than two hundred people that Abigail and I are dating. Bragging that he knew years ago we would be a *perfect match*. Oblivious of reality, my father couldn't be further from the truth.

String and post lights glow around us, gradually outshining the fading sun. For the umpteenth time, I scan the crowd for Oliver. When his set ended, he probably stayed with Hailey and Trip or sought out Kirsten, Skylar, and Delilah—his other close friends.

The air around me shifts and grows insufferable with each breath. Goose bumps dance over my skin as my stomach cramps uncomfortably.

"Would you stop fidgeting?"

I jolt then stiffen as my mind registers my father's voice. Clench my fingers into fists until my knuckles burn. Gnash my molars as irritation ripples through my veins.

Twisting to look at my father, I keep my expression blank. "If I actually wanted to be here, if any of this interested me, it'd be a nonissue."

His top lip twitches as annoyance sparks in his eyes. Countless unspoken words linger in the air between us. But he won't give them a voice. Not now. Not when the majority of the town watches on. Not when his true persona may jeopardize his mayoral role and the townsfolk's perception of him.

One thing matters to Jefferson Thornhill-West. His public persona. After that, my mother and brother.

"Did you not agree to join Abigail today?" He glances down at his watch, purses his lips, then shifts his gaze to the sky. "Your behavior reflects on her now that you're together."

I jerk back an inch as my nails dig into my palms. "You have got to be fucking joking."

"Watch how you speak to me, boy."

With a subtle shake of my head, I shift my attention to the crowd and let my eyes lose focus. For a moment, I lose sight of my surroundings. Then fire licks my skin as fury heats my blood. In a blink, everything sharpens.

"I'm not a fucking boy," I grit out. "And I'm not some damn toy to dress up and flaunt around town." My hands twitch at my sides as I glance at his profile. "I am *not* you. Nor do I ever want to be."

I need to get out of here. Now.

One foot in front of the other, I walk away from my version of hell.

"Where are you going?"

I don't stop or spare a glance over my shoulder, which will undoubtedly anger him more. "To piss."

Weaving through the endless sea of townsfolk, I slow when I spot Oliver in the distance with friends. Vivid, addictive smile on his handsome face, he laughs a beat before Skylar shoves his shoulder. And then his laughter dies down as awareness lights his expression. His attention darts from one person to the next in the crowd until our eyes lock.

Under his surveillance, I come alive. For the first time in hours, I take a full, deep breath.

An odd pang surfaces in my gut. An edgy spasm in my side. Both of them small, bitter reminders that I'm not an anonymous person in Stone Bay. That I have eyes on me.

I jerk my chin away from the main festivities. Oliver gives me a nod, but waits to follow.

The farther I get from the food and games and entertainment, the fewer people I pass. Twilight fades as darkness sets in. The last tent glows behind me as I trek farther and head for the trees, desperate for the obscurity, eager for the anonymity.

Leaning against an evergreen trunk, I face the festival and wait for Oliver. Equally as eager to see me, he doesn't make me wait long.

Backlit by the party lights, I lick my lips as my eyes trail down his silhouette. The closer he gets, the more my eyes adjust and take all of him in.

He's changed since the show. A black graphic tee hugs his biceps, but rests comfortably over his chest. Loose-fitting jeans sit low on his hips and only serve to amplify his natural swagger. And fuck me, he looks mouthwatering.

The moment he spots me next to the tree, he picks up his pace. Heart pounding in my chest, he gifts me a smile I swear he reserves for me.

"You're still here."

Pushing off the tree, I nod as I inch closer to him. "You looked great on stage." I tap the side of my legs over and over.

"Couldn't take my eyes off you." Saliva pools in my mouth and I swallow. "The crowd loved you."

Oliver stands inches away, the heat of him dancing over my skin. His finger hooks in the belt loop of my pants and he tugs me closer. "Don't want to talk about the show."

"No?"

The show is the last thing I want to talk about. But the swirl of nervous energy and adrenaline throughout my body has me rambling and twitchy.

Breath warm on my lips, he shakes his head. "Later."

"Later," I repeat and take a deep, shuddering inhale.

Before I exhale, Oliver's mouth is on mine. Urgent and greedy and unrelenting. He licks the seam of my lips and I quiver before opening up for him. His eager hands drift to my hips, grip me with bruising force, and haul me forward until the bulge beneath his zipper rubs the length of my erection.

Fisting his shirt, I deepen the kiss as I moan into his mouth. I take and taste and grow impossibly harder. My body begging for more—his hands, his lips, his tongue on my skin. Desire thrums through my veins and fuels my already intense feelings for Oliver.

I surrender to the desires I've hidden for so long. Forget about obligations and Stone Bay and any preconceived notions I've had shoved down my throat all my life. I live in the moment and free my mind and heart.

Releasing his shirt, my hands drift down his chest. Lower and lower. Dipping beneath the worn cotton of his shirt, my fingers skim the waistband of his jeans and the soft skin just above it. He sucks in a sharp breath and tries to pull back. But I keep him pinned in place.

"Ollie..." His name is raspy, breathy, a plea. "Let me feel you."

His hands on my hips fist impossibly harder before his grip

loosens and drifts up my body. Forehead pressed to mine, he cups my cheeks and stares into my soul.

I see the fight in his eyes. The eagerness to say yes because he wants this as much as I do. The resistance because he fears what will happen once we take this step. Once we become more than friends.

"I'm scared, too," I confess softly. "So damn afraid."

Worry creases the corners of his eyes as they dart between mine.

"Afraid of what we may lose. Frightened we may never be the same." I close my eyes, inhale deeply, then meet his gaze with renewed strength. "But I'm more terrified of not being with you. Petrified of not admitting what I want, taking my shot, and missing out on the greatest relationship of my life."

Oliver's expression softens as he melts into me. "Levi..."

"Let me feel you."

When he doesn't respond, when he doesn't pull away or spew a rebuttal, I take it as a good sign. That he's considering it.

His thumbs stroke my cheeks once, twice, and then his lips are on mine again. Softer this time. Tender yet starved. With each stroke of his tongue on mine, the air around us thickens. Intensifies. Amplifies.

I pop the button on his jeans and pause. He doesn't retreat or break the kiss. No, he curls his fingers into my hair and deepens the kiss.

My heart pounds viciously in the confines of my rib cage as I drag his zipper down. My hands shake as I graze the waistband of his boxer briefs. He gently rocks his hips forward and moans into my mouth, encouraging me.

In this moment, time is measured in heartbeats. Nothing and no one exists except him and me and the feelings we've shared but have been too frightened to admit.

My fingers dip beneath his underwear and we both gasp. A loud *thump* echoes through the trees a moment before a *boom, crack, fizzle* ripples in the air. The night sky turns red as I gently fist his length.

Thick and hard and throbbing in my hand, I slowly stroke the length of him. His jaw slackens as my hand moves up and down, root to tip. I lick his bottom lip. Relish in the pleasure written in his expression. Swipe my thumb over the head of his cock and smear the precum.

Fireworks light the sky in various colors and highlight the undiluted lust in his eyes. I stroke him harder. Faster. Shove his pants and underwear lower.

And before I second-guess myself, I drop to my knees. Lick the length of his cock, then wrap my lips around the head and take him to the back of my throat.

"Oh, fuck." He fists my hair and hisses.

While the sky ignites, I fuck Oliver with my mouth. Show him how much I want this. How much I want him.

"Shit." His grip on my hair tightens. "L… Jesus, fuck."

His dick swells in my mouth. I reach around and clutch his ass. Hold him in place as I suck faster and add a little teeth. His muscles lock up a breath before he comes down my throat. I dig my fingers in his ass and suck him off until he trembles beneath my hands.

Releasing him, I stare up at the man I've wanted as more than a friend for far too long. He pulls up his underwear and pants, adjusts himself, then drops to his knees so we're eye to eye.

In his gaze, I see awe and wonder and something akin to love. He lifts a hand to my jaw and strokes the pad of his thumb over my lips.

"You're a literal fantasy."

A smile stretches my cheeks painfully. "Right back at ya."

He drops his forehead to mine. "What now?"

One firework after another brightens the night sky through the trees.

"Not sure." I drop a chaste kiss to his lips. "But as long as it involves you, nothing else matters."

ELEVEN

OLIVER

can make you see the world in a different light.

For years, I fantasized about what it'd be like to be with Levi. I created this perfect image of us in my mind. My heart fluttered at the mere idea of holding his hand, of lacing our fingers together and walking around town as a couple. A light sheen of sweat spread across my skin as I pictured his lips on mine countless times. And my cock ached at the slim possibility of having him in my bed, naked, moaning my name and begging for more.

In my endless stream of wishful thoughts and amorous dreams, I never had a clear sense of the future. Nor a true grasp of the potential reality. My lustful delusions of me and Levi always had this hazy aura. An ugly reminder that we would never be anything more than best friends.

Now, those fantastical thoughts have more definition. A hint of clarity. A touch of substantiality.

But not fully.

Levi West may be mine in all the ways that matter, but he

isn't mine completely. And that stings more than not having him at all.

Is it inconsiderate and foolish of me to want us to go from friends to lovers in a blink? Without a doubt, but does that change the fact that I do? No. Although Levi has told me point blank he wants me, wants more, it isn't that simple. Not when his family sets ridiculous, unattainable goals and expectations for his life. Not when they force him into relationships he does not want. Not when we have to tiptoe around others and hide the real us.

"You okay, Ollie?"

I startle as Kirsten sidles up to me and stares at my hands. The same hands that have been putting a filter and grounds in the coffee maker basket for who knows how long.

Unsure how many scoops I've added to the filter, I dump the grounds back in the container and start over.

"Yeah. Just have a lot on my mind."

I pop the basket into the coffee maker and press the brew button.

Kirsten leans into my side. "Want to talk about it?"

Can I talk about it? I want to. God, do I want to. But I don't want to break Levi's confidence.

In the past three weeks, so much in my life has changed. I've never been this happy. I've also never been this reserved. It feels as though I am constantly teetering on a tightrope, trying to maintain my balance. Swayed by my heart and head, I revel in my new relationship with Levi while I simultaneously question if I can keep what we have a secret.

Levi hasn't asked me to stay tight-lipped about us, but I assume he wants as much since everything we do is behind closed doors or in isolated places. Not to mention, he and Abigail Calhoun are still fake dating.

"Not here." I scan the restaurant for prying eyes. "Maybe later."

Kirsten rubs a hand up and down my bicep as her expression softens. "Whenever you're ready."

"Thanks, K." Needing to get out of my head, I flip the attention on Kirsten. "How's our favorite hot officer?" I waggle my brows. "He looks fucking yummy in his snug, short-sleeve uniform shirt." A dreamy sigh leaves my lips as I fill ice waters for new customers. "Bless the summer months."

"Ollie," she chastises as she bumps me with her hip, then chuckles. "Travis is more than man candy."

I load the glasses on a tray. "Is he, though?"

Her lips curve up in a dopey smile. "Yes." The way she says it is as if she's trying to convince herself. "But I have to admit… my man is more than easy on the eyes."

"Mm-hmm." I pick up the tray and start for the newly filled tables in my section. "Like I said, yummy."

"Oh, I forgot to mention."

I pause and turn to look at her. Her dreamy smile from a moment ago turns mischievous. I narrow my eyes at her.

"Trudie put Old Lady Hensen in your section." She juts her chin toward a table near the window. A table obscured by a group of brawny workers. "Have fun."

On a groan, I exit the server alley and move from one table to the next, delivering water glasses. I let them know I'll be back in a moment to take their orders. And then I head for the table near the window, to Old Lady Hensen and her grabby hands.

Across the table and out of reach, I set a glass of water in front of her. "Morning, Ms. Hensen. Do you need another minute to decide?"

The corners of her eyes crinkle as she squints at the menu through her glasses. "Must be time to get my eyes checked again." She points to something on the laminated page. "What does this say?"

I move around the table and stand next to her. Bend slightly and read the menu where her finger sits. "Spinach Florentine quiche." Quiche comes out more like key-eee-uh-sh as I inch back from her.

Because, as per usual, Old Lady Hensen takes advantage of my hospitality and grabs my ass.

Although the action is meaningless and a way to get her jollies in her old age, it's still unwelcome and awkward. Most of us brush it under the rug. Joke about how she's just some dirty old lady. But after three years of ass grabs, I'm over it.

"Ah, yes." She tips her head back slightly and peers at the menu through the bottom of her lenses. "I see it now. Must've been a smudge on my glasses." Her eyes meet mine, a purposeful smile wrinkling her weathered skin. "I'll have the quiche and a hot tea. Thank you, Oliver."

I scribble down her order. "I'll get that in for you."

Bolting from her table, I tend to my other customers. When her order is ready, I let someone else run it to her table. I check on her a couple times, staying out of arm's reach, but otherwise avoid her table.

As the morning rush thins and I have more downtime than work, thoughts of Levi trickle back in. Rather than think about our relationship, I focus on other things in his world, like work.

He hasn't mentioned much recently about the huge case he and Tymber are working on. Whenever I bring it up, he skirts around the details. For obvious reasons, his work is confidential. He isn't allowed to share specific pieces of information. I would never ask that of him or put him in a compromising position.

But it's difficult to miss the additional strain in his posture since taking on the case. Every now and then, this dazed, haunted look takes over his expression. Accented by the bruisy crescents beneath his eyes, some days he appears lifeless.

Worst of all, he keeps it bottled up. He keeps *too much* bottled up.

Between the stress of work, the pressure from his parents, maintaining the facade with Abigail, and spending time with me, the burden of carrying so much weight is slowly chipping away at him. He won't be able to burn the candle at both ends for much longer.

Loading a tray with the sweetener packet holders from the empty tables, I take it to the server alley and refill them. Halfway through the task, Kirsten rests her chin on my shoulder from behind.

"How about a movie night?" She straightens and moves to my side. "Since you have an out-of-town show tomorrow, we should all hang tonight."

A night with friends, junk food, and laughter is exactly what I need. Something to distract me from my incessant thoughts.

"Sounds great. What should I bring?"

Kirsten pulls her phone from her pocket, taps the screen, and shakes her head. "Just you." Her gaze lifts to mine, a soft smile on her lips.

My phone buzzes in my back pocket and I pull it out to read her message.

K

Movie night tonight. My place. Dinner on me.

I tap the heart reaction and type out my own response as others pop up in the group chat.

SKY

I'm on snack duty. What time?

DEE DEE

I've got drinks. Just us 4??

Someone's a bit demanding. Side effects of my favorite hot officer 😌

Kirsten play-slaps my arm. "You're ridiculous, Ollie." Her fingers fly across the screen again.

K

6-6:30 and us 4 only

The backs of my eyes sting as I stare down at the screen. Kirsten didn't indicate *why* tonight is the core group only. But since the three of them are in romantic relationships now, we usually only have these types of get-togethers when one of us needs extra support or advice.

And this round, it's me in the hot seat.

Halfway into my third slice of pizza, Kirsten changes the entire tone of the evening with a single word.

"Alright, Ollie. Spill."

Since our teens, the four of us have been close.

With our unique differences, we were labeled as too eccentric, goofy or reticent by our peers. We weren't outcasts in school per se. Just comfortable in our individualism. And because of that, we easily gravitated toward each other. Not all at once, but in separate friendships that came together in time. And since my, Kirsten's, and Skylar's freshman year and Delilah's junior year, we've been this close-knit quartet.

There is beauty in knowing someone for years. A comfort. A feeling of kinship. But with it comes them knowing when you are out of sorts. In most situations, it's nice to have friends you can gush about life with. But when you're hurting, when you harbor secrets that aren't yours to tell, it makes sharing more of a challenge.

"Not sure I can."

Kirsten narrows her eyes, Skylar tilts her head, and Delilah gives a knowing, sympathetic smile.

Hand over her mouth while she chews, Skylar mumbles, "So confused. What does that even mean?"

It means exactly what I said, I want to say but keep to myself.

Levi hasn't told me *not* to tell anyone about us. But he hasn't said it's okay to do so either. Add in the facts that the town believes he's dating Abigail and everything we do is in dark, secluded places, I'm assuming there are to be no shared details of our relationship.

Will Levi fault me for seeking advice from my friends? I don't think so. He knows they'd keep quiet if I asked them to.

I toss my slice of pizza down and wipe my hands with a napkin. "It means I hate secrets. It means I haven't been told to keep one, but it's insinuated by the situation." Sinking into the couch, I tip my head back and stare at the vaulted ceiling. "It means I want to tell you, but would possibly break someone's trust in the process."

A hand rests on my knee a moment before delivering a gentle squeeze. "Whether you share or not, we're here, Ollie," Delilah says with a gentle, compassionate tone.

If anyone gets where my head is at, it's Delilah. Her love story and mine aren't too far apart. Unrequited love is a bitch, especially when you're gay or lesbian and you're unsure the person you like will reciprocate your feelings.

"Thanks, Dee Dee." I rest my hand on hers and return her reassuring grip. "Right now, all I need is my friends."

Food set aside, they climb onto the couch and swarm me. Wrap me in awkward hugs and tickle my sides. Press sloppy kisses on my cheeks and ruffle my hair.

The movie plays as we huddle on the couch and comfort each other. I may not have opened up to them, I may not have told them the one thing I've dreamed about for years has finally happened, but it doesn't matter. All they know is I need them, and they've come to the rescue. They saw me hurting and surrounded me with warmth and love without hesitation.

Although it eases the ache, it doesn't wipe it away fully. For now, that's okay.

———————

June 14th

I had a dream last night that felt more like a memory. But when I try to conjure up the memory, I can't quite see it.

About a week after the Memorial Day Festival, L texted to meet up with him and A at Dalton's. A's boyfriend was also going to be there, and they were grabbing beers and burgers. My insides twisted when I read the text. Something felt off as I read the invitation. But I ignored it and went anyway.

The entire night, it felt as if I was an interloper. An outsider as my boyfriend, if he is my boyfriend, was on a fake date with his fake fucking girlfriend. I zoned out frequently. Desmond appeared to do the same.

It was fucking weird, but I didn't say anything. I wanted to spend time with him.

And then, last night I had a dream, or flashback, of that night. Like I was seeing things I missed in person. It might be all in my head. My mind might be jumbling up what actually happened with my irrational, borderline-jealous thoughts. But in the dream, I caught A staring at L longer than usual. I saw the way she looked at him. Like she wanted him to be more than her friend. Like she didn't want their relationship to be fake anymore.

I haven't told L about it. I don't want him to disregard it as foolish or impossible. I don't want to be placated.

But fuck, it's eating away at me. I know he doesn't want her as anything other than a friend. I remind myself of this every time my thoughts spin out of control. But it's still hard as hell.

I feel like the third wheel.

I should tell him. He'd want me to share my insecurities with him. He'd want me to be open and honest. But right now, I just can't. Maybe when his workload tapers off and he's not so stressed. The last thing I want to do is be an additional burden.

TWELVE
NUMBER 263

Day Ten

My stomach cramps a breath before pain blooms on the right side of my body. I press the heel of my hand to my side and inhale slow, methodical breaths. The sharp stabbing sensation dulls into a throbbing ache as I lightly massage the area. After several passes, I breathe easier.

A small collection of empty child-sized water bottles and containers sits off to the side of my narrow prison. In a corner near the door, excrement litters the floor. My stone cell reeks, but the putrid odor is inescapable.

With no access to the outside world, to the sun or moon, I have no concept of time. I'd base the days on my sleep cycle, but with my body reserving energy and sleeping in fits and starts, it is unreliable. Mixed with the screams and laughter and randomly played deafening music, my mind shuts down at every possible opportunity.

My stomach twists with another cramp and I know it's from lack of water and food. Mere hours may have passed since a water bottle and container of tasteless slop were set in my cell, but it feels like weeks.

Three.

Three bottles of water.

Three measly portions of food—if you can even call stale crackers and insipid goop food.

Enough to keep my body functioning, but nothing more.

Back against the wall, I draw my legs to my chest. I stare into the darkness and pray for someone to rescue me. Anyone. But as quickly as the wish flits through my mind, it vanishes.

If no one knows where I am, how will they save me? How will I be set free from this hell?

I hug my legs closer to my torso. My body screams in protest at the simple action. Muscles weak and bones weary, I lick my cracked lips and loosen my hold. Give my weakening muscles an ounce of reprieve.

The door flies open, the bright light in the hall momentarily blinds me, and a man steps into my cell. As my eyes adjust to the light, I glance up at his face.

Black fabric covers his face and neck and clings to him like a second skin. Holes expose his eyes, mouth, and the base of his nose. He wears a long-sleeve black shirt, black cargo pants, gloves, and boots. He has no food or water in his hands.

This isn't an obligatory visit.

Digging my heels into the floor, I crush my spine to the wall and try to evade him.

A robotic laugh echoes off the walls as he inches closer. And then another man steps up behind him. More or less as tall. Equally as brawny and menacing. Side by side, they stare down at me on the floor. One reaches for his groin and rubs up and down several times. The other backhands him in the chest.

And then they pounce. I scramble to escape, but it's no use.

There is nowhere to go. Especially when I'm chained to the floor.

Thick arms wrap around me and hoist me off the floor. When I first woke up in this room and someone came at me, I fought back. I kicked, punched and screamed. But now, not as much. Sure, I squirm and try to wiggle free. I grunt and mutter my abhorrence. But the more time that passes, the less I fight. The longer I'm here, the longer I'm deprived of basic human necessities the less strength—physically and mentally—I have.

While one man painfully pins me to his chest and squats, the other shortens the length of my chains anchored to the floor by securing a different link to the eyebolt. When he finishes, my knees crash down on the concrete, and I fall onto my side.

Maniacal, synthetic laughter rings in my ears as the two men exit the room. But they don't close the door.

Hope surges in my chest but dies out before I take my next breath.

A different man enters the room. This one shorter, leaner, a little twitchy. Clothed in dress slacks and a polo shirt, he, too, wears a mask over his head.

Uncertain what will happen next, I remain on my side on the floor near the anchor, my eyes locked on his every move.

An arm's length away, he squats down and tilts his head to the side, studying me like a new and fascinating trinket.

My insides twist in an unorthodox way. Bile claws at the walls of my stomach and creeps up my throat.

He reaches forward and grazes my cheek with his knuckles. I jerk away but barely move an inch. Mechanical laughter fills the room as he repeats the action, then clutches my chin.

"When they told me how attractive you were," he says, "I thought they were exaggerating." The man jerks my chin up and shifts my head left, then right. "But they weren't wrong.

You're quite ravishing." He rises to his full height and inches back. "Not that your looks will save you."

His words momentarily throw me off.

"Up on your knees," he orders in a deep, inhuman voice.

When I don't move right away, he takes a step back and then swings his foot forward, connecting with my shins.

I howl in pain and curl into a fetal position, clutching my legs to my chest.

"I said get up on your fucking knees." His robotic command is louder, harsher, and I detect a hint of his own voice.

Pushing up off the floor, I clamber to my knees. My shins and knees burn against the concrete, but I don't voice my pain. I don't give this asshole the satisfaction.

The man walks in slow circles around me, the soles of his shoes sticking to the floor and squeaking with each step. He stares down at me as if I'm prey. As if I'm some pawn in his fucked-up game.

"Let's see what you're made of, Two Sixty-Three." He stops in front of me and tilts his head a moment, contemplative. "Let's see how long you last." Twisted laughter bounces off the walls. "Let's see how much you love it."

I have no idea what's about to happen, but it can't be good. And without a doubt, I won't enjoy a single second of it.

"Consider this a small sample of what's to come."

Before his words register, his fist connects with my cheek. An explosion of pain and fire sears my face. Flashes of light dance across my vision. I reach for my cheek but fall short when the chain jerks to a stop. And then the same excruciating pain lances my other cheek.

I drop my chin to my chest in the hopes of avoiding another blow. But it's impossible.

Fingers slide through my hair, curl into a tight fist, and yank my head upright.

"Ah, ah, ah." The man waggles a finger inches from my nose. "Did I give you permission to hide your face?" He jerks my head back further until his masked face fills my vision. "The answer is no, Two Sixty-Three." He releases my hair with a shove. "Be good and stay upright."

Blow after blow, the man punches and kicks my head, my chest, my hips, my legs. His grunts, groans and laughter blend with the white noise in my ears. Bruises and blood mottle my dirty, bare skin. The taste of metal dances over my tongue. Each hit lasts a lifetime and permanently etches itself on my soul.

Death would be too kind with how I feel in this moment.

But then he adds humiliation to the list.

Unbuckling his belt, he releases the button on his slacks, drags down the zipper, and pulls his dick out. He spits on his palm and jerks off inches from my face. I avert my attention and he fists my chin, twisting my head so I am forced to watch. So I have to witness his pleasure, how much he gets off as he subjugates me further. He tells me how much I deserve this— to be on my knees, to be punished, to live the rest of my days in the servitude of others' needs. An unwavering pledge on his tongue, he tells me this is how my life will be from now on.

And then he comes on my face and chest, tucks himself away, refastens his pants and belt, and exits my prison cell.

I collapse on the ground, curl into myself, and silently cry. I send a silent wish out to the universe and beg for my life back. Body numb and eyes stinging, I lay motionless on the concrete with my chin tucked and weep as the man's words carve themselves into my soul.

A large bottle of water is thrown in the room and a plate

with a sandwich is slid across the floor. Then the door closes and I'm swallowed up by darkness once more.

Except this time, I prefer the dark. I beg for the escape and isolation. One breath after another, I pray for death.

But death never comes.

THIRTEEN

LEVI

I EXIT MY CAR AND WEAVE THROUGH THE LOT TOWARD THE entrance of Gigi's Italian. The light balm from the bay mingles with the sound of classic Italian music. Clusters of people linger near the door as they wait for an open table.

Earlier today, Abigail sent a text suggesting we go out tonight. Though it's difficult to tell through nonverbal communication, the tone of her text came across as some-what frantic. When I asked if everything was okay, she said her parents were asking about us more often. Then she said she told her parents we had a date at Gigi's tonight.

Everyone with the last name Calhoun is all smiles at the news. Me, on the other hand, not so much.

It's bad enough I suggested this whole fake dating bullshit in the first place. Gaining a friend out of the situation? Not so bad. But now, said friend is making plans for us and telling others without consulting me first… unacceptable.

My father has made it his mission to govern my life and mold me into someone I am not nor will be. Over the past month or so, Abigail seems to have joined forces with my father and is tossing out manipulation tactics like Halloween candy. I will not tolerate either of them.

As I near the host stand, Abigail spots me and gives me her brightest smile. A voice in the back of my mind tells me not to trust that smile.

"Finally, you're here." Her whole body comes to life as she steps closer and rests a hand on my forearm. "I'll let the host know."

Confusion mars my brow as I watch her talk with the host. The voice in the back of my head speaks louder and tells me to leave. That something isn't right.

She touched me.

None of our family is here. No one we need to flaunt our lies in front of is present.

So why did she touch me with a level of intimacy we don't share?

Lost in my head, I miss her return. I fail to pull away before she hooks her arm with mine and gives a gentle tug.

"Our table's ready."

Mildly bewildered, I nod and let her lead us to where the host waits. As we move through the restaurant, it feels as though every set of eyes is on us. Judging us together a beat before they whisper to their tablemate.

With as much finesse as possible, I ease my arm free of Abigail. When we reach the table, I let her choose her seat first, then sit opposite her with my chair farther than normal from the table. I tuck my feet under my chair and lean back in my seat, maintaining my personal space.

I open my mouth to ask her if something happened between her text and now, but the server sidles up to the table.

After a thorough rundown of the chef's specials tonight, they ask for our drink orders. Abigail taps her lips for a moment, then chooses a local red wine. I almost order the same, but stop myself. A twinge in my gut tells me to keep a clear head. So, I order a sparkling water. Abigail's pout at my order amplifies the pang, and I don't fucking like it.

Ignoring the menu, I study her as she reads hers. Less notable now, her smile never fades. If she's happy, that's great. But the longer I stare at her, the more I feel it isn't general happiness that has her so gleeful.

"What's up with you?" I blurt out the question, not caring how it comes across.

Her entire expression scrunches to the middle of her face for a split second. Then that damn smile returns.

"Can't I just be in a good mood?"

I tilt my head, narrow my eyes, and scrutinize her. From her expression and attitude to her attire and the way she looks at me, I evaluate every inch of her.

In a short, cream-colored dress with thin straps and a low *V* over her breasts, she has more skin than ever on display. Sitting tall in her chair, she leans in my direction slightly. A subtle smile tips up the corners of her faintly parted lips.

My stomach cramps the longer I study her. The voice in the back of my head more or less yelling at me to get out now.

With a gentle shake of my head, I inhale a deep breath, count to five, and exhale.

"Everything good with Desmond?"

Lifting her menu, she drops her gaze and swallows. "Not sure. We broke up."

Shit. Now I feel like an asshole.

No one feels great after a breakup. She's probably masking her pain with artificial joy. And here I am, giving her a hard time. I should be consoling her. I should be the friend that asks what they can do to make it better. Hell, her breakup is probably part of the reason she wanted to go out tonight.

"Sorry to hear." And I genuinely mean it. "He seemed like a good guy. Goes to show appearances aren't everything."

Before she responds, the server returns with our drinks and takes our dinner orders.

Once the server leaves, silence is an encapsulating bubble around our table. I remain tight-lipped and give her a moment to gather her thoughts. To tell me why she and Desmond are no longer a couple. I picture countless scenarios, but nothing sticks. I didn't know Desmond well. But the last I saw them both together, they appeared genuinely happy as a couple.

"I broke up with him," she finally admits.

Of all the reasons I anticipated hearing from her, I didn't expect her to say it was *her* who broke up with *him*.

"Why?"

With a shrug of her shoulders, she picks up her glass and sips her wine. "Felt like the right thing to do."

All I know of their relationship is what Abigail has shared, which isn't much. But in the past month and a half, I've heard only wonderful things about him. She spoke of a future with him. Marriage and children and being with someone she loved.

I lean forward and rest an arm on the table as I try to make sense of her news. The more I think about it, the more confused I become.

"Did he cheat on you?"

If that's the case, I may need to pay a visit to his work and give him a piece of my mind.

Her brows furrow as she shakes her head. "No."

No? Then what? What did Desmond do that would make Abigail not want to be with him anymore?

And then she reaches across the table, sets her hand over mine, and curls her fingers slightly. Her expression softens as she stares at me across the table.

The nagging voice in my head screams and the spasm in my midsection explodes into nausea-inducing pain. I jerk my hand away from hers and push back in my chair.

No. No, no, no, no, no.

"It doesn't feel right to be with Desmond when I no longer feel the same for him."

I ball my fingers into fists in my lap. Breathe heavily through my nostrils. Do my best not to cause a scene in the middle of the restaurant.

Abigail rolls her lips between her teeth. "Not when I want to be with someone else."

My fingernails dig into my palms as my molars gnash together. Anger bubbles from each of my pores and radiates around me like a venomous cloud.

"I mean, our families already think we're dating. It'd be easy to not pretend," she prattles on.

"No," I bark out louder than expected.

She flinches, then lifts her hand from the table in a gesture for me to hear her out. "We like each other."

"Not like that," I insert before she says anything else.

"But—"

"No." I shove my chair back farther and rise. "That's not what this is, was…" I wave a hand in the air. "When I suggested this, it wasn't because I actually wanted to be… *anything* to you. It was to shut my damn father up." I pull out my wallet, grab a couple twenties, and drop them on the table. "I didn't want it to begin with. Now…" I pocket my wallet. "This is over. We're done. No friendship. Nothing." One step, then another, I walk away. "Fuck off and lose my number."

Several patrons glance my way as I head for the exit. Not that I give a fuck.

When I step outside, my anger fizzles out and the additional weight I've carried for weeks falls away.

The facade is no more. The days of selling my soul to appease my father have come to an end.

In my car, I take out my phone and send Oliver a text.

Hang out?

I crank the engine to life and wait for him to reply. When several minutes pass without a word, I go to his social media page and check the band's schedule. On the pinned post, it says Hailey's Fire is playing in Smoky Creek tonight.

I tap the link for the band's social media profile and open their live stream. My eyes shamelessly roam over Oliver as he plays. Not much sweat dampens his shirt, which means they haven't been playing long.

Closing the app, I stow my phone and buckle my seat belt. Within seconds, I exit the parking lot and make my way to Opal Trail. The moment I reach the outskirts of town, I shift gears and smash the accelerator. The world passes in a blur of occasional streetlights in the fading sunlight.

———

I reach Smoky Creek in less than half the time it'd take anyone else. Perks of a fast car on quiet roads.

Easing off the accelerator as I enter town limits, I scan the storefronts for Brickton and Sons Tavern.

I drive by countless shops, restaurants, offices, and standard businesses you'd find in most towns. I pass the occasional person or couple, but for a Friday night, not many people milling about. Smoky Creek is small, like Stone Bay, but there doesn't seem to be much *life* to it.

The first true signs of life emerge a couple miles into Smoky Creek. Endless cars fill the street parking along the main road. The farther I drive, the more cars and people I come across. Minutes later, I arrive at the town's hotspot for the night.

Brickton and Sons Tavern.

Either this is the place to be on weekend nights, or most of the town fills the bar to see Hailey's Fire play. Less than a quarter of Stone Bay visits Dalton's when Oliver's band is on stage. If this crowd is for them...

Warmth fills my chest as I search for a parking spot on the street. Pride and adoration and this prickle of something desirable yet foreign surge in my bloodstream.

Half a mile later, I cut the engine, exit the car, and wander down the sidewalk. Hands in my pockets, I focus on the throng of townsfolk near the bar. Just before the tavern comes into view, the music hits my ears. A smile instantly curves the corners of my mouth and I pick up my pace.

Weaving through the overcrowded tavern, I make it to the bar and order a drink. Frosty glass in hand, I slip between people until I near the makeshift stage at the back wall. I move off to the side, away from the thick of the crowd, and hover in the periphery with my eyes glued to Oliver.

"You've been fucking incredible, Smoky Creek," Hailey says when the song ends.

Whistles and cheers and excited expletives ricochet off the walls at a deafening volume.

"We're slowing it down for our last song." Hailey presses a finger to her lips. "Don't tell anyone in Stone Bay, but this is the first time we've played 'Fallen Stars' in public."

She lifts her guitar strap over her head and swaps it for an acoustic on the side of the stage. Oliver rises from his stool behind the drums, runs a hand through his hair, wipes it on his shorts, then picks up the other acoustic guitar. He grabs a barstool, sets it in front of Trip's microphone near Hailey, then takes a seat.

I sift through countless memories of watching the band play in Oliver's garage. I search for a time when the two of them played acoustic together. But I come up blank. The title of the song doesn't ring a bell either.

As long as I've known Oliver, he has played the guitar as well as the drums. But not once, to my recollection, has he played guitar during show nights.

I down the last of my drink as the first chords of the song fill the air. While Hailey drops her head and focuses on the tune, Oliver leans closer to the microphone and closes his eyes.

"It's always been us, a sea of blue and green." A few notes fill the air. "Our silent conversations and blurry fragments of a dream."

As Oliver plucks the strings of his guitar, I swallow and inch closer to the stage.

"Just out of reach, I wanted to take your hand. But it wasn't my place to touch you. Not like that."

Perspiration dampens my skin as I listen to Oliver croon lyrics to hundreds of Smoky Creek residents. Lyrics I know, without a doubt, are about us.

"So I stood by your side with a cheek-burning smile. I played the goof, the fool, while I died a little inside."

The more he sings, the harder my heart pounds in my chest.

"From the start, all I wanted was you. From the start, little did I know you wanted me too."

The backs of my eyes sting as my throat clogs with emotion.

"In the shadows, we hide. Tall trees, scraped knees, stars falling in the night."

A cramp flares to life beneath my diaphragm as guilt gnaws at my soul.

"But I'd live forever in the dark to keep you at my side. My best-kept secret. My reason. My life."

My fingers drum on my thighs as I wait for the song to end. Every cell in my body aches for him. To go to him. To touch him. To kiss him.

"From the start, all I wanted was you. From the start, you wanted me too."

Like the rest of the crowd, I'm stunned silent and can't take my eyes off Oliver.

"Forever mine… until every star falls from the sky." The song starts to fade as Oliver whispers the last lyrics into the mic. "Until every star falls. Every star falls. Every star falls." He inhales deeply. "Until I fall."

Hailey and Oliver stop playing and a heavy silence hangs in the air. No one breathes or speaks or moves for a solid seven seconds. Everyone stares at the duo on stage, awestruck and emotional.

And then, it's as though the volume gets turned back on. The crowd cheers louder than before. Hoots and hollers and *fuck yeah*s boom throughout the tavern.

Wide smiles on their faces, the band takes a bow a beat before Hailey throws devil's horns to the crowd.

"Thanks for being fucking awesome, Smoky Creek. We fucking love you," Hailey bellows into the mic.

As the raucous cheer from the patrons settles and the overhead music kicks on, the band gives one last wave and turns to exit the stage.

My knee bounces as I wait for Oliver to look up. For his eyes to lock with mine. Seconds feel like hours as my pulse whooshes loudly beneath my ears. As I all but silently beg for him to meet my eager gaze.

And the second he steps off the stage and sees me, feet away, all the air gets sucked from the room. He freezes and narrows his eyes as if I'm a figment of his imagination.

My heart hammers painfully as my rig cage constricts my lungs.

He inches closer but keeps his distance. His eyes continue to roam my face, still uncertain I'm actually here. That I drove to his out-of-town show to see him.

Those vacant feet between us make me twitchy. Anxious. Unsettled. Small as it is, I hate that there's a shred of distance between us right now, especially after that song. All I want to do is step into his space, frame his face with my hands, and crush his lips with mine.

Rather than resist what I want, for the first time in my life, I follow through. I give into what I want, what I feel, what we both feel.

In two long strides, I'm toe to toe with Oliver. His eyes widen as his chest visibly rises and falls. Lips slightly parted, his breath dances over my skin.

"Hey—"

I cut him off as my hands cup his cheeks and my lips claim his. Oliver flinches, but I don't relent. When I lick the seam of his lips with my tongue, every muscle in his body softens.

And then his hands are on my hips, fisting my body with bruising force. He hauls me into him, his dick hardening in his shorts as he deepens the kiss. As moans spill from his mouth and mingle with mine.

The noise, the people, the bar… all of it disappears as I give into desire. As I allow myself to be truly selfish for the first time.

Oliver breaks the kiss. "What—"

I lean into him and take his mouth again. Desperate and greedy and insatiable.

He returns the kiss, his hands skating up my sides until they frame my face. He breaks the kiss again, soft laughter dancing between us.

"I'll kiss you all night if that's what you want." He drops a chaste kiss on my lips. "But I need a momentary break." The corners of his mouth twitch as he fights a smile and fails. "Maybe a little hydration."

I inch back. "Shit." My brows tug together. "Sorry."

He laughs harder while his thumbs stroke my cheeks. With a subtle shake of his head, he says, "Never apologize for kissing me." He drops his forehead to mine. "Ever."

I close my eyes, take a deep breath, and give an infinitesimal nod. "Yeah." I open my eyes and reluctantly pull back. "Alright."

The world around us comes back into focus, but I refuse to look anywhere except at Oliver.

We join Trip and Hailey at a table off to the side. Food and drinks get ordered as we shoot the shit and townies stop by the table to sing their praises. As the hours pass, the crowd thins to what is a typical night at Dalton's.

The entire time, Oliver doesn't take his hand off my thigh beneath the table.

When our plates empty and we drain the last of our drinks, Oliver leans into my side, his breath warm on my ear. "Want to get out of here?" He inches back until our gazes lock.

Silly fucking question. I've wanted to leave with him since I kissed him.

Not wanting to appear overeager, I give a subtle nod. "Yeah. Don't you need to pack up?" I jerk my chin toward the stage.

"Owner said we could come back in the morning." He shrugs. "I have a room booked at the inn."

Those words are an instant shot of adrenaline and lust in my veins, but I try to not let it show. "With Trip and Hailey?"

Please say no.

Throaty laughter fills the air as Oliver covers his mouth with a loose fist. "Uh, no." He shakes his head for emphasis. "It's nothing personal. Just not in the mood to listen to and watch them fuck for hours."

I choke on my own breath, and it only serves to make Oliver laugh harder.

"Jesus, Ollie."

"What?" He rolls his eyes. "Just telling it like it is."

He rises from his stool and I immediately miss the contact of his hand on my thigh.

"Be right back. Going to close out our tab."

Before I'm able to hand over cash for my part, he's halfway to the bar. For a moment, he chats with the bartender and I ogle the brilliant smile on his beautiful face.

The day started with stress and darkness. It almost ended in a similar fashion.

But I'm tired of hiding a part of myself. A very large part of my identity. It's time to embrace who I am. It's time to walk through the world as myself. My true self. Not all at once. I don't think I'm mentally prepared for that. But tonight helped. Being around people who don't know me, who don't have set expectations of me… it's a start.

So long as I have Oliver, I don't fear what happens next.

"Ready?" he asks as he approaches the table.

More than ever.

I slip off my stool. "Ready."

Oliver waves to Hailey and Trip. "Bartender said after ten tomorrow morning."

"Cool." Trip sips his beer. "Night."

"Night." Oliver waves.

Our stride is casual as we exit the tavern and walk down the street for my car. But there is no mistaking the exquisite tension building between us. Each step we take is a step closer to a fantasy I've jacked off to countless times over the years.

As the engine warms, Oliver indicates where the inn is. When I put the car in gear and drive down the street, he reaches across the console, lays his hand on my upper thigh, and gently massages the muscles inches from my groin.

Less than five minutes later, I park the car in front of his room at the inn.

Dick hard as steel, I inhale a stuttered breath and turn to look at Oliver. An expression I've never seen on him etches his features. Undiluted need. Ache. Lust.

And when my gaze trails down his body, I see exactly how much he wants me right now.

Without a word, I unbuckle my seat belt, exit the car, and wait for him to do the same. In six lengthy strides, we stand outside the door as he fumbles for the key card.

The second we slip inside, everything changes.

FOURTEEN

OLIVER

I've played this moment in my mind an infinite number of times over the past seven years. Fantasized over what it'd be like to touch and taste Levi. Openly claim him with my hand on him or our fingers laced together. To tell the world this man belongs to me, and I belong to him. To take him to my bed and permanently alter the shape of our souls.

Not once during those hedonistic daydreams did I believe it'd become a reality. Nor did I foresee Levi initiating this monumental shift in our relationship.

It's both thrilling and terrifying.

The soft click of the door as it closes jump-starts my heart. My pulse soars as I step farther into the room. Frenetic energy trickles through my bloodstream and wakes every nerve ending in my body as Levi stands inches away. My breaths come in slow, stuttered sips as I stare at the quilt-covered queen bed in the middle of the room.

This is really fucking happening.

His fingers graze mine for the briefest of seconds and I suck in a sharp breath. Heat and thrill and something foreign yet addictive dance across my skin. My eyes roll back and close as I absorb this new, potent sensation.

And then the feeling is gone.

My eyes pop open and shoot to his as I reach for his hand. As our fingers weave together, I read the uncertainty in his expression.

"What's wrong?" The question leaves my lips in a whisper.

He drops his gaze to our joined hands, his thumb trailing the length of mine in delicate, carefree strokes. With a subtle shake of his head, he says, "Just nervous."

Inhaling a shaky breath, I gently tighten my hold on him. His eyes drift back up to mine, the cool blue of his irises now darker. Bolder. An unspoken declaration.

I swallow past the bubbling anxiety expanding in my chest. "Me too."

God, am I fucking nervous.

Levi moves to stand in front of me, takes my other hand, and inches close enough for his breath to paint my lips. Notes of cedar with the hint of something distinctly him fill my nose.

Hour-long seconds pass as my heart rattles my rib cage, the vicious rhythm of my pulse ricocheting in my ears. I drop my gaze to his lips as the memory of kissing him in public hours ago ambushes my thoughts. As if he hears my introspection, his tongue darts out and wets his lips.

My grip on his hand tightens.

And with that simple reaction, he eviscerates the last of the space between us and claims my mouth with his.

He releases my hands and lifts his to frame my face. His fingers bruise my flesh a beat before they drift into my hair and curl into loose fists. The desperation in his touch, mixed with the taste of him on my tongue, has me dizzy.

A moan vibrates my chest and spills from my lips onto his tongue.

His fingers fist my hair harder as he deepens the kiss. As his tongue wars with mine.

And then we're moving across the room.

I reach for him and clutch his hips. Fist the cotton of his shirt in my hands as we stumble to a stop. Haul him flush to my frame as the kiss turns frenzied. Greedy. Borderline violent.

My hands skim the waist of his pants from his hips to the line of buttons on his shirt. With a slight tremble in my fingers, I pop the buttons free. Graze the soft skin of his abdomen with the tips of my fingers. Smile into the kiss as he quivers beneath my touch.

I shove the shirt open and down his arms but stop at his wrists when the cuffs catch. Lips still on mine, Levi yanks at the material. When it doesn't give, he breaks the kiss, grumbles under his breath, unfastens the buttons, and tosses the shirt aside.

Eager as I am to step back into him and take his mouth again, I inch back and rake my gaze over his chest. Glimpse the faint definition of his pecs and abdominals. Peek at the ink telling a story on his arms. Visually trace the stiff peaks of his nipples. Skim down his midline to the light dusting of hair below his navel that dips beneath his pants. Unabashedly stare at the thick bulge straining his slacks beneath his zipper.

My dick twitches, and I lick my lips.

A groan echoes through the room and my eyes dart up to meet his.

"You're killing me, Ollie."

I tuck my lips between my teeth to fight my smile. Shuffling forward, I hook a finger in a belt loop on his slacks. "Oh, really?"

Eyes fixed on mine, he reaches for the bottom hem of my shirt, fists it for one, two, three ragged breaths, then drags the fabric up my torso. It sails across the room and joins his shirt on the floor.

Nimble fingers explore my skin at a painfully slow pace. The soft pads of his fingers, the harsh bite of his nails, the delicious bruise of his grip. I revel in the way his gaze roams my body. Bask in the hum dancing over my skin. Come alive as his fingers drift lower and skim the waistband of my underwear peeking out of my shorts.

With one hand, he pops the button on my shorts as if he's done it countless times. He tugs at my zipper next, my shorts falling to the floor without effort.

My cock strains the cotton of my boxer briefs, eager for his touch. Hopeful for his mouth. Begging for much more.

Toeing off my shoes, I reach for the button of his slacks, followed by the zipper. I shove the fabric down his thighs and inch back as he kicks off his shoes and pants.

"I need to fucking touch you," he growls out as he fists his cock through his briefs.

Without a word, my fingers circle his wrist and I haul him across the room. He stumbles for a couple steps then steps impossibly close as we enter the bathroom. Releasing my hold on him, I crank the water in the shower.

On a slow spin of my heel, I meet his waiting gaze. I peel one sock off, then the other. Hook my thumbs in the waistband of my underwear and thrust the last shred of fabric hiding me from him to the floor.

His dick spasms at the sight of my swollen, lengthy cock.

"Join me?"

Not waiting for his answer, I step into the shower and leave the curtain partially open.

Under the hot spray, I rinse away my night on stage and mentally prepare myself for what may happen next.

"Fuck, this shower is small," Levi says as he steps in and closes the curtain.

I chuckle and open my mouth with a witty retort. But the words never leave my lips.

Because as I inch out from under the spray, his cock nudges my ass and I stop breathing.

As water rains down on us, he traces the length of my spine with his finger. I assume he'll stop when he reaches the top of my ass, but Levi surprises me at every turn. Slowly, too damn slowly, his finger dips between the globes of my ass. Lower. Lower. Until he's *there*.

Just as he adds a bit of pressure, I whirl around, shove him into the wall, and drop to my knees.

I'd love nothing more than to let Levi explore my body. To let him learn with a hands-on approach. But I don't want the first time we have sex—other than oral—to be in the shower.

"Ollie, what—"

Gripping the base of his cock, I circle the head with my tongue once before I take him to the back of my throat.

A hiss leaves his lips as he threads his fingers through my hair. "Fuck…"

My gaze flits up his body until I reach his slack-jawed expression. I study his hooded eyes and the barely perceptible shifts in his features as I fuck him with my mouth. I change my pace and note which he prefers. And then I add a little teeth and relish in the pain as he fists my hair harder.

"You feel so good wrapped around my cock."

I reach around and clutch his ass with both hands. Hold him in place, relax my jaw further, and take him deeper at a slow, punishing pace.

He hangs his head, his hair falling in his face. But his eyes never leave mine. Not for a single second.

His breaths come faster, harsher. A guttural moan vibrates his frame as his cock swells in my mouth.

"Oh, fuck." The cheeks of his ass flex. "Fuck." He grips my hair painfully. "Ollie… fuck."

Hot cum hits the back of my throat and I moan. Hands still on his ass, I hold him in place and bob up and down his length until I swallow every salty drop.

With a pop, I release him and rise from the floor. A victorious smile stretches my face painfully as I slink back under the spray and stare after him as he catches his breath.

In a blink, Levi shoves off the wall, grips either side of my face, and crushes my mouth with a punishing kiss. The pads of his fingers bruise my flesh a beat before one of his hands drops and fists my cock. He breaks the kiss but hovers close enough for his lips to occasionally graze mine.

"You like my cock in your mouth?" His question has an edge to it.

My lips part as he strokes my length with the perfect amount of pressure. I grip the edge of the inset shelf on the wall and give it some of my weight.

"Obviously," I reply, my tone a hint satirical.

He hums. "And you like my cum on your tongue?" The tip of his tongue darts out and licks my top lip.

The slight tease of his tongue mixed with his perfect strokes of my cock is an exquisite combination. Add in all this dirty talk about blow jobs and cum, it won't be long before mine paints the tile.

My greens lock onto his blues. "Any fucking day of the week."

"Good."

The corner of his mouth twitches a breath before he grips my biceps, spins us around, thrusts me against the wall, and falls to his knees. Water rains down on his back as his fingers clutch my thighs. Eyes on my dick, he leans in and circles my tip with his tongue.

"Now it's my turn for a taste." His hands drift around to the backs of my thighs. "Fuck my mouth, Ollie." His nails bite my skin. "Make up for all the times you didn't get to fuck me but wanted to."

"Fucking hell…" I mutter.

I comb my fingers through his lengthy locks and curl them at the back of his head. Rocking my hips forward, I nudge his lips with my tip.

"Open up and relax your jaw."

Levi does as I say, but his grip on my thighs stiffens.

I gently yank his hair so he'll meet my gaze. "You're safe with me, L." I nod in reassurance. "Always."

His eyes dart between mine as he inhales a few steadying breaths. Whatever he sees in my gaze, it's enough to ease his anxiety. His grip on my thighs loosens as his shoulders sag in obvious relief.

I cup the angle of his jaw and stroke the apple of his cheek with my thumb. "Never feel pressured to do anything with me. Ever."

Levi shakes his head. "I don't."

A faint smile curves a corner of my mouth as I arch a brow. "Prove it."

And until I growl his name and come down his throat, Levi does exactly that.

We towel off enough to not soak the sheets.

I rip the quilt from the bed, shove Levi down onto the mattress, and crawl up his body until my cock grazes his. He clutches my hips, grinding me against him as I claim his mouth. I fist his hair as he palms my ass.

Fire licks every inch of my skin as one of his hands trails up my spine, his other arm banding around my waist. He grips the nape of my neck, pins my body to his, and then flips me on my back.

Hovering a breath above me, he reaches between us and wraps his fingers around my cock. "I want to fuck you." His words are a growl. "And not just your mouth."

I grip his jaw with bruising strength and pull him close enough his lips ghost mine. "Not sure you're ready for that."

With a cock of his brow, one corner of his mouth kicks up. "I know how to fuck, Ollie." His tongue darts out and licks up the center of my lips.

Tilting my head to the side, I snake my hand around the nape of his neck, comb my fingers through the strands, grab a fistful, and yank his head back. "Mmm... I don't doubt it." I lift off the mattress and lick my way up the column of his throat. Nip his chin with my teeth and meet his smoldering blues. "But have you ever fucked a guy?"

He releases my cock, takes both my hands in his, drags them above my head, and rocks his hips in the cradle of mine. "Pretty sure the mechanics are the same."

"True." I circle his hips with my legs, lace our fingers together, and flip us back over. "But not quite."

Bracing my legs on either side of him, I release his hands and sit up. Ever so slowly, I trace his soft skin with my fingers. Over the lean muscles of his pecs, pausing momentarily to toy with his nipples. Down the almost indiscernible ridges of his abdomen. Across the contours of his hip bones.

Sucking in a sharp breath, he clutches my thighs. "Quit being a fucking tease."

My greens flit to his blues as I fist his cock with savage

force. I don't stroke or roll my thumb over the swollen head. I simply hold him and cluck my tongue. "So impatient."

"Ollie, please…" His plea is a whisper, a hiss and an invocation all in one.

Loosening my grip on his cock, I slowly stroke up. "Anyone can fuck, L." I drag my hand down his length, then back up at a torturous pace. "But you're not just anyone." Continuing my leisurely strokes, I lower my lips to his chest and circle his nipple with my tongue. "Make no mistake"—I bite his nipple and he hisses—"I will fuck you. Hard." Kissing my way across his chest, I pay equal attention to his other nipple. "But not until you're ready." I release his cock, drag my fingers down to cup his balls, and then dip a finger between his ass cheeks and massage his puckered hole. "This isn't your car. We can't go from zero to a hundred in seconds."

Levi gently rolls his hips and adds pressure to my finger on his hole. I match his pressure and breech his clenched muscles. His fingers are in my hair as a hiss echoes through the room.

I kiss my way up his chest, his neck, the thin layer of scruff on his jaw until I reach his lips. "Breathe, baby." I take his mouth in a gentle kiss. "You need to relax."

Luminous blue eyes lock on mine as he inhales deeply. His hands in my hair drift down my back and explore. On the exhale, his whole body sighs.

"That's it, baby," I coo.

I drop my lips to his in a fevered kiss as I continue to tease his hole. With each circle, he adds more weight, more pressure. But as my finger dips inside, his nails claw at my skin.

Easing my finger out as I break the kiss, I rest my forehead on his. "There's no rush." I drop a chaste kiss to his lips. "Wait a sec."

I roll off him and the bed and go to my duffel bag on the

dresser. Riffling through the contents, I locate the small bottle of lube and box of condoms.

"Do I want to know why you brought condoms?"

I toss the bottle and box on the bed. Crawling back up Levi's body, I pepper kisses from his hip to his lips. "Habit," I mutter over his lips. "Promise."

Levi clutches my jaw and pins me with a fiery gaze. "Better fucking be."

Every ounce of humor vanishes between us as I hold his gaze. "All I've ever wanted is you." I cover his hand with one of mine. "Now that you're mine, I won't fuck it up."

Levi lifts off the mattress and captures my mouth with his. Tells me wordlessly that I *am* his. That he *is* mine. That we've belonged to each other for much longer than either of us is willing to admit.

I frame his face with my hands and deepen the kiss. Stroke his tongue with mine and memorize his taste. Moan as his arms band around my middle, his hands drifting to the nape of my neck and globes of my ass, pinning me to him. Become fevered and wild as his finger slips between my ass cheeks and he rocks his hips beneath mine.

Blindly, I search for the lube with my hand. When I make purchase, I reluctantly break the kiss and pull back. I pop the top, coat my fingers with the slick liquid, squirt a few drops on my cock and his, snap the lid shut, and toss it aside.

As I drop to hover inches above him, Levi reaches between us, wraps his dexterous fingers around both our cocks, and strokes us together in one fluid motion. Fire surges in my veins as I slowly rock my hips in time with his touch.

Reaching down, I slip my lubed fingers beneath his balls and slick his puckered hole. Circle the tight muscles again and again, adding more pressure with each circuit. When I dip my finger inside, we gasp in unison.

"Holy fuck," Levi hisses out.

In slow, measured thrusts, I pump my finger in and out. Go a little deeper with each stroke. Curl my finger and tease his prostate. Grow impossibly more aroused as he rocks his hips, stroking us faster, and silently begs for more of my finger.

I ease out and add a second digit. Precum beads my cock as his lips part. As his faint whimpers fill the air. As he rolls his hips faster, harder, and fucks my fingers with abandon.

"Look at you, baby." I lick his lips, then nip the bottom. "Fucking my fingers like a good boy."

His breaths come faster as he strokes us franticly. Without a doubt, he's seconds from coming.

But I don't want him coming from finger play. I want my cock inside him when he detonates.

When I pull my fingers out, he groans his displeasure.

"What the hell?"

On a soft chuckle, I free my cock from his hold, swipe a condom from the box, and sit back on my haunches. I rip open the foil, toss the empty packet aside, and roll the condom down my length. I add a little more lube, then drop so we're nose to nose.

"I want to come inside you," I whisper against his lips. "I want *you* to come while I'm inside you."

He fists the back of my neck, mutters, "Fucking hell," and then yanks me down until our mouths collide.

We kiss as though we'll never have the opportunity again. I guide his legs farther apart with mine, loosely fist my cock and spread the lube evenly on my length, line my tip up with his entrance, and ever so slowly press the tip of my cock to his tight hole.

An eternity passes in a matter of seconds as we hold our breaths and I sink the head of my cock inside him.

"Jesus fuck," he hisses out as his nails pierce my flesh.

I ease out, give him a brief moment of reprieve, then rock my hips forward. Give him more of my length. Read the pleasure on his face as he takes a few inches.

He curls the fingers of his free hand in the sheet as he bows off the bed. His hot breaths on my lips come faster.

"More." The word is part growl, part mewl on his lips.

I peel his hand from the back of my neck, lace my fingers with his, and drag our joined hands above his head. Lowering until our lips meet, I kiss him with unfamiliar tenderness. And then I give him more of my length. More of me.

His fingers grip mine with unimaginable strength, though it's not painful. Sweat slicks our skin as we moan and devour and discover a new us. An us we've both hidden for far too long. *The real us.*

"So damn tight," I grunt out. "So damn perfect."

He tears his hands from mine, palms my ass cheeks, and squeezes harshly as he rocks his hips and slams our bodies together over and over.

"Oh, shit," he mutters between pants. "Holy fucking shit."

Close. He's so fucking close.

As he tops from the bottom, I reach between us, fist his cock, and stroke him at the pace of our thrusts. Our heavy breaths synchronize as we edge closer to our orgasms.

"Ollie..." My name is a strangled gasp on his tongue seconds before he comes.

Hot cum spurts from his cock and marks his abdomen, his pecks, the base of his throat. The sight of his reddened skin, of the pleasure written on his expression, of his cum on his skin because of me...

My fingers clutch the sheet on either side of his head as I explode on a roar inside of him. "Oh fuck, L." Spasms ripple through my limbs as I come hard. Harder than I ever have.

Levi frames my face and pulls my mouth down to his.

Kisses me with unparalleled hunger, devotion, and something... else. Something warm and irresistible and foreign yet familiar.

When the kiss ends, I collapse beside him on the bed and pull him into my side. I wrap him in my arms, press my lips to his head, and close my eyes. "That was..."

"...incredible," he finishes.

"Fucking phenomenal," I add and tighten my hold on him.

"Beyond fucking phenomenal."

Silence fills the space as we catch our breaths. As we reflect on this new step in our relationship.

I reach for the floor and grab one of the towels. Wipe the evidence of our first time from his skin. Toss the towel aside and revel in the moment.

And then his body relaxes fully. His breathing evens out.

I tip my head and peer down to see he's fallen asleep. A soft smile curves the corners of my mouth as I bask in the feel of him in my arms, where I've always wanted him. Where Levi has always belonged.

Slipping off the condom, I tie the end and toss it on the floor. I sink further into my hold on him. Inhale a slow, deep breath, then press a chaste kiss to his forehead and whisper, "Love you, L," just before sleep takes me too.

June 16th

We had sex last night and it was by far the most incredible moment of my life. Every moment with him is surreal, but last night... nothing will top last night. Right now, he's asleep in the hotel bed, fully naked, with the sheet low on his hips. I've spent the last thirty minutes studying every inch of his exposed skin. Tracing it with my eyes as my fingers twitch at my side, eager to touch him again.

For seven years, I've wanted Levi West. Now, he's mine. Really mine.

And while he slept last night, I whispered my biggest, scariest confession. I'm in love with him. I don't know if I'm brave enough to say it out loud while he's awake. The last thing I want to do is freak him out. After last night, all I want is to keep him so fucking close.

FIFTEEN

LEVI

For the third time in less than an hour, I close my eyes, inhale a slow, steadying breath, and let my mind drift to happier thoughts. Anything to quell the vicious churning in my stomach from the grotesque images and words on the computer screen.

Naturally, Oliver is at the heart of every blissful memory I own. He is the first thing I think about when I wake each day. Hell, he has been my first thought for several years. Only now, it feels different. Better. Perfect. Limitless.

Since the night of his show in Smoky Creek, since I kissed him in front of hundreds of people, erasing every single line between us, life feels more consequential. As if I unearthed buried treasure deep within myself. A new sense of meaning. Purpose. Not that I didn't have either before. I did. I do.

But with Oliver in my arms, life is more transcendent and worthwhile.

For the first time in my life, I feel alive. Whole. Fully myself. Real.

Now, I need to figure out how to break the news to my family.

Fuck my life.

The saint that Oliver is, he's waiting to share the news with his closest friends—Skylar, Kirsten, and Delilah. I didn't ask this of him, but he granted me the courtesy anyway. He won't openly talk about us as an official couple until I give him the go-ahead.

It's not as though his closest friends aren't aware.

Over the years, I've seen the way they side-eyed us when I joined their gatherings. I caught hints of their whispers whenever Oliver and I were close. But I kept those little tidbits to myself. Smiled at the idea of someone knowing that we were more than friends, even though we hadn't owned as much yet.

Having people in our corner, cheering us on and loving us as we are, makes my rib cage constrict and nose sting. It's a level of acceptance I've always craved but have never truly known.

Though it's a pipedream, I hope my family will welcome the real me and my relationship with Oliver with open arms.

Inhaling a soul-cleansing breath, I turn my attention back to the screens hovering over my desk. Dissociate from reality and flip on the analyst part of my brain. Enter the darkest parts of the world with zero emotions.

I scan the various threads I have followed for weeks. Look for anything new or notable in the discussions. Read the cryptic messages and do my best to decipher them. To learn something, anything new about the growing list of missing persons in the region.

"Sick fucks," I mutter as I skim a thread, the anonymous poster bragging about their recent *conquest.*

On another thread, a few highly disturbing images are posted. I save them and run them in a facial recognition program against the missing person profiles provided. In a matter of seconds, each image gets a hit on the list. I note them and add screenshots of the thread to our list.

As I read more on the thread with the images, I decipher and learn of a future auction. These people—children and adults—will be available to the highest bidder.

For hours and days and weeks, I have tried to find out more about this auction. When it will be held. Where they plan to sell humans as if they are inanimate objects. How the hell I can access it because it sure as hell isn't promoted in any of the threads I've been on in the past eight weeks.

Knowing these pieces of shit, they have another dark, fucked-up place for the truly trusted *customers*.

"Knock, knock."

I startle in my seat as Tymber enters my office.

"Sorry, man." He winces when I meet his weary gaze. "I actually knocked, but you didn't answer."

Pushing back from my desk, I drag my fingers through my hair. "No need to apologize." I suck in a ragged breath. "I detach from everything while working on this shit."

"Find anything new?"

With a subtle nod, I turn back to the screens and pull up my latest discoveries. Tymber stands behind me and scans the screen as I pull up the images. I don't miss his sharp, strangled inhale.

"Identified three. They'll apparently be up for auction, but I don't know when or where."

"Fuck…"

"My thoughts exactly." I shove away from my desk and spin around again. "Without seeming desperate, I'm trying to weasel my way in. But they have the auction site locked down. Someone probably needs to vouch for you to get in." Doesn't mean I will stop trying to gain access. Doesn't mean I will give up on these people or their families.

Tymber sits in one of the guest chairs in my office, rests his elbows on his knees, and drops his head in his hands. Frozen for minutes, we sit in silence and mull over how dark and fucked up this entire situation is. How we have taken on such a colossal job, unaware of how it would affect our lives forever.

I've read and seen some monstrous things. Gruesome and heinous things I'd love to permanently erase from my mind.

If only it were so easy.

After several hour-long minutes, Tymber straightens in his seat and levels me with his gaze. "I don't want to give up."

"Me either."

"But I don't know how much longer we should work this case."

My brows pinch in the middle as my pulse picks up. Molars gnashing, I shake my head. "Fuck no, man."

"Levi—"

"No," I bark out, rising from my seat, agitated and fidgety. "I'll be the first to admit I don't know how much more I can handle." Heat blooms in my chest as anger flares in my veins. "But I'm in too fucking deep to cower." Eyes on him, I point to my screens. "All that shit..." My fingers ball into tight fists. "That's surface level." The backs of my eyes sting. "Imagine what those damn *kids* are going through. It's only going to get worse."

"Fuck. I know." Tymber rises from the chair and paces the length of my office.

"If we give up, we might as well say they don't fucking matter."

Tymber covers his face with his hands and rubs his eyes. "I know," he says, exhaustion evident in his voice.

"This is bigger than us, man."

My mind drifts to Oliver, and I think about what it would

feel like if I lost him. If he vanished without a trace. If he was one of the countless people missing in the area.

The sting behind my eyes grows tenfold as a relentless, breath-stealing pang expands beneath my sternum. My vision blurs as the nightmare plays out in my head. My breaths come in jagged bursts as my heart beats in stuttered *th-thumps*. An unfamiliar wave of dread pulls me under and suffocates me.

The room swirls around me as I try and fail to catch my breath. My pulse echoes in my ears in a deafening *whoosh, whoosh, whoosh*. Inch by inch, the room darkens, shrinks, becomes an inescapable coffin. A chill settles in my bones as my limbs shake uncontrollably.

"Levi."

Distantly, I hear my name as my body jerks back and forth.

"Levi, can you hear me?"

The voice is louder but still out of reach. Foggy. Indistinct.

Thwack.

I jerk back, stumbling as the room slowly comes back into focus. My hand goes to my cheek as a sharp sting blooms on my skin.

"Shit. Sorry." Tymber winces as he studies my face. "I had to."

"What?" I ask, confusion lacing my tone.

Tymber takes a tentative step in my direction. "You were having a panic attack." He runs a hand through his hair. "Your skin was… gray." He takes another step and ducks to meet my bewildered gaze. "Sorry I hit you, but you weren't breathing."

I rub my cheek. "Thanks."

He scratches his beard and nods. "Yeah. Sure." His hand drifts to the back of his neck and massages the muscles. "Let's call it a day." His hand falls to his side. "Start fresh in the morning."

Part of me wants to argue with him. Tell him I have made progress and it is foolish to quit while I am ahead.

But then the rational part of my mind steps into the foreground and agrees with Tymber. I need the break. I need rest before I tackle more on this case. A clear head and a good meal. Time with Oliver to decompress and smile.

I hate it, but my sensible side is right.

"Probably best," I mutter.

Tymber rests a hand on my shoulder and gives a firm, quick squeeze. "We'll figure this out."

Lips screwed up and shifting from left to right, again and again, I nod. "I really hope so, man."

"We will." His hand falls away as he steps back. "But only if we're at our best."

He's right. I know he is. But fuck, it's hard to stop looking. Painful as it is to see all this fucked-up shit, all I want to do is find these assholes. All I want is to find these missing people and return them to their loved ones.

———

I park behind Oliver's Camry, cut the engine, and stare at the window on the second floor of the garage for a beat. Breath by breath, I force out the darker thoughts from earlier. Tell myself it's just my mind creating false worst-case scenarios.

"Ollie's safe," I whisper as my eyes close. "He's here, out of harm's way and within reach."

On a deep inhale, I open my eyes, swallow, and exit the car. One foot in front of the other, I climb the stairs to his apartment above the garage and key the code into the lock. After one last cleansing breath, I reach for the handle and twist.

As I enter his space, a faint melody from an acoustic guitar floats through the air, washes over me, and blankets me in immeasurable comfort. With a few simple notes played on his guitar, my worry from earlier fades away.

Eyes glued to his back as he sits hunched over his guitar, I close the door quietly. I shuffle into the apartment, toe off my shoes, and pad across the room. Focus on him, his music, the lyrics he croons to himself. Close my eyes and let his raspy voice stitch every fissure in my soul back together.

The room goes quiet and my eyes pop open. Oliver sets his guitar aside, leans forward, and scribbles in a journal on the table.

"Hey," I say as I round the couch.

Oliver jolts in his seat. "Oh, shit." He clutches his chest. "Didn't hear you come in."

Sitting next to him on the couch, I eliminate every inch between us, frame his face with my hands, and press my lips to his. Kiss him as though it's the first time and last all in one.

When his hands cup my cheeks, I deepen the kiss. Moan into his mouth and get lost in the feel of him. Let his warmth eviscerate the chill in my bones. Let the feel of his hands on my skin ground me to the earth, to the moment, to him.

All too soon, he breaks the kiss and rests his forehead on mine. His thumbs caress my cheeks as we breathe each other in.

"Everything okay?"

I press a chaste kiss to his lips. "Shitty day."

He nods but doesn't press for details.

"What was that song?" I ask, wanting to change the subject.

When he doesn't answer, I peek at him through my lashes. His eyes are still closed, the corners slightly crinkled with uncertainty.

My hands fall away from his face as I kiss my way to his ear. "You don't have to tell me. I was just curious."

Oliver inhales a shaky breath, inches back, and holds my blues with his brilliant greens. A faint blush colors his cheeks as he rolls his lips between his teeth. He swallows and opens his mouth to speak but then closes it.

The corners of my mouth tip up into a faint smile at his sudden self-consciousness. If he's this hesitant to tell me, it can only mean one thing.

With a shake of his head, he rolls his eyes. "It's about you," he blurts. "The song."

When he turned sheepish, I had a sneaking suspicion. "Okay." I shrug and leave, revealing more is up to him.

He twists to face me on the couch and reaches for my shirt, gently fisting the material. "Sorry you had a shitty day." He leans in and drops the barest of kisses to my lips. "How can I make it better?"

The corner of my mouth twitches at his request. Leaning forward, I press into him, rest my head on his shoulder, and clutch the cotton of his shirt. Breathe in his leather and musk scent with a hint of something distinctly Oliver. I melt into him and let the world disappear.

For now, it's just him and me and nothing else. For this small blip in time, everything is perfect.

"You already made it better," I mumble into the crook of his neck after several minutes. Straightening, I drop another kiss on his lips. "Hungry?"

He cups my jaw, stares at my mouth, and strokes my bottom lip with his thumb. "I could eat." He licks his lips then lifts his gaze to mine.

I take his thumb between my lips and suck for one, two, three breaths. Oliver's basil-green irises morph into a molten forest green before I release the digit.

"Or we can skip food to satisfy other cravings." He arches a brow.

Rising from the couch, I extend my hand and try to ignore the bulge in my pants and his. "Later." I tip my head in the direction of the door. "Let's go out."

———

"I want to tell my family," I blurt after the server delivers garlic bread to the table.

Soft green irises greet me when I glance across the table. A gentle smile on Oliver's lips as he reaches for his water. "Whenever you're ready."

My heart thrashes in my rib cage as a light sheen of perspiration dampens my skin. Beneath my diaphragm, a whir of energy sparks to life and swirls steadily. I curl my fingers until my nails bite my palms, then shake them out.

"Why am I so fucking nervous?"

Beneath the table, Oliver presses his leg against mine. The contact is an instantaneous balm.

"It's a big deal." His lips shift side to side. "I'd be shocked if you weren't nervous."

Tired of caring about other people's opinions of me, I extend an arm and rest my hand close to his on the table. One breath followed by another, his eyes glass over, flitting from my gaze to my waiting hand. Almost indiscernible, his brows twitch before he takes my hand with his.

Warmth and comfort and thrill dance across my skin and thrum through my veins the moment our hands connect. In a single move, everything feels right. Perfect. As it's meant to be.

With gentle, lazy strokes, my thumb caresses his hand. "I already know how my father will react." I shudder as an image of his red, severe expression dances across my vision. "Wish I was more certain about my mom." My gaze drops to the flickering candle in the middle of the table. "I'm so damn tired. Of the facade. Of the secrecy." I meet Oliver's patient stare. "Of not holding my boyfriend's hand in public."

God… calling Oliver my boyfriend, saying it out loud for anyone to hear… Liberation washes over me as a lifetime of invisible burdens lift from my shoulders.

"Whatever you decide to do, whenever you choose to do it, I'll be here," he declares and tightens his hold. "I'll always be here."

His proclamation is a warm, gentle caress around my heart. A hit of dopamine to my bloodstream. The most incredible, unparalleled high.

And damn, it has me eager to spill how deeply I feel for him. How deeply I've *always* felt for him.

A constant temptation, that four-letter word edges closer to the tip of my tongue, daring to jump.

But I hold back a little longer.

Hands connected the entire time, we eat dinner in comfortable silence.

After I pay the bill, we leave the restaurant and head back to Oliver's place. During the drive, I tell him I don't want to wait. That I want to tell my family tomorrow. And then I ask him to come along. Without hesitation, he says yes.

When we step inside his apartment, I feel more at home than any previous time. Like I've finally found my footing, my place, and acknowledged that Oliver *is* my person.

We strip off our clothes and take our time with each other's bodies. With unhurried lips and fingers and strokes, we say more than any words will ever express. And after I spill inside of him, he hauls me to his chest and holds me with unrivaled ferocity.

I love you, Oliver Moss.

It's my last thought before I fall asleep in his arms.

SIXTEEN

NUMBER 263

Day Twenty-One

A PAPER PLATE WITH A PARTIALLY EATEN SANDWICH SITS INCHES from my face on the floor. Cockroaches crawl on the remnants of the food, scavenging for their own meal. My eyes lose focus as I stare at them, jealous. I envy their ability to slip under the door or through a crack in the wall and escape this hellhole.

With each breath I take, my hope diminishes further. The longer I exist in this grimy prison, the more I surrender to the idea of never being found.

I honestly have no idea how long I've been here. I have no idea *where* here is.

Not that I have a way to tell anyone where I am.

Still, I say a silent prayer often. I plead with whoever hears my cry.

Save me from this hell.

Most days, my prayers are followed by more beatings. Different men in polished attire, straining erections, and black masks to hide their identities.

My mental faculties slip more and more with each visit.

Every time one of them walks into my cell, I bite back the urge to laugh. I fight my desire to mock them. Their masks have become my only form of amusement.

Wealthy, powerful men who probably have countless people cowering to their every whim... wearing masks so the abducted, shackled people they violate don't see their faces. So they can never be identified if one of us escapes.

Sick pieces of shit.

Dragging my hand closer to my body, I inhale deeply and send all my strength into my arms as I slowly sit up. My limbs tremble with the simple movement as my bones protest. I draw my legs to my chest and hug them, but only for a moment. The position no longer provides me with a sense of comfort.

The longer I am here, the more I lose myself—not just mentally but also physically.

I reach for the water bottle near the plate and the cockroaches scatter.

"Don't let me interrupt your meal," I rasp out, my voice unrecognizable to my own ears.

Twisting off the cap, I sip the last of the water and toss the bottle in the general direction of my trash pile. My stomach cramps, silently begging for more nourishment, but I ignore it. Dwelling on the fact that I'm slowly starving to death is futile. There is nothing I can do about it, so it's pointless to worry.

Footsteps echo outside of my cell, and I scramble to sit on my haunches. My shins scream in pain as they bear down on the concrete, but like the pain in my stomach, I disregard it.

Metal scrapes metal and grates my eardrums as the door swings open. My gaze flits up to the silhouette of a guard as he enters the room. As per usual, he rubs the crotch of his pants until the second guard enters the room.

"Finally learning your place, I see," his robotic voice

praises me. He inches closer and grabs a fistful of my hair. "Doesn't mean you won't be taught a lesson every day for the rest of your pitiful life." Releasing his hold on my hair, he shoves me back.

My scalp burns. The backs of my eyes sting. My pulse beats violently in my rib cage. They enjoy it when I cry or lash out, so I remain the epitome of calm. Either way, they will beat me until I'm unable to sit back up.

Guard One glances over at his buddy. "Bring him in."

Guard Two nods and exits the cell. In no time, he returns with another man.

"Leave us," the new man orders. He wears a mask, but his voice isn't disguised.

The guards back out of the room and close the door. Darkness swallows us and a sense of doom floods my veins.

Since I've been in this place, I've been malnourished, beaten, and humiliated. Each instance has chipped away at my body and soul.

But something about *this* man is different. His energy is distinct. Volatile. Malicious. Horrific.

A faint *clink* echoes in the room a moment before golden light flickers to life. The man holds a Zippo close to my face as he appraises my features. Warmth grazes my cheek and I momentarily bask in the sensation.

He steps back and moves toward the door. Holding the Zippo high, he lights an oil lamp just within his reach. The room brightens as he stows the lighter in his pocket.

"Not a soul has been looking for you, Two Sixty-Three." He glances down at the floor, careful not to step in the mess as he walks around me in the center of the cell. "No one from your former life loves you." He stops in front of me, fists my chin, and jerks up until our eyes lock. "One of us may be your only hope for love."

A sharp pain expands beneath my sternum as faint memories try to surface.

"They don't love you, Two Sixty-Three. They don't want you." His finger caresses my lips. "If you're good and do as I say, one of us could love you." He forces his thumb into my mouth and presses down on my tongue. "Do you want me to love you, Two Sixty-Three?"

I gag as his thumb nears my throat.

He rips his thumb out. "Do you?" he shouts a breath before the back of his hand connects with my cheek.

I disconnect from my body as he continues to assault me with his fists and feet. My mind drifts to the hazy memories of someone soft, warm, and comforting. For whatever reason, I can't see their face or hear their voice. I've forgotten their name. Maybe it's my mind's way of protecting what I hold sacred.

I miss them. Desperately. More than a limb. More than the sun.

And the faintest sliver of hope in my heart says they miss me too. I cling to that fragment with the last of my strength.

"You are property. That's all you'll ever be. A possession. A plaything. Material goods until you're no longer useful."

His foot connects with my rib cage. Pain lances my lungs as a sickening crunch fills the air.

"Mine to punish and fuck whenever I please."

Chin to my chest, a tinge of iron on my tongue, his Santoni leather oxfords come into view. I stare at the craftsmanship of the shoes. Mentally detach from the situation as I study the stitches and laces. Do my best to ignore the tinkering of his belt as I examine the bottom hem of his slacks.

A soft hand strokes my temple. I close my eyes and relish the comforting caress. But it doesn't last long.

His fingers comb through my greasy hair and yank my

head back. "Look at what you do to me, Two Sixty-Three." Inching closer, he brushes my hollow cheek with his stiff dick. "Look at how much my body wants you."

Tightening his hold on me, he paints my lips with precum. Drags the tip of his dick back and forth over my closed lips. And then he forces his length into my mouth. He pistons his hips rapidly and laughs when I choke on his dick.

The backs of my eyes sting as I fight off tears. I refuse to let them see me cry. I won't let them take that last piece of my soul.

Bile claws its way up my throat but doesn't surface. My body doesn't have the strength to vomit.

As he grunts and pummels my mouth, I dissociate from the situation. As this man gets off by violating me, I close my eyes and mentally leave my body.

I search for a happy memory. Anything to divert my attention and remind me of a better life. My life before I was taken.

Salt in the air. A hint of stars in the night sky. Someone holding my hand. Warm, soft lips pressed to mine. Happiness. Love.

A guttural moan followed by the man orgasming down my throat rips me from my memory. My arms dangle as I sway like a rag doll. When he finishes, he shoves me away.

"If you participate, it makes you more valuable." He tucks himself back in his slacks, zips up and fastens the button, then secures his belt. "In this place, Two Sixty-Three, you want to be priceless. It guarantees your future."

The warping corners of my mind make me want to laugh in his face and whisper, *What future?*

I remain silent.

Provocation only ends with more violence. Reticence and submission are rewarded with food and water. Yielding gnaws at my soul, but at least I live another day.

Although I've prayed for death more times than I can count, maybe all I need is one more day.

So I surrender.

He opens the door and extinguishes the light. A guard sidles up to him with a plate and water bottle. My newest abuser stares down at the measly scraps and shakes his head.

"We need to talk about portions."

"Yes, sir."

"No one likes their cock sucked by skeletons."

"Yes, sir."

Water and food are set on the floor within inches of the eyebolt. The guard backs out, closes the door, and leaves me in solitude. Footsteps echo and quiet outside my cell.

I take a deep breath, grab the plate and bottle, and devour the food. After a few small sips of water, I lie down on the floor and close my eyes.

Salty air.

Starry night.

Holding hands.

Warm kisses.

Happiness.

Love.

SEVENTEEN

OLIVER

Bass vibrates my seat as electronic music spills from the speakers in Levi's car. The summer sun warms my skin as the salty wind whips through my hair. Tall evergreens line one side of the road as businesses teem with residents and tourists on the other.

Beautiful as the day is, I struggle to enjoy it. Toying with a loose thread on my shorts as we weave through town toward his house, I recall Levi's words from earlier.

After breakfast with my parents, Levi said he didn't want to wait to tell his family about himself *and us.* On the next breath, he asked me to come with him.

Proud as I am of him for taking this step—officially coming out—I am nervous as hell. His father doesn't *hate* me, but he isn't fond of me either.

Deep down, I know it isn't my fault Mr. West feels the way he does. I've not done anything untoward or egregious to Levi or anyone else in their family. I think he dislikes me because Levi and I have always been close. Add in the fact that I am gay and his son is spending most of his free time with me; Mr. West is far from happy.

Long before Levi and I were friends, his father set impossible expectations. Mr. West wants both of his sons in politics with stunning women at their sides. He wants some antiquated version of a picture-perfect family that everyone in Stone Bay looks up to and idolizes. He wants his children to live fictitious lives and perpetuate these false ideologies for future generations.

Levi refuses to be molded into a replica of his father. His aspirations lie outside of politics and people-pleasing. He has no desire to sit on a proverbial throne and let townsfolk worship him. And he doesn't want a woman on his arm.

All Levi wants is to live his life according to his own rules, to be loved and to love someone in return.

Some might say that's not asking for much. But for Levi, asking this of his father is monumental.

The car slows as we pass the fire department. Less than a mile later, he flips the blinker on and turns onto Founders Way. My knee bounces when the sign for West Terrace comes into view.

Levi downshifts then rests his hand on my thigh as the roof of the main house peeks through the trees.

"Let me do the talking, okay?"

I flip my hand over and lace my fingers with his. "No problem."

He chuckles. "We'll go inside and I'll ask my parents and grandparents to join us in the sitting room. If Parker's home, I'll invite him too."

His thumb lazily strokes the length of mine.

"Once everyone is present, I'll let them know things with Abi didn't work out because we both have feelings for other people."

He guides the car around the last of the trees.

"And then I'll tell them about us."

"You have it all worked out, don't you?"

His sunglasses-covered gaze warms my profile. I turn to take in the sight of him and melt when his lips turn up at the corners.

Fuck, I love it when he smiles.

"Not everything, but enough to let them know the truth about me and us."

Earlier, I would have thought it'd be impossible to love Levi more. But he continues to prove otherwise.

"What the hell?"

At his bewilderment, I glance toward the house and see an unfamiliar car parked in the driveway. "Who is that?"

Levi whips around the vehicle and parks in front of it. He cuts the engine, rests his head against the seat, and sighs as he pinches the bridge of his nose.

"Calhoun," he says after a moment.

My eyes widen as I peer over my shoulder at the vehicle. "As in Abigail or her parents?"

"It's not Abi's car." He brings my hand to his lips. "But I assume whoever's here… they're talking about her and me and the breakup." He audibly exhales. "Fuck."

"Maybe we should wait."

"No." He releases my hand to cup my cheek. "I don't care why they're here." Levi leans into me and presses a tender kiss to my lips. "I'm telling them." He drops his forehead to mine and steals my breath with his penetrating gaze. "You and me" —his thumb strokes my cheek—"that's *all* I care about."

Silence drags on for timeless minutes. If we could stay in our bliss bubble forever, I'd die happy.

Unfortunately, our bliss bubble will have to wait.

Levi inches back and exits the car. When he meets me on

the passenger side, he takes my hand, gives it a gentle, reassuring squeeze, then leads us to the door.

Each step forward thrills and terrifies me in equal measure. The fantasy I've harbored for years has become a reality. I only hope his family accepts this newly revealed side of him with open arms.

Pushing open the front door, Levi leads us into the grand foyer. I take in the entrance of the main West house with fresh eyes. The last time I walked through these doors was in high school. Not much has changed since then, yet it feels much different. Less of a home and more of a display.

Light chatter meets my ears a moment before Levi's mom enters the room and greets us with a bright smile.

"There you are, darling. I started to worry." She lifts her hands to clasp his shoulders before pulling him into a tight hug. "Such wonderful news," she mutters, then takes a step back. Her eyes meet mine briefly. "What a good friend you are, Oliver. Here to support Levi."

My brows knit together in confusion. *What is she talking about?*

I glance at Levi and see he is equally perplexed by her comment.

Before either of us can ask what she means, she spins on her heel and returns to whatever room she came from. With hesitant steps, we cross the foyer and enter the sitting room.

On a couch with their backs to us, the Calhouns sit poised as they chat with Levi's father opposite them. A boisterous energy floats through the room. Something about it sets my teeth on edge.

"Here he is," Mrs. West announces as we enter the space. "Our handsome Levi."

Levi's mom has always been nice—at least in the presence

of others—but her excitement seems a bit much considering the circumstances. Breakups aren't joyous occasions, especially in this household.

Abigail peers over her shoulder with a brilliant smile on her face. It falters when she sees me, but not for long.

"Mom, what's going on?"

Levi releases my hand, leaves me at the entrance of the room and goes to stand where he can look everyone in the eye.

"Quit playing coy, son," Mr. West says with a forced chuckle. "Abigail has already shared the wonderful news."

A knot forms in my gut as I wait for someone to elaborate. Minute-long seconds tick by without an answer as the pang in my stomach twists and morphs into a gnarly beast.

"What news?" Levi demands with a growl, his fingers balled into fists at his sides.

"Mind your tone," Mr. West says more politely than he would without select guests.

Mrs. West sidles up to her husband and pats his thigh. "He's probably just nervous, Jefferson. Ease up." As she says the last two words, she squeezes his leg.

"Will someone tell me what the hell is going on?" Levi's voice booms throughout the room.

Time stands still for a split second as all eyes dart in his direction. Then everything moves in slow motion as Abigail rises from her seat, walks over to where Levi stands and loops her arm with his.

Dazzling smile on her face, Abigail lifts her left hand and wiggles her fingers, a behemoth diamond sparkling in the light. "I know you told me to wait, but I just couldn't." She giggles and clutches his arm harder. "I had to share the news of our engagement."

My heart falls to the floor as my body turns to ice.

What. The. Fuck?

It isn't true. And it's not a part of their fake relationship either. Levi would have told me immediately. He would have warned me about something this monumental.

Yet my mind refuses to grasp reality. It only believes the lie.

I stumble back and hit the wall. A shiver rolls up my spine as the room blurs and narrows.

But it's Levi's thunderous words that snap me back to the present.

"What the actual fuck, Abi?" He rips his arm from hers and steps back. "We are not fucking engaged." He scoffs. "Hell, we're not even a couple. We never were."

Levi moves closer to me as everyone's eyes widen.

"It was fake from the goddamn start." He jabs his chest. "My idea to get you all off our backs." His eyes narrow on her. "Because we're both in love with someone else. People our families wouldn't approve of."

A nervous laugh falls from Abigail's lips as she inches closer to her parents. "There's no one else, Daddy." She shakes her head vehemently. "I swear."

"Wow, Abi." Levi gives her a disbelieving look. "Are you that scared of your parents knowing about Desmond?" His gaze shifts to Mr. and Mrs. Calhoun. "He's a great guy. Laid-back, thoughtful and madly in love with your daughter." He tilts his head and narrows his eyes. "Did you break up with him to do all this?"

"I don't know what you're talking about," she lies with too much ease.

"Either way, I put an end to this whole fake relationship bullshit two weeks ago." He slices the air with his hands.

"No, we're enga—"

"Shut the fuck up, Abi," Levi yells.

"My apologies, Ray, Angel," Mrs. West says at the same time Mr. West barks out, "Levi, a word in the other room."

Meanwhile, I try to blend into the wall and escape this new form of hell.

"No!" Levi shouts. "I came here for one reason."

My pulse whooshes in my ears. My hands tremble at my sides. Anxiety swells beneath my diaphragm.

This is it.

Watery eyes meet mine and hold them for one, two, three breaths. The corners of his mouth tip up in the softest smile. Then he breaks the connection to face his family, lifts a hand and points in my direction.

"I am in love with Ollie."

A gasp echoes throughout the room and I have no clue who it came from. Nor do I care.

Levi West just told a roomful of people he is in love with me.

He erases the distance between us, takes my hand in his and locks onto my teary gaze. "I've been in love with him for years." With an infinitesimal nod, he mouths *I love you* before turning back to his parents. "I'm tired of hiding who I am to please you." He laces our fingers. "This is the real me; take it or leave it."

Stunned in silence, his parents and the Calhouns stare at us. When no one speaks up, Levi tightens his hold on my hand and starts for the front door.

As we exit the house, everyone stirs back to life and voices boom in the background. I can't make out what they are saying, but their volume and tone speak for themselves.

Anger. Lots and lots of anger.

Rushing to his car, we get in and he cranks the engine. Less than a minute later, he parks outside the pool house. Out of the car, Levi waits for me at the front and takes my hand when I step up to his side.

"What are we doing?" I ask as we enter his home on the West property.

Levi spins around and walks backward, his luminous eyes never straying from mine. When we reach the door leading to his bedroom, he stops and swallows.

"Can I stay with you?"

A surge of adrenaline spikes my bloodstream as my heart rattles my rib cage.

Levi is in love with me—he is mine—and just asked to stay at my place.

The backs of my eyes sting as emotion swells in my throat and saliva floods my mouth. Telling him yes dancing on the tip of my tongue, but I'm too overwhelmed to articulate the actual word.

Lips tucked and rolling between my teeth, I slowly nod my acquiescence.

The corners of his mouth tip up in the most addictive smile. He steps into me, frames my face with his hands and kisses me with unfathomable hunger. I melt into his touch, the kiss, his taste. Get lost in his warmth, the way his tongue caresses mine, his moans as his fingers slip into my hair.

All too soon, he breaks the kiss and drops his forehead to mine. Our heavy breaths mingle as we come down from the temporary high.

Will it always feel like this with him? Powerful. Soul-consuming. An endless need for more.

God, I hope so.

His thumbs stroke my cheeks as he drops a chaste kiss to my lips. "I love you, Oliver." He nods almost imperceptibly. "So fucking much."

Tears well in my eyes as I inhale a shaky breath. I clutch his

wrists and meet his spellbinding blue eyes. "I love you, Levi."
I grip his wrists harder. "Moje srce." *My heart.*

June 29th

Today made me dizzy. The highs, the craziness, the confessions. L told me he's in love with me. He announced this monumental truth in front of his parents and the Calhouns. I think I left my body for a moment when he said the words. I doubt he wanted to tell me like that, but after the shit A tried to pull, he needed everyone to hear him.

A has obviously gone insane. I mean, who does what she did? Who spends a shit ton of money on an engagement ring for themselves to pretend they're getting married to someone they're not even with? Yeah, they agreed to fake date to shut their parents up. None of it was real, though. L put an end to the charade weeks ago, but it's obvious she didn't hear a word he said. Her problem not ours.

Either way, I'm glad that shit's fucking over and we can move on.

L moved in with me today. Well, kind of. He packed up most of his closet, work stuff and anything of importance, shoved it in every nook of his car, and brought it to my place. While he packed, I talked to Mama. She and Papa were cool about it since I pay rent. I just wanted them to know before we showed up with duffel bags and L's car spent more time at our house.

I've dreamed about this moment for years. It's hard to believe that he's here, that he's mine, that we're together and in love. But I'll happily count my lucky stars because L is worth every single one of them.

EIGHTEEN

LEVI

The further I dig in this case, the more atrocities I unearth. By no means am I an idiot. With the number of missing persons in the area and their ages, I've had my suspicions. But hunches are nothing more than persistent gut feelings, and I need concrete proof.

Hundreds of people go missing every year in Washington and Oregon for various reasons. In all my research, the number of disappearances was never this high in such a short period of time. Statistics don't lie.

Unfortunately, my intuition is spot on with this case. Four words are all it takes for bile to claw its way up my throat. With four words, the horrid truth is validated.

In black and white, the most despicable and degrading phrase stares at me from the screen.

Fresh filets coming soon.

For weeks, I've held on tight to the smallest sliver of hope. I've said countless silent prayers to whoever listened and begged for a simpler outcome than this. In this case, prayers are worthless.

This isn't a run-of-the-mill transaction. No, this is vile, barbaric and inhumane. A fucking gavel-clapping transaction to the highest bidder. These pieces of shit spend tens of thousands of dollars… to own, enslave and conceal people until they are no longer *useful*.

"Fuck…"

I twist in my chair, grab my garbage can and hurl the meager contents of my stomach into the liner. Several minutes pass before my body stops heaving. Straightening in my seat, I take a swig of water from the bottle on my desk, swish it a few times, then spit it in the can.

Capping the bottle, I close my eyes, pinch the bridge of my nose and inhale several cleansing breaths. When the cramps in my stomach ease a little, I turn back to my screens and shut off my emotions.

"This is the only way," I tell myself in an attempted pep talk. "This is how you bring all these people home."

I read the thread on the screen again. No definitive date is announced in the conversation, but a vague period in their cryptic language is there for everyone to see.

> *New deliveries arriving at port daily.*
> *Available not long after the gust passes.*

"New deliveries" easily translates to the hundreds of abductees. The "port" is wherever they are being held. Those two points are rather obvious, to me at least. The back half of the clue takes reading it several times to decipher. Only someone whose been in this world for a while or with in-depth analytical skills will pick up on the latter.

…not long after the gust passes.

The gust.

August.

In roughly two months, these sick motherfuckers are selling kids to the trashiest humans in existence.

I need to get to them before then. I need to shut this shit down now.

"But how?" I mutter to myself.

The rational part of my mind says I should let Tymber in on the news. Together, we can brainstorm and possibly cut this off sooner rather than later. It's the right thing to do.

So, of course, I ignore my logical brain. I opt to keep the news to myself and trudge down the darkest path of all. An avenue no one should take alone. An approach that should be met with a team, not one or two people.

Donning my invisible cape, I walk the path of the vigilante.

fall_or_rise39

any chance at sampling the catch before the gust passes?

I close my eyes, inhale deeply and remind myself over and over that this is just a job. All I need to do is meet up with one of these assholes and wiggle my way into their regime. Play the part and I can get these kids back to their families.

hook_n_release_cap
@fall_or_rise39 this is your first time at the market, so you don't know the rules. To prevent contamination, there are no samples.

"Dammit."

I shove away from my desk, bring my hands to my face and rub my eyes. Running my hands through my hair, I open my mouth, ready to scream, but am cut off when my computer pings with a new message.

Rolling closer, I scan the thread I've messaged in but see nothing new. In the sidebar, however, a new chat blinks with an unread message.

I inhale a slow, methodical breath and click on the chat.

hook_n_release_cap
wasn't trying to be an asshole in the thread.
Gotta keep things on the up and up to weed
out the unsavory folks.

The unsavory folks?

"You have got to be shitting me." My fingers ball into fists for one, two, three vicious heartbeats before I relax my hands. "Play the fucking part." That's all I need to do to find this lowlife.

fall_or_rise39
I get it. Never know who the fuck
you're talking to. I respect it.

hook_n_release_cap
maybe we can arrange something. A meetup.

"Fuck yes."

I take a deep breath, pause for a moment and contemplate how to respond. The last thing I need to do is come off as too eager.

fall_or_rise39
I'll leave it up to you and the rules.

The screen blurs as I stare at the blinking cursor. Minutes tick by with no response. My knee bounces over and over as I drum my thumb just as quickly on the desk.

"Come on," I mutter. "Take the bait."

On the verge of screaming, their message finally comes through.

hook_n_release_cap
it's your lucky day. WA or OR?

Thrill shoots through my veins as I reply.

fall_or_rise39
WA

hook_n_release_cap
coastal or inland?

fall_or_rise39
coastal

hook_n_release_cap
tomorrow afternoon

"Holy shit."

Unsure who I'm meeting, it's best to do this as publicly as possible. With tomorrow being Independence Day, the town will be bustling with residents and tourists. If I suggest the festival as a location, it's less likely he will know I am from Stone Bay.

fall_or_rise39
tomorrow's good. Town not far from me has
an event for the holiday. Meet in Stone Bay?

Again, they go silent for several minutes. The possibility of catching this prick is worth every brutal blink of the cursor.

hook_n_release_cap
I know the town. Noon. Near the food tents.
Wear a fisherman's cap with a blue ribbon.
I'll find you.

This is really happening. I'm luring this sleazeball in and they are taking the bait.

fall_or_rise39
got it

I exit the chat and exhale a breath I didn't realize I'd been holding.

"Holy. Fucking. Shit."

Pushing back on my chair, I rise and pace the room. I contemplate telling Tymber the new development but decide it's best to keep it to myself. For now, at least. He will be at the festival tomorrow. If shit goes sideways, I'll shoot him a text or flag down one of the officers in attendance.

What I need to do now is call it a day. Sign off, make a quick stop at the bait and tackle shop for a hat, and head home to Oliver.

"Tomorrow, I'll get this asshole."

NINETEEN

LEVI

THE SUMMER SUN WARMS MY SKIN AS OLIVER AND I WALK HAND in hand through the crowd. The scent of fried sugar, salty cheese and grilled meat lingers in the air. Hundreds of residents mingle with countless tourists and chat about the festival's music itinerary. Pop-up tents offer an array of food, an assortment of drinks, merchandise and information from local small businesses, and endless arts, crafts, and festive entertainment for all ages.

The Fourth of July Festival is Stone Bay's biggest annual event. To no one's surprise, the festival is grander than the previous.

People throughout the state flock here for the festivities. Many book rooms at the ski resort or inn or reserve one of several rentals from the Seven and stay in town for several days. The tourism dollars from this week alone total more than any other season. As a thank-you, the town ups the ante each year and adds new festivities for a more memorable experience.

The gates open at nine in the morning and most attendees stay until they shuffle out close to midnight. I've never spent the entire day at the festival but plan to today. Were Hailey's Fire not on the roster today, if I hadn't made plans to meet up with the schmuck from online, I would've convinced Oliver to stay in bed with me all day.

"Hungry?" Oliver gives my hand a gentle squeeze as we approach a long row of food tents.

I shrug. "A little."

"I need something in my system before we play." He slows to a stop after a few tents. "Anything look good?"

Staring down the line, I spot a banner for Rosenberg's Deli and tug Oliver toward the line. "Maybe something light. Don't need you retching on stage."

His hand still in mine, we get in line. Oliver twists to face my side and clings to my arm, resting his chin on my shoulder, his gaze raking over my profile. A soft hum vibrates his chest against my arm.

For years, I've wanted this with him—a relationship greater than friendship—but part of me wasn't ready. Painful as it was to hold back my feelings, agonizing as it was to stay silent and wait, I wouldn't change a single footprint on our journey. Each step we have taken steered us to where we are now.

Although it hurt to hear about Oliver with other people every now and then, although I had my fair share of meaningless sex with random people to quell my urges, those past partners were necessary. Had we given in to our libidinous desire for each other years ago, we might not have lasted.

The moment I met Oliver, I knew he was different than other guy friends. The more we talked, the more I was convinced we'd be more than friends. Still insecure about my sexuality at the time, I had no idea how or when our relationship would shift, but my instincts knew it was inevitable.

Seven years is a long time to conceal your feelings for

someone. Seven years is a long time to keep them close without giving in to what you both want. But without those excruciating years, we wouldn't appreciate each other and what we have now.

"Love you, moje srce," he whispers before he presses a kiss to the angle of my jaw.

Oliver straightens a beat before we shuffle forward in line. When we stop, I step into him, clasp his chin and lift until his line of sight locks with mine. The tip of my nose caresses the length of his as I haul him closer. My pulse soars, dick aching as his lips part, his breath painting my skin.

The world disappears as I obliterate the last inch of space between us and take his lips in a ravenous kiss. On a hum, his lips part a breath before his tongue strokes the length of mine. He fists my shirt at my hips and pulls me impossibly closer. The bulge behind his zipper presses my swelling erection. I deepen the kiss, a groan spilling from my mouth to his.

Someone clears their throat and cuts off our first public display.

Me, from months ago, would have been too jittery or self-conscious to kiss Oliver out in the open. Hell, I would have been apprehensive about holding his hand. But after a lifetime of suppressing who I am, after stifling my attraction to Oliver for far too long, all I want to do is tell the world he is mine.

"Love you, Ollie." I drop one last chaste kiss to his lips.

We order sandwiches and drinks then join his friends and bandmates at a table.

Trip and Hailey talk enthusiastically about their performance in less than an hour.

Skylar picks at her food as she leans into her boyfriend, Lawrence, and says she wants more private cooking lessons from him. Lawrence responds with a suggestive arch of his brow. He doesn't say a word. He doesn't need to. With that simple response, a smile brightens Skylar's face as she wiggles in her seat.

My gaze drifts to Phoebe and Delilah. I study their intimacy a little longer. Observe the way Delilah softens when Phoebe tucks a flyway strand of hair behind her ear. Of everyone at the table—aside from Oliver—Phoebe intrigues me the most.

Along with Travis, Delilah, and myself, Phoebe is one of the Seven. As kids, we spent a lot of time together. Whenever our families gathered for social events or town meetings, the youngest generation of the Seven was shoved into the same room and encouraged to build friendships. On every occasion, Phoebe removed herself from the group to sit on the sidelines and write. If anyone approached her, she greeted them with a callous expression and verbally bit their head off.

With age, her cool demeanor turned glacial. No one wanted to be within five feet of Phoebe Graves.

Earlier this year, Phoebe and Delilah were thrust together when several dead women were discovered in town and a key piece of evidence put Delilah's family's business on the radar. Many assumed Phoebe would crush Delilah's soul with her vitriol. But we were all surprised.

In a matter of months, Delilah thawed Phoebe's heart. With every obstacle they overcame, I envied their strength and courage more.

Oliver nudges me with his elbow. "Everything okay? You're quieter than usual."

I lean into his side and give him my weight for a moment. "Yeah." I shrug. "Adjusting."

He sets his sandwich down and wipes his mouth. "Is this too much at once?" He rests his hand on my thigh. "We've hung out with everyone before, but it was different."

I lay my hand over his. "It's not too much." My knee

bumps his leg as I turn toward him. A smile tugs at the corners of my mouth as I lean closer. "Is it selfish to want you all to myself?"

His hand on my thigh flexes as he groans. "No." Inching back, his vibrant basil-green eyes flit to my blues. "Would it make me an asshole to abandon our friends to spend time alone with you?"

He said our *friends.*

"What're you two whispering about over there?" Kirsten asks, diverting everyone's attention to us.

"Do you really want the answer?" Oliver gives her a pointed stare.

Kirsten purses her lips and shakes her head. "Nope. I'm good."

Laughter echoes around the table.

"We need another movie night," Kirsten suggests. "Maybe next week when the town is less chaotic, so Trav can join us."

Like every officer at the Stone Bay Police Department, Travis is on duty all day. He joined us for a quick bite but will soon be wading through the crowd until the festivities end.

I uncap my water and take a sip. "I've heard about these movie nights. Lots of food and gossip. Not much movie watching."

Travis barks out a laugh. "Spot on, man."

"Hey," Oliver, Kirsten, Skylar and Delilah say in unison before falling into a fit of laughter.

After we agree to plan a movie night next week, conversation around the table quiets. Travis finishes his sandwich, gives Kirsten a kiss on the head, and blends into the crowd as he resumes work.

Minutes later, Hailey and Trip toss their trash in the bin and head for the stage. Oliver lingers for a moment, his fingers toying with the hem of my shorts.

"Come hang backstage while we play."

Sleazeball's message in the chat from yesterday flashes in my mind.

As much as I want to watch Oliver play from the side of the stage, I can't miss the opportunity to meet this person.

Maybe I should cap how long I wait. Give them fifteen minutes, twenty tops. If they don't show, it is safe to assume they stood me up. Honestly, wouldn't shock me if they do.

My stomach twists as I make a poor excuse to not join him. "Mind if I look for Tymber first?"

Hurt shadows his features for a split second. "Of course not." He licks his lips then swallows. "Work?"

Technically, waiting for this creep is work-related. "Yeah." I take his hand in mine and lace our fingers. I let his warmth and strength soothe my sudden nervousness. "I'll come back-stage soon." I lean in and press my lips to his. "Promise."

Trailing a finger along my jaw, he gives me one more kiss. "'Kay. I'll let the event staff know."

Oliver gathers his trash, rises from the table, and ambles away from the table. I follow him with my eyes, not missing the slight slump in his frame.

When he disappears in the crowd, my gaze drifts back to the table. Phoebe openly studies me with a quizzical expression. Her keen, icy stare makes me want to crawl out of my skin. Good to know she hasn't lost her touch.

I check my watch and note I have less than ten minutes. The last place I want to be when I meet this asshole is near friends. But I don't want to rush away from the table and garner more attention from Phoebe.

After eating a few more chips, I ball up my sandwich paper, wipe my hands, and collect my trash. All eyes shift my way as I push back on my chair and stand.

"You're welcome to stay with us, Levi," Delilah offers.

I scratch my temple and nod. "Thanks. I'll be back in a bit. Going to look for Tymber."

Delilah gives me a kind smile. "Okay. We'll be near the stage if we're not here."

"Cool. Thanks." Not wanting to prolong our temporary goodbye, I walk off and toss my trash in the closest garbage can.

Weaving through the crowd, I head for the opposite end of the food tents. When I no longer see our friends, I pull the folded hat from my back pocket. At the farthest tent from everyone I know, I stand off to the side and put the hat and my sunglasses on.

The soul-vibrating sound of Oliver's drums echoes throughout the amphitheater. I let the familiar beat ease the expanding knot in my gut.

Feet rooted to the earth, fingers twitching at my side, I scan every face in the crowd. No one pays me any attention as the first Hailey's Fire song booms from the speakers.

As song one ends, a middle-aged man approaches me, says hello and asks if I know where the bathrooms are located. I point him in the general direction and he walks away.

Midway through song three, my stomach rolls and I swallow down the sudden urge to vomit. I survey the nearby crowd and search for the source of my unexpected dread. Not a single soul looks my way.

When the fifth song starts, I check the time: 12:18 p.m.

"No-show," I mutter as I rip the hat from my head. "*Dammit.*"

The pang in my stomach grows exponentially as I walk off. I do my best to ignore it as I wander toward the stage. I inhale one deep breath after another and attempt to clear my head. As I pass a garbage can, I throw away the hat.

By the end of the fifth song, I pass the event staff and head for the side of the stage. Before the next song starts, Oliver meets my gaze and smiles. It's an instant balm to my soul and I mouth, *Hey.*

The rest of their set goes by quicker than expected. When Hailey thanks the crowd and tells everyone to join them at Dalton's tomorrow night for an encore, cheers and whistles ring through the air.

We hang out near the stage while the next band plays and Oliver cools down. Every now and again, a twinge in my stomach steals my attention. And every time I search for the origin, I come up blank.

For hours, we meander the amphitheater, play games, win prizes, and chat with people at a few tents before joining our friends. While they talk about Hailey's Fire's set, I zone out and try to bury the residual pang that just won't end.

All too soon, the sun dips beneath the horizon and people crowd the lawn. A sense of claustrophobia smacks me hard in the chest.

As if he picks up on my discomfort, Oliver wraps an arm around me and pulls me into his side. "What's wrong?"

I close my eyes, lean into his comfort, and rest my head on his shoulder. Absorb his warmth. Breathe in his scent. Melt into his touch. "Just feel off." I turn and kiss the side of his neck. "But this helps."

He lays his head on mine. "We can go."

I shake my head. "When the fireworks end."

"Okay." He kisses my hair. "If we need to leave sooner, let me know."

Tightening my hold on him, I glance up at the sky and get lost in the sea of fiery colors. As the grand finale lights up the night, I kiss my way up Oliver's neck.

His fingers comb through my hair as our lips meet. My hand drifts beneath his shirt, the pads of my fingers dancing over his abs as I deepen the kiss. Giving me more of his weight, he lowers me to the blanket on the lawn.

For the second time today, the world ceases to exist. The night sky glows above us, the spray of pyrotechnics falling around us like stars.

One of my arms circles Oliver's waist as my other hand drifts to his hair. He devours me and grinds his erection against mine without shame. I moan into the kiss and lift my hips, silently telling him I need more.

When he breaks the kiss, I lock onto his intense, amorous gaze. My dick twitches, desperate for him.

He notices.

"Home." He presses a chaste kiss to my lips. "Now."

I push up on my elbows and take his mouth again, greedy for him.

Home.

I'm already there.

TWENTY

NUMBER 263

Day Forty

"Your friends are worried about you, Two Sixty-Three."

At the mention of friends, I lift my head slowly and narrow my eyes at the masked guard.

"My friends?" A faint glimmer of hope coats my words, but not for long.

Booming laughter bounces off the walls of my cell as the guard presses a hand to his stomach. When he regains his composure, he shakes his head. "Poor word choice on my part, I suppose. Not friends. You don't have any of those. I should've said visitors."

The last shred of optimism vanishes into the void along with my shriveling body and withering soul. I collapse onto my side on the floor and pray for the ground to open and swallow me whole.

The hell mentioned in books and churches sounds like a vacation compared to my current prison. I'd take fire and brimstone over physical and sexual assaults any day of the week. I'd take anything over the isolation, humiliation, and unwelcome degradation. Anything.

I don't respond to the guard. There is no point. Whatever I say will get spun around and twisted to poke fun at me and my situation.

"Your most recent visitor says you're looking gaunt. They're not pleased. Apparently, you're not eating the food we give you."

I don't fucking care, is what I want to say.

Instead, I remain tight-lipped.

"No one wants to fuck a stick, Two Sixty-Three."

Another guard enters the room with a tray.

"So it's time to put more meat on those bones."

I don't want to gain weight. I don't want to be more appealing to these sadistic motherfuckers.

If anything, I want this nightmare to end.

I'd rather die than do a damn thing to please these sick monsters.

The first guard grabs something off the tray and holds it in front of my face. A slice of bread with a thick layer of peanut butter.

My stomach quivers as the scent invades my nose. My fingers twitch in my lap, eager to reach for the bread, take it, and shove the whole piece in my mouth.

But I refuse to make it easy for them.

I may not have the strength or energy to fight, but I still have my mind. Although, that's slowly slipping too.

Lifting my cuffed hands, I pretend to reach for the offering. I meet the guard's gaze, display the weakest smile, and swat the food away.

"Always a thorn in my fucking side, Two Sixty-Three." He shakes his head, fetches the bread from the floor, and folds it in half. "This is your fault." He clutches my hair with his free hand and yanks my head back. "One day, you'll learn it's in your best interest to do as you're told. Now"—he shoves the bread against my mouth and forces it between my lips—"eat your fucking food."

I choke on the nasty bread as it's plunged down my throat. The guard smacks my back with brute strength until I stop coughing.

One piece at a time, I am force-fed several fatty foods— peanut butter, avocado, cheese, scrambled eggs, bacon, rice. With each bite I swallow, my stomach gurgles and knots.

I have no idea how long I've been here, but I do know it's been weeks since I've eaten anything substantial or nutritious. My body is no longer used to normal portions, variety or nutrient-dense food. It's become accustomed to the water, crackers, goop, and meager helpings.

Once they appear satisfied with what I've eaten, Guard Two exits my cell. Guard One lingers a moment, walking a circle around me near the eyebolt. His menacing gaze heats my skin as his boots clap on the concrete.

My stomach churns for an entirely different reason.

When he reaches my right, he pauses. Before my next inhale, his fist connects with my temple.

Blinding light steals my vision as I fall to the floor. My head smacks the filthy concrete and another burst of light flashes behind my eyelids. A pain I'm all too familiar with throbs in the confines of my skull as a loud ringing floods my ears.

I stay down with the hope of not getting punched again. Not that it will stop his boot from connecting with my head, ribs or limbs.

Considering they shoved food down my throat minutes ago, I doubt they want to beat me until I puke it up.

"I will break you, Two Sixty-Three." He takes a step toward

the door. "You will be obedient by the time I finish my job." Another step. "And when I'm done, you will thank me."

Never.

The guard grips the handle on the door and pulls it closed as he steps out. But the door doesn't shut completely.

"Boss just handed out an update," a muffled voice says.

I lift my head and inch closer to the door. Close my eyes and focus all my energy on hearing the conversation just outside of my cell.

"And?" Irritation laces Guard One's voice.

"We need to spend more time with the defiant detainees. Break their will and make them compliant."

A growl echoes in the air. "Does he think we sit around with our thumbs up our asses all day?" He huffs. "Don't fucking answer that."

"I'm right there with you, man." There's a pause before he continues. "Either way, we need them ready in the next couple of weeks."

"Maybe his ass should come down here and fucking help."

"You know that won't happen."

"Yeah."

The sound of metal creaking makes me wince as the door closes another inch.

"A couple weeks?"

"Yep. Then our little birds leave the nest."

"Can't fucking wait. This batch has been particularly stubborn."

The other man chuckles. "Definitely testing our patience."

More creaking fills the air a second before the door fully closes and the locks outside are secured.

"I anticipate Two Sixty-Three will fetch a pretty penny at the auction," Guard One says loud enough for me to hear.

"If I had the money, I'd shell it out to keep that one under lock and key."

With that final comment, the contents of my stomach make a reappearance.

I push away from the mess and move to the cleanest part of my cell. Slowly, I lower to the floor, lie on my side and draw my knees to my chest.

Auction.

In a couple weeks, they plan to *sell me* to one of the countless dirtbags that's paid me a visit.

The backs of my eyes burn as my throat swells. Saliva pools in my mouth seconds before the first tear trails down my cheek.

"Please," I croak out into the darkness. "Let me die. I beg you."

I repeat the words over and over in my head until they are the only ones I know.

Let. Me. Die.

TWENTY-ONE

OLIVER

I bang the drums in time with Hailey and Trip as our second-to-last song comes to an end. Sweat rolls down the back of my neck as the space quiets for a pulse-pounding second. A beat later, every patron in Dalton's claps, whistles or hollers excited expletives.

Exhausted doesn't remotely cover how I feel after back-to-back shows, but the crowd's enthusiasm makes every second on this stage worth it.

"How's everyone doing?" Hailey screams into the mic.

As always, the crowd goes wild in response.

"Before we play our last song of the night, we just wanted to say how much we love you."

More cheers.

"Our Stone Bay family and those of you visiting us from parts unknown." She bounces in place. "You mean the fucking world to us. We wouldn't be on this stage without you."

The cheers grow impossibly louder.

While Hailey talks to the packed pub and gives us a moment of reprieve, I glance over at the table with Levi and the rest of our friends.

Kirsten, Skylar and Delilah talk animatedly about something. Phoebe appears to be giving Travis and Law a dose of her insight. And Levi... he hasn't taken his eyes off me. I have no idea if he has struck up a conversation with anyone at the table or if he is content sitting and listening while he gives me all his attention.

Hailey announces our final song and kicks it off with a few chords before Trip and I join in. For the next three and a half minutes, I focus on my drums and get lost in the music. In what feels like seconds, the song ends and we thank everyone for coming out tonight.

After one last wave, we step off the stage and join our friends.

As I near Levi, he reaches for my hand, hauls me between his legs, wraps his arms around my waist, and presses his lips to mine. I moan into his mouth as his tongue caresses the length of mine. Fist his shirt and crush my chest to his. Deepen the kiss as we ignore everyone and everything around us.

Fuck, I love him. So damn much.

Snorts and laughter erupt around us and it's enough to steal my attention. Reluctantly, I break the kiss and peek over Levi's shoulder to see several sets of eyes on us.

"What?" I ask with a hint of mock irritation.

The corner of Skylar's mouth tugs up in a gentle half smile. "Am I not allowed to be happy for you?"

I playfully roll my eyes. "I suppose so."

Taking the stool next to Levi, I order food and a drink.

Light chatter sparks to life around the table while music from the jukebox plays from overhead speakers. Delilah asks when our next show is since we just played two days in a row. Hailey tells everyone we have a couple weeks off, her enthusiasm evident.

"It's not that I don't love being on stage"—Hailey drinks half her glass of water—"but it takes a lot out of you." She loops her arm with Trip's and rests her head on his shoulder. "I'm happy for the downtime."

Plus, all three of us have jobs not involving the band.

I lay a hand on Levi's thigh beneath the table as I smile at Hailey and Trip. "Same. I'm thinking of locking this one away"—I nudge Levi's arm with mine—"all weekend."

"Won't hear me complain," Levi says loud enough for the entire table to hear.

The table falls silent for two breaths. Then it's as though everyone wakes back up. Some laugh while others cover their mouths to hide smiles. Beside me, Levi sits a little taller, uncaring of how his comment is taken.

I love this new brazen Levi.

Levi has always had this addictive air about him. An unwavering self-assurance I gravitate toward. A magnetism that lures me in and holds me captive. I doubt I'm the only one affected by his charms. The difference between Levi and most people is he doesn't use his charisma as a weapon. Nor does he act as though he is more important than anyone else.

When it comes to his intelligence and what or who he holds close, Levi is unshakable. Some of his truths may take longer to find their voice, but they always find their way to the surface. And if anyone is brave enough to question his stance or intellect, he will argue his side on the matter until the other person sees reason.

Levi's confidence and intelligence are his sexiest traits. Doesn't hurt that he is fucking beautiful.

"We should pack up," Trip says as Hailey yawns.

I glance at the time on my phone—just after eleven—and nod.

Levi nudges my leg with his. "Want help?"

Leaning into him, I press a chaste kiss to his lips. "Sure."

As we rise from our stools, Kirsten grabs my arm and pulls me into her. "We're heading out."

"Us too," Skylar and Delilah say in unison, then laugh.

Hugs, back slaps and good nights are exchanged. Law mentions covering our tab. Levi takes money from his wallet and presses it to Law's chest until he accepts it. Amused by the whole situation, I linger in the background with a shit-eating grin on my face and a loose fist pressed to my mouth.

"Relentless," Levi mutters as we walk toward the stage.

"Indeed." I chuckle. "So are you."

He scoffs as we start breaking down my drum kit. "Am not."

I pin him with a glare.

"Okay, fine," he huffs out. "Maybe a little." He lifts his hand and pinches his thumb and finger together. "But you love it."

I soften at his words and shrug. "I love *you*."

He leans in and presses a chaste kiss to my lips. "Love you, too."

With the instruments and equipment packed up, we carry it out to Trip and Hailey's van. Once everything is secure, we exchange more hugs and goodbyes.

Levi slips his hand around mine and guides us back inside Dalton's. "It's been a while since I've beaten your ass in pool," Levi states with cool arrogance. "We should play a few games."

I steer us toward the bar and we order drinks.

"Last I checked, we're tied for wins."

Levi leans into my side. The tip of his nose glides along the line of my jaw until he reaches my ear. "Are you sure?" he whisper-asks, his breath warm on my skin. "My tally says otherwise."

My fingers tighten in his as he nips the lobe of my ear. I close my eyes as a shiver rolls up my spine.

I swallow and will my erection away. "I'd like to see this tally," I say, voice raspy.

The bartender sets our drinks in front of us. Levi hands him cash and tells him to keep the rest.

With our drinks in hand, we weave through the pub to the billiard tables. We sit off to the side as we wait for a table to become available. Within minutes, Levi stands at one end of a pool table and racks the balls. I chalk our cues and taunt him with innuendos centered around sticks, balls, and holes.

He smiles and laughs. Both are a balm for my soul.

One game blends into another. We tease each other when either of us misses or fails to drop a ball. We brag about our wins until the other slaps a hand over the other's mouth.

This night, this moment, his endless smiles and laughter… they will live rent-free in my memories and heart for as long as air fills my lungs.

Hours pass by in what feels like minutes and it isn't long before last call is announced.

We down the last of our drinks and finish our fourth game. Levi wins the final game, evening out tonight's tally. He blathers on about still being in the lead overall. I let him have the small victory.

Pool table back to rights, we carry our glasses to the bar and say good night to the woman wiping down the counter. Levi reaches for my hand and weaves our fingers together as we exit the pub.

"When we get home, Mr. Billiard Aficionado, you can show me all the ways you know how to use your stick."

Levi snort-laughs. "Happy to share my expertise."

I press the button on the fob as we approach my car.

Levi jerks us to a stop near the trunk, spins me to face him and walks me backward until I bump the car. His hands frame my face as he invades my space and presses his lips to mine. I snake an arm around his waist and drag my other hand up the length of his spine until my fingers curl around the nape of his neck.

Shamelessly, he mouth-fucks me in the low-lit parking lot. Grinds his steel-hard cock against my length. Slips his fingers into my hair and all but rips my clothes off in public.

Reaching between us, I stroke him through his shorts. He rips his mouth away and drops his forehead to mine.

"Fuck, that feels good," he says, words breathy and gruff.

I release him and he groans.

"I'll make it better at home," I promise.

Inhaling deeply, he steps back and meets my gaze. "Then take me the fuck home."

I laugh as we go to either side of the car. As I reach for the door handle and glance at Levi across the car roof, all the air leaves my lungs. His eyes widen as he stares back at me.

On fast feet, a stocky man approaches Levi from behind. I open my mouth to say something, to warn him, but I don't get the chance. As the words surface, dark fabric is shoved over my head and I'm dragged backward. I fight against the person's hold.

Nearby, Levi curses and fights with whoever grabbed him. His words turn garbled and quieter. And then, I hear nothing.

"Levi!" I thrash harder and manage to break free. "Levi!" I repeat his name as I reach for the fabric over my head.

A fragment of the parking lot comes into view as debilitating pain lances my temple. I collapse on the ground as warm liquid coats my face. I try to open my eyes, needing to see if Levi is okay, but can't muster the strength. Pain explodes through my body as one kick after another is delivered to my gut, my ribs, my head.

Lifeless on the ground, I hear one of them say, "Let's go."

Then the world fades to black.

TWENTY-TWO

OLIVER

A consistent, dull ache reverberates in my skull. A thunderous *whoosh, whoosh, whoosh* echoes in my ears. I can't think straight. Can't hear anything except the deafening sound of my blood pumping.

Body stiff, I shift my arms and instantly regret it. A sharp burst of pain shoots from my fingers to my neck and upper chest.

I suck in a harsh breath between my teeth, my lungs expanding and pressing against my rib cage as a scorching knife pierces my chest over and over. Hissing, I curl my fingers into loose fists.

"Dušo?"

A hand rests on my shoulder delicately.

"My handsome dušo. Can you hear me?"

"Mama?" Her name is sandpaper on my tongue.

A shaky inhale, followed by a sniffle, filters through the whooshing in my ears. "It's Mama, dušo." She presses her lips tenderly to my forehead. "Papa went for coffee. He'll be so happy you're awake."

I peel my eyes open and wince when dim light filters in.

With slow blinks, my eyesight adjusts. Scenic prints in plastic frames hang on generic white walls. A small television is mounted high on the wall across from where I lie. Mint green curtains are pulled together over what I assume is a window. A machine with a screen is on my left, colorful lines and numbers on the display. A plastic bag with clear liquid hangs from a post, a thin tube at the base.

I follow the length of the tube with my eyes until it reaches the back of my hand. My gaze drifts to the white thermal blanket draped over my legs and torso to the rails on either side of the hospital bed.

Hospital. I'm in the hospital.

I glance up at Mama, take in the bruisy crescents beneath her eyes and her disheveled hair. It's a rare occasion if Mama puts on makeup, styles her hair or spruces up her attire, but she always looks put together. Happy. Vibrant.

Right now, she is none of those things. Everything about her is different. Out of sorts. Unkempt. Dispirited.

"What happened?"

My brow furrows as I attempt to sift through my memory. The past several days are blurry and just out of reach. I close my eyes and force my mind to think, think, think.

"Tesoro?" Papa's gentle baritone is laced with confusion as it drifts through the room. "Is everything okay?"

"He's awake." Deep affection and endless gratitude fill those two words.

The shuffling of feet makes me open my eyes.

Papa clambers across the room, setting two cups down and sidling up to the opposite side of the bed from Mama. His usually smooth jawline is peppered with thick black stubble. Beneath his eyes, dark half circles paint his olive skin. His hair pokes haphazardly in several directions, a complete juxtaposition from his everyday slicked-back style.

"Oliver," he weeps my name. "I'm so happy you're okay." Tears glisten in his eyes a breath before one trails down his cheek. "We've been so worried."

I repeat my question from minutes ago. "What happened?"

Papa hovers over me as his hand reaches out then pulls back. Uncertainty flits across his expression as he resists connecting with me physically.

"The police called just before three this morning." Lifting a hand to his face, Papa wipes his eyes. "As the last employees left Dalton's, they saw you unconscious on the ground in the parking lot." The corners of his eyes crinkle as his chin starts to wobble. "You were covered in blood."

I filter through his words with delicate precision as I try to piece together last night. Closing my eyes, I take a deep breath, ignore the sounds, pay little attention to my tender muscles and achy bones, and focus my thoughts. One at a time, memories trickle in.

Hailey's Fire had a show at Dalton's last night.

We were exhausted but happy to play.

Food and drinks, ribbing and laughter.

Packing up the gear.

Pool and innuendos.

Last call.

Kissing Levi in the parking lot.

A scary as fuck man storming up to Levi as we tried to get in the car.

Darkness.

Levi struggling.

Quiet.

"Levi!" I shout as my eyes pop open. My throat burns from the simple action, but I ignore it. "Where's Levi?" My gaze flits from Mama to Papa.

Brows pinched at the middle, Papa shakes his head. "We

don't know, figlio." He rests his hand lightly over mine. "You were alone when they found you."

"No." I shake my head and pain ricochets through my skull. The backs of my eyes burn and the room blurs. "No. He was there." Panic bubbles in my chest. Unease swells in my throat. My limbs start to shake as my mouth goes dry. "W-with me." Tears spill down my cheeks in parallel lines.

"We'll find him, dušo." Mama presses her lips to my forehead. "Promise."

"H-how?"

Papa gives my hand a gentle squeeze. "I'll make some calls." His gaze darts to Mama. "Let the doctor know he's awake and ask when we can take him home."

Without hesitation, Mama presses a button on the bed rail. She nods toward the door. "Go, moja ljubavi. Make calls." A tender smile lifts the corners of her mouth. "I won't leave Ollie's side."

On a deep inhale, Papa takes one of the cups, heads for the door and disappears into the hallway.

A silent river of tears coats my cheeks as I close my eyes and try to recall any other sounds or images from last night. A faint flash of the parking lot appears behind my eyelids. My hands tremble uncontrollably as I lock onto the memory and study it harder. As I scavenge for the smallest clue as to where Levi may be.

An ill-defined image of the man who approached Levi comes into view. Stalky build. Tall. The hood of his sweatshirt was up and covered most of his head.

"Mrs. Moss," a warm voice says. "Did you need something?"

I open my eyes and peer up at a man in pale-green scrubs.

"Oh"—cheeriness fills his expression—"Oliver is awake." He taps a few buttons on the tablet in his hand. "I've just notified the doctor. She'll be in shortly to do a thorough exam."

An understated smile lifts the corners of Mama's mouth for a brief second. "Thank you."

He nods and inches closer to the bed. "On a scale of one to ten, how would you rate your pain, Oliver?"

I do a quick mental sweep of the dull aches and sharp pains. "Maybe a seven." My answer feels more like a question than a statement of fact.

The nurse taps on the tablet screen. "We'll wait until after the doctor examines you before we administer more pain medication. It's best if you let her know how you feel without suppressants."

I nod as a woman in a white coat and navy scrubs enters the room. She sidles up to the nurse and he hands her the tablet.

"Glad to see you're awake, Oliver." The corners of her eyes wrinkle as a toothy smile brightens her expression. "I'm Dr. Sharma. Is it okay if I ask you some questions?"

"Yes."

"Thank you." Dr. Sharma glances at Mama briefly before meeting my gaze again. "Because you're an adult, I have to ask if it's okay for your mother to be in the room while we talk."

I meet Mama's eyes and nod. "It's fine."

The clock on the wall ticks on and on as Dr. Sharma asks several questions about my injuries. When she reaches what I think is the end, I open my mouth to ask when I can go home. But I'm cut off as she starts a new round of questions focusing on my memory. Thankfully, this part of the exam is brief.

Next, she waves a penlight in front of my eyes then adds notes to the tablet. After some nerve and muscle tests, she gives a subtle nod.

"Aside from your physical injuries, everything appears to

be normal. Your memory of the event is cloudy, which is to be expected. Our minds have a way of blocking out trauma while we heal."

She taps the tablet screen several times.

"I'd like you to remain here for the night. In the morning, you can go home. I'll write a script for the pain. Other than a couple cracked ribs, you have no major injuries."

She presses the lock button on the tablet and hugs it to her chest.

"Time and rest, Oliver. I'll detail things to avoid during recovery. If all goes accordingly, your ribs should be good as new in six weeks."

"Six weeks?" I toss back incredulously.

A sympathetic smile dons her face as she shrugs. "Unless you're a fast healer, six weeks is standard."

No way in hell will I fucking lie around for six goddamn weeks. I need to find Levi.

I inhale deeply then groan as pain shoots through my midsection. "Thanks, Dr. Sharma."

"You're welcome." She checks the bag attached to my IV line. "I'll have the nurse bring in some pain med—"

"No." My stomach twists at the idea of losing more time. "Not yet. Maybe when I need to sleep."

"Are you sure, dušo?"

I meet Mama's concerned gaze and nod. "Yeah, Mama. I need to speak with the police and Levi's boss. It's best to do both with as clear a head as possible."

"Levi's boss?"

"I'll explain."

Dr. Sharma heads for the door. "I'll give you privacy. Whenever you're ready for the pain meds, press the call button."

"Thank you."

The doctor exits the room, but I wait a moment before speaking up. Not that I'm well informed.

"Levi was working on something big with his boss. He couldn't share details due to confidentiality, but it was a significant project. Dark. Heavy. Stressful." I swallow past the expansive knot in my throat. "If he's… missing"—tears well in my eyes once more—"Tymber may know how to find him."

Mama gently squeezes my fingers. "Okay, dušo." She nods. "I'll text Papa and ask him to call Tymber."

One of the longest hours of my life passes before Travis Emerson enters my hospital room.

"Hey, Ollie. How're you holding up?"

I wave a hand up and down my body. "Could be better."

"True. We're just glad you're alive. Soon as Kirsten heard the news, she told Sky and Dee Dee. They're ready to smother you with food and care." He chuckles.

A cloud of unease fills the room as I don't respond in kind. But before Travis speaks up again, Tymber walks into the room.

On a good day, Tymber is quite formidable. The trait comes in handy with his line of work. But today isn't a good day, and Tymber looks as though he hasn't slept in weeks.

"Tymber." Travis offers him a hand to shake, and Tymber takes it. "Why are you here?"

"I asked him to come," I say.

Both men glance my way.

"Nice to see you, Oliver." Tymber steps closer to the bed. "Wish it was under better circumstances."

"Me too." I inhale a small, shaky breath. "I know I need to

give you a statement, Travis, but I also wanted Tymber here because of the situation."

Travis's brow furrows. "Alright." He takes out his phone and taps on the screen a few times. "Whenever you're ready, Oliver."

My gaze darts between the two of them. "Last night is still a bit hazy, but I remember bits of what happened after everyone left Dalton's."

I spend the next several minutes giving an account of what I remember. As I near the end, I lock on to Tymber's weary expression. "I don't know what you and Levi are working on, but the little he shared, I know it's extensive."

Closing my eyes, I muster up the strength to say the next part. A chill blankets me from head to toe as my limbs tremble. Curling my fingers, I fist the blanket and meet their waiting stares.

"This wasn't random. They weren't vagrants. They weren't mugging us." I swallow as the next part edges the tip of my tongue. "I think someone t-took him," I say, the words shaky and hollow.

Tymber's expression turns a ghastly shade of gray as he turns to my parents. "Would you mind stepping out for a moment? It won't take long."

Concern mars my parents' features, but they agree to give us privacy.

When it's only the three of us, Tymber tips his head back and pinches the bridge of his nose. After a deep inhale, he levels his gaze.

"Levi and I were asked to help on a missing person case. But the case was one of hundreds, and we couldn't ignore the similarities when we compared several of them. I need to look through his computer at the office, but I know he's been in communication with a group of people on the dark web."

Travis's head snaps in Tymber's direction. "I'm sorry, what?" His voice vibrates the air.

Tymber gives Travis an apologetic smile. "We can talk more later."

"No," Travis barks. "We can talk now." He points to the floor.

"I *will* share more later, but what I *can* say in present company"—Tymber's gaze returns to mine—"is that we uncovered a major human trafficking ring."

My body goes numb as I stop breathing. My eyes burn as every inch of my body shakes violently. The heart monitor next to the bed beeps faster and louder as the room shrinks around me.

No. I shake my head in disbelief. *Please don't let it be true.*

I slam my eyes closed and gasp for breath, but no air fills my lungs.

Something presses down on my foot, and I flinch.

"No!" I scream as my eyes fly open. My fists slam down on the mattress over and over. "No, no, no, no, no!"

My parents dash into the room and scurry to my side.

"Shh, dušo." Mama touches my cheek. "I've got you."

"What did you say?" Papa barks out, his voice laced with unfamiliar venom.

Mama continues to soothe me with quiet words as she presses the button on the bed rail.

"Tell me," Papa demands.

"We believe Levi has been... abducted," Travis says too calmly.

Mama gasps at the same time Papa clutches his chest. Papa's warm eyes meet mine, tears rimming them as he swallows. He inhales a shaky breath as the first tear falls. A mixture of fear, sympathy and relief washes over his face.

Since waking up, my parents have fretted over and smothered me with an obscene amount of love and gratitude. But the moment I questioned where Levi was and explained what I could remember, all I got was gentle reassurances in soft tones.

It pisses me off.

"I need to get out of here," I say. "I need to find him. Now."

"We'll find him," Tymber states with more confidence than any of us feels.

"How?" I bark out. "You've been working on this for a while. Obviously, he got too close and they took him."

The heart monitor beeps faster once more.

"So tell me, how will *you* find him?"

"Dušo," Mama chastises.

"It's okay, ma'am." Tymber runs his fingers through his hair. "Oliver, I promise I will do everything within my power to find him. He keeps extensive notes on his computer. I will go through all of them until we find him."

"And now that I've been apprised of the situation, Stone Bay police will work alongside Mr. Woulf, missing persons, and additional law enforcement." Travis rests his hand on the footrail of the bed. "We will not rest until we find him, Ollie." His eyes hold mine, unwavering. "I swear to you."

His word means more than Tymber's right now.

"I'll hold you to it, Travis," I say on a shaky exhale. "Now, please leave. Go find my boyfriend."

TWENTY-THREE
LEVI

A TREMOR RIPPLES THROUGH MY BODY AS I HUG MY LEGS CLOSER to my chest. Resting my head on my knees, I inhale slow, methodical breaths and close my eyes. It doesn't matter whether my eyes are open or closed; there is no light in the room. But something about closing my eyes gives me comfort.

A loud gurgle sounds from my stomach seconds before it twists into a vicious cramp. The last thing I ate was a measly fistful of stale crackers thrown at my face. The last thing I drank was a small bottle of water, also tossed at my head.

Both were… days ago. At least, I think it was days ago. I have no fucking clue.

Time doesn't exist in this hellhole.

My mind drifts to Oliver. The absolute terror on his face seconds before a hood was dropped over my head. His thrashing and screaming as he fought one of our assailants repeats like an endless nightmare.

Is he here?

Is he locked in a cell like this one?

Is he alone and scared and as worried about me as I am for him?

Please, don't let him be here.

I did this. I opened the lid to Pandora's box, let the monsters out, led them straight to us, and all but identified myself when I put on that fucking hat at the festival.

Stupid. Fucking. Idiot.

Music comes on outside of the room and is cranked to a deafening volume. Since I woke up in this place, I have learned music means one thing. Torture. They use fast-paced, squealy rock music to mask the screams as people are beaten.

I know this because it has happened to me.

The shiver-inducing screech of the metal hinges mingles with the violent music as the door to my cell is opened. Bright light infiltrates the room and I wince.

A large man stands in the doorway, his biceps thicker than my thighs. I've seen him twice before now—when he threw crackers at my face and sometime later when he came in to punch and kick me for several minutes.

"There you are," he says in a robotic voice. "Our new pretty toy."

My fingers curl into fists as I press my back to the wall. "I'm not *yours*," I bite out, though the words don't sound as harsh in my dehydrated state.

Mechanical-sounding laughter bounces off the walls as he steps farther into my cell. "That's where you're wrong. The second you started chatting with us online, you were ours. We just waited for the perfect opportunity."

"Huh?"

He takes another step closer and shakes his head. "We've been doing this a long fucking time. We do our research too. Not hard to weed out the impostors when you know your audience."

I may not be some sick and twisted pervert looking to buy, corrupt and destroy people, but I think I played the part well. Hell, I barely spoke with anyone. For the most part, I loitered.

But maybe that was the biggest red flag.

These bastards don't linger. They're eager for every scrap of filth they can get their hands on from the start.

"Noted." I lift my gaze to meet his. "Just let me go home. I don't even know where the hell I am. I won't tell a soul."

He scoffs as he closes the small distance between us and squats down.

"You still don't get it."

I stare at him and try to puzzle out what he means. With a lack of food and water, my brain isn't functioning at full capacity. I'm not connecting the dots.

Rising to his feet, he digs into a pocket of his cargo pants. He sets a small bottle of water next to my feet. From another pocket, he removes a different container and deposits it next to the bottle, the contents unidentifiable.

"You are home, Two Sixty-Three. Best you get used to the accommodations."

TWENTY-FOUR
OLIVER

I stare at the ceiling as dawn peeks through the blinds. Faint shadows dance across the subtle texture beneath the paint. For a moment, the pale pink and orange colors steal my attention. Give me something to focus on other than reality. Gift me an inkling of respite.

As quickly as the calm filters in, it vanishes.

I don't deserve to feel an ounce of comfort. Not while the spot next to me in bed remains cold, empty and lifeless. Not while the most important person in my life is missing and existing in hell.

All that matters is finding him and bringing him home.

Rolling onto my side, I bury my face in his pillow, close my eyes and inhale deeply. I picture Levi here with me, pulling me into him and pinning me to his chest. Imagine him throwing a leg over my hip as he hugs the air from my lungs. I recall his warmth and affection and the way he never wanted to let go.

Though his scent has faded over the past thirty days, I refuse to wash his pillowcase. I refuse to clean any trace of him from my space. His underwear and socks sit in the dresser untouched. His clothes hang in the closet as he last left them.

As for his dirty laundry, all but some of his shirts remain in the basket.

On the nights when my sobs seem endless, I slip one of his dirty shirts over my head and breathe him in. Whisper promises into the darkness that I will do whatever it takes to find him. That I will never stop looking. Between tears, I murmur how much I love him.

"I love you, moje srce," I mumble into the pillow.

Taking one last deep breath, I shove away from his pillow and force myself out of bed.

Since coming home from the hospital, my daily routine has been much the same. Roll out of bed after a fitful night of unrest, do basic hygiene, dress for the day, sit down with my parents for breakfast but don't eat it, then head to Tymber Woulf Security and Investigative Services until well after dark.

Several times a week, Travis comes into TWSIS and the three of us brainstorm over new information. Tymber spends most of the day sifting through code on Levi's computer line by line, looking for one tiny fragment that would give us a better idea of where to search for him. I sift through hundreds of files on the missing people in the hopes of finding common denominators among them.

Yesterday, we tacked a large map of the Northwest to a corkboard. While Tymber reads code and Travis coordinates with various law enforcement offices, I make a list of who went missing and where then add a pin to the map for each person. Our hope with the pins is to get a different perspective. If several people were taken in the same area or the abductions surround an area, it may lead us to where everyone has been taken.

"You're too thin, dušo," Mama says, the heavy weight of despair in her voice. She brushes the back of her fingers down my cheek. "I know you don't want to, but please make sure you eat." She takes my hands in hers. "You need your strength to find him."

I give her hands a quick squeeze and nod. "I'm trying, Mama." The corners of my mouth twitch. "Promise."

Releasing my hands, she cups my cheeks, pushes up on her toes, and presses a kiss to my forehead. "Let me pack something for you to eat later."

I follow her into the kitchen and watch as she fills a storage container with food. A voice in the back of my head begs me to tell her not to add anything too heavy. I ignore it and let her add whatever she wants. If one thing is certain, it's that food is one of Mama's love languages. Same goes for Papa. In some respects, I've also made it one of mine, although I don't do most of the cooking.

Snapping the lid on, Mama puts the container in a bag, adds a napkin and utensils then ties the cloth handles once. "I don't expect you to eat it all"—she hands me the bag—"but I wanted you to have options."

I take the bag, step into her, wrap her in my arms, inhale her familiar and comforting scent, and press a kiss to her cheek as I release her. "Thank you, Mama. Volim te." *I love you.*

"Volim te više, dušo."

Crossing the room, I hug Papa goodbye and promise to check in when I reach TWSIS—something new we have implemented since Levi's abduction. If checking in gives us a glimmer of peace, it's worth the simple text message.

Wind ruffles my hair as I drive through town. The summer sun beats down on me through the windshield and warms my skin. Townsfolk stroll leisurely down the sidewalk, some with children enjoying summer vacation. Smiles and laughter surround me as I pause at a stop sign and wait for pedestrians to cross the street.

I don't return a single smile. Nor do I wave or say hello. Their joy is incomprehensible.

All I feel is numb. Alone. Crestfallen.

Until Levi is back in my arms, happiness is an illusion.

Parking in the small lot at TWSIS, I exit the car, grab the food bag, and follow the same path I have for weeks. As I wind my way through the office, employees glance up, pause, then give me the same woeful smile they have every single day. I do my best to not look at their pitiful gazes.

"Anything new?" I ask as I enter Levi's office and close the door.

Tymber pushes back in the chair and rolls away from Levi's desk. He runs his hand through his hair and exhales an audible sigh. "These fuckers are cryptic as hell."

I set the bag on an empty chair. "Probably how they've stayed hidden for so long."

"Some conversations can be read at face value." He reaches for one of several lidded cups on the desk and takes a long pull of caffeine. "But other chats, they talk in fucking riddles." He slams the cup down. "And because Levi's too brilliant for his own good, he deciphered the riddles. Just wish he would've jotted his findings somewhere." Resting his elbows on his knees, he drops his head in his hands. "Or told me more of what he figured out."

Moving to the table covered in files and photos, I stare down at the sea of faces and pray we find not only Levi but all of them too. Some of these kids have been missing more than six months. Their loved ones must be thoroughly devastated at the lack of news or progress. Well, there was momentum while Levi worked the case. But like Tymber said, Levi didn't leave detailed notes on all his discoveries.

That one thing frustrates me daily as we work tirelessly to

learn what he found out. But my exasperation fizzles out before it has the chance to stick.

Tymber returns to his task on Levi's computer. We work in amiable silence as we continue our search for answers.

As I press a new pin into the map and note on the list who it relates to, an idea sparks.

"We need a fresh perspective." I turn to face Tymber and he pauses his task. "Someone who will look at this without bias or former knowledge of the situation. Someone who thinks differently than me, you or Travis."

Tymber spins in the chair and crosses his arms over his chest. "Sounds like you have someone in mind."

I nod.

"Are they trustworthy?"

"Implicitly."

"Who?"

"Phoebe Graves."

"The Gazette reporter?" A muscle in his jaw tics. "You sure about her?"

"A year ago, I would've said absolutely not."

The recent murders in Stone Bay and Phoebe's ruthless determination to find answers flicker to life in my memory. At any time during the case, she could've written headlining stories for the paper and turned the town upside down. As she and Delilah looked for clues to bring the killer to justice, Travis asked for discretion. Phoebe held up her end of the bargain and waited until after the trial to publish an article that was tamer than many of us expected.

Does Phoebe enjoy keeping a tight lid on stories? Absolutely not. Will she be circumspect and maintain confidentiality while we work? Without a doubt, yes.

"But I'd trust her with my life now."

A low hum fills the room as Tymber mulls over my response. Tipping his head back, he closes his eyes and drags his hands over his face. When he levels me with his gaze, resolution fills his eyes.

"Bring her in. I'd like to talk with her first. Make sure she knows how serious and classified the situation is before putting her to work."

"Do you mind if Delilah Fox, her girlfriend and one of my best friends, lends a hand as well? They worked on the St. Agnes case together."

"Same rule applies." He picks up his cup, shakes it, sighs, and sets it back on the desk. "At this point, the more help we have, the better."

Tymber presses a button on the phone and a mechanical buzz echoes from the speaker.

"Yes, Mr. Woulf?"

"I know you're not my secretary, Lauren, but I will love you forever if you do a coffee run."

"I'll hold you to it." Indistinct sounds crackle through the line. "Want me to use the company card?"

"Please."

"Anything other than coffee? I'm going to Poke the Yolk."

Guilt washes over me at the mention of the restaurant where I work but haven't been to since the start of July. Gracious as Deidra, my manager, and the owners have been at letting me have time off, it doesn't stop the pang in my gut from flaring to life. They know I am not in the right headspace to smile and tend to people. Deidra promises my job is secure until I am able to return.

The restaurant isn't the only responsibility I've ignored.

Practice with Hailey and Trip has come to an abrupt halt. We also canceled two shows. Even if we find Levi this week, it's likely our show in early September will be scrapped too. Although Hailey and Trip have been completely understanding, I feel as if I've let them down. As if I'm ruining the future of the band. They assure me the band will be fine and the venues will book us again as soon as we are ready.

Tymber glances at me and lifts a brow.

"Cherry Coke." I shrug.

"Lots of coffee and Cherry Coke, Lauren. Oh, and the pancake breakfast."

"On it."

The phone disconnects and the room goes silent. Tymber returns to his task on the computer and ends our talk.

I pull out my phone and send a text to Delilah.

> I need your help. Well, you & Phoebe.

Mere seconds pass before her response fills my screen.

> DEE DEE
>
> Anything. What's up?

> can't say much over text but it's about finding Levi

> whatever you need Ollie

> will you & Phoebe come to TWSIS so we can talk?

> be there asap

"Not sure how much help I'll be, Ollie, but I'm happy to do whatever I can." Delilah wraps me in a breath-stealing hug.

"Thanks, Dee Dee."

Delilah releases me and steps back.

"The Gazette's been slow, so I have loads of time," Phoebe chimes in.

Tymber narrows his gaze. "Not a word of this in the paper."

"Ever?" Phoebe asks incredulously.

Inhaling a slow, deep breath, Tymber pinches the bridge of his nose. "Not until *I* give the all clear."

Phoebe hooks her arm with Delilah's, gives her girlfriend a soft smile, then turns her attention to Tymber and nods. "Won't be a problem."

"Then welcome to the team." Tymber turns his attention my way. "Do you mind bringing them up to speed?" He turns back to his task before I answer.

For the next hour, I share what we know about Levi's work and what he discovered. With each new revelation, I witness the color drain from Delilah and Phoebe's faces. When I finish, I glance up and wait for them to say something.

Delilah remains stoic as her eyes roam over papers and photos on the table. Phoebe, on the other hand, has regained some of her strength. I study her expression and can't deny the hope I feel at seeing her steely determination.

Bringing them into the fold was the right move.

"Where do you want me?" Phoebe asks.

I hand her a stack of files. "These are the most recently reported cases before Levi was taken."

Without a word, she takes the folders, ambles over to an empty spot on the floor, and starts sifting through the contents.

Delilah rises from her seat and takes a step toward Phoebe. She pauses as she passes me and meets my weary gaze. "We will find him, Ollie." And then she joins Phoebe on the floor.

August 5th

I will never give up on finding L, but I hate to admit I am starting to lose hope. It's been a month since I last touched him, hugged him, kissed him. I miss the deep baritone of his voice. I miss the way I came to life under his touch and how it never felt like enough. I miss the way his bright blue eyes watched me, as if he feared forgetting one of my features. But most of all, I miss him. So fucking much. It's never been so damn hard to breathe or focus or move forward. Without him, there is NO forward. He is my future, my soul, forever moje srce.

Thankfully I had enough sense to ask for more help today. And those extra eyes and hands... they may be exactly what we need to find him.

Until you're in my arms again L, I won't stop. Not ever.

TWENTY-FIVE
LEVI

Day Fifty

"IN THE SHADOWS, WE HIDE," I MURMUR TO MYSELF AS I SCRATCH the same spot on the wall over and over. "Until every star falls."

A stab of pain shoots up my finger to my wrist and along my forearm, but it's bearable compared to the countless other afflictions I've experienced in this cell.

So I ignore it.

I go back to scraping the wall.

Moisture coats the tip of my finger and I bring it to my lips. I drag my sandpaper tongue over the wetness. Taste something metallic and cringe. Pull the finger from my mouth and go back to my task on the wall.

"In the shadows," I repeat again and again, the words almost inaudible.

A tug at the tip of my finger, followed by a soft ripping sound and a fresh shock of pain, makes me hiss. I pop my finger back into my mouth and suck, only to realize my fingernail has detached from the nail bed.

The backs of my eyes sting as a shiver rolls throughout my body. Finger still between my lips, I pin my hand to my mouth with the other. I close my eyes and hum the words that have been swirling in my head for days. Familiar yet foreign words. I rock back and forth on the concrete and let the strange melody in my head soothe my pain.

It doesn't last long, though. It never does.

Music roars to life and I yank my finger from my mouth.

Digging my bony heels into the floor, I shove myself as far into the corner as the chains attached to my cuffs and shackles allow. I draw my legs to my chest and hug them as best I can with my arms. The cuffs hang loosely on my wrists but are not slack enough to slide free. Every bone in my body complains as I fold myself in half and crush my femurs to my rib cage.

"Every star, every star, every star…" I say faster and faster.

I clamp my fingers around the tops of my shins. My long, jagged nails bite the skin with ease. I focus my attention on the pain as I repeat the words over and over.

The door to my prison flies open. A man stands in the doorway. Although he is feet away, his menacing form feels as though it hovers inches above me.

My stomach churns out of habit, but nothing else happens. I haven't eaten anything for a while. They have given me more food to make me less emaciated and more appealing to the dressy men who come to visit my cell.

For days, I have been force-fed. And for just as long, I have purged all the contents of my stomach shortly after they leave.

I'd rather die in this hell than do a single damn thing to make these assholes happy. If starvation is the answer, then that is how I will end this.

"I've got a present for you, Two Sixty-Three." The man steps into the room and shoves a hand in a cargo pocket.

Yanking on the chain, I try to escape his reach. It's impossible, I know, yet I still pray a cuff will wiggle loose and I'll be free.

A wicked voice in my head tells me I will never be free. This is my life now.

In my time here, my eyes have adjusted to the darkness. The room and its contents are easier to see when the door is closed. When the door opens, the brightness messes with my vision. It takes me longer to make out finer details.

It's not until a second before he brings his hand to my neck that I make out the slight shimmer of the needle. As the syringe registers in my mind, it's too late. The thin metal has already pierced my skin.

I jerk my head away from the sting and reach for my neck.

A moment of déjà vu hits as warmth spreads from my neck to my chest and out to my limbs. The room becomes hazy as my body melts into the floor.

"What..." The word is sludge on my tongue.

"Time to sleep, Two Sixty-Three."

Within seconds, my eyes close. For the first time since I've been in this place, a sense of peace washes over me. I bask in the sensation as my body becomes weightless.

Just before sleep takes me, green eyes and dark hair flash in my mind. In that minor blip of time, it feels as if I'm home again.

My tongue is heavy and dry as my mind slowly wakes up. Exhaustion gnaws at every muscle, bone and cell in my body. It feels as though I'm floating and drowning at the same time.

I lift my hand toward my face but only make it an inch before my arm is jerked back. Confused, I peel my eyes open. The room is blurry, unfamiliar, and a bit brighter than before.

Where am I?

The floor rattles a little before the room teeters.

I slam my eyes shut, inhale several slow, deep breaths, and hum the melody I've had in my head for a while. When I exhale the tenth breath, I ease my eyes open again. I take my time glancing around the space as my gaze adjusts to the new setting.

Across from me, just out of reach, a woman sits on the floor. Her legs are folded to her chest, a leather strap wrapped around them and pinning them to her torso. Thick metal cuffs hang loose on her wrists, a clasp on them connected to cuffs on her ankles. Trailing up her legs, I pause at her throat. A wide, worn leather collar encircles her neck, a metal ring at the front.

For several breaths, I stare at the strip of material. The simple piece of animal flesh is also a symbol. A representation of what we have become to the world in these people's eyes.

Property.

As I think the word, the band of leather around my own neck chafes my skin.

Slowly, I lift my gaze to the woman's face. Her eyes are on mine, but she doesn't *see* me. There is no life in her eyes, in her expression, in her soul. She is just a body—frail, inanimate, praying for death.

I turn my head to survey the rest of the room and it sways. I close my eyes again and wait for the feeling to pass. Whatever they stuck me with must still be wearing off.

When the ground steadies and stills, I open my eyes and scan the room. What I'm met with is unexpected and unsurprising at the same time.

As far as I can see, other captives sit pinned to the wall. Many are unconscious, their head slumped and close to their knees. But quite a few are awake. One by one, we meet each other's gazes. Some are lifeless while others are riddled with panic.

Not a soul speaks. We know better.

Without a doubt, especially with so many of us in the same space, guards are in the room. Trying to talk to another prisoner is an open invitation for punishment.

Are we being moved?

Did we all get the same injection? Did they knock us out so they could move us without resistance?

I have no idea where we were before, but if they are moving us… this can't be good.

Closing my eyes, I sift through my mind. Search for thoughts from *before*. Try to remember something. *Anything*. A clue as to what this might mean.

The past is foggy. Like a dream I can't quite grasp. A part of my life just out of reach.

But if ever there is a good time to remember *before*, it's now. *Think.*

A glint of something lingers in the periphery. Something important.

But what?

And then a memory drifts in.

Before here, I was working on a project. A big project. Something massive and life-changing.

What was it?

Think, think, think.

I pinch my eyes tighter as I dig deeper. I latch on to the memory and try to bring it into focus.

Images of screens flash behind my eyelids. Colorful lines of code on them. *Research*. A stack of file folders and pictures are scattered everywhere, but the details are hazy.

You can do this. You have to do this. Think.

What was I researching? What was I looking for?

One breath at a time, the details sharpen. The lines on the screen become legible. The scattered pictures become clearer. The cover of the file folder comes into view.

I was looking for… missing people.

My eyes fly open. I glance left then right. Take in the countless others pinned in place.

I was looking for *these* people.

But where the hell are we? I never learned where the abductees were taken. Had I, none of us would be here right now. And if I didn't figure out their location, how would anyone else sort it out? How the hell will anyone find *me*?

Simple answer… they won't. No one will find me. Or these people.

And if this rocking motion means what I think it does, we are no longer in the same place. So even if they figure out where we *were*, it's too late. We are already gone.

"In the shadows, we hide," I whisper as the backs of my eyes burn. "Until every star falls."

I don't know why those words bring me comfort. I don't know why those words make me want to live when every cell in my body begs for the end. Whatever the reason, these words are all I have left. So, I hold on to them with every ounce of mental strength I have left.

If anyone can hear me, please hurry. I won't last much longer.

TWENTY-SIX
OLIVER

Elbows on my knees and head in my hands, I press the heels of my palms to my eyes and curl my fingers in my hair. One steadying breath after another, I work to calm the perpetual anxiety living in my chest.

As I do most days, I focus my thoughts on the minor details we've discovered since Phoebe and Delilah joined the mission a little more than three weeks ago. I concentrate on the map inundated with pins and strings and try to see it from different points of view. I stare at it with a faux predator's mindset and do my best to think strategically rather than irrationally with my heart.

Today marks fifty-three days since we were beaten in a parking lot and Levi was abducted. Since he was stolen from my life and robbed of his.

Fifty-three days have passed since I last held him in my arms and pressed my lips to his. Since I last told him I love him and heard him say it in return.

In those fifty-three days, I've aged just as many years.

Fuck, I miss him. My best friend. My boyfriend. The one

person who understands me when no one else does. The only person that makes me want a longer life, just so I have more time with him. I miss his profound intelligence and the explosive way he loves. I miss his addictive eyes and broody silence. I miss the smell of him on my skin and the smile he reserves for me and gives no one else.

I miss him more than a limb. More than every damn limb.

Words will never adequately describe what I feel for Levi. Love is nowhere near enough. Levi is embedded in every cell of my body. He is rooted deep in my bones. Tattooed on my soul.

When they took him from me, they pried my rib cage in two and wrenched my heart from my chest. They stole the air from my lungs and left me to wither to dust.

A life without Levi is meaningless and dark.

Fifty-three days have passed since I last looked into his eyes. Fifty-three exhausting and excruciating days. But if I have to spend every day of the rest of my life looking for him, I will. And I'll count every single one of those days. Whatever it takes, no matter the cost, I will not rest until we find Levi.

He is worth every second, every breath, every heartbeat.

"Holy shit!"

My head snaps up and I lock onto Tymber at Levi's desk. "What?" I shoot up from my seat and cross the room, eager for more information.

"Holy fucking shit!" Tymber shouts with more enthusiasm.

I step up behind him and stare at the countless rows of code on the screens. To me, it's gibberish. But to tech-savvy people, it's simply another language.

"What?" I ask again, anxiety and impatience evident in my tone.

Tymber points to the screen, peers over his shoulder, and

meets my gaze. A glint of hope shines in his weary eyes. "I found something." His attention returns to the screen. "At least, I think I did."

My eyes scan the screen where he points, but none of it makes sense when I read it. I huff out my annoyance. "I have no clue what that says."

Everyone else in the office crowds around Tymber and focuses on the screen with the same perplexed look in their eyes. Not a single one of us breathes as we wait for Tymber to relay the news.

Shortly after Phoebe and Delilah joined the search party, Levi's parents walked through the front door of TWSIS. A mixture of surprise, heartache, and uncertainty swirled in my chest at the sight of them. When they said they wanted to help find their son, that whirl of emotion grew tenfold.

Levi may have a strained relationship with his parents, but seeing them in that moment... His family let go of their past differences. For the first time since I've known Levi, his parents' love for him outshines their status and outward appearance.

By the time they walked into TWSIS, they'd spoken at length with Chief Emerson at the Stone Bay Police Department, as well as county, state, and federal law enforcement. Though the departments are working together to locate this human trafficking ring, they directed the Wests to TWSIS, dubbing it the local headquarters for this case.

"It's a coded message in one of the chat logs." Tymber spins in the chair and faces the group. "Levi lingered for the most part, reading and deciphering various chats and announcements. But there were a few threads he interacted with to get more information. Some of which he told me about but never gave in-depth details."

"And?" Infinite hope shapes the small word as Mrs. West waits for Tymber to continue.

"If I'm translating it correctly"—his eyes dart between me and Levi's parents before he swallows—"the auction he mentioned before he was taken, it will happen soon."

"An auction?" Mr. West asks in disbelief.

Mrs. West gasps and covers her mouth with her hand.

I stare at the code on the screen, looking for something to contradict Tymber's interpretation. Anything. But a faint voice in the back of my head says it's pointless.

Levi hunted this trafficking ring and fell victim in the process. Now, he may be sold to some sick, rich fucker halfway across the world. If that happens, I might lose him forever.

And that's not an option. I can't lose him. Not like this. Not ever.

Every inch of my body turns to ice as fear and panic swirl low in my belly and twist their way up my spine.

"When?" I demand. "How long do we have?"

Tymber turns his attention back to the screen and points again. "This comment says *not long after the gust passes*." He twists and points to a different screen, one with Levi's personal notes on the case. "When this popped up in the thread, Levi deciphered the comment as an auction happening at the beginning of September. He decoded *gust* as August."

Not a single day has passed since Levi's abduction that I didn't know the date or how many days he's been missing. Yet, I still take out my phone, wake it up with a tap, and stare at the date on the screen.

August 28.

August ends in three days.

Three. Fucking. Days.

We are out of time.

We have to find him.

Right the fuck now.

"Fuck," I mutter. The backs of my eyes burn and my nose stings as this new reality takes center stage.

An arm wraps around my shoulders a moment before the air is hugged from my lungs. Mrs. West shushes and rocks me gently.

"We'll get him back," she says, her proclamation laced with conviction.

I close my eyes and count to ten. Silently absorb some of her confidence and let it bolster my own.

In the days since Levi's parents walked through the doors of TWSIS, I've witnessed a big change in their acceptance of my relationship with Levi.

Mrs. West had treated me with kindness over the years, but she'd still sided with her husband when it came to Levi's future. They'd wanted him with a prominent woman and to produce future West heirs. Like some of the other Stone Bay founding families, they never asked Levi what he wanted for his life.

Before he spoke his first words, most of Levi's life had been mapped out for him. Appearance, profession, marriage. When Mr. and Mrs. West envisioned Levi's future, they didn't include the idea of him choosing his own career path or falling in love with a same-sex commoner.

Fifty-four days ago, they disliked that their eldest son was in love with me—an ordinary man.

Since his disappearance, they have put aside their archaic ideals and embraced me with open arms. For the first time in years, they see me as someone their son loves rather than someone robbing him of his future.

"I'll call Emerson with the news," Mr. West says.

Tymber grabs his phone. "And I'll call my buddy at missing persons."

The room erupts in chaos as Mrs. West releases me and takes out her phone. She taps the screen a few times and brings the phone to her ear. In seconds, she prattles instructions to whoever she talks with.

Phoebe and Delilah are near the map with the pins and string, pointing and chatting quietly. I join them and stare at the map with a new perspective. Tough as it is, I try to insert myself into the shoes of these bastards and think like a heinous criminal.

"If I was a sadistic motherfucker selling hundreds of human beings, where would I be?"

Delilah, Phoebe, and I get lost in our thoughts as we gaze at the map of Washington and Oregon.

"In my case"—Delilah starts then pauses to take a deep breath—"they took me to a place that people rarely visited. Somewhere away from homes, businesses, and general traffic."

Delilah makes a good point.

"So we should look in more rural areas?"

Turning to face me, her steel-blues meet my greens. She tips her head from side to side. "Yes and no." Returning her attention to the map, she studies it for a beat. "They'd need somewhere big. Even crammed together, that's a lot of people."

Phoebe takes her eyes off the map and roams Delilah's profile. "What's going through that pretty head of yours, Fox?"

Delilah's eyes narrow on the map as she rolls her lips between her teeth.

"If this is too much—"

"No." Delilah cuts Phoebe off. She closes her eyes, inhales deeply, and gives herself a moment to move past her own dark memories. A sense of calm fills her features when she opens her eyes. "I need to do this."

Phoebe slips her hand around Delilah's and nods. "Okay."

The clap of boots on the tile echoes through the room as

Travis and Chief Emerson enter the office. Chief walks over to where Mr. and Mrs. West stand with Tymber. Travis heads in our direction.

Delilah doesn't take her eyes off the map. "You asked where this person would be."

None of us say a word as we wait for Delilah to continue.

"Step back and *really* look at the map," she says.

We all do as she suggests. I study the board and try to see what she does. I shove aside the written-in-stone facts and look at what is literally in front of me.

"Majority of the pins are close to bodies of water," Travis murmurs. "Holy shit." He steps within inches of the map and trails a finger over several pinheads. "Inlets, rivers, bays, the state's coast. All within a few miles."

"Tymber says they talk in code but often sound like fishermen," I say.

Without another word, Travis spins on his heel and moves across the room. I follow him with my eyes and watch as the other half of the group reacts to this discovery.

A hand on my arm startles me.

"Sorry." Delilah gives me a gentle smile.

I shake my head. "No need to apologize."

Her hold on my forearm tightens. "We'll find him, Ollie."

The backs of my eyes sting as my vision blurs. Saliva pools in my mouth as emotion swells in my throat. "How can you be so sure?"

Turning to face me fully, Delilah invades my space, wraps her arms around my middle and hugs me, unlike anyone else since this whole fiasco began. I drop my head to her shoulder, close my eyes, and let my tears fall freely. Delilah hugs me with inconceivable strength as everything I've felt for the past fifty-three days streams down my cheeks. Up and down, Delilah gently strokes between my shoulder blades.

When my tears slow, Delilah inches away to meet my eyes. "Call it intuition, instinct or whatever you want, but I *know* we'll get him back." She takes my hands in hers. "I feel it in my bones."

Unable to speak past the emotion in my throat, I nod.

She strengthens her hold. "This isn't the end. You and Levi will love each other for decades to come."

More tears stain my cheeks as I hold her resolute gaze.

God, I hope she's right.

August 28th

We haven't brought L home yet, but today was a better day. After weeks of no change, we found something in L's computer history. A clue. It's vague as fuck, but it's more than we had yesterday. Right now, any new information is better than nothing at all.

Then we figured out something else. Not sure if it'll lead us in the right direction, but I sure as hell hope so. Almost everyone went missing near the water. In a matter of minutes, the news went out to other law enforcement. T says the Coast Guard and police are flying up and down the coast, over all the smaller bodies of water, and a little inland.

Everyone seems optimistic after the discovery. They're all more animated and energized. But for whatever reason, I'm not. It feels weird to be auspicious so soon. I hold on to hope that we'll find him.

But I don't want to be so clouded by it that we miss something important.

I just need him to come home. I just need to wrap him in my arms and tell him I love him.

My life is pointless without you, moje srce.

TWENTY-SEVEN

LEVI

Day Sixty

A THICK HAND STRANGLES MY BICEP AS I AM GUIDED DOWN A long, narrow corridor. The guard should know he doesn't need to hold me with such a firm grip. He doesn't need to lead me with such force.

Not anymore.

I no longer have the physical strength to fight. I barely have the strength to walk.

Head hung, I stare down my bony frame and wonder if this really is *my* body. My gaze roams over my grimy underwear. Before I was taken, my underwear hugged my waist and thighs. I saw the slight definition of my muscles beneath the fabric. Now, they dangle limply and threaten to fall off my prominent hip bones. Now, the cotton barely grazes my legs.

The evidence of my unsanitary condition paints my skin, coats my hair, tarnishes my breath, and embeds itself under my lengthy nails. Without a doubt, I smell putrid. Lucky for me, I became desensitized to foul odors some time ago.

Glowing lights brighten the corridor and I study the floor and lower walls as we walk.

Pristine white tiles with black grout run the length of the corridor floor. Unlike the location of my first cell, this place smells uncontaminated. Sterile. A blend of chemicals and artificial fragrances. A brighter white than the floor, the walls are spotless. Perfect. As though they have never been touched.

Searing pain erupts in the muscles in my legs and my gait stutters. On my next step, my ankle starts to twist as I plant my foot. I hiss as fire shoots up the side of my shin.

Before I twist it fully and fall face-first onto the floor, the guard tightens his hold and yanks me upright.

He clucks his tongue. "Can't break one of our favorite toys before the big event."

Big event?

I lean into his hold to take some of the weight off my ankle. As we weave through a maze of hallways, I dig into my memories and search for any details about an event.

My memories are thinning cirrostratus clouds. I see them in my mind's eye, but most aren't clear. Many hang on by a thread. The longer I'm isolated and locked away, the quicker I forget things, especially from before.

In the beginning, I recited important facts over and over. Said them with intention. Forced myself to think of something other than my present situation.

But as time moved forward and my future seemed bleaker, I narrowed my focus. I repeated simple things, such as my name and where I'm from. I stowed everything else in the back of my mind and left it for when it was safe to remember.

Now, I need to dig up one of those memories. I need to remember what this big event is and what it means for me.

The guard takes a sharp turn at the next corridor. I stumble and scramble to put one foot in front of the other. Before I get my bearings, he opens a door with a key card and hauls me inside a shiny room.

A man in white scrubs and a dark-blue coat steps into view. His dark eyes scan me head to toe as his lips form a tight line. He shakes his head as his gaze shifts to the guard.

"How many times do I need to speak with Cap about living conditions prior to game day?" The man crosses his arms over his chest and huffs.

Cap?

The guard releases me and throws his hands up next to his face. "Don't get pissy with me, man." He mirrors the other man's posture and cocks a brow. "Cap gives orders and I follow them."

The room goes quiet. My gaze darts between the two men as they have a verbal standoff.

Dropping his arms, the guard inches closer to the man in the scrubs. "We all know what happens when orders aren't followed." The guard lifts his hands and brushes the other man's shoulders before slapping his back. "Get him ready. I hear several offers are on the table for our pretty little spy."

Spy?

How am I a spy?

I don't know if it's morning or night, let alone the day of the week or year. How the hell am I a spy?

A loud *bang* echoes off the metal walls and I jump. My gaze races around the room for the source. When I don't see the guard and notice the door is shut, I assume the noise came from his departure.

"No need for alarm…" The man reaches for my hands and lifts them to read the number on my cuffs. "You're safe in here, Two Sixty-Three."

Safe?

No one in this place is *safe*.

"Come." He walks toward a large steel tub and gestures to it with his hand. "Let's get you washed up."

Glued to the floor, I don't move. I tremble in place as my mind becomes a blob of mushy confusion.

The man cranks the faucet and water flows freely. He sticks his hand beneath the steady stream and adjusts the knobs. Then he adds clear liquid from a nondescript bottle and bubbles puff up and cover the water's surface.

The backs of my eyes sting as I stare at the bath. The tremor in my limbs strengthens.

A bath. I'm going to cry over taking a bath.

Such a simple task, yet a luxury I took for granted my entire life.

With slow, composed steps, the man approaches me with his hands held up. "I'm not here to hurt you, Two Sixty-Three." He reaches for and takes my hand. One foot in front of the other, he walks me to the tub. "The last thing I want to do is cause you pain."

I flinch at his words. A spark crackles in the center of my chest. While anger creeps into my thoughts, my body tries to remember what rage feels like.

I narrow my gaze at him. "This place is hell," I choke out, my voice withered and gravelly. "You people are advocates of the devil."

A solemn look blankets the man's expression. "Like you, I am not here by choice." He turns off the faucet. "I may not be in your position, but I am as much a prisoner as you." Inhaling a deep breath, he gestures to the water. "Now, please, get in the tub. You'll need more than one bath and your time with me is limited."

Stepping away, he gives me his back and privacy. The crackle in my chest from a moment ago softens.

I shove my underwear down, grab the edge of the tub, and

step into the bubbly water. As the heat hits my skin, I hiss through my teeth and grip the tub lip tighter. After a brief pause, I ease myself into the hot water. The temperature is equal parts heaven and hell.

Closing my eyes, I lean back and rest my head on the edge. I filter through my foggy memories and try to remember the last time I took a bath. Maybe when I was a child?

For the first time in what feels like years, I relax. My body weeps and celebrates as the heat soothes my shriveled muscles and the water washes away the thick layer of muck.

What was I trying to remember before the guard brought me in here?

A faint floral fragrance floats in the air and quiets my mind. Exhaustion creeps to the surface and my body unwinds further. For a moment, I get lost in the only peace I've had in who knows how long.

"A washcloth," the man whispers.

I peel my eyes open to see white fabric draped over the lip of the tub. Again, such a simple thing—a square of cotton to help clean your skin—yet I've taken it for granted my entire life.

The man returns to a stool beside a table, opens a file folder, and writes on a paper inside. He pays me no attention as I soak up this temporary bliss and gently wipe the grime from my body.

Once I've scrubbed the areas I can reach, he sidles up to the tub and gently washes my arms and back. He reaches into his pocket, retrieves nail clippers, and cuts my lengthy, jagged fingernails. After a quick dunk of my hair, he tells me to remain in the tub as he drains the darkened water. When it empties, he asks me to cover myself while he rinses the residual dirt in the tub down the drain.

The second bath passes by faster and with more focus. He

hands me a new washcloth with a bar of soap and instructs me to wash what I'm able to reach. After he washes my arms and back, he swaps the bar of soap for a bottle of shampoo. Like a child, he eases me into the water and cleans my hair.

The action fills me with comfort and unease.

When my hair is done, he fetches a towel from the table and sets it on the floor beside the tub. "Do you need help getting out?"

My brows pinch together as I stare at the thinning layer of bubbles. I shake my head.

Returning to the table, he gives me his back once more and writes more inside the file folder.

My chest constricts.

Once I'm dried off, he sets clothes on an empty stool and turns away. My stomach cramps as I stare at the pile of clothes. Since I was taken, all I've worn is the same pair of underwear. Now, I've been given an entire outfit, including shoes.

"Can't break one of our favorite toys before the big event."

The new, pristine room, the bath, the clothes… they are cleaning me up for all the men who visited my cell. They are making me *presentable* for the sadistic perverts.

Acid claws its way up my throat. I press a fist to my stomach and bend at the hips. Unsteady on my feet, I teeter forward and start to tip.

The man wraps an arm around my shoulders and holds me upright. "Shh, Two Sixty-Three."

I wish he'd stop fucking calling me that. My name is…

I close my eyes and pinch them tightly.

What the hell is my name?

Inhaling a shaky breath, I scour my mind.

Levi.

My name is Levi.

The man guides me to a stool and sets me on it. He helps

me put on the underwear and pants. Unlocking one of my cuffs, he hands me the shirt and I tug it over my head. When the cuff is locked again, he gives me the socks and sets the lace-free shoes at my feet.

Once I'm dressed, he reaches for something on the table and hands it to me—a toothbrush. "Let's get you finished up before they return."

I stare at the narrow piece of blue plastic with a small patch of bristles. My vision blurs as I take in yet another simple part of daily life I've forgotten about so easily.

Mint wafts through the air as the man squirts toothpaste on the bristles. As he recaps the tube, I gingerly stick the brush in my mouth.

With gentle strokes, I move it back and forth over my teeth. My gums ache. My teeth wiggle too easily. I pinch my eyes closed as the unbearable pressure of the bristles ripples throughout my jaw. Once I've gone over each tooth, I hand him the toothbrush.

He hands me an empty cup to spit in, then one with water to swish.

After I rinse and spit, I drink the rest of the water.

The door flies open and the guard steps inside. "Almost like new again," he says, a smile in his voice. "Time to go back to your room."

Shuffling me out, he clutches my biceps and thrusts me down the hallway. As we move through the lifeless corridors, I scan the walls for any distinguishing marks. A chip in the paint. A nick in the plaster. Something identifiable that will remind me where I've been inside this endless labyrinth.

Several doors line the next hallway. Roughly six feet apart, each of them is painted with a number. As I read them, my stomach curls in on itself. The numbers in this hallway descend from three hundred.

How many hallways are there?

How many people are shoved in these closet-sized rooms?

How many people have been the same prisoner number as me?

Two hundred seventy-one.

Two hundred seventy.

The sound of countless footsteps steals the quiet.

Two hundred sixty-nine.

Two hundred sixty-eight.

Two hundred sixty-seven.

A deafening *bang* fills the air. I lift my hands to cover my ears.

The hand around my biceps squeezes hard. In an instant, I am dragged down the hall. The door to my cell is whipped open.

Shouts and gunshots ring through the air. Rather than duck, I turn in the direction of the noise. Several people dressed in black storm the hallway.

The guard shoves me in my cell and I fall to the floor. He lifts his gun and fires it at the people in black.

As the door slams shut, I hear someone yell, "Levi!"

TWENTY-EIGHT
OLIVER

The past week has been nothing short of chaos. From the moment Tymber uncovered the lead on Levi's computer, everything switched gears. Moved faster. Became more urgent.

Because time is not on our side.

At least one of us, if not more, is working to discover the location of where Levi had been taken at all hours.

A day and a half ago, the Coast Guard surveyed an unusually high level of activity on a supposedly uninhabited island four to five miles off the coast of central Washington. Several docked boats and yachts, with many others coming and going.

The night of the discovery, law enforcement loitered in a boat far enough from the island to not be seen as they watched the activity level go from high to extreme. Releasing a drone with a night vision camera, they were able to get a better view of what we were up against. They watched as unconscious people of all ages were carried off boats, thrown in a pile on a trailer, and carted off to what appeared to be a door.

With the naked eye, the door was connected to a space barely large enough for three people. After taking the fifth person through the door, law enforcement surmised there was a level beneath the surface. A building beneath the earth and trees. To what extent, no one had a clue.

Yesterday, law enforcement and Tymber made a plan.

Ambush the island, imprison who we can, but take out uncontainable threats, and get inside the door.

Tymber and Travis argued with me when I informed them I was coming along. For hours, we went back and forth. They wanted to keep me safe. They didn't want to worry about me while entering the unknown.

But I didn't back down. I didn't give them a choice.

Like it or not, I would be in the room when we found Levi. Period.

This is why I am now suited up in way too much tactical gear, without a weapon, and following behind Tymber as we wander long, clinical hallways with numerous doors on stealthy feet.

"Levi!" I holler, no longer concerned about being quiet.

We stormed the island fifteen minutes ago. Officers from various law enforcement agencies have taken out or detained no less than thirty individuals—and we've just grazed the surface.

They know we are here, so now it's about finding Levi and freeing the people within these walls.

Pop, pop, pop.

Bullets fly through the air. Bodies fall to the ground—thankfully, none on our side. Alarms wail through the halls at deafening levels. Masked people appear out of thin air with weapons created for war and death.

With hands shaking and anxiety twisting my insides, I push forward.

"Levi!"

The team veers to the side, avoiding a body on the ground. As we reach the masked man, I pause when silver glints from the waist of his pants. I squat and reach for the clip hooked to his belt loop.

Keys. Three brass and three silver. And a key card.

Disobeying orders, I shuffle out of line and move to one of the doors. I flip through the keys on the ring and try to unlock the door.

"Oliver, no." Tymber rests a hand on my shoulder. "We don't know what's behind these doors."

I peer over my shoulder with narrow eyes. "If it's the people who took Levi, don't you think they'd be out here trying to kill us?" I purse my lips. "I'm opening the door."

His fingers curl around my shoulder in either frustration or acquiescence. I don't stop to ask which.

The second brass key slides into the lock and I twist it. A loud click sounds as the key stops. With a twist of the handle, I ease the door open.

Huddled in the corner of a walk-in closet-sized room is a girl in a white sundress too big for her body. Practically a skeleton, she visibly trembles as she tries to blend into the wall.

"You're okay, miss," Tymber says in a voice so soft I'd never guess it was his. "We're here to take you home." He holds his hands up and keeps his distance. "We just need to take care of the bad guys first." Inching back, he grabs a bucket on the floor and props the door open. "Stay here while we do that. Okay?"

She doesn't speak or nod. She doesn't give any indication she heard or understands what's been said.

Tymber backs out of the room and tells someone that there may be victims behind the doors.

I stare at the scared girl for one, two, three ragged breaths. Then I stumble back into the hallway, turn my head, and look at the countless doors.

He's here. Behind one of these doors, I will find him.

The backs of my eyes sting and my vision blurs. I blink the imminent tears away.

"Later," I mumble. "Focus on finding him."

Key firmly in my grip, I move to the next door and unlock it. A woman old enough to be my mother jumps back and starts crying. I grab the bucket in her room and prop the door open. Rather than soothe her with hopeful words, I shuffle to the next door.

One door after another, I unlock the doors and search for Levi. When I reach the last door in this hallway and still don't find him, my heart clenches beneath my sternum.

Then I remind myself that this place is immense.

If I have to open hundreds of doors before I find him, so be it. I refuse to give up. Until Levi is in my arms again, I refuse to let a single part of myself rest.

Rounding the end of the hall and moving to the next, I unlock more doors.

My rib cage strangles my lungs tighter and tighter as I open one door after another and don't find Levi on the other side.

Silence echoes in the air for a split second as the alarm shuts off. Then, all I hear is my jagged breaths and footsteps on the tile.

"I'm here, moje srce," I say, the words garbled and thick with emotion. "And I won't leave without you."

Stepping around a man in a puddle of blood on the floor, I go to the next room. The key slips into the lock and I twist it as I have more than a hundred times already. I open the door and glance into the room, mentally ready to grab the bucket, prop the door, and move to the next.

But as I reach for the bucket, I freeze.

On the floor, legs bent and crushed to his chest, cheek pressed to his knees, Levi rocks back and forth.

"Levi?" His name is a tender question on my tongue as I narrow my eyes and take him in.

The man on the floor doesn't look like Levi. Not *my* Levi. But deep in my bones, I *know* it's him.

In this life and every other possible existence, my soul unequivocally recognizes his.

Every cell in my body screams with joy in finding him. But the delight fades fast. A shiver rolls up my spine and goose bumps erupt on my skin as my eyes roam over him. As I listen to his muted voice as it says something indiscernible.

Uncertain what to say or do, I move the bucket to prop open the door with unhurried movements. As I straighten my spine, I take a tentative step into the room. On the next step, I stand within a foot of him.

He doesn't move, doesn't look up, doesn't pay me a single ounce of attention.

I shove the keys in my pocket, take a slow, deep breath, and bend my knees to squat in front of him.

Levi jerks back and shuffles across the room until his back slams against the wall.

My heart wrenches in my chest as the air evaporates in my lungs.

Every instinct in me says to close the distance between us and comfort him, to wrap him in my arms and tell him he is safe. Every fiber in my makeup says to inch closer and soothe his concerns with calm reassurances and tender touches.

But I can't.

Levi isn't scared. He is downright petrified *of me*.

The last thing I want to do is retreat. But it's not about what I want right now.

Levi needs to not feel threatened, endangered or powerless—three things he has inevitably experienced during his captivity. He needs a sense of safety and strength. He needs the opportunity to dig deep and unearth his fortitude.

Dropping to my hands and knees on the floor, I reluctantly push myself away from him. Less than a foot—I'm unwilling to add any more distance.

"Levi," I whisper as I dip my chin in an attempt to meet his gaze. "It's Ollie."

Eyes on my hands, his cracked lips move over and over, but I still can't hear what he says.

Before we left for the island, law enforcement prepped us for possible scenarios we'd encounter. The biggest situation being how the victims may behave as we happen upon them. Some have been missing more than six months. Others, a few weeks. Unaware of their living conditions or treatment since their disappearance, we had no clue what version of hell we were walking into.

Levi is one of the most courageous and headstrong people I know. But after weeks or months in hell, even the most unyielding of minds can be broken and trampled.

I test the boundary between us and scoot forward an inch or two.

He doesn't flinch and shrink away.

Progress.

"Levi," I murmur, keeping my tone passive and low. With immeasurable restraint, I lift my hand, flip it palm-side up, and extend it toward him. "It's Ollie," I repeat. "I'm here to take you home."

"In the shadows, we hide," he mutters on a loop as he studies my hand.

My heart soars at his words. My words. *My lyrics.*

Thrilled as I am, I school my features and do my

damnedest to remain impassive. The last thing I want to do is spook him.

Wanting to connect with him and earn his dismantled trust, I take a deep breath and whisper a different line from the song.

"Forever mine… until every star falls from the sky."

Lifeless blue eyes flit to mine and narrow. Incredulous, he studies my face for any sign of familiarity. Slowly, he relaxes his limbs and tilts his head. Inching closer but maintaining some distance.

I don't move, don't speak, don't offer anything further. I resist every urge to lunge forward, wrap him in my arms, and press my lips to his.

Levi needs to make the next move. He needs the control that was stolen from him.

"Ollie?"

The backs of my eyes burn and my nose stings as my name leaves his lips. Saliva pools in my mouth as emotion clogs my throat.

Rolling my lips between my teeth, I slowly nod. "Yeah." I blink a few times. "It's me."

His brows and lips twitch as his chin wobbles. "Ollie?" he repeats as though he's unconvinced. "You're really here?"

My vision blurs as a slow, gentle smile tugs at the corners of my mouth. The first tear rolls down my cheek as my hand extended between us trembles. "I'm really here, Levi."

I fight the inclination to call him by the term of endearment I gifted him months ago. Damn, do I fight it.

Not knowing what state any of the victims would be in, we were coached to only speak with them simplistically. We were told to use their name repeatedly—if we knew it—so they would feel a sense of identity. Though it sounded off-putting, we were told to speak with them in a calm, even, plain voice with basic words.

It guts me to talk to him like a frightened child. It shreds my soul to not touch him.

But this isn't about what I *want*; it's about Levi and what he *needs* right now.

Control. Security. Familiarity.

Love.

He scoots closer and lifts his hand. My heart rattles my rib cage as his fingers extend toward mine.

Boots pound the floor behind us and Levi thrusts back. He folds himself in half and wraps his arms around his bent legs. His entire frame shakes as his eyes pinch closed.

"Ollie?" Tymber's voice echoes through the hallway as his shadow casts over me on the floor. "Shit," he mutters.

I hold up my other hand and signal him to stop.

"Levi?" I hate that I have to start again, but I'll do it every minute of every damn day if I need to. "It's okay, Levi." I glance over my shoulder, give Tymber a synthetic smile, then return my gaze to Levi. "Tymber is here."

Levi eases his eyes open and meets my gaze. "Tymber?"

I nod. "Yes."

Levi glances past me and squints. He cranes his head and inches closer once more. "Tymber?" he repeats.

Behind me, Tymber slowly lowers to the floor and makes himself as small and passive as possible. "Hey, Levi." He inhales a deep, shaky breath. "So good to see you, man."

The muscles in my arm burn as it remains lifted between me and Levi. I refuse to lower it. Doing so may make him think I no longer want him or to help him.

Hour-long minutes tick by as he inches across the floor and erases the distance between us. Unwavering, I hold his gaze. My heart thunders in my chest as anxiety flips my stomach upside down. Through every apprehensive second, I maintain cool, collected body language.

"You're taking me home?" Levi asks, needing our assurance.

A rogue tear rolls down my cheek as a corner of my mouth quirks up in a half smile. "Yes, Levi." I nod. "We're taking you home."

His eyes drop to my hand for a beat. He raises his arm, meets my gaze once more, then takes my hand. He curls his cold, thin fingers around my palm and gives it a light squeeze.

My pulse stutters as I inhale a shaky breath.

I found him.

I have him.

I'm bringing him home.

At an unhurried pace, Tymber leads us down the hallway toward the only known way in or out. He walks several paces in front of us, ready to take anyone out with his fists or the baton and Taser on his belt.

As we near the elevator, I caress Levi's hand with slow, steady strokes of my thumb. We pause at the door and I turn to face him.

"We're below ground," I say, then pause, waiting for my statement to register. When a hint of recognition gleams in his eyes, I continue. "We need to take this elevator up to leave. Okay?"

His eyes dart to the door. A light tremor ripples through him and turns into a noticeable shudder within seconds.

"Tymber and I will be with you the entire time." I stroke his knuckles with my thumb. "I promise."

Lips and chin quivering, his gaze returns to mine. "Okay," he whispers.

On a nod, Tymber takes a walkie-talkie out of his pocket and turns it on. Pressing the side button, he holds it close to his mouth and says, "Objective three complete. Coming up elevator now, over."

"Communication received topside, over."

Tymber presses the call button for the elevator. When the doors open, Levi inhales several ragged breaths as he stares at the claustrophobic space.

I stroke his knuckles over and over. "We'll be right beside you the entire time."

His grip on my hand tightens. He clamps down on his lips with his teeth, subtly nods, and takes a tentative step toward the elevator. Seconds turn into minutes, but neither of us rushes Levi. Once we're inside, Tymber presses the button and we ascend to the surface.

As the door opens, Tymber moves in front of us. To not overwhelm Levi further, he creates a temporary barrier until Levi appears comfortable enough to be at the forefront of attention.

Unfortunately, it doesn't stop Levi's parents from rushing us.

"Levi," Mrs. West says, voice shaky. "My sweet boy." She crowds him and reaches for his face.

He rips his hand from mine and stumbles backward, his eyes wide.

"Felicity." Tymber steps between her and Levi and sticks out his arm. "Let him come to you."

She lifts a hand, covers her mouth, and nods. "You're right." Her glassy eyes lock onto Levi. "I'm sorry, Levi. It's just"—she sniffles—"I'm so happy to see you."

Levi comes back to my side, but he doesn't take my hand. My fingers twitch at my side, eager for his touch again. As much as I want to initiate holding his hand, I keep mine pinned to my side and let him decide.

No matter what, he needs to be in control. He must decide what happens next.

"Mom?"

Mrs. West's lips curve up into a shaky smile as tears stream down her cheeks. "Yes, it's Mom."

A complete surprise to everyone, Levi steps away from me and all but runs into his mother's arms. He circles his arms around her middle, tucks his head in the crook of her neck, and sobs as she strokes his hair.

Bitter jealousy sinks its claws into my heart. I stop breathing as I stare at them. My hands shake at my sides. The world wobbles beneath my feet. Imperceptibly, I shake my head over and over. My vision turns hazy as I teeter in place.

Minutes pass by in sobs and loud whooshes.

No one pays me any attention. Not that they should right now.

An unfamiliar cloud of melancholy blankets my soul as a foreign pang expands in my chest.

More people crowd the area as groups of others are brought up from below.

A man croaks out, "Sydney," as a frail young woman passes me toward him and his wife. She looks bewildered. Lost. When he repeats her name, she furrows her brow. Like Levi, she probably hasn't heard her name in months.

I wonder what number was on her door.

After one last glance at Levi as he embraces his mom with unimaginable strength, I avert my gaze, put one foot in front of the other, and head for the boat. On the fifth step, my name echoes through the air.

I pause, close my eyes, inhale deeply, and count to five. Opening my eyes, I school my expression, turn around, and face Levi.

"Yeah?" I feel as empty as the single-word question, but I do my best to not let it show.

Levi releases his mom and moves to stand within arm's reach. "Thank you."

His gratitude is a jagged knife to the heart.

All I want is to hold him, console him, tell him I love him.

But I've been instructed to reserve my emotions. To let him make the first move.

I understand why. Doesn't mean I have to agree with or like the reason.

Tears rim my eyes as I stare into his somber blues and nod. "You're welcome." My voice cracks on the last syllable.

His brow furrows as he crosses his arms and hugs himself.

When I pictured our reunion, it was unclear. Regardless, I never imagined I'd feel so… *dejected*. I never envisioned him embracing his parents and not me. It's a selfish conclusion but one based on our history.

Now that Levi is safe, he needs to heal. And maybe the initial stages of healing don't include me in his life. As much as that hurts, I need to set aside my own desires and let Levi recover in his own ways and time.

My lips curve into a lifeless smile as I lift a hand, wave, then turn on my heel. "See ya." The impersonal farewell shreds my heart and rips apart my soul.

I *feel* his eyes on me until I disappear from view, keeping my gaze forward. I disregard his obvious confusion and choose not to respond to it.

One heavy foot in front of the other, I leave him with his parents and let him decide his future.

Below deck on the boat, I find a vacant corner and press my back to the wall. Sliding down until my ass hits the floor, I draw my legs up and hug them, drop my chin to my chest, and let my tears flow freely.

Time passes in endless footfalls and whispered words.

Law enforcement remains on the island to make arrests and free hundreds of missing people.

Those of us who came for Levi are on a separate boat and preparing to leave this hellscape.

Relief washes over me that we found them. But I'm far from happy.

As the boat picks up speed, Tymber rests a hand on my back. "Give him time, Ollie. He'll come back to you."

I pray he's right.

September 4th

We found him and brought him home. He's safe now. But he's not with me. I know it's shitty of me to be selfish right now, to want him in my arms, my space, at my side, but I can't fucking help it. I missed him so fucking much. I felt incomplete without him. Cold. Faulty. Lifeless.

He chose to embrace his parents. I hate that he picked them over me, but I also understand. They're his family. I'm just me. Either way, my heart fucking hurts.

I'll never forget the fear on his face when I entered that tiny-ass room and got close to him. The way he shot back in terror. It was in complete opposition to his reaction at seeing his mom. He bolted to her and hugged her with a bruising embrace. He hugged his mom as if she was all he needed.

I was lucky I got to hold his hand.

I realize I'm a fucking asshole for feeling jealous.

It's ludicrous of me to want him all to myself after he's experienced the worst trauma of his life. I was delusional to think he'd come back to my apartment and life would slowly drift back to normal.

Doesn't mean it isn't what I wanted. For sixty days, all I've wanted is him by my side again. Safe. If I'm lucky, after a while, maybe those wishes will come true. I need them to come true.

Come back to me, L.

I love you.

I need you.

I don't want a life without you.

TWENTY-NINE

LEVI

I've gone from one prison to another.

Every breath I take, every word I say, every sip of drink and bite of food I swallow… all of it is scrutinized with pensive looks, phony smiles, and subtle tilts of the head.

If I stay in my room for too many hours of the day, my parents whisper about me wanting isolation or confinement. If I leave my room and spend most of the day sitting on a bench alone in the garden, they question in hushed tones if me wandering alone outside is okay this soon after my abduction.

Every aspect of my life is now dissected into micro-moments. Every action—or lack thereof—starts a mumbled debate between my parents.

"How do you feel?"

I'm asked this no less than a hundred times a day.

"What can I get you?"

On the hour from sunrise to sunset, my mom or one of the house staff chime in with this one.

"Do you need more time with Dr. Hampton?"

This question annoys me the most.

When I got off the boat at the Stone Bay marina, my parents

whisked me to the hospital. Within minutes, doctors and nurses crowded around and bombarded me with questions, tubes, and needles. After months of solitary confinement in the dark, limited food and drink, and frequent abuse, I went from skittish to manic in seconds.

Thrashing and screaming, it took several hospital staff members to hold me still and eventually restrain me to the bed. As the last leather strap was secured around my ankle, my mind flashed back to the filthy room I spent the past two months in. I saw the metal cuffs around my wrists and shackles around my ankles. The eyebolt on the floor. I felt every ounce of freedom I'd gained since Oliver opened the door and found me slip away.

Within an hour of my arrival at Stone Bay Memorial, Dr. Gina Hampton entered my room. Speaking in soft tones, she asked my parents to leave the room so she could talk with me in private.

My parents didn't like that.

I wasn't eager to be alone with a stranger so soon, but I also didn't want my parents in the room while the doctor asked me intrusive questions about my abduction.

Every day since my return, I take a seat across from Dr. Hampton, cut myself open verbally, and release some of the demons that haunt me when I close my eyes. For an hour each day, sometimes more than once a day, I relive the darkest moments of my life. Then I do mental exercises to help me move past the terrors I experienced in that grimy, claustrophobic cell. I share how relieved I am to be home but also how frustrated I am with the extreme level of attention.

My parents' incessant invasion of my space makes my heartbeat erratic and my breaths come in short, quick sips. It makes my hands shake and my vision blur. It makes me restless. Fidgety. Angry.

Their endless inquisition and attendance have become a new prison.

For the first time in my life, my parents are attentive without an agenda that benefits them. They tiptoe around me and choose their words wisely. They dote on me in ways I've only seen Oliver's parents treat him.

From grade school to my early teens, I wanted a fragment of this adoration from my parents but never got it.

Now that I'm the center of everything they think, do, or say, I wish they'd just leave me alone.

Not to worry. Their constant affection and consideration won't last.

Soon enough, my relationship with my parents—which I've discussed with Dr. Hampton as my memories have returned—will go back to what it was before. Broken. Distant. Meaningless.

The only relationship I worry over and care about is the one I have with Oliver.

Two weeks have passed since I took Oliver's hand and followed him out of hell. Our exchange was so generic and too short. But if I focus hard enough, I still feel his thumb softly stroking my knuckles. I still feel his warmth and the magnetism that has always existed between us.

That small touch has comforted me often since my return. When the darkness creeps in, I close my eyes and imagine Oliver and his hand holding mine.

But I haven't felt him since that day two weeks ago. Haven't heard the gentle rasp of his voice. Haven't stared into his mesmerizing basil-green eyes and forgotten about the world.

A life without Oliver is less than. Inadequate. Insufficient.

I am a fragment of who I should be without him at my side.

The day before yesterday, a new, relentless pain flared to

life. Beneath my sternum, something snaked around my heart and squeezed until I couldn't breathe. It stole my thoughts and invaded my soul.

When I mentioned it to Dr. Hampton, she said when we release trauma, we make ourselves vulnerable. We revive parts of our life from before and bring it near the forefront. Former emotions surface and blend with the present.

"Life before your trauma will return. It may come in slow drips or a flash flood. The experience is different for everyone. Don't fight what you feel, Levi. Embrace it. Breathe through it. Believe that your version of normal will return with time and patience. Though you won't be the same Levi, you will heal. You will have future happiness."

A fool, I am not.

The next several years will be daunting. Harrowing. The biggest challenge I will ever face.

But it will be worse without Oliver.

"Need to see him," I mutter into my pillow.

A gentle knock sounds on my open door—another thing I'm annoyed by; the lack of privacy—and my body wilts. Without peering over my shoulder, I know it's Mom. Were it my father, the rap of his knuckles would've rattled the wood. My name would've immediately followed in his authoritative baritone.

Although my father has been... compassionate since my return, it'd take a hell of a lot more to change Jefferson Thornhill-West. Had it been my mom that was taken, he would have set the world on fire to get her back. He would have complied with any demands.

Mom rounds the end of my bed. "How are you, darling?"

Ugh.

Sick and fucking tired of being asked how I am, is what I want to tell her.

Instead, I bite my tongue, take a deep breath like Dr. Hampton instructed me to do in these moments, then give my mom a gentle smile I don't feel whatsoever.

"Fine."

Taking a seat near my feet, she rests a hand on my leg.

I flinch.

Her mouth turns down at the corners as she puts her hand in her lap. "Sorry."

I say nothing.

It isn't her fault that touching happens on my terms now. Physical contact must be of my volition.

"Dinner will be ready in ten minutes." She wrings her hands. "It'd be nice if we could all sit together."

Since returning home, I've only left my room for appointments and to sit in the garden sporadically. Dr. Hampton said it was better for my recovery if I was in a familiar place instead of a sterile environment. So last week's therapy sessions and physician follow-ups, the doctors visited the West estate.

During my seventh session with Dr. Hampton—she came to the house two to three times a day, depending on my headspace—I told her the house felt like another prison. I never left my room—not for meals, not to speak with anyone, not to roam the estate. Every time I did, my parents or brother or one of the house staff fawned over me like a wounded creature. They always asked the same monotonous questions. They treated me with unwelcome fragility.

I may have gone through the worst fucking experience of my life, but I am not some brittle, helpless lamb. I don't need or want people to treat me as though I'll break at any moment. And I sure as fuck don't want their pity or uncertainty.

Hell might not have shattered me, but my family may soon.

An inkling of relief coursed through my veins when Dr. Hampton switched all my future appointments to her office.

Like all things in my life right now, there's a downside. Until she gives the all clear, I'm not allowed to drive. Something about possible triggers and flashbacks while I'm behind the wheel.

Whatever.

At least our sessions give me purpose. Something to look forward to. For a few hours each day, I get to leave the house and exist outside the lifeless walls of the West estate.

The biggest, most pathetic highlight of my day.

My days wouldn't be so treacherous if I had entertainment. Some form of stimulation. Something other than the bare walls and bland colors in my old bedroom. I have nothing. No pictures or books. No television, video games or computer. No phone, *dangerous* objects, or access to anyone outside the house. Not without asking my parents.

Prisoner.

I am slowly suffocating in this place.

I need to get out.

Blinking out of my reverie, I glance up at my mother. Hope glints in her eyes as she waits for me to answer.

The last place I want to be is at the dinner table with my family as they blather on about insignificant things. But if I want out of this house anytime soon, I need to *show signs of improvement.*

"I'll come down in a moment," I say after far too long. As the words leave my lips, a knot forms in my belly.

Her lips instantly curve into the brightest smile as the corners of her eyes tip up. She rises from the bed and clamps her hands tighter. "Wonderful." She takes a step away from the bed, then pauses. "I love you, darling."

"Love you too."

As quickly as she entered my room, she disappears.

Swinging my legs off the bed, I sit up and plant my feet on

the floor. Eyes unfocused as I stare out the window, I take several deep breaths to stave off the expanding pang beneath my diaphragm. It helps, but not much.

I curl my toes in the carpet, ground myself, push up to stand, and pad across the room, ignoring the mirror next to the closet as I pass. I don't need a mirror to know I look like shit. Staring down my gaunt frame is evidence enough. Stumbling my first few steps every time I get up to walk is testimony of my feebleness.

I hate how weak I am.

Hand on the rail, I descend the stairs slowly. Several minutes pass as I ease my way down thirty-something steps, but I keep a cool head.

As my bones, muscles and organs recover from malnutrition, starvation and dehydration, my physical activity has been limited. What little mobility I do get in, the stairs are the most gruesome. Painful as it is to traverse from one floor of the house to another, I need the strength training. I need to restore my body to what it was before my life got flipped upside down. And I need to do it in my own time.

On my first day home, my parents offered to bring in a physical therapist. I declined. Wonderful as it would be to recover quicker, the last thing I wanted was one more person to fret over my *delicate state*—my mother's words, not mine. I'm capable of walking and lifting but need to do it at my own pace.

"There you are, darling," my mother says as I enter the formal dining room. "Come"—she rises from her seat, darts to my chair and pulls it out—"sit. It's so nice to have the family together for dinner again."

I open my mouth to ask where Parker is but snap it shut when he enters the room as I sit.

Sharply dressed in a navy-blue suit, Parker is the younger

carbon copy of our father. Entering his junior year of college in a few days, he lives, eats and breathes political science, as does his girlfriend of three years, Brittany. Parker is the epitome of everything my father wanted for my future.

At least one of his children makes him happy.

A few steps behind Parker, Brittany crosses the dining room to my mother and kisses both her cheeks. The joy that radiates off my parents is stifling.

Conversation sparks around the table. Parker and Brittany share their excitement for fall term. Father talks about the boost in tourism with the festival today. Mom shares upcoming events at the performing arts center.

I stare at my salad and try to tune them out.

Two weeks. I've been home for two fucking weeks. After vanishing for two goddamn months, being assaulted and violated and deprived of everything essential, I hugged my mom and put my life in her hands.

It's only been two goddamn weeks and she's talking about some fucking musical. They're all carrying on frivolous conversations as if the most heinous situation in my life didn't fucking happen. They're chatting in light tones with smiles on their faces as if the darkest fucking cloud in existence didn't engulf me and threaten to never let me leave.

Do they give a damn about me? Do they care about the pandemonium swirling in my head? Do they care that I think about my own death no less than a dozen times a day?

"How do you feel?"

"What can I get you?"

"Do you need more time with Dr. Hampton?"

Is that what they pay the long line of doctors for? Thousands of dollars to strangers who futz over me and get me back to my "old self." Meanwhile, the rest of the West family resumes a worry-free life.

Pain stabs my palms as my fingers curl into tight fists in my lap. Heat crawls up my neck and spreads across my cheeks. My heart hammers in my chest as the rapid *whoosh, whoosh, whoosh* of my pulse clogs my ears.

I'm so fucking angry I could scream.

"Sorry I'm late."

Momentarily confused at the new voice, I loosen my fists.

Heels clap on the marble as I lift my gaze and follow the swish of blue fabric. My eyes reach her face as she pulls out the chair to my left. A bright, cheerful smile lights her expression.

"Hi," Abigail says with too much enthusiasm.

My nails dig deeper into my palms as I grind my molars. Fire licks my veins. Madness grabs hold of my rib cage and rattles the walls of my chest viciously.

"What the fuck are you doing here?"

"Levi," Father snaps.

"Jefferson," Mom retorts.

"I... uh..." Every ounce of light vanishes from Abigail's eyes. "Your parents thought—"

"Thought what?" I cut her off, my eyes darting to my mother then my father. "Maybe we can mold Levi into someone he's not because he's fucked in the head," I say in a mocking tone as I wave my hands. "Maybe he'll forget who he was, and we can manipulate him into what *we* want."

"Levi..." Devastation blankets my name as Mom reaches for my hand.

Shoving back in my chair, it topples to the floor as I stand. "No!" One wobbly step followed by another, I back away from the table and shake my head as my eyes go from one person to the next. "I'm not a goddamn puppet." I slap a hand to my chest and fist the fabric. Close my eyes, take a deep breath, then open them on the exhale. "Don't use my abduction as a tool to turn me into someone I'm not."

"Son, we aren't—"

"Yes"—I aim all my anger at my father and his deadpan expression—"you are." I drag my fingers through my hair and savagely tug the strands. "Why the fuck is she here?" I thrust a hand toward Abigail. "She isn't *family*. She doesn't belong at this table."

Mom scoots her chair back and slowly stands. "We just thought it'd be nice to have someone familiar at dinner."

Fury ripples through my body and I visibly shake as I take another step away from the table. "Then invite my fucking boyfriend," I grit out.

"The way you let him go..." Mom shakes her head. "We weren't sure..."

I can't be here anymore. Imprisoned and having people forced upon me, it's almost worse than that dark, dingy cell.

Without a second thought, I spin on my heel, stagger on the first few steps, then regain my footing as I dash for the front door. Footsteps echo in the foyer as my name floats through the air on repeat. I ignore them, push harder, whip the door open, and step outside.

I suck in a sharp breath as the brisk September air hits my skin. Streaks of pink and orange paint the sky as the sun dips below the horizon. My eyes dart from one car to the next in front of the main house and I mentally stumble over what to do now.

My feet trudge forward of their own accord. Down the steps, past the line of cars, along the drive, I put one foot in front of the other. I pick up speed and put as much distance as possible between me and the house.

I veer left, abandon the driveway, and traverse the manicured lawn. Goose bumps dance over my skin as I spot the pool house several yards away. Cicadas chirp as I reach the forestry surrounding the West property and enter the woods.

Sticks and foliage crunch beneath my bare feet as I weave through the trees. Crisp, piney air fills my lungs and energizes my soul as I move on faster feet.

Streetlights peek through the trees. The hum of passing cars hits my ears as I approach the property fence. Following the eight-foot chain link, I stare through the trees on the opposite side and look for a landmark. When the soft glow of Poke the Yolk's sign comes into view, I scale the fence.

Unsure where to go, I wander along Chalcedony and stare inside businesses as I pass. Many on this stretch of the road are closed now, but some stores and restaurants are brightly lit with patrons coming and going.

It's calm. Desolate. Quiet.

Too quiet.

When I reach Garnet, I go right and cut over to Granite. People mill about the sidewalk. Cars occupy most of the parking spaces along the street. The cacophony of countless conversations mingles with a hint of music.

Earlier this week, Dr. Hampton said crowds and loud noise were something I needed to ease into. That they may frighten or disorient me. Trigger bad memories.

But as I stand in the middle of dozens of residents and visitors, all I feel in this moment is free. As people pass me on the sidewalk and pay me no attention, all I am is *normal*. Just Levi.

I pause, close my eyes, and inhale deeply. Let the hustle of everyday life blanket me head to toe. Let it restore one of a thousand facets of my life.

God, I've missed this.

Being average and inconsequential.

On my next breath, I zero in on the faint sound of music. Angle my head and figure out where it's coming from.

Eyes popping open, I trek down the sidewalk with unfamiliar speed and determination. My pulse whooshes in my ears and the muscles in my legs are on fire as I dart through the crowd. The *thump, thump, thump* of a bass drum reverberates in the air as I near Sloppy's BBQ.

I know that bassline.

The music rattles the storefronts as the crowd grows. Hot cider, cocoa or various local brews are sipped. Burgers, barbecue, pizza, a variety of Asian street foods, and countless sweet treats are devoured. People sing and dance and enjoy the start of fall with a smile on their faces.

I cross to the other side of the street and zigzag between bodies toward the music.

The song ends and I freeze. Cheers erupt and drown out whatever's being said to the crowd. Then, generic music floats through the air.

No.

I shove through the crowd. A few people throw curses in my direction, but I ignore them. I keep moving forward.

Minutes feel like hours. The drum doesn't thunder again.

My breaths come in jagged bursts. The muscles of my legs are ready to give out. Invisible fingers wrap around my heart and curl into a fist, squeezing, shredding, pulverizing.

I smack into a hard chest and bounce back.

"Sorry." I shake my head and step to the side.

"Levi?"

I freeze at the sound of my name and lift my gaze. When my eyes lock onto my favorite shade of green, the ground wobbles beneath my feet.

Oliver.

THIRTY

OLIVER

For three staggering, disbelieving heartbeats, I thought I was seeing things. Wouldn't be the first time since July.

Then I said his name and he stopped.

Levi.

He's here.

Why is he here? Who brought him?

I quickly scan the crowd and don't spot any familiar faces. My attention is back on him in a blink.

Fuck, I've missed him. So goddamn much. For months, I have been hollow. A shell. A soul without purpose or heart or animation.

Without Levi, I am not alive. Just merely existing.

Indecision mars his brow as his blue eyes roam my face. The crowd, the town, the world fades into white noise. Under his inquisitive stare, thrill courses through my veins for the first time in months. As he takes in every curve, dip and angle of my profile, I do the same of his.

Shorter than he typically wears it and a bit unruly—as if he's run his fingers through it repeatedly—Levi's hair skims the middle of his forehead. The natural shine and temptation in his blue irises are absent, a glum, matte-blue in its place. Bruisy crescents paint the skin beneath his eyes. A faint shadow darkens his sunken cheeks and bony jaw. Although he's gained weight in the past two weeks, he appears frail and unsteady.

God, I want to touch him.

A simple brush of my finger against his. Maybe a lift of my hand to gently caress his cheek.

I want to wrap my arms around him, pin him to my chest, and reacquaint myself with the way his body molds against mine. I want to breathe in his clean, cedar scent, embed it in my senses and memory, and never forget it. I want to press my lips to his and kiss him with profound tenderness.

More than anything, I want to tell him how much I love him. How much I miss him. How it feels like I can't fucking breathe without him.

Instead, I stand statue-still with my lips sealed.

Levi must be in control of his life going forward. He may need help with certain aspects while he heals, but ultimately, he should be at the helm of his future.

With what he's been through, I refuse to be the person who steals his choices. As desperate as I am to have Levi in my life, the decision isn't mine to make.

Shuffling closer and standing within inches of me, he licks his lips, tucks them between his teeth, swallows and releases them. On a shaky inhale, his eyes dart between mine. "I need you."

The backs of my eyes sting as I nod woodenly. Saliva floods in my mouth as my breath catches in my throat. I swallow and blink a few times, not wanting to cry and distress him.

In the small space between us, I lift and offer my hand. His gaze drops. For a beat, he stares at my hand. I don't breathe, don't move, don't say a word.

I just wait.

His blues lock onto my greens as his fingers curl around my hand. With one simple touch, one easy connection, the earth steadies beneath my feet. He laces his fingers with mine and I instantly feel whole.

"We can go back to my place." I jerk my head in the general direction of my house. If we shortcut through the trees, we'll reach the stairs to my loft apartment in no time.

Levi nods. "Let's go."

I tighten my hold on his hand. "Need to text Trip and Hailey. So they know to pack up my drums."

"We don't have to go now." His breathing picks up as his eyes dart to the crowd.

"Hey." I caress his knuckles with my thumb and wait for his gaze to meet mine. Inching closer to him, I whisper, "Moje srce."

Blue eyes flash to mine. A hint of that luster I've missed so damn much rims his irises. A glint of his passion simmers just beneath the surface.

"I promise they won't be upset."

With a gentle tug, I take one step, then another, and slowly guide us through the crowd. When we reach the clearing beside the stage, I pull out my phone and type a text in the Hailey's Fire group chat. Levi tries to release my hand so I can type with both.

Not a chance in hell.

I strengthen my hold on him, but not in a possessive or controlling way.

> Bumped into Levi. Headed back to my place. You cool to pack up my shit?

> HAILEY
> Go. We got you.

TRIP

Absolutely. Chat later.

I shove my phone back in my pocket. "All good."

We follow a faint footpath through the trees and come out on my street a few minutes later. Two houses down, we climb the stairs that lead to my apartment above the garage.

Levi doesn't let go of my hand the entire time.

It only makes me want to hug him, kiss him, *love him* more.

Unlocking the door, I gesture for Levi to go in first. Hands inseparable, I shuffle in behind him and ease the door shut but don't lock it. For a moment, we loiter in the small entryway.

At his side, I peer up at his profile. Watch him as he takes in the space with a new perspective. Study his nuances as he steps into the home we shared briefly.

I trail the pad of my thumb over his knuckles. "Hungry?"

He blinks then turns to meet my gaze. "Yeah."

The longer he looks at me, the more I see hints of the old Levi. No matter what, though, he will always be *my* Levi.

"Anything sound good?"

His expression brightens. The corner of his mouth twitches, a half smile tugging up his lips for a second.

Damn, I missed his smile.

"I would kill for some pizza and a Pepsi."

Laughter bubbles in my chest and spills from my lips. God, it feels good to laugh again.

Pulling out my phone, I call the pizza place around the corner. With the fall festival crowd and the main drag of Granite Parkway closed, it'll take forever to get here, but I don't care.

"Hey, Jenny, it's Ollie."

The manager rambles on about the crowd and jokes about running out of cheese. As often as I order, I'd usually go back and forth with her or give her a hard time about business being so good.

But not tonight.

"Can I order a couple pizzas and sodas for delivery?"

"It'll be an hour or more."

Glued at my side, his hand still in mine, Levi visually roams the apartment.

"Not a problem."

"Okay. Fine."

"I need a Pepsi, Cherry Coke, and two large pizzas, both with roasted garlic, grilled onions, and pineapple."

Levi's gaze snaps to mine. I don't hear anything Jenny says.

"That's all," I say, hoping it answers whatever she asked. "Cash." I rattle off my phone number and address then disconnect the call.

"You didn't have to do that," Levi whispers, his brows twitching and chin quivering.

I shrug. "You know I'll eat any kind of pizza." I stroke the length of his thumb with mine. "But yours is my favorite."

His fingers threaded with mine, grip impossibly tight. "Thanks… I guess."

"You have good taste." I tip my head toward the couch. "Want to sit?"

He gives a gentle tug of my hand and leads me across the room. Warmth floods my chest as we sit and his thigh brushes mine. Still connected, he strengthens his hold.

His gaze drops to our hands as he lifts his other and starts tracing my fingers, my knuckles, and up to my wrist. Fire dances under my skin where he touches me. Electricity crackles in my veins and wakes dormant parts of my body. My pulse zings and my breathing stutters as he caresses me with unmatched tenderness.

I open my mouth to tell him how much I missed his touch but snap it shut when he speaks up first.

"There's no good time to do this…"

My heart falls to my feet.

No.

"I want to tell you about… my abduction."

Mentally, I sag with relief. Not that hearing about his time in captivity is something I relish. But it sure as hell beats what I thought he was going to say—that he didn't want to be together.

Lifting my other hand, I cradle both of his. "Only if you want to."

A sad smile mars his expression as his blues connect with my greens. "I don't really *want* to." He rolls his lips between his teeth. "But I *need* to." He audibly inhales. "Does that make sense?"

I hug his hands with mine and methodically nod.

And until the food arrives, Levi shares every dark and horrid detail of his abduction. The entire hour and eighteen minutes, I listen to every word. I give him every ounce of my attention. I keep my emotions at bay and don't let my feelings overshadow his.

Traumatic as it is for him to say and relive, agonizing as it is for me to hear and not yank him into my arms and drown him in love, we both live through his retelling of the past two and a half months.

When I deposit the pizza, soda, and two glasses with ice on the coffee table, our first slices get eaten slowly in silence. Midway through the second, he speaks up again.

"I want the impossible."

Covering my full mouth, I ask, "What do you mean?"

He huffs out a laugh. "Normal. All I want is my version of normal."

I wipe my mouth and sit straighter. "May seem impossible right now." My hand twitches at my side, eager to touch him, comfort him, give him strength. Rather than take his hand, I press my leg to his and give him some of my weight. Give him a modicum of love and courage through the innocent contact. "But we'll find normal again." I swallow. "Together."

He leans back and his arm presses against mine. Then he drops his head on my shoulder and melts into my side.

My nose and the backs of my eyes sting. A charm of hummingbirds takes flight in my chest. One shaky breath followed by another; I rest my head on his and close my eyes.

Damn, I fucking love him.

"How do you say *my forever* in Bosnian?"

I blink away my tears and scrunch my brows together. "Uh… the translation is a bit different. More like *mine forever*. Moj zauvjek."

He inches back, sits up straight, and holds me captive with glassy blue eyes. "Help me find normal again, moj zauvjek."

Without thinking, I cup his cheek. Stroke his prominent cheekbone ever so gently with my thumb and nod. "Until my last breath, moje srce."

THIRTY-ONE

LEVI

My knee bounces as I sit on the edge of Oliver's bed—*our* bed—and give myself a mental pep talk. So far, all it is doing is making me more antsy. No matter what I think or say or do, I can't seem to sit still this morning.

And it pisses me off.

I rest my hands on the tops of my thighs and press down. "Just stop," I mutter under my breath. Pinching my eyes closed, I will this ceaseless burst of energy into extinction.

As if my mind wants to torture me further, my knee bounces faster.

Just. Fucking. Stop.

I ease my eyes open, clamp my thighs just above the knees, and exhale my frustration.

Across the room, with the door open, Oliver drags a razor down the thick layer of shaving cream along his jaw. Every other stroke, he leans closer to the mirror and angles his chin down or up or off to the side. He appears so at ease—with himself, with me, with life.

I'd kill for a fraction of his tranquility.

Eyes fixed on his hands, his fingers, the way he shifts his

lips as he shaves around them, a sense of calm soothes some of my fidgety nerves. Enough to make my foot settle and knee relax.

Oliver. He has always been a balm for my soul.

Needing further distraction from my restless thoughts, I rake my eyes down his body.

Towel hanging low on his hips, water drips from his curly hair and dots his chiseled chest. Corded muscles in his arms flex as he swipes the razor over his skin then waves it under running water. Setting the razor down, he wets a washcloth and rubs off any residual shaving cream.

Pivoting, he exits the bathroom, pads across the room, and goes to the small walk-in closet. Just before he steps inside, he tugs the towel free and flashes me his sculpted ass.

My skin heats at the sight. My cock twitches beneath my zipper. An undeniable hum courses through my veins.

Fuck, I want him.

So damn much.

But every time I attempt to do anything more than hold his hand or caress his cheek or lean into a side embrace, memories from *then* invade the present and I nosedive into a panic attack.

Almost four goddamn weeks of therapy and normal hugs still freak me out. I can barely touch Oliver or be touched by him without seeing the sadistic motherfuckers that came into my cell and violated me.

Why can't I erase the nightmares from my mind? Why can't I move forward and forget those horrific sixty days?

A hug. All I want is a hug from my boyfriend. Warm arms wrapped around my middle. Strong chest pressed to mine. Nose in the crook of my neck as he breathes me in. Undeniable love radiating between us.

I miss the feel of him in my arms. The way his body

molds perfectly to mine every time. The way he knows exactly how to hold me in every moment. Gentle or strong or greedy.

I miss the taste of him on my tongue. The way every kiss with Oliver is as potent and heady and addictive as the first. His moans that tell me he needs more. His whimpers as I deepen the kiss and push us further.

I miss how everything clicks into place when we're connected in every possible way. How the world completely disappears. How everything is perfect when he's inside me, or I'm inside him.

Before *that night*, I miss the way we were before then.

The only way to get back there is to heal and resume life as it once was. Not fully. One manageable step at a time is how I rediscover *normal* and take back my life.

A little more than a week ago, I bolted from my parents' house. Wandered the streets until I bumped into Oliver. Thought I was hallucinating when he called my name.

For the first time in weeks, I wasn't seeing things. *Thank god.*

He brought me back to his apartment—*our* apartment—and made me feel safe. At home for the first time in weeks. With his hand in mine, he eased some of my burdens. Not expecting anything in return, he shouldered some of my weight. And after I cut myself open and spilled the atrocities of the last two months, he promised to help me find normal again. Together.

That night, I took my first step toward normal. I made my address the same as his. Again.

Today, the next big step is walking through the front door of TWSIS.

By no means am I ready to dive into work. But I do want to find a daily routine of sorts. Part of that routine includes easing back into a job I love—even if I'm only doing grunt work for months.

"Ready?" Oliver asks as he steps out of the closet in jeans, a Poke the Yolk T-shirt, and black Vans. A hoodie draped over his shoulder.

I love how Oliver doesn't question my decision to go to work today. How he doesn't try to steer me away from activities or places or people.

If anything, he supports my decisions. Even encourages them.

When I brought up work a few nights ago, Oliver told me Tymber comes into Poke the Yolk every morning, orders the same thing, then mentions how much he misses me in the office. Not my work. Not my financial worth to the company. *Me*.

His relayed message would've come across as endearing to some. For me, it said I was wanted. Necessary. That my absence didn't go unnoticed. I am more than just some whiz behind a computer screen.

One simple message further solidified my resolve.

More than his support, I love that Oliver doesn't *push*. He doesn't ask what I will be doing in the office. He doesn't sprinkle everything I want to do with doubt. He doesn't suggest activities I dislike because they're *good for recovery*.

Oliver trusts me to make the right decisions for myself.

And it's his confidence in me that makes me love him even more.

"Mm-hmm." I rise from the bed, grab one of his hoodies from the closet, tug it over my head and inhale deeply, then meet him at the door.

We jog down the stairs to his car and I scan our surroundings. He unlocks it with the fob as I round the hood for the passenger side, hop in, and lock the doors. As I click my seat belt in place, he cranks the engine and tugs on his hoodie. While we wait for the car to warm up, I connect my phone to the stereo and scroll through playlists.

Much to my dismay, it's still recommended I don't get behind the wheel.

Dr. Hampton says we'll do a test drive in a week or two. But until she gives the all clear, my parents have hidden the keys to my car and bolted the garage.

On the upside, my replacement driver's license, bank cards, and cell phone arrived at Oliver's—*our*—place a few days ago. Although I don't currently *need* any of them, holding those small plastic rectangles and having more accessibility to the world gives me a sense of normalcy and inclusivity.

I select a playlist I haven't listened to in over a year, set my phone in my lap, melt into the seat, and let the music drown out my incessant thoughts.

Oliver reverses out of the driveway, shifts gears, then reaches across the console and takes my hand in his. The entire drive to Poke the Yolk, his thumb gently strokes the length of my knuckles and assuages my anxiety.

Dawn barely colors the sky as we exit the car and cross the lot for the employee entrance of the restaurant. Inside, Oliver peels off his hoodie, hangs it on a hook, then fetches an apron.

"Come on." He tilts his head toward the open door separating the office from the kitchen.

I've been back here a couple times—weekend days when Oliver closed—but never when Max, one of the cooks, was on the clock.

"Morning, Max."

Peeking over her shoulder, her brows tug together. She lifts her wrist, checks her watch, then narrows her eyes at Oliver. "You're early." Turning back to the griddle, she flips pancakes and eggs. "Should I get used to it?"

Oliver scoffs. "Not if you're smart."

She holds up a spatula. "Noted. Breakfast?"

"Please." Oliver prattles off his order then looks to me. "Whatever you want. You can take it for later."

Food has been a weird subject since my return.

Doctors talked with me at length on how to ease back into normal eating habits. They gave me a list of *gentle* foods—whatever the hell that means—and when I should introduce heavier items into my diet.

My parents hired a chef exclusively for me. They wanted to make sure the doctor's list was strictly adhered to. If the list said vegetable soup for dinner five times a week, that's what was delivered to my room.

I hated those damn food lists.

Oliver is oblivious to the doctor's recommendations.

With the exception of the night of the Fall Fest, when he ordered pizza with my favorite toppings, he lets me choose what I eat. Most days, it's Emina's dishes for breakfast and Nero's massive entrées for dinner. Belly ache be damned, I clear my plate during every meal.

"French toast, scrambled eggs, and turkey sausage."

"On it." Max holds up her spatula again, shaking it twice.

Oliver fills two mugs with coffee and we take a seat at the small table in the back. Kirsten enters the kitchen and chats with us for a moment. Like Oliver, she doesn't ask how I am. Like me, she knows what it's like to be under the microscope after a traumatic situation.

We eat breakfast in relative, comfortable silence. Oliver clears his plate, but I save a slice of French toast and sausage link for later.

With my leftovers in a box and a to-go cup filled with coffee, I squeeze Oliver's hand and tell him I'll see him when his shift ends. Wanting to avoid the town gossip mill, I exit through the back. Surveying my surroundings, I cross the lot and head for the street.

TWSIS doesn't unlock its front door for another hour, but I spot Tymber's car in the lot as I dash across Opal Trail.

The nervous energy I had an hour ago flares back to life. Only now, it's accompanied by skepticism and insecurity.

Can I do this?

Can I walk back into TWSIS and not lose my shit?

Can I work there without reliving the horrors I unearthed while hunting for the person who eventually became my captor?

Will I ever be able to sit behind a computer screen again?

Will I be able to do what I love without constant flashbacks?

Only time will tell. But I pray I don't lose another piece of myself to those assholes.

I take a seat across from Tymber on a couch in his office. "I have no expectations for my first day back." Dropping my chin to my chest, I stare at my fumbling fingers a moment before I shove them beneath my thighs.

"This place is as much your baby as it is mine."

The backs of my eyes sting as I meet his gaze. "Means a lot." Nodding, I roll my lips between my teeth.

"Just glad you're home."

Home.

Yes, this place is as much my home as Oliver. Just a different type of home.

"Any idea what you want to do today?"

I shake my head. "Thought I'd loiter for a bit. See what calls to me."

My gaze shifts to the cluster of screens over his desk and a torrent of anxiety swells beneath my diaphragm. I inhale a shaky breath and meet his tired eyes.

"It'll be a while before I'm online again," I admit.

"Not worried about it." A strained smile curves the corners of his mouth. "With the big case closed, things are much quieter now."

Unsure what to say, I take a sip of my coffee.

"The case files have been removed from your office." He shrugs. "In case you'd like to go in there and clean."

Maybe that's what I need right now. To wipe the slate clean. Erase anything that may trigger my time away.

And I can start by scrubbing any evidence of that case from my office.

The paperwork may be gone, but the hours I spent at my desk, sifting through the darkest recesses of the world, poison the air and walls and furniture. Before I dive back into work, I need to eradicate the hell I brought to light.

———

"Five hours and this place is unrecognizable." Tymber whistles as he glances around my office.

"Still have lots to do, but it's a start."

Moving closer to Tymber, I cross my arms over my chest and scan the room. Give today's work a thorough once-over.

Compared to my previous setup, no one would think this is my office.

Which is exactly what I need.

Clean slate.

Tymber points to the desk in the middle of the room. "Don't move that on your own, man." He reaches behind himself and rubs a hand up and down his lower back. "Back pain isn't just for old people."

I want to laugh. I want to tease him and tell him he *is* old, even though five years is all that separates us in age.

But I do neither.

Instead, I blurt, "How did you figure out where I was?"

Beside me, Tymber stiffens.

The temperature in the room plummets.

The topic I've spent the better part of four weeks avoiding is thrust center stage, *by me*.

Tymber slowly turns to face me, his expression guarded. "Levi, I…" He lifts a hand to the back of his neck and squeezes. His gaze falls to the floor for one, two, three breaths before meeting mine again. "I'll never keep shit from you." Dropping his hand, he crosses his arms over his chest. "You're like a brother."

I wait for him to continue, but several minutes pass in silence.

"But…"

Something akin to familial love passes over his face. "I don't want to be a source of pain."

The back of my eyes sting. "Appreciate it." I sniffle and swallow past the sudden swell of emotion. "But I need this." I roll my eyes. "If therapy has taught me anything, it's that I need to conquer my demons in order to heal and move forward."

Tymber tips his head toward the couch and chairs shoved together. "We should sit down."

THIRTY-TWO

LEVI

"How was work, dear?" Oliver asks in a teasing tone as I slide into the passenger seat.

Without hesitation, I laugh. And Oliver… melts at the sight.

Damn, it feels good to laugh.

A hint of a smile on my lips, I shake my head. "Busy. Cathartic."

"Busy?"

"Mm-hmm." I buckle my seat belt. "Spent most of the day rearranging my office."

He steers the car out of the lot, then takes my hand. "Definitely busy." Weaving our fingers together, he gives them a gentle squeeze. "Get everything where you want it?"

"No. I did make progress, though."

His thumb strokes the length of mine, up and down, over and over. "Good. Can't wait to see it when you're done."

Leaning into the headrest, I roll my head to look at him. *Really* look at him.

His eyes may be on the road, but I know he sees me in his

periphery. When the corner of his mouth quirks up, he proves me right.

Our relationship may not have picked up where it left off in July, but I don't doubt we will find our way back to that version of us.

Time and patience.

Seven years ago, Oliver came into my life. Unbeknownst to him, he consumed every thought, fantasy, and future wish. Before either of us gave our feelings a voice, I knew—deep in my bones—Oliver and I would eventually be together.

Even then, I felt the way his eyes studied my profile, the column of my throat, my ass when he thought I wasn't paying attention.

Whenever Oliver is near, I pay attention. Always have. Always will.

Back then, I concealed my frequent stares with dimly lit rooms. Masked my desires by talking about anything other than sex and relationships. Disguised my yearning for more than friendship but kept him closer than anyone else in my life.

Now, I ogle him without shame. Touch him without fear of consequence. Love him out in the open.

Our physical relationship may not be what it was months ago, but we will find our way back to that place. With Oliver, love is timeless. Limitless. Eternal.

Although my lips won't form the words since my return, I love Oliver Moss.

Moj zauvjek.

Mine forever.

"Dinner with my folks? Or just us tonight?" He throws the car in park and cuts the engine.

I love Mama and Papa Moss. They are complete opposites of my parents. Warm and gentle and giving. Open and affectionate and inspirational. Down to earth and accepting and supportive.

I am forever grateful for them. Not only for their generosity and love but also for the remarkable person they brought into the world. The man I get to call mine.

"Will they be upset if we eat alone tonight?"

His basil-green eyes hold mine as he slowly shakes his head. "Never." A smile softens his expression. "Want me to go snag us dinner from the main kitchen? They won't mind."

I will never turn down Mama or Papa Moss's cooking. "If they won't mind."

Oliver squeezes my hand then releases it as he opens his door. "I'll be up in a moment."

While he jogs toward the door leading into the main house, I exit the car and slowly make my way up to our apartment. Our sanctuary.

Although it quiets more each day, I still hear the boom in my father's authoritative voice from a week ago.

"You will not leave this house."

I didn't want a confrontation with my family, but anticipated nothing less when I asked Oliver to drive to the estate. The clothes I'd brought to the apartment months ago still had a place in the closet. But I wanted to get the last of my things—clothes, art, notebooks, things from college. Most of it is replaceable, but I didn't want my parents to have anything to use as a tool to lure me back.

For weeks, my father played the doting, concerned parent role well. Gentle embraces, hushed words, and frequent smiles —they were a juxtaposition to the man I'd known my entire life. It's said that trauma impacts loved ones as much as victims. With each sentiment and kind act, I believed my abduction changed my father for good.

The moment my courage surfaced, the moment I made a

decision he didn't agree with, he tried to bully me into submission. With one ugly demand from his lips, he not only made me feel like a prisoner again, but he also erased every positive ideology I had for him.

One day, years from now, I hope we find even ground.

Jefferson Thornhill-West isn't a bad man. He just has underlying issues he needs to overcome. At least he and Mom seem more accepting of my relationship with Oliver.

As I plop down on the couch, the door opens and Oliver comes in with a small casserole dish. Garlic and lemon perfume the air, and my stomach growls.

He sets the dish on the kitchen counter. "Linguine and clams." From the cabinet, he grabs two wide, shallow bowls. "Snagged a chunk of parmesan too."

Warmth blooms on my skin as I rise from the couch. Eyes on Oliver as he divvies seafood pasta, my heart pounds faster, harder beneath my sternum. He reaches for the grater and the backs of my eyes sting.

My sudden onslaught of emotion isn't about him catering to me or stealing cheese from his parents' kitchen. The tears in my vision and swell in my throat are for his attention to detail.

Oliver doesn't ask me my favorite color or style of music or food dish. He doesn't need to. For years, Oliver has watched every little thing I do. Same as I do him. Without asking, he learns all the things that matter. He picks up on my pet peeves and preferences.

When you love someone, you commit every little piece of them to memory. You do everything within your power to make them feel seen, heard and adored. You love them without reservation or expectation.

I sidle up to him, lean into him, and drop my head on his shoulder. My eyes roll closed as I inhale deeply.

He rests his head on mine and we stand there, unmoving, for a beat.

Moj zauvjek.

Pressing his lips to my hair, he hums. "Let's eat."

I breathe in his leather and musk scent, lift my head, and nod. "I'll grab drinks."

Random movie playing on the television, we eat dinner on the couch. When the last of the daylight fades, Oliver reaches for the lamp on the side table and flips it on.

Empty bowls on the table, I give him my weight and rest my head on his shoulder again. He takes my hand, entwines our fingers, and lays his head on mine.

One breath, one heartbeat, one minute at a time, Oliver replaces the darkness with light and warmth and love. For as long as we live, I vow to give him as much, if not more, in return.

My champion.

My heart.

My soul.

Moj zauvjek.

Neither of us moves as the credits roll up the screen. Were it not for his occasional lazy strokes on my hand, I'd assume he'd fallen asleep. Like me, he is enjoying the physical contact. The intimacy. The small step toward the old us.

And I'm about to pop the bubble.

Heart hammering in my chest, I whisper, "I want to go back."

He shifts and gives me a little more of his weight. "Hmm?"

I close my eyes and inhale a shaky breath. "Where you found me. I want to go back."

Oliver stiffens for one, two, three erratic heartbeats before he softens. "Why?" His voice is hoarse as the single word scratches my ears.

"I wasn't in that place long, but I think seeing what's left of it will help me move on."

To my knowledge, the grimy, rancid prison I spent most of my time in hasn't been located. If it has, the details are under lock and key. Which is fine by me. Not a chance in hell I'd set foot in those walls ever again.

Oliver tightens his hold, lifts our joined hands, and cradles them to his chest. His breaths come in short, fast, audible bursts. His heart hammers beneath our clasped hands.

"I…" he starts then stops.

It wasn't just me in hell for months. Oliver existed in his own version too.

But I need this. To see the place vacant and dismantled. To know that no one else will be stripped apart by those assholes and treated as though their lives, their personhood doesn't matter.

I nuzzle into the crook of his neck. "Please." Clutching the hem of his shirt with my free hand, I fist the fabric and anchor myself to him.

Inhaling a shuddering breath, he brings our joined hands to his lips. "That place holds bad memories for me too."

I'd be a fool to think otherwise. "I know."

"You're not going alone." He shakes his head over and over.

Lifting my head from his shoulder, I stare at his backlit profile and wait. Minute-long seconds tick by before he chastely kisses my fingers then twists to meet my waiting gaze.

His glassy green eyes stop my heart. Rob me of oxygen. Have me gripping his hand with impossible strength. Heartache and despair shape the tears threatening to fall down his cheeks.

I release his shirt and lift my hand to his cheek. Cup his jaw and caress his stubbled skin.

I love you. Why can't I say the fucking words?

"Not a chance in hell I'd go alone."

"I have conditions."

A tear rolls down his cheek and I wipe it away.

"Good."

He sniffles. "A group of us goes." Concern mars his features. "I don't trust either of us to be okay."

Valid point. My abduction impacted us both, just differently.

"Reasonable request." I nod.

Blinking away his tears, he swallows and sits a bit straighter. "First sign you're triggered, we're turning around and coming home." Resolution shapes his tone, but it doesn't come across as a demand. Every ounce of his inflection comes from a place of love.

"Okay."

He visibly relaxes at my acquiescence. The muscles of his jaw soften as his tongue peeks out to lick his lips.

"You tell Dr. Hampton before we go," he whispers.

As much as I hate the idea—because she may try to stop me—Oliver is right. Plus, she may offer advice on how to approach the situation.

"I'll call her in the morning."

"We wait until the weekend." He leans into my touch. "So I can coordinate with everyone."

Five days feels so far away and too soon at the same time.

Returning to the small island off the coast is a big step toward closing this horrific chapter in my life. And his. We can't go in without a plan. I need to prepare mentally. So does Oliver.

The nightmares that rob us of sleep each night may not be the same, but they center around the same situation.

In five days, we may be able to start healing.

"This weekend." I nod.

Oliver twists and presses his lips to my palm. "Let's go to bed."

For the first time in months, I dreamlessly sleep through the night.

THIRTY-THREE
OLIVER

The boat teeters as we surge over choppy waves. I clutch the rail and dig my heels more into the floorboard. In front of me, Levi does the same, his knuckles blanching around the metal.

Is this a good idea?

Returning to the place of living, breathing nightmares… is this the right decision?

When Levi mentioned the trip to Dr. Hampton, she offered to come along. To be a neutral party and guide him through his feelings as they surface. To be another person he can lean on while he seeks liberation from what will haunt him for years to come.

Naturally, Levi declined her offer. But he promised to speak with her as soon as we dock in Stone Bay.

Levi insisted on as few people as possible. I did my damnedest to fulfill his request.

The plan was to only invite Travis and Tymber. But the moment I asked Travis if we could use his family's boat, Kirsten wanted to know why. In the middle of Poke the Yolk, I leaned in close and whispered the plan. The first words out of Kirsten's mouth were, *"Sky, Dee Dee, and I are coming too."*

Yesterday afternoon, I learned Lawrence and Phoebe were tagging along.

I love how everyone wants to support Levi and be at his side as he works through his trauma. Our friends are incredible.

However, the entire drive home from work yesterday, I feared his reaction to the news. When I told him over dinner, he was less bothered than I foresaw.

Maybe it's because Skylar, Kirsten, Delilah, and I have been friends for years. Maybe it's because he's spent time with all of us together or in smaller groups countless times and we are more his family than the people who share his blood.

Whatever the reason, I'm glad he accepts the extra support when he needs it most.

A hand on my shoulder steals my attention. I glance back to see Kirsten, a sympathetic smile on her face.

Leaning in so only I hear her, she says, "Trav says we're a couple miles away. With the waves, maybe twenty-five to thirty minutes."

When she inches back and meets my eyes, I nod and mouth, "Thank you."

I shuffle closer to Levi but don't crowd him at the bow. Resting my free hand on his waist, I tell him without words that I am here and not going anywhere. Ever so slightly, he presses his weight into my hand.

Less than ten minutes pass before the faint shape of tall evergreens breaks up the horizon. In another five, it's easy to discern the island—a little over a mile long and three-quarters wide. With its jagged rock face and dense forestry, an onlooker would think the small stretch of land uninhabitable.

Which made it the perfect place for illicit activity.

The boat banks a little left and Levi reaches for my hand. As we circle around the island and approach a hidden alcove with sporadic docks, my hand loses feeling as his fingers curl around mine with ineffable strength. When the boat slows and the motor quiets, Levi's audible, rapid breathing hits my ears.

With a gentle clutch of his hip, I step into him, my front a breath away from his back. "I'm here, moje srce." I rest my forehead on the back of his head and breathe him in. "I've got you." I press my lips to his hair. "I'm not going anywhere."

His hand on mine tightens, his silent way of saying thank you.

Travis eases the boat next to one of the long wooden docks and ties off the boat. One at a time, we disembark the boat and wait.

As discussed ahead of our trip, we will let Levi guide every step of this journey. Although we were all impacted by what happened, our side of the story is tame compared to what Levi experienced. Coming back to this place, triggering his memories, must be on his terms every step of the way.

Levi takes my hand and laces our fingers. Like a pebble skipped across the water's surface, trembling ripples from his body to mine. I absorb those apprehensive vibrations and blanket them with love. Stroke the length of his thumb with mine as I study his profile and wait for his next move. Send every ounce of strength and courage from my body to his as his eyes scan the trees.

No one moves, no one says a word. In a semicircle around Levi, we shower him with endless support.

And then, he takes his first step toward the island.

This early in the day—the sun shining brightly overhead, the wind whipping through the trees, and various wildlife milling about—the place appears less ominous. Doesn't change how any of us see it. None of us will look at this island or others like it without unease.

We step off the dock and follow a path created by small vehicles. Pine needles and twigs crunch under our boots as we wander through the thin forestry into a denser canopy. Salt, earth and pine linger in the air. Birds squawk overhead. The occasional chipmunk scurries through the brush.

It's all very… disorienting.

Levi pauses and I whip my attention to his face. His eyes widen, and I follow his line of sight to see a small structure through the trees.

Where did that come from?

I scan the woods and spot another similar building farther out. Too nice to be a shack built by the homeless, but meager enough that the inhabitant isn't cozy.

Travis clears his throat. "Guard stations." He sidles up to me and points in a different direction. "The island has several, but most are near the main door."

With my attention focused on finding Levi the last time I was here, I missed the finer details of my surroundings.

"They're being dismantled like everything else," he adds.

Good. Everything those assholes built needs to burn.

We trek the path farther. Gradually, the trees start to thin again.

Levi shakes so hard it rattles my bones. His fingers crush mine as his breathing picks up.

One foot in front of the other, we approach a solitary door with narrow, tall walls around it. An elevator shaft to the darkest parts of the underworld. No one presses forward without Levi taking a step first.

Levi peers past me to Travis. "Are we—" He closes his eyes, inhales a deep breath, and swallows as he meets Travis's patient gaze. "Are we able to go inside?"

With a well-practiced, emotionless expression, Travis nods. "Law enforcement hasn't shut off the power yet. Until everything is deconstructed and filled in, we still have access."

Shifting his gaze back to the door, Levi secures his hold on my hand. "I need to go down there," he whispers. "If only for a minute, I need to see it's truly over." Resilience coats his final words.

After years of pining, sexual frustration, sleepless nights, unimaginable obstacles, and the world trying to rip us apart, I didn't think I could love Levi more. I've never been more wrong.

As he straightens his spine and walks toward the elevator that leads to the desolate halls of misery, fire expands in my chest. A blaze so powerful it robs me of breath. Clenches my heart. Jolts my soul. A firestorm constructed by love and bravery and perseverance. An indestructible force that forms a protective shield around us.

Our scars may never fully heal, but we will overcome this part of our journey. Together.

Shuffling into the elevator, Levi presses the button and we descend. Hour-long seconds pass as we wait to reach the bottom.

Levi's faint quivers transition into full-fledge tremors as a ding echoes through the elevator car. The second the doors open, Levi dashes out and tugs me along. As everyone steps out, Levi pauses and stares at the sterile, lifeless walls.

His jagged breaths grow louder, a soft, pained whimper edging each exhale. He crushes my bones in his grip. A steady *tap, tap, tap* bounces off the walls as his tremors make his teeth clatter.

I lean into him. "I'm right here, moje srce," I assure him. "The entire time, I'll be right next to you." I rest the side of my head on his. "We leave when you want to. Just say the word."

Giving me some of his weight, he nods. "Thank you."

Several minutes pass before his tremors calm to a soft vibration. He lifts his head, swallows, then takes a step toward one of the numerous hallways. When he reads the number on the first door, he backtracks and moves to another hallway. The one where they kept him.

Eerie silence fills the stagnant air as Levi leads us to his final prison cell. The closet-sized room where I found him a month ago.

As we near the door, his feet move faster and more unsteadily. My pulse whooshes in my ears as my vision tunnels to *the* door.

God, he was so fucking scared and perplexed when I stepped into the room. A complete juxtaposition to the strong and brilliant man I've known for years.

But I refused to leave this shithole without him.

Only death will rip us apart. Even then, my soul will raze the universe to find his.

Inches from the propped open door, Levi stops and stares at one piece in his hellscape puzzle. The last piece.

I wait for his next move, ready for anything.

Instead of pushing the door open like I expect, he drops to his knees and pulls me down with him. Releasing his hold on me, he brings his hands to his face as he starts to rock in place. A sob rips from his throat and echoes off the walls.

I don't think, don't hesitate, don't hold back as I wrap him in my arms and hold him tighter than comprehensible. He doesn't shove me away. His feet slide out from beneath him and he collapses in my arms, giving me all his weight.

"You're safe. I've got you," I whisper over and over as I lull him. Tears stain my cheeks as I kiss his hair. "I love you. I love you. I love you."

We cry on the floor for almost an hour before Levi quiets.

He sits up and wipes his cheeks. Takes a deep breath, then another. On shaky legs, he rises, takes my hand, and walks toward the elevator.

"Let's go home."

October 5th

Today was hard as fuck. I wanted to puke several times, but kept my shit together for L. Until he broke down and cried more than I've seen anyone cry in my life. Other than calling Dr. H, he's been quiet since we left. He's probably processing. I sure as hell am. I just hope he comes to me if he needs to get anything off his chest. I hope he knows I'll be there for him no matter what. More than anything, I hope today helps both of us move forward. L deserves peace and love. I hope he knows he'll always have both with me.

THIRTY-FOUR

LEVI

"How's work been this week?" Dr. Hampton asks, pen in hand and poised over the pad on her lap.

Last week, I told Tymber I was done filling time with random tasks in the office. With a strained smile on his face, he said he was excited to have me online again.

I will be the first to admit I'm not ready for a job that will consume every waking hour of my life. But I am ready to get back to what I love most—helping others by putting my knowledge and skills to use.

In the month since my return to TWSIS, I'd revamped my office three times, organized the supply closet twice, rummaged through the breakroom, thrown away several expired and questionable food items, and coached each employee no less than two full days each.

The past four weeks of low-stress tasks and zero pressure were exactly what I needed to ease myself back into my old work routine. I remained active with the team and contributed to the company I helped build.

As of two days ago, I am back at my desk and doing what I love… with minor restrictions.

"Great." I cross my legs at the ankles. "Dusting off the cogs a bit, but it's nice to be back and have a sense of purpose."

"What about the workload?"

Here is where the restrictions come into play. Limitations *I* put in place.

"Minimal." A sardonic huff leaves my lips. "But that's my doing."

"We haven't talked much about your schedule from before. By your reaction, I assume this is not what you're used to." She scribbles notes on the pad.

I shove my hands in the front pocket of my hoodie—Oliver's hoodie—and clamp my fingers painfully. "Not at all. Most of my workdays were ten to twelve hours long. Depending on the project, sometimes I'd work from home after I left the office." I shrug and purse my lips. "I love what I do."

A soft smile tips up the corners of her mouth. "It doesn't always feel like work when we love what we do."

"Exactly."

"Does work feel different now?"

"A little." I shift my attention to the window and stare at the evergreens lining the bay. "I still love it."

I pause, but Dr. Hampton doesn't push me to continue. Instead, she lets me decide when to speak and how much to say. The backs of my eyes sting as I consider my next words.

"After what happened, parts of the job seem trivial."

"How so?"

With Dr. Hampton's expertise, I've been able to process what happened without guilt or shame. She has taught me how to find the smallest shred of positivity in each moment as we work through my experience. Every time I have a nightmare or flashback, I follow one of several mental exercises she has taught me. Rather than surrender my energy to the horrors I lived through, I channel my attention on what and who is important. I breathe through the dark memories, tell myself they are in the past, and remind myself I am safe and home now. Then, I focus on something positive in my life. It's not a slow process, and I do my best not to rush it.

Some days, the exercises work. Other times, the images are too vivid, too front of mind, too gruesome to forget.

Oliver has been my rock and guiding light through everything. When a panic attack or nightmare surfaces, he centers me with softly spoken words and gentle touches. A simple reminder he is by my side. But as we attempt to move forward, our lives ease back into our former routines. Which means it is impossible to spend all hours of the day together.

Thankfully, the other solid friendship I have is with my business partner. Tymber is more like a brother than a colleague, and I'm fortunate to have met him years ago. Like Oliver, Tymber gives me freedom to breathe and make my own decisions. But when I need extra support, he steps up without hesitation.

After a nightmare or flashback, I see the world through a different lens. Frivolous activities and situations no longer hold the same weight they once did. And that perspective has bled into every facet of my life, including work.

"I work at one of the top up-and-coming security and investigative companies in the Northwest." I scoff. "Because of me, one of the biggest known human trafficking rings was shut down." Tipping my head back, I stare at the ceiling and take a deep breath. "Chasing potentially unfaithful spouses seems like a foolish waste of time and resources now." I level my gaze and roll my lips between my teeth. "But I'm also terrified to work on a case as heavy as my last."

Dr. Hampton jots notes on her pad. Eyes narrowed and lips bunched, her expression turns curious. "I'm unfamiliar with the logistics of your company, but is it possible for *you* to specialize in an area of security or investigations?"

My vision blurs a moment as I tilt my head left then right. "It's never been brought up before, but I suppose it's possible. Why?"

Gathering the pad and pen, she sets them on the table beside her chair and clasps her hands in her lap. "If there's one thing I've learned over the years, it's that everyone heals differently and in their own time. We've been working together close to two months and your progress has been remarkable."

When Dr. Hampton remains silent a moment, I say, "But…"

A kind smile lights her expression. "I think you would truly benefit from working on cases where you reunite people rather than unearth a scandal."

I mull over the idea. Abductions aren't something I'm quite ready to handle yet, but Dr. Hampton probably has a different concept in mind. "I like the idea, but kidnappings are… off the table. For now."

Her eyes soften. "It may be years before you're comfortable with darker cases, and that's normal. I'd anticipate nothing less. I was thinking more along the lines of helping a loved one find someone they haven't seen or spoken to in years due to a discord between other family members." She sits straighter and crosses one leg over the other. "It would fulfill your desire to help others, as well as make a positive impact—for them and you."

I repeat her words in my head over and over. The idea has merit; the more I consider it, the more a new warmth blooms in my chest. A mixture of intuition and passion. Of purpose and courage. Now that it's out in the open, I'd be a fool to ignore it.

"I'll talk it over with Tymber." I nod.

"Wonderful." She reaches for her pen and paper. "Let's discuss more personal topics now."

I pull my hands from the hoodie pocket and stuff them beneath my thighs.

"Have you spent more time with other people?" She flips through her notes and reads an entry from a previous session. "A couple weeks ago, you mentioned a cookout with friends."

The day flashes in my mind.

A little more than a week after we visited the island off the coast, Skylar and Lawrence hosted a gathering at their house. It was the same group that'd been on the boat, the same people Oliver has been friends with for a while.

So, I said yes to the invitation.

The day had its ups and downs.

"Overall, it was a nice time." I take a deep breath and count to ten. "But after a few hours, I became restless. I wanted to leave but didn't want to force Ollie to go." I smile. "He was having a good time."

"But you weren't anymore?"

I shake my head. "Out of nowhere, it went from casual and comfortable to overwhelming."

"What happened next?"

My heart races beneath my sternum as my tipping point resurfaces. "I don't know exactly how it happened, but one of the guys snuck up on one of the ladies. It was meant to be funny." My brows scrunch together. "She screamed so loud." I close my eyes as my stomach twists in knots. "I fell off my chair and curled in on myself on the ground."

Dr. Hampton writes on the paper. "What ran through your mind in that moment?"

"Flashbacks of the screams I'd hear over the music before a guard came to my cell."

"How long did the flashback last?"

I uncross my legs and my knee immediately bounces. "Felt like hours but Ollie says it was less than a minute."

"Did any specific word or action bring you back to the present?"

My foot settles on the floor and my knee stops as I nod. "Oliver." I audibly exhale as my pulse settles. "Well, more like his arms around me mixed with the scent of his cologne."

She adds more to the pad. "Often, it's easier to figure out what will trigger past trauma. Similar sounds, places, smells, circumstances or sights. But many don't consider the ways to diminish or eliminate a trigger. Obviously, we won't know what will activate those memories until it happens. That's the unfortunate part. But we can work on how to come back to the present when they do happen."

"How?"

"You said it was Oliver's hold and scent that helped."

I nod.

"Oliver is one of your pillars. He provides you with comfort, strength, freedom, courage, security, and love—all things that were taken from you during your abduction. His embrace and smell are pleasurable to you. A happy trigger, if you will. They remind you that you're home, safe, and with him. Does that make sense?"

I never looked at it from that angle. "Yes."

"An exercise I'd like you to practice over the next couple of weeks is learning other happy triggers. Not just with Oliver, but anyone you spend considerable time with. This way, you have more than one person to help bring you back to the present. Also, many people use an object to ground them when triggers occur. A touchstone. It can be any object—a stone, coin, jewelry, etcetera. Find something you can always keep on you."

I nod.

"Last appointment, you mentioned your relationship with Oliver was good but that you missed how it was prior to your abduction. Has there been any change?"

My knee starts to bounce again. "Still good. Pretty much the same." I clutch the underside of my thighs. "I want us to get a place of our own but haven't told him."

"What holds you back from asking?"

Fear of rejection. Him thinking it's silly or too soon. Me not getting better and it causing a rift between us.

The fact that I can't fucking tell him I love him.

"I'm worried he won't want to and it'll be the start of the end."

Again, she sets her pen and paper aside. Scooting to the edge of her seat, a soft smile grazes her lips. "It's normal to fear losing someone you love, Levi. You've told me quite a bit about Oliver. I may not know him the way you do, but I have a strong enough picture of him to believe it'd take a true force of nature for him to walk away from you."

"I don't want him to say yes and not mean it."

"Then tell him as much."

Sounds too easy. Too good to be true.

"Is there more to it?"

As usual, Dr. Hampton knows me better than I know myself.

"He's told me several times since I've been back that he loves me." I drop my gaze to my lap. "But I can't say the damn words to him."

"How does the idea of saying the words make you feel right now?"

Taking a deep breath, I test the words in my head.

Ollie, I love you.

Nervous energy swirls beneath my diaphragm. I close my eyes and focus on the sensation. Break it into parts. Dissect it until I reach the missing or tattered piece. After a moment, an unwelcome thought crosses my mind.

What if I say it and he thinks it's not genuine? What if he thinks I'm saying it to appease him?

"Jittery."

"Do you know why?"

I inhale a lungful of air and answer on the exhale. "I've never questioned the way Ollie feels about me or how I feel about him." I clamp my lips between my teeth until it hurts. "But what if he questions my feelings now? What if he thinks my *I love yous* are from a place of obligation? What if he thinks I'm saying I love you to cope?"

"I want you to picture Oliver."

I close my eyes. "Okay."

"In your mind, ask him any or all of those questions. How would the Oliver you know respond?"

Tears sting the backs of my eyes as I open them. "He'd cup my cheeks, look me square in the eye, and tell me he knows how I feel. Then, he'd tell me he loves me."

Warmth radiates off Dr. Hampton as she gives me a kind smile. "You have your answer." She glances at her watch, then gathers her pen and paper. "Often, people spend a lot of time brewing over what they think someone will say rather than having an open conversation and hearing how the other person feels. Over time, that supposition grows and festers until it's unmanageable and they explode. By then, they're so stuck on a false ideology it's difficult to believe the truth. Even from the source."

The truth of her words is a punch to the solar plexus. It renders me speechless, breathless, thoughtless.

Dr. Hampton rises from her chair. "In addition to learning more about your happy triggers and finding a touchstone, I'd like you to have an open conversation with Oliver about what we've discussed today."

Rising from my seat, I follow her to the door. "Okay."

"Talk through any nervousness at your own pace. And remember that you don't have to discuss everything in one conversation. It's okay to break them into smaller, more manageable chats."

"Thanks, Doc."

She rests a hand on my shoulder. "You're welcome. I'm here if you need me." With a smile, her hand falls away. "See you on Monday."

I exit her office, scan the parking lot, then dash to my car—another piece of normal I got back ten days ago—a few spaces away. Unlocking it, I slide behind the wheel, lock the doors, and crank the engine. After I secure my seat belt, I scan the lot again and reverse out of the space.

As I drive through town, I mull over how to broach the subject of moving with Oliver. I also practice saying I love you out loud several times while I'm alone.

The jittery sensation roars to life in my chest again, but this time it feels different. Almost as though I'm telling Oliver I love him for the first time.

"I love you, Ollie," I say for the umpteenth time as I park in the empty driveway. This time, the words come out stronger.

I can do this.

Because I have Oliver, I can do anything.

THIRTY-FIVE

OLIVER

Engine idling, I sit in my car in the driveway and stare at the back of Levi's car. The corner of my mouth twitches as I recall countless times we drove out of Stone Bay and flew down the highway without a care in the world. Just me and him with the wind in our hair, music cranked up, and the comfort we have always had with each other.

Damn, I miss those carefree days. A lot.

Without a doubt, we will have more wild and easygoing days in the future. Navigating the unknown until that time comes is a true labor of love.

But Levi is worth the wait.

I cut the engine, grab the bag on the passenger seat, and open the door. Locking the car with a press of the fob, I jog up the stairs to the apartment, enter my code and push through the front door.

Across the open floor plan, Levi sits on the couch in a daze. Eyes fixed on the television, he watches the screen but doesn't appear to be paying attention to the show. Maybe working half a day for his appointment put him in a funk. Half days are weird like that.

"Hey," I say, stepping farther into the apartment. I hold up the bag and shake it. "Hungry?"

He blinks a few times then meets my gaze. "Yeah. I could eat."

I wander to the kitchen and set the bag down on the counter, pulling out a couple food boxes. As I grab plates from the cabinet, my mind wanders off.

Will it always be like this with us now? Us tiptoeing around reality.

Less than two months have passed since we rescued Levi from hell. It's been less than a month since we returned to the only location he knows and connects to his trauma. Compared to the day he left that horrific place, he is immeasurably better. Every day, I glimpse more and more of the former Levi.

Then why the hell is my mind so insistent on us fast-forwarding past the hard stuff? Why the hell am I not mentally giving him the grace he deserves? What kind of person does it make me, wanting our relationship and lives to go back to the way they were before? To move forward as if those things didn't happen.

A huge fucking asshole, that's what kind.

Breathe. We will find normal again.

Guilt gnaws at my insides as I divvy the food onto our plates. Shame slithers through my veins as I do my best not to compare our relationship before to how it is now.

Patience. I need to practice more patience.

Closing my eyes, I inhale a slow, methodical breath and focus on the positives. A handful of good things that make me smile.

Positive: Levi is here with me by choice.

Positive: I can touch him more without him trembling or pulling away.

Positive: Although it's modest, I see the small efforts he is putting in *for himself and us.*

Positive: Every day, I get to wake up beside him and fall asleep with him curled into my side.

Positive: I love him. God, do I love him.

The last thought overrides every shitty thought I had a moment ago. It squashes and buries them deep in the earth.

I love him, and that is what matters.

Carrying the plates to the couch, I offer one to Levi then take a seat next to him. "How was work?" Then, I shove a forkful of savory stuffed French toast in my mouth.

I make a point not to ask about his therapy sessions. Not because I don't care about them. More like it isn't my place to pry about them. Levi's sessions with Dr. Hampton are private. A safe space for him to discuss difficulties and be vulnerable about things impacting his life. If he wants to talk about his sessions with me, he must be the one to broach the topic. He must take the first step.

"Good." He bites the end of a piece of bacon. "A little dull since I left after a few hours."

"Yeah." I chuckle. "Remember back in high school when we loved short days?" I shove another chunk of French toast between my lips, cover my mouth with my hand, and continue. "We'd spend the rest of the day playing video—"

"Let's move in together," Levi blurts, then sets his plate on the table.

Brows scrunched and eyes narrowed, I meet his waiting gaze. "I..." I set my plate next to his and wipe my hands on my pants. "We... already live together," I say, confusion saturating each of my words.

Levi twists in his seat and his knee bumps my thigh. He reaches for and takes my hands with his. When he drops his gaze to our hands, I do the same.

Lazily, his thumbs stroke back and forth over my knuckles. With each pass, a fresh spark lights under my skin. I lock onto the action, refusing to blink, not wanting to miss a single second.

Since his return, this is one of the few times Levi has initiated physical intimacy. I refuse to miss a single second.

"Yes, we live together already."

In my periphery, he lifts his chin. I peek up to see his eyes on my profile. Slowly, I level my gaze to meet his.

"But I want a place that is *ours*. I want a place that we choose. A place that we paint and decorate and do all that couple-y shit in."

"Couple-y shit?" I laugh and inch closer to him.

The corner of his mouth tips up slightly. "I want a place that can be a fresh start for us both." He rolls his lips between his teeth a moment. "Ollie, this place holds so many firsts for me and us. But I want more firsts with you. Not that we couldn't have some of them here." He shakes his head. "But I think in order for me to truly get over some of my mental hurdles, I need a new space and room to grow."

My apartment above the garage doesn't hold bad memories. Not that I recall. But I also see how these walls flaunt our past, like framed photos. I love so many of the good memories we created here, but I understand how Levi may feel inadequate because he is no longer the same person in those older images.

"You hate the idea, don't you?"

I flip my hands and take his, giving his fingers a gentle squeeze. "No, moje srce. I'm just trying to see it through your eyes."

The television plays in the background as our food goes cold on the table. Neither of us cares.

"Today was good with Dr. Hampton."

I stop breathing and snap my attention to him. Every possible distraction fades away as I focus on Levi.

"We discussed work and how it felt to be back. She gave me a great idea of how to blend work with helping others. More on that later." Levi's eyes dart between mine as a subtle smile tips up one corner of his mouth. "But then we talked about how things are with you and me."

My rib cage constricts as my heart hammers beneath my sternum. With a faint gasp, I wait for him to say more.

"I told her I wanted us to get our own place but that I hadn't brought it up with you. The good doctor that she is, she asked why." His fingers draw shaky lines over my skin as he pins me with his devastating blue eyes. "Because I'm fucking petrified you'll say no and we won't be the same."

Every muscle in my body reacts, eager to reach for him, wrap him in my arms, and never let go. But I keep my hands in his. Wait for him to finish sharing his vulnerabilities.

"The thought of losing you..." He slowly shakes his head over and over. "It scares me more than anything."

"I'm not going anywhere," I vow. "Not now. Not ever."

"I hear you and believe you." His face screws up. "But there's this small voice in the back of my head that makes me question everything." He releases my hands, curls his into fists, and shakes them near his chest. "For fucking months, they drilled it into my head that I had no one. That I was unworthy of happiness or love or freedom." His voice grows louder, harsher, angrier with every word. "That I was trash. A plaything. A punching bag." He pushes to his feet and paces the room. "I fucking hate that I can't make that damn voice go away."

With measured moves, I rise from my seat and round the table. I mentally prepare for countless scenarios. But mostly, I just want to stay close and present as he unleashes his frustrations and anger.

"How do I make it go away, Ollie?" he pleads as his fingers dive into his hair.

I take a step in his direction. "Every time you hear that voice, I want to know. No matter where we are, what we're doing, who we're with, if you hear that voice, you tell me. If we're not together, you call or text." I take another step. "In return, I'll remind you of what's real. I'll replace those falsehoods with open, honest truths. Even if they're uncomfortable."

"You swear?"

I close the distance between us, take his hands in mine, and pour every ounce of strength, love, and courage from my heart into his. "Forever, moje srce."

He nods. "There's one more thing."

Lifting a hand to his jaw, I stroke his soft, fuller cheek and follow the action with my eyes. "What's that?"

He takes a deep breath and waits until my gaze meets his. A little more of that shimmer has returned to his addictive blues. Oh, how I've missed that sparkle.

"I love you," he whispers.

My eyes widen a beat before my vision blurs. Joy and thrill and love expand in my chest. My heart throbs and weeps and bursts with euphoria. As I open my mouth to say those three little yet enormous words back, I stumble. Swallowing past the emotion, I part my lips and try again.

"I love you so fucking much, moje srce. Until my last breath."

He drops his forehead to rest on mine. "Moj zauvjek."

Mine forever.

Then he takes me by surprise, erases the breath between us and presses his lips to mine. Every cell in my body sparks to life and melts simultaneously. The kiss is chaste, gentle, his lips softly caressing mine. But fuck… it is everything.

Badly as I want to deepen the kiss, I resist the urge. There is something to be said about subtle, sweet kisses. It is a promise and a tease and slow worship. It speaks from the heart and soul.

I love every kiss Levi has given me, but right now, after he said he loves me for the first time in too many months, this kiss is my favorite.

Too soon, he breaks the kiss and inhales a shaky breath. "Thank you."

My brows tug together. "Why are you thanking me?"

Soft, stilted laughter leaves his lips. "I'm a fucking mess, Ollie." He reaches up and cups my cheek. "And you're still here."

"Where else would I be?"

"Anywhere." He shrugs. "But you stayed."

"I stayed."

"I love you, Ollie." His thumb strokes my cheek. "I've wanted to say that for weeks, but it wouldn't come out."

Fisting his shirt, I haul him into my chest. "I won't lie; hearing the words makes it more real. But Levi"—I rest my hand over his on my cheek—"I've always known how you felt, even when neither of us said it."

His eyes glaze over. "Really?"

"Yeah." I nod. "As for the other thing"—I inhale deeply, count to three, and exhale—"yes."

Confusion mars his brow. "Yes?"

Slowly, I eliminate the space between our mouths and kiss him chastely. "Let's find a place of our own."

October 30th

After all the chaos, after all the ups and downs, life feels less heavy and uncertain. For the first time in months, L told me he loves me. When I told him I knew, it wasn't a lie. It's nice to hear the words. It's nice to feel different versions of his affection. But he is part of me and I am part of him. His pain is my pain. His love is my love. His soul is my soul. There isn't a damn thing on earth that will change this. Forever my love. Forever moje srce.

EPILOGUE
LEVI

I TAKE A DEEP BREATH AND TIGHTEN MY HOLD ON OLIVER'S HAND. In return, he gives me subtle reassurances with small strokes of his thumb along the length of mine.

Those gentle caresses are my favorite.

With a single touch, without saying a word, Oliver soothes my anxiety. A true balm to my soul, he always knows the right thing to say or do in every moment.

Hundreds of people mill about at the amphitheater. The aroma of salty and sweet fried treats floats through the air. Balloons are blown and twisted into animals, hats, or swords. People wait in lines for the dunk tank, jumbo-sized Jenga and Connect 4, Twister with the dots painted on the grass, cornhole, and more. Laughter and buoyant conversation blend with loud music played by a local DJ.

The pre-summer sun warms our skin and boosts everyone's mood. The entire town and countless tourists are present and excited for Stone Bay's annual Memorial Day festival.

As for me, I'm equal parts thrilled and uneasy.

Since mid-October, Oliver has helped me ease into group social situations. Most of them involved our core friends—Skylar, Lawrence, Kirsten, Travis, Delilah, and Phoebe. Occasionally, Delilah's siblings would join the fold and share a meal or celebration with us. What I love most about our circle is we don't treat each other differently because of past circumstances.

Some of us have been through crazy shit. Those moments changed our outlook on life. Opened our eyes and made us see just how precious life is. Earlier this year, Skylar, Kirsten, Delilah, and I joked about forming our own recovery group. Just the four of us. Soon thereafter, I got a message from Delilah—a group chat text.

DEE DEE

For those moments when we need to get heavy stuff off our chest

The chat gets used a couple times a month. Most of the conversations are about things we have discussed with our significant other but want comfort from someone who has been in our shoes.

"My stomach is ready to eat itself. What about yours?" Oliver's question snaps me out of my introspection.

"Yeah. Skimped on breakfast so I could eat my weight in grease and sugar today." I chuckle.

God, it feels good to laugh easily now.

"Brats, shrimp, donut burgers, tacos, some fancy French word I can't pronounce," Oliver says as he points to different food tents. "Ooh, the bacon and potato tent."

He tightens his grip and hauls me toward the mile-long line.

"Nervous about playing today?"

Hailey's Fire has played a handful of shows since Dalton's

on July 5th. When I was taken, everything band-related was canceled until further notice. No shows. No band practices. Hell, I hadn't heard Oliver play anything on his own until a few months ago.

As much as I wanted to ask him why, I never did. Deep down, I knew the answer. His need to distance himself from his music had many layers. It's difficult to write or play something when your mind isn't in the right headspace. Like other creative art forms, you have to *feel* it, connect with it. Otherwise, it falls flat.

"A little." Oliver tips his head from side to side. "I *know* I can do it. The Fall Fest and shows we've played at Dalton's over the past few months prove as much." He shrugs. "Just feels weird to be on a big stage again."

"I'll be front and center if it helps."

Oliver, Trip, and Hailey managed to convince the event coordinators—my mom and Marilyn Langston—to make a VIP section right in front of the stage. Enough space for our group and select family members to sit close and enjoy Hailey's Fire comfortably without fighting the crowd.

Turning into my side, Oliver rests his chin on my shoulder. "It does."

We shuffle forward in line. I point to the chalkboard menu as it comes into view. "What sounds good?"

"All of it." He laughs. "But I shouldn't eat too much before we play." He straightens and studies the options. "Hmm. Maybe the loaded potato tornado." Leaning back into my side, he kisses my neck. "What about you?"

I tilt my head from side to side as I decide between my top two choices. "The pierogi sampler." I nod.

Minutes later, we place our order. When Oliver's name is called, we both go wide-eyed as we take in the huge portions.

"Let's go find everyone and chill for a bit."

Winding our way through the crowd, I startle when a little girl with face paint disguising her features bolts past us and bumps my hip. A man calls after her and apologizes as he jogs past us.

Needing a moment, I pause, take a few deep breaths, and count with each one.

Inhale… one, two, three.

Exhale… three, two, one.

Oliver grazes the top of my hand with his finger. The simple touch steals my attention and assuages my distress. I glance down at our hands and smile. Comfort and pleasure blanket me head to toe as I stare at the silver glinting in the sunlight. A solid silver band on his left forefinger and a matching one on my right. Our promise to each other until we choose another ring in the future and one of my few touchstones.

"Better?"

I lift my gaze as I lace my fingers with his. "Better," I repeat in affirmation.

We meet up with everyone in the VIP area by the stage. All our friends are present except for Travis, who is working the event. Also joining us are Oliver's parents, Delilah's siblings, and Tymber. Later, the Messer family will join us. We eat and chat, catching up since we last spoke or saw one another.

As it nears time for Hailey's Fire to take the stage, I notice other smaller closed-off sections near the stage. When I read the signs on a few, I chuckle under my breath. *West. Langston. Barron. Calhoun. Kemp.* There isn't a section for each founding family—not all of them want to be feet from the stage during a rock concert—but the families that want their name in the limelight paid for their own VIP experience.

Whatever. The money just gets funneled back into the town.

I don't miss that the Calhoun section is next to ours. *Joy.*

The last time I saw Abigail was a week before Christmas in the grocery store. Oliver and I were loading a cart with way too much food, excited about our first Christmas together as a couple. When we rounded the end of the baking aisle, our cart almost rammed hers… and Desmond's.

She apologized profusely, although I think it was for more than our carts almost colliding. Desmond and Oliver remained stoic, and I stayed tight-lipped as she rambled.

It was awkward as fuck. But it was closure for me and her. The end of an uncomfortable chapter in our lives.

If Abigail sits in the section beside ours, I pray Desmond is with her. After everything they've been through as a couple, he deserves to love her out in the open.

"Wish me luck." Oliver leans in and presses his lips to mine.

I try to deepen the kiss, but he breaks it before I'm able. I push out my bottom lip.

"Not that you need it"—I fist his T-shirt and press my lips to his with a chaste kiss—"but good luck."

Oliver, Hailey, and Trip exit VIP and head for the stairs on the side of the stage. As they do one last instrument check, the seats under the amphitheater canopy fill with enthusiastic residents and visitors. Abigail and Desmond enter the Calhoun section, hand in hand, followed by her brother and nephew, Ray III and Tucker. James, Estrella, and Sydney Messer join us in our VIP section. As Tymber sparks a conversation with James and Estrella, I check in with Sydney.

Of the hundreds of people who were in the same situation, Sydney is the only person I've spoken to.

A few months ago, her parents reached out to Tymber and asked if I would speak with them. Sydney was struggling to readjust to her previous life. Not that I blame her; she'd been in hell twice as long as me. Her parents asked if I'd be okay with meeting sometime. They thought that Sydney might have an easier time recovering if she had someone in her life that related.

Over the past three months, I gained a little sister. In return, Sydney has reclaimed part of herself. We may have connected because of our trauma, but it isn't the only reason we talk anymore. Oliver showed me what a real family looks like. Love and happiness. A place where you belong.

With Sydney, I've discovered something similar. A sibling of sorts. Someone I connect with in a familial way. A support system for years to come. I may limit what I share with her about my experiences during that time, but when she has dark days, she has someone to lean on or chat with who understands.

"Happy fucking Memorial Day, Stone Bay."

Applause and whistles fill the air as Hailey hollers into the mic. I snap my eyes to the stage and lock onto Oliver behind his drum kit.

"Sorry, parents. This isn't a PG show." She laughs. "But I'll try to keep the curse words to a minimum."

The crowd joins in on her laughter.

"It's been almost a year since we've been on this stage." She presses a hand to her heart and taps a couple times. "We're so grateful to be here." With a small step back, she peeks over her shoulder at Oliver and nods.

Energetic rock music booms around us for the next forty-five minutes. Sweat soaks Oliver's shirt. Trip bangs his head throughout most of the set. Lyrics rip from Hailey's lips as her fingers crank out notes on her guitar. When she's not singing, Hailey jumps around on the stage or leans against Trip as they play.

When the song they usually play last comes to an end, I

clap and cheer and give Oliver the biggest smile. He winks and drops his sticks near the bass drum.

"We love you, Stone Bay."

Deafening cheers echo through the amphitheater.

"Before we leave the stage, we've got one more for you."

My gaze flits to Oliver and I furrow my brows.

Oliver rises from his seat and smiles as he joins Hailey and Trip at the front of the stage. Stools and mics are set up. A stagehand brings them each an acoustic guitar.

A low hum dances under my skin as I watch him settle on the stool. As Oliver quietly chats with Hailey and Trip a moment, I think back to the last time he stepped out from behind his drums.

In a couple weeks, it will be a year since that night. When I drove to Smoky Creek and listened to him play his acoustic guitar and croon lyrics about life and love and us. That night was the first time I kissed him in public and didn't care who saw us.

"Fallen Stars."

A song he wrote for us. A song I haven't heard him play since that night. A song that got me through some of the darkest nights of my life last year.

Eyes closed and chin tucked close to his chest, Oliver strums the opening chords of the song. But it isn't "Fallen Stars." Hailey and Trip pluck strings on their guitars and sway to the melody.

I know this song.

How do I know this song?

"A shocking surprise, you came out of left field. Broody and quiet with undeniable appeal." Oliver's fingers shift on the neck of the guitar. "A nameless boy, that's who I was. Then our eyes met"—he lifts his head and meets my eyes—"and the world stopped and stumbled."

The backs of my eyes sting and I swallow.

"Blue, you branded my heart. Reserved, you tattooed my soul."

The tempo slows as Oliver tucks his chin once more.

"Hoarder of game pieces, you always needed control."

The corner of his mouth twitches as he becomes one with his guitar.

"Even then, we danced in the shadows. Pretenders. Impostors. Lovers in disguise."

Saliva pools in my mouth as emotion swells in my throat.

"And all I wanted was to be your light."

Since the day Oliver entered my life, he has always been my light. A voice of reason. The one person I could always count on. The one person that made me want to be a better version of myself. My biggest motivator, advocate, friend, and hero.

"I'll take the long road. Spend forever on your right."

Again, he lifts his head. His brilliant green eyes lock onto and hold my blues.

"Be yours until the end. But only if you're mine."

Vision blurry, I mouth, *forever mine.*

A bright, toothy smile spreads across his face.

"Take my hand and never let go. Spend forever on my left. Be my home."

The melody slows once more.

"Let me be your light, be your light, be your light." He closes his eyes as the drawn-out notes float through the air. "Say you're mine, always mine, forever mine." His dazzling blues meet my blurry gaze. "Forever mine."

The final chord echoes around the silent crowd. And then everything comes alive as whistles and cheers fill the amphitheater.

Frozen in place, my eyes don't leave Oliver.

Freed of his guitar, he rises from his stool, takes Hailey and Trip's hands, and bows. Then he hops off the stage into VIP and weaves between everyone to reach me. Wrapping his arms around my middle, he lifts me off the ground and kisses me as if no one is watching.

When I'm back on my feet, I frame his face with my hands. "When did you write that?"

He rests his hands on my hips and keeps me close. "Been working on it for years but finished it about a month ago."

"How do I know the song but not the lyrics?"

Oliver rolls his lips between his teeth. "Before you left for college, I played part of it in your room." A faint blush colors his cheeks. "I hummed while I sang the lyrics in my head. When I finished, you made a comment and freaked me out. I thought maybe I'd sung them out loud. But I didn't."

"I think I loved you then," I confess. "But I was scared to admit it."

"I know I loved you then, moje srce." He presses his lips to mine. "But I didn't want to risk losing you."

My thumbs slowly stroke his cheeks. "Yours until the end, moj zauvjek."

"Mr. Ollie! Mr. Ollie!" a young boy shouts.

Oliver and I break apart and he peeks over his shoulder to see Tucker Calhoun jumping in place. Smile on his face, Oliver walks to the wall separating our section from the Calhouns.

"Hey, man!" Oliver holds up his hand for a high five. "Tucker, right?"

His jaw drops as his eyes grow impossibly wide. "You know my name?"

Oliver chuckles. "Yeah, I do."

"Wow." Tucker slaps Oliver's hand. "Will you sign my T-shirt?" He taps the white fabric and brandishes a marker.

"Tucker..." Ray mutters.

Oliver smiles and looks at Ray. "It's no bother." He shifts his attention back to Tucker. "In fact, I think it's supercool." Oliver takes the marker from Tucker. "This is my first autograph. Ever."

"Whoa! I'm the first person to ask for your autograph?"

"Yep." Oliver uncaps the marker and scribbles his signature on the cotton. "Which means it's the most valuable."

When Oliver finishes, Tucker stares down at the black squiggles. "Never washing this shirt."

"Thanks, man." Ray holds out his hand and Oliver takes it. "You made his year."

"Glad I made him smile." Oliver shifts his attention back to Tucker. "See ya around, Tucker. Be good for your dad."

He nods emphatically. "I will, Mr. Ollie."

When they walk away, Oliver turns to me and smiles. "First fan."

Slowly, I shake my head and point to my chest. "Number one, right here."

Oliver reaches for my hand and laces our fingers. "True." He presses his lips to my forehead. "More potatoes and bacon, then home?"

"Yes. Feed me and then take me home." I tighten my hold on him. "I need to hear that song again."

"Anything for you, moje srce."

Two Years Later

"Go, Ollie." Kirsten all but shoves me out the back door of Poke the Yolk. "You don't want to miss your flight."

"We don't have to be at the airport until ten. It's only three." I hold my phone up and flash her the screen.

"Do you still need to pack?"

My face heats. "Maybe," I mutter.

"Mm-hmm." Smile on her face, she shakes her head. "Did you also forget it takes two and a half hours to drive to the airport?"

I look anywhere but at her. "Maybe."

"Go." She points to the parking lot. "Get to the airport early. Eat dinner. Mentally prepare for the best vacation ever."

She's right, but I have no plans to tell her as much. "Fine," I huff out. "I'll go."

"Love you, Ollie." She blows me a kiss. "Have fun."

Unlocking my shiny new SUV, I slide behind the wheel and press the ignition button. The engine is so quiet compared to my old Camry—may she rest in peace—that I often question if it's actually running.

When my previous car bit the dust, Levi insisted on buying me a brand-new car. I told him I had enough saved to buy a great used car, but he wasn't having it. A car. That was the subject of our first legitimate fight as a couple. But my argument died on my tongue the moment a tear hit his cheek and he said all he wanted was for me to be safe.

So, no used car.

Now, I am the proud owner of a forest-green beast on wheels. And because Levi has the means, it has every safety feature and upgrade possible. I still don't know what all the buttons and prompts are for, but I'm learning.

Pressing the button for the garage, I park beside his Ferrari in the bay. I cut the engine, close the garage, and exit the car. When I step inside the house, a full suitcase and carry-on sit near the door.

We're going on vacation.

All of a sudden, reality sinks in. It's an instant shot of anxiety and thrill to my bloodstream.

"Levi?" I toe off my shoes, pick them up, and climb the stairs to our bedroom.

When I reach the landing, the sound of the shower running hits my ears. As I cross the room, I drop my shoes and ditch my clothes. On quick feet, I enter the bathroom, open the foggy glass door, and step into the shower.

With his back to me, I lightly tap a knuckle on the shower door as I close it. A simple, faint sound to let him know he is no longer alone.

Next week marks three years since his abduction.

Although Levi has made major strides during recovery, the occasional nightmare crops up and jolts him awake. Large crowds still make him anxious, but not as much as they did years ago. Most of all, he does not like surprises—not the type that involves people appearing out of nowhere or loud noises. He may never be okay with them again.

I've never known anyone as courageous and resilient as Levi. Every day he is part of my life, I consider myself lucky and privileged.

"Hey." He turns around, tips his head back under the spray, and rinses the shampoo from his hair. "You just get home?"

"Yeah. Kirsten shoved me out the back door and demanded I get home ASAP." I roll my eyes.

Levi chuckles. "Good. I don't want to rush, but I'd like to leave in a couple hours. Maybe stop for dinner near the airport."

I join him under the spray, fisting his hips as I press my lips to his. "Two hours is plenty of time to fuck and pack."

With a hum, his hand comes to my throat just under my jaw—something new he started doing when sex entered our relationship for the second time—as he backs me up against the tile.

At first, his hand around my throat startled me. We'd been rough in bed before, but this was different. We'd never done anything this… intense. Ruthless. I didn't mind; it just took me by surprise.

Every now and again, our sex is gentle. Sweet. The most intimate experience of my life. On those nights, he hands me the reins. He lets me love him with delicate caresses, tender kisses, and slow strokes.

I love those soft moments as much as I relish the rough ones.

Often, Levi is assertive, aggressive, and possessive in the bedroom. Dominant through and through. His need to be in control takes over. Drives his every move.

He needs the power, and I willingly give it to him.

Erection thick and hard as it rubs the length of mine, he licks the seam of my lips. "Want me to fuck you in the shower?" With his free hand, he clutches the globe of my ass before trailing his finger to my hole. "Fill you with my cum before we fly off to paradise?"

I arch a brow then smile. "In the shower. After I finish packing." My tongue darts out and I lick my lips. "In the family bathroom at the airport."

He groans. "The amount of fucking we're doing on this trip… I'd be shocked if our dicks don't fall off."

I chuckle. "My dick likes yours too much to let either of them fall off."

"Good."

Levi spins me around, presses his front to my back, and teases my ass with his cock. The telltale *pop* of the lube we keep in the shower echoes off the walls. He inches back and coats his cock, his knuckles grazing my ass in the process. Then his finger is between my cheeks, circling my hole and coating it thoroughly.

Bending slightly at the knees, he lines his cock with and nudges my entrance. He reaches around, grips my throat with one hand and fists my cock with the other. Then he rocks his hips forward and thrusts inside.

Our joined moans bounce off the tile as he eases out then plunges back in, deeper. His hand on my cock moves at the same tempo as his hips—desperate, feverish.

"Fuck, you feel good." His confession comes out gruff as he pumps his hips faster. "Perfect."

One hand on the tile, I reach for his hair and fist it with the other. "Harder." I tip my head back and rest it on his shoulder. "Fuck me harder."

A man on a mission to please us both, he fulfills my wish.

His hands tighten around my throat and cock as he fucks me boneless.

"That's it," he coos in my ear as my dick swells in his palm. "Paint the wall with cum."

Fire coils around my spine as he strokes me faster. My breaths come in quick gasps as my balls tighten and draw up. I fist his hair with bone-crushing strength. Whimper and meet him thrust for thrust as my orgasm builds.

He drags his tongue from the curve of my neck to my ear, then takes my earlobe between his teeth and bites. Hard. It's a direct line to my cock and I explode, hot ropes of cum staining the tile.

"Good fucking boy," he grunts out just before he unloads inside me. His body jerks as the last of his release spills out. "Moj zauvjek."

I close my eyes and nod. "Always."

At a quaint restaurant not far from the airport, we talk animatedly about our two-week vacation. The sights we want to see. The food we want to eat. Lazy days. Sunsets and sunrises. Sex. Lots and lots of sex.

It's my first true vacation.

Levi says he was three years old when his parents took him to Europe. He doesn't remember anything about the trip, not even where they visited. So he considers this trip his first vacation too.

"Not working for two weeks will be weird," Levi says, then takes a bite of his dinner.

A year and a half ago, Levi and Tymber formed a new division of Tymber Woulf Security and Investigative Services—We Meet Again. Several months in the making, they wanted the new branch of the company to kick off without issues. Hundreds of hours went into planning and implementing. By the time the announcement was made, they were champing at the bit to help people locate lost loved ones. Since they cut the ribbon for We Meet Again, people have lined up for their help.

The most rewarding part of the job... seeing people's reactions as they are reunited.

When the caseload is heavier than normal, I pitch in and lend a hand. But it's rare for Levi to ask for help, not because of pride. He simply loves being at the helm on most cases. Connecting people. The cases he divvies up between his five employees, always knowing everything happening with each one.

I love that he found his true passion. To this day, he continues to scour the internet and the globe for secrets. Only now, those secrets are less scary.

"Yeah. I've never planned to do nothing for weeks." I laugh. "Let's see how long we last."

Our plates are cleared from the table and we pay the bill. We leave the restaurant hand in hand and drive a few miles through the city toward the airport. Levi steers the SUV into long-term parking, and it isn't long before we hoist our luggage from the back.

Hours to spare, we mosey through the airport and security. We grab dessert at a restaurant near our gate and buy a couple books at a small shop. Soon thereafter, we board the plane, stow our carry-ons, and wait for takeoff. The stewards in first class provide us with pillows and a blanket since it's an overnight flight.

Once we're in the air, I lift the armrest between our seats, recline my seat as Levi does the same with his, and curl into his side. Levi's cedar scent, mixed with his warm embrace, has me falling asleep in minutes.

A soft tap on my arm wakes me almost seven hours later.

"Good morning. We're landing soon," the steward whispers. "Would you like coffee, juice, or water?"

"Coffee would be great." I point to Levi. "For him as well."

The steward nods, taps the screen of their tablet, and moves to the next row.

I gently rouse Levi. "Rise and shine, sleepyhead." I press my lips to his hair.

He groans into the crook of my neck. "I don't wanna."

I chuckle. "An overnight flight wasn't *my* idea. So suck it up."

Lifting his head, he opens one eye and scowls. "It'll be worth it. We'll exit the airport and see the sunrise."

"The perfect start to our trip."

"Exactly."

With a little caffeine in our system, the wheels touch down far from home. The pilot steers the plane toward the gate and soon we disembark from the plane. We wander through the airport, barely a soul in sight. We stop to use the bathroom and splash our faces before we head to baggage claim.

As we near baggage claim, I spot a woman with a sign.

Oliver & Levi

I peek over at Levi. "What's this?"

"Come on." He tips his head toward the woman. As we approach, he lifts a hand, waves, then points to us as he speaks. "Levi and Oliver."

"Aloha, Levi. Welcome to Hawaii." The woman holds out a beautiful lei with vibrant flowers and greenery. Levi bows his head, and she places it around his neck. Then she turns to me. "Aloha, Oliver. Welcome to Hawaii." I am presented with a matching lei that she places around my neck. "Enjoy your time with us." With a short nod, she walks away.

My nose and the backs of my eyes sting as I turn to Levi. "Sneaky." I press a kiss to his lips. "But I love it."

Once we have our luggage, we order a ride and drive toward our bungalow on the beach. The entire ride, we stare out the windows and point to all the places we want to visit. As the driver steers the car into the driveway, a hint of pink and orange paints the sky.

The bungalow is modern and stunning. Dark bamboo, soft-gray tile, and endless windows with black and charcoal embellishments, fixtures, and linens. A small kitchen and dining table. A massive bed and adjoining bathroom. And a huge communal area on a covered, outdoor patio to sit and relax or socialize.

Stowing our bags in the bedroom, we kick off our shoes, step out the back door and walk until sand sifts between our toes. On our first vacation, we watch the sunrise in paradise.

One week later, we get married on the same beach as the sun sets.

"Fallen Stars"

It's always been us, a sea of blue and green / Our silent conversations and blurry fragments of a dream / Just out of reach, I wanted to take your hand / But it wasn't my place to touch you / Not like that / So I stood by your side with a cheek-burning smile / I played the goof, the fool, while I died a little inside / From the start, all I wanted was you / From the start, little did I know you wanted me too / In the shadows, we hide / Tall trees, scraped knees, stars falling in the night / But I'd live forever in the dark to keep you at my side / My best-kept secret / My reason / My life / From the start, all I wanted was you / From the start, you wanted me too / Forever mine… until every star falls from the sky / Until every star falls / Every star falls / Every star falls / Until I fall.

"Forever Mine"

A shocking surprise, you came out of left field / Broody and quiet with undeniable appeal / A nameless boy, that's who I was / Then our eyes met and the world stopped and stumbled / Blue, you branded my heart / Reserved, you tattooed my soul / Hoarder of game pieces, you always needed control / Even then, we danced in the shadows / Pretenders / Impostors / Lovers in disguise / And all I wanted was to be your light / I'll take the long road / Spend forever on your right / Be yours until the end / But only if you're mine / Take my hand and never let go / Spend forever on my left / Be my home / Let me be your light, be your light, be your light / Say you're mine, always mine, forever mine / Forever mine.

FALLEN STARS WORD/PHRASE TRANSLATIONS

dušo - Bosnian for *sweetheart; my soul*

čimbur - Bosnian breakfast dish

moje srce - Bosnian for *my heart*

moja ljubavi - Bosnian for *my love*

volim te - Bosnian for *I love you*

volim te više - Bosnian for *I love you more*

figlio - Italian for *son*

tesoro - Italian for *treasure*

moj zauvjek - Bosnain for *mine forever*

aarluk - Inuit word for *orca*

WEST
family tree

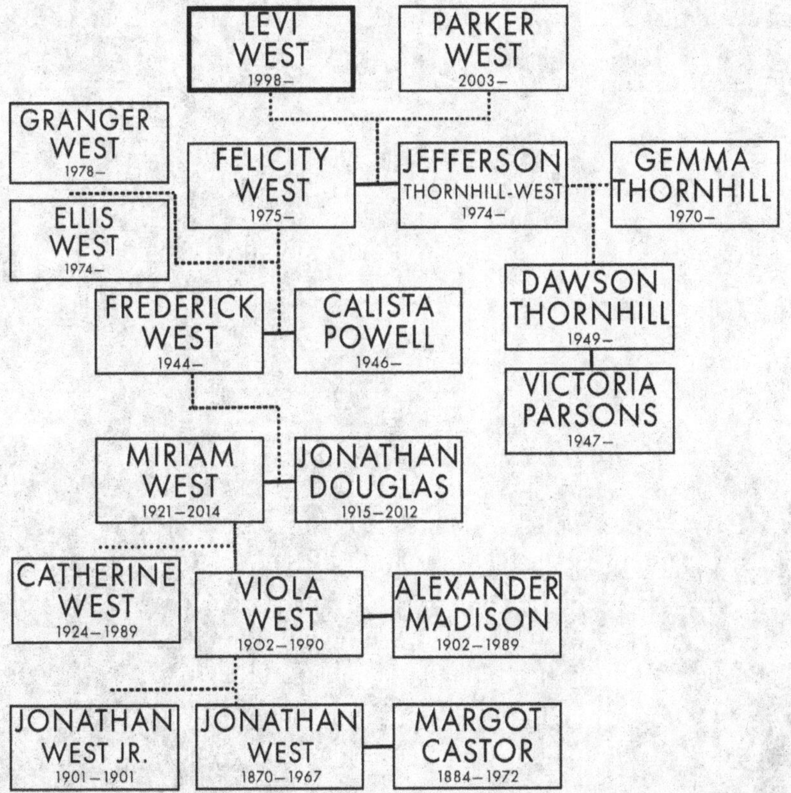

PLAYLIST

Here are some of the songs from the **Fallen Stars** playlist. You can find and listen to the entire playlist on Spotify!

I'm yours | Isabel LaRosa
Panic Room | Au/Ra
War of Hearts | Ruelle
Sorry | Halsey
Fire On Fire | Sam Smith
Hurts Like Hell | Tommee Profitt, Fleurie
Can You Hold Me | NF, Britt Nicole
Monsters | Ruelle
Meet Me on the Battlefield | SVRCINA
Without You | Ursine Vulpine, Annaca
Emergency Contact | Pierce The Veil

MORE BY PERSEPHONE

Shattered Sun

When your heart is split in two, how do choose who to love more? While Ben—her childhood best friend—and Travis—the hottest cop in Stone Bay—fight for Kirsten's affection, someone else has their eye on her. When she questions everyone and everything, Ben and Travis vow to protect her. In the process, she falls for both men. Before it's too late, she needs to decide which man she loves more.

Fractured Night

Shallow. Heartless. Egocentric. The top three words people use to describe Phoebe Graves. Somehow, I've always seen past her icy facade. Seen beyond her callous exterior. And those minor glimpses… they make me want her more. The moment my fantasies start becoming reality, I question how long it'll last before Phoebe abandons me for something bigger.

Depths Awakened

A small town romance which captivates you from the start. Mags and Geoff are two broken souls who have sworn off love. Vowed to never lose anyone else. But their undeniable attraction brings them together and refuses to let go.

One Night Forsaken

One night. No names. No romance. Just fun. Nothing more—at least, that's what she tells herself. Until he appears in her coffee shop months later with that addictive smile. She swore off commitment. He vows to never love again. But the more they fight it, the more life brings them together.

Every Thought Taken

As young children, an unshakable friendship brought them together. As teens, they discovered an undeniable love. Then life pulled them in different directions–into darkness and light–and slowly ripped them apart. Years later, he returns home in the hopes of a second chance with his first love and to conquer the demons of his past.

Distorted Devotion

Free-spirited Sarah lives life to the fullest. When a new love interest enters her life, she starts receiving strange gifts and letters. She doesn't want to relinquish her freedom or new love, but fears the consequences.

Transcendental

A musician in search of his muse and a woman grieving the loss of her husband. Two weeks at an exclusive retreat and their connection rivals all others. Until she leaves early without notice. But he refuses to give up until he finds her again.

The Click Duet

High school sweethearts torn apart. When fate gives them a second chance, one doesn't trust they won't be hurt again. Through the Lens (Click Duet #1) and Time Exposure (Click Duet #2) is an angsty, second chance, friends to lovers romance with all the feels.

The Artist Duet

A tortured hero with the biggest heart and a charismatic heroine with the patience of a saint. Previous heartache has him fighting his desire to be more than friends with her. But she is everywhere, and he can't help but give in. The Artist Duet is an angsty, friends to lovers slow burn.

CONNECT WITH PERSEPHONE

<u>Connect with Persephone</u>
www.persephoneautumn.com

<u>Subscribe to Persephone's newsletter</u>
www.persephoneautumn.com/newsletter

<u>Join Persephone's reader's group</u>
Persephone's Playground

<u>Follow Persephone online</u>

instagram.com/persephoneautumn
facebook.com/persephoneautumnwrites
tiktok.com/@persephoneautumn
bookbub.com/authors/persephone-autumn
goodreads.com/persephoneautumn
amazon.com/author/persephoneautumn
pinterest.com/persephoneautumn
threads.net/@persephoneautumn

ACKNOWLEDGMENTS

Family… I love you so fucking much!

Rosa at Fairy Proofmother Proofreading! Every time I think I have "proper" writing and punctuation figured out, you prove me wrong lol. Bless your knowledge and expertise. Love you!!

Christopher John at CJC Photography! Thank you for being so gracious with me as I navigated my first professional photo for a book cover. You made the process seamless.

Eric & Jeff! Thank you for taking such incredible photos and being so kind. I'm honored to have you both on my cover.

Abi of Pink Elephant Designs! You make my books so damn pretty and I'm so grateful for your magic and skills.

Emina @theromanticbosnian! Thank you for being so wonderful and friendly and helpful when I popped into your DMs. I appreciate you and your help with making sure the Bosnian translations in Fallen Stars were accurate.

To all the bloggers and ARC readers that continuously promote my stories, get excited about books I'm terrified of putting out in the world, or read and love my words. I love you all so much!! Your support means more than you know. I love seeing your posts and joy about my books.

To everyone that picks up one of my books, I love you! Whether Fallen Stars is your first Persephone Autumn book or your 20+ book, I never take a single one of you for granted. All the fucking hugs!!!!

ABOUT THE AUTHOR

USA Today Bestselling Author Persephone Autumn lives in Florida with her wife and psycho cat. A proud mom with a cuckoo grandpup. An ethnic food enthusiast who has fun discovering ways to vegan-ize her favorite non-vegan foods. Most days, you'll find her with a tea latte or fruity concoction in her hand. If given the opportunity, she would intentionally get lost in nature.

For years, Persephone did some form of writing; mostly journaling or poetry. After pairing her poetry with images and posting them online, she began the journey of writing her first novel.

She mainly writes romance and poetry, but on occasion dips her toes in other works. Look for her non-romance novel publications under P. Autumn.